M000104167

WIZARDOMS: OBJECTS OF POWER

FATE OF WIZARDOMS, BOOK FOUR

JEFFREY L. KOHANEK

FALLBRANDT PRESS

First Edition

ISBN: 978-1-949382-26-6

PUBLISHED BY JEFFREY L. KOHANEK and FALLBRANDT PRESS

www.JeffreyLKohanek.com

ALSO BY JEFFREY L. KOHANEK

Fate of Wizardoms

Book One: Eye of Obscurance

Book Two: Balance of Magic

Book Three: Temple of the Oracle

Book Four: Objects of Power

Book Five: Rise of a Wizard Queen

Book Six: A Contest of Gods

* * *

Warriors, Wizards, & Rogues (Fate of Wizardoms 0)

Fate of Wizardoms Boxed Set: Books 1-3

Runes of Issalia

The Buried Symbol: Runes of Issalia 1

The Emblem Throne: Runes of Issalia 2

An Empire in Runes: Runes of Issalia 3

Rogue Legacy: Runes of Issalia Prequel

* * *

Runes of Issalia Bonus Box

Wardens of Issalia

A Warden's Purpose: Wardens of Issalia 1

The Arcane Ward: Wardens of Issalia 2

An Imperial Gambit: Wardens of Issalia 3

A Kingdom Under Siege: Wardens of Issalia 4

ICON: A Wardens of Issalia Companion Tale

* * *

Wardens of Issalia Boxed Set

JOURNAL ENTRY

And so, we have reached the midpoint in our tale. While much has occurred, in truth, little has been revealed. This will soon change. In the following entry, additional players enter the game, the stakes rise, and numerous truths shall be exposed.

Before I continue, I shall take a moment to recap what has occurred thus far.

A menagerie acrobat named Rhoa stole the amulet known as the Eye of Obscurance, the same amulet pursued by master thief Jerrell Landish. Jerrell, who goes by the name Jace, agreed to track down this acrobat, claim the Eye of Obscurance, and use it to assassinate Lord Taladain, the Wizard Lord of Ghealdor.

Jace eventually caught up to Rhoa's menagerie outside of Starmuth, where he agreed to team up with Rhoa and a dwarf named Rawk with the shared goal of seeing Lord Taladain dead. Soon afterward, the trio met me in a small Ghealdan village, where I, Salvon, invited them to ride with me to Fastella. With my assistance, the four of us laid plans for Lord Taladain's final performance.

However, Lord Taladain's daughter, Narine, who had recently returned from her eight-year stay at the University in Tiadd and now a skilled wizardess, sought to prove herself an asset to her father. Unfortunately, her brother, Eldalain, viewed her as a threat.

While Prince Eldalain was away, we delivered a memorable troupe performance for Lord Taladain, killing the man in the process, an act made possible by the Eye of

Obscurance. In the process, it was discovered that Rhoa possessed a natural immunity to magic.

To avoid her brother's wrath, we agreed to smuggle Narine and her bodyguard, Adyn, out of the city. Our small group did not remain together for long, forced to split apart when High Wizard Charcoan's soldiers attempted to arrest Narine while in Starmuth. Jace, Narine, and Adyn fled the city on a ship bound for the Farrowen city of Shear, while the rest of us journeyed by land toward Lionne.

Rhoa, Rawk, and I were soon captured by Captain Despaldi and brought to Marquithe to face our fate before Lord Malvorian. We escaped our cells below the Marquithe Palace, where we discovered Rawk's uncle, Algoron, secretly working for Malvorian.

We were led to Malvorian's throne room, discovering Jace, Narine, and Adyn already there. A confrontation of magic, swords, and death ensued. While Malvorian, Thurvin, and Despaldi were defeated, Jace was severely wounded in the process. As destiny would have it, Narine acquired an enchanted bracelet, enhancing her magic and enabling her to save his life. Malvorian was not so lucky.

Our party of heroes escaped the city, on the run once again, Despaldi and his men in pursuit for killing his master.

With two wizard lords dead, a shift in the balance of magic occurred. Creatures of legend, mighty and dangerous, began to appear – something unheard of for two millennia.

Upon reaching the Pallanar border, we sought the assistance of a retired soldier named Brogan Reisner and his archer companion, Blythe. After a confrontation with Despaldi and his men, we journeyed to Illustan, the capital of Pallanar.

While meeting with Wizard Lord Raskor and his wife, Ariella, a dragon attacked the city. The wizard lord confronted the beast, only to discover that dragons were immune to magic. With quick thinking, Narine crafted an illusion and led the dragon from the city, saving the populace. Raskor eventually succumbed to wounds inflicted during the confrontation.

All the while, the Farrowen Army captured the Ghealdan cities of Starmuth and Marquithe, converting the purple flames of Gheald to the blue of Farrow, redirecting the prayers of Devotion to Lord Thurvin, the new Wizard Lord of Farrowen, feeding the wizard's power. Dorban was eventually added to the list, the city captured because of the heroics of Lieutenant Garvin and a thief named Rindle.

After Lord Raskor's demise, a Seer named Xionne and her dwarf guardian, Hadnoddon, appeared in Illustan, demanding we all accompany her on a journey to the legendary city of Kelmar. With an escort of Pallanese soldiers, we sailed to Eastern Pallanar and made for the Frost Forest. A trio of wyvern attacked at night, the skirmish killing all but one of the soldiers and nearly costing Brogan his life.

Days later, the heroes arrived in Kelmar, city of the Seers, a secretive sect of prophets who lived inside the lonely mountain Paehl Lanor. There, the sisters and our heroes sifted through prophecies, seeking to reveal which were true and which were false. During an attempt to divine the truth, the Dark Lord, Urvadan, attacked Xionne, for he was behind the troubles in the world and the shift in magic. His minions, an army of goblins, then snuck into Kelmar, striking with a surprise attack. The swift thinking, courageous actions and unique magic of our heroes and their weapons were the only thing preventing Kelmar from annihilation. In the end, our heroes survived and were sent off in different directions, tasked by prophecy to recover two objects of magic hidden in different corners of the world.

While at Kelmar, Jace and Narine had discovered a journal revealing an undiscovered use for magic. At the same time, Lord Thurvin of Farrowen was gifted a similar book by a dark and mysterious benefactor. The man unleashed this new magic upon Captain Despaldi, imbuing the man with dangerous magic never before seen.

The last subject of our story, a princess named Priella, the last surviving offspring of Lord Raskor, is as important as any of the others. Upon returning to Illustan after her father's death, Priella manipulated events, placing herself among the applicants to become wizard lord. As fate would have it, Pallan chose Priella, gifting her with the power of a god.

Only the second woman in history to acquire such power, it has yet to be seen how the world will look upon her legacy.

While half the world has been disrupted, most remain unaware of the Murguard falling, their battlements no longer containing the darkspawn who call the Murlands home. The exceptions are those who live in Kyranni, the wizardom bordering The Fractured Lands. There, the darkspawn invasion shall begin as the Dark Lord seeks to choke all light from the world and plunge all to shadow.

This is where our story resumes.

-Salvon the Great

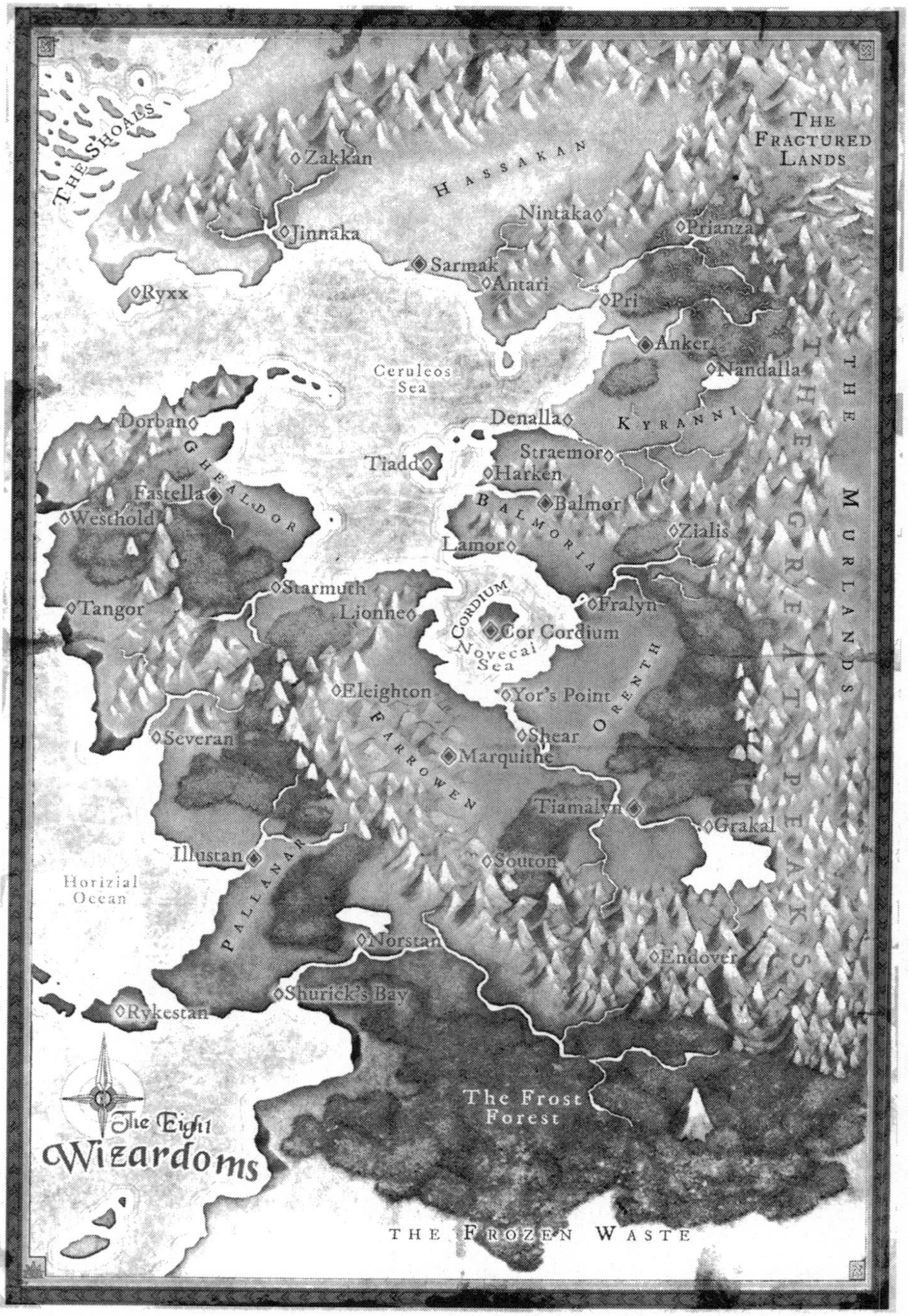
The Eight Wizardoms
The Shoals
Zakkan
Hassakan
The Fractured Lands
Nintaka
Prianza
Jinnaka
Sarmak
Antari
Ryxx
Pri
Anker
Nandalla
Ceruleos Sea
Dorban
Denalla
Kyranni
Gheal'dor
Tiadd
Straemor
Harken
Fastella
Balmor
Balmoria
Westhold
Zialis
Lamor
The Murlands
The Great Peaks
Starmuth
Tangor
Lionne
Cordium
Fralyn
Cor Cordium
Novecai Sea
Orenth
Eleighton
Yor's Point
Farrowen
Shear
Severan
Marquithe
Tiamalyn
Grakal
Illustan
Souton
Pallanar
Horizial Ocean
Norstan
Endover
Shurick's Bay
Rykestan
The Frost Forest
The Frozen Waste

PROLOGUE

Naginata in hand – wooden shaft smooth and dark, sharp blade oiled – Captain Eviara Tivik stalked the top of the city wall. She gazed toward the jungle to the east, leaves bathed in the dark amber of dusk, the sun hidden below the western horizon. A half-mile of open land stood between the wall and the jungle. Most called it "the killing zone".

Armed soldiers waited along the wall, staring off into the distance, faces grim. Some held bows, others, spears. A handful held swords and shields, but those would be the last line of defense, needed only if there was a breach, the same as the soldiers crowding the streets below.

Every ten strides, she was forced to circumvent one of the cranes mounted to the top of the wall and manned by a soldier. Beside each, a female diver, armed with a naginata, stood ready, one end of a rope secured to a harness on each diver's back, the other to the nearest crane. When those divers looked in her direction, Eviara gave a firm nod, mostly out of respect. In this battle, those warriors would likely die first.

She reached a tower roof where a cluster of wizards – men in burnt orange robes, women in bright orange dresses – huddled together, discussing strategy. The surrounding area was empty. Soldiers often avoided wizards, even when at war.

At the center of the cluster was Wizard Lord Kelluon Gree, dressed in orange-trimmed black robes. He was tall, even for a Kyranni, skin dark, eyes darker, bald head smooth. His black goatee had a streak of gray down the center, and Eviara absently wondered how long the gray had been there. *Was it there before he became wizard lord?* It was a question only he could answer. Nobody else in Anker was alive back when he rose to the throne.

Kelluon dismissed the wizards, the men and women dispersing, half in each direction. He then turned toward Eviara. "Are we ready, Captain?"

"As ready as one can be, Your Majesty. Most of the soldiers have served in The Fractured Lands, so they have an idea of what to expect." She ran a hand across her shorn hair before absently tugging at the braid in the back. "I had long feared the darkspawn might break beyond the Murguard posts, but never to this extent. Never in my lifetime, at least."

Kelluon grunted and put a big hand on her shoulder. Despite her height of six feet, he towered over her. "We have lost many soldiers already. I just pray we receive good news from your scouts."

She turned toward the east again. "The scouts I sent to Nandalla should have returned by now. After what happened in Prianza, it leaves me concerned…" Her voice trailed off, thoughts drifting.

The scouting report from Prianza had come in a week earlier, a tale of horror containing little hope. The city walls had been breached in a dozen places, buildings destroyed, fires ravaging what remained. The darkspawn had abandoned the city, but the scouts found no survivors. Nine thousand Kyranni citizens had called Prianza their home.

I pray Kyra received those poor souls.

"I fear Nandalla has fallen, as well," Kelluon said. "Devotion last night… It was even worse than the days since Prianza fell, the absence of more prayers noticeable."

Eviara closed her eyes in silent prayer. While the other cities were small compared to Anker, those deaths meant less blessings to feed Kelluon's magic. As wizard lord, his abilities were paramount to protect his wizardom, and every person lost reduced his power by some measure.

"I must go," he said. "Night is upon us, and I cannot miss Devotion. My magic is required now more than ever. I will return soon."

As the wizard lord headed for the guard tower, Eviara turned back toward the jungle.

The sky was decidedly darker, the edge of the jungle difficult to see in the gloom. She watched the men light the braziers that sat between the wall and the foliage, twenty in total, each spaced a few hundred feet apart. Once finished, they raced back toward the wall, eager to return before monsters attacked. When they were safely inside, the portcullis closed, and all fell still.

Eviara wondered if tonight was the night the Dark Lord's host would strike Anker. Not knowing when it would come was a cause of frustration and anxiety. The progress of the darkspawn horde turned out to be difficult to track, the monsters fading into the jungle during the day, only to emerge miles away the next evening, their pattern and direction random and seemingly without thought. For years, she had held fast to the idea that goblin magic users operated under their own design, barely possessing enough intelligence to point their army in the proper direction. Until the Murguard fell, it was widely believed that an inherent need to sacrifice humans to appease Urvadan was as far as they could think. She and her fellow Kyranni officers now acknowledged that someone, or something, intelligent guided them.

What has changed? she wondered. There were rumors of war in faraway Ghealdor and new wizard lords rising in Farrowen and Pallanar, but how could those distant events have anything to do with the darkspawn?

A man down the wall shouted. Eviara turned toward him, following where the soldier pointed.

It was subtle at first, but then she saw movement at the edge of the jungle.

"Goblins," she muttered before cupping her hands to her mouth. "Enemy spotted! To your stations!"

The goblins gathered beyond the light of the braziers, their numbers building but none advancing. *Strange,* she thought. Three years of fighting in The Fractured Lands had proven darkspawn never waited. When darkness fell, they attacked with a mad rage. *What are they planning?*

A figure burst from the jungle to the southeast, a quarter mile from where the monsters huddled. It was a woman, running toward the gate. At the same moment, the darkspawn rushed the wall, a flood pouring over the field. It would be close, but Eviara feared the monsters would reach the gate first.

Eviara burst into a run, streaking past soldiers as she headed toward the gate tower. "Open the gate! Open the gate! Let that soldier inside!" She dashed into the tower as the soldiers cranked the portcullis up. "Only open it enough to let her in, then close it."

"Yes, Captain," the soldier's voice followed her as Eviara raced down the curved stairwell.

It was a hundred feet to the ground level, ten stories she cleared in the span of twenty breaths. At the bottom, she darted out the door and into a crowd of Kyranni soldiers.

"Prepare to defend the gate!" Eviara shouted. "Beware. It closes the moment our scout reaches the city."

Through the rising bars, she sighted the running woman, face twisted in effort. Goblins raced in from the side, arms flailing, gripping swords and spears, red eyes round as they hooted in excitement. Some slowed to loose arrows, narrowly missing the running soldier, a few arrows coming through the gate to strike raised shields.

When it was clear she would not make it, Eviara shouted, "With me! We attack before they can reach her!"

Her naginata in hand, she raced forward, ducking beneath the rising gate and rushing beyond the wall. Spinning and bringing her weapon around in a broad arc, she met the goblin horde. The blade at the end of her shaft sliced across the torsos of three goblins, eviscerating the squealing monsters. Her fellow soldiers struck the attacking mob in a clash of steel, blades, and blood.

She glanced back as the scout ran through the gate, then turned around just in time to dodge the thrust of a spear. Twisting again, she rammed the butt of her weapon into the monster's midriff, the next jab connecting with a bone-shattering blow to its jaw.

While dozens of goblins lay dead, thousands still rushed toward them.

"Retreat!" Eviara shouted. "Back to the city!"

Kyranni soldiers were experienced, most having served time in the Murguard. They knew to harry the enemy during a retreat, never turning their backs until they were beyond the gate.

The moment Eviara and her soldiers were inside, she shouted, "Close the gate!"

The portcullis slammed down, the thick, iron barbs impaling a half-dozen goblins, trapping the horde outside. Twenty had made it beyond the gate but were rapidly dispatched. In the end, only three Kyranni were wounded, none dead.

She pushed past soldiers and found her scout, a woman named Halata Kain. Between breaths, Eviara asked, "Did you reach Nandalla?"

Halata nodded as she gasped for air. "The city was intact when I arrived." She wiped her brow, black hair sticking to her forehead. "They gave me shelter, but it didn't last. Darkspawn attacked that evening." The woman shook her head. "It was horrible. Even with wizards on our side, the city is surely lost. I was lucky to escape."

Eviara grimaced. Now that the woman was safe inside the city, she needed a report. "I expected you back two days ago."

"I tried but was forced to travel three times the distance to circumvent the monsters." Halata's eyes took on a haunted look. "They are everywhere."

With a sigh, Eviara closed her eyes. *Blessed Kyra, what must we do to survive?* Opening them again, she put her hand on Halata's shoulder. "Go rest and get food."

The Tower of Devotion flared brightly, beams of orange light bursting across the sky, connecting to the other major Kyranni cities. Those surrounding Eviara fell to their knees and began the chant, offering Devotion to their wizard lord. The expression of faith would grant Kelluon the magic of their god, but with Prianza and Nandalla fallen, the lives and prayers of those citizens had been lost forever.

Hurry, Kelluon. We may need your magic tonight.

While the others chanted, Eviara turned toward the gate tower. She had a battle to fight.

Body covered in sweat, Eviara strode along the top of the wall, calling out commands. Below, divers at the end of their lines twirled with long, sweeping strokes, naginata blades slicing through goblin flesh, limbs, and bodies, adding to the pile at the base of the wall. Her squad leaders called out targets, archers firing upon command. An hour had passed since the fighting began, her soldiers tiring, so she called for a shift change.

The crane operators reeled the divers back up, while archers kept the horde at bay. Male wizards ran in, one every fifty feet. One waved his hands, a resounding thunderclap echoing in the night. The wizards then began launching fireballs upon the monsters nearest to the wall, the goblins shrieking as they burned and set the piles of dead on fire in the process. This continued while the new divers relieved the old, fresh archers replacing those who were exhausted, their quivers empty.

By the time Eviara's troops were ready, the wizards were drained, breathing heavily, beads of sweat running down their faces. A bloom arose from the goblin horde, balls of flame arcing up from three of the braziers.

"Look out!" Eviara shouted.

The fireballs struck, one landing just ten strides away, setting a crane and the man on it ablaze. Two wizards were among those burning, arms flailing as they tried feebly to escape. More fireballs emerged from the night, and Eviara urgently commanded the archers to fire upon the goblin magic users. Arrows sailed through the sky, but they fell short of the nearest shaman, striking and killing ordinary goblins instead.

A roar echoed in the night, the sound sending a knife of fear slicing through Eviara's soul. She had hoped they would not face a rock troll. Moments later, she realized they had even bigger problems.

Four giant, gray bodies emerged from the darkness, each rock troll standing three stories tall, thick of body, massive feet stomping on goblins in their way.

"Prepare the ballistae!" Eviara shouted, the command relayed along the wall.

They only had two of the war machines, each newly built and mounted to the wall to add to their defenses. She ran to the nearest ballista and slowed as two men positioned it, a third standing behind, gazing through the sight. A four-foot-long bolt, three inches in diameter, rested in the launch chamber, cocked and ready. The trolls stormed toward the wall, and the man pulled the trigger. The missile flew toward the nearest troll and struck true, the bolt impaling the monster's neck. Lurching but not stopping, the troll continued forward, while the three men urgently cranked the launch arm back. Warriors along the wall loosed arrows at the massive monsters, some soldiers launching spears. Nothing had any effect.

Before the next bolt was in place, the troll struck the wall.

A hundred feet tall and eight feet thick, the wall had stood for two thousand years. Yet the impact shook it violently, soldiers stumbling, a handful falling off to their deaths. Two more trolls struck moments later, the beasts pounding on the wall with fists the size of a man.

Four male wizards rushed over, each waving his hands and calling upon his magic. A bolt of lightning arced from each, all striking the same troll. The massive, gray body shook, smoke rising from its greasy, black hair as its skin fried. Another troll roared, bent, and scooped up a handful of dead goblins, some burning. It launched the goblins, bodies smashing into the top of the wall, others striking the wizards. Eviara watched in helpless horror as two wizards fell toward the city below.

Another pile of goblins came flying toward her. She dove behind the merlons as the bodies struck, some hitting the merlon, three sailing into the city beyond, one landing on the wall in a twisted, bloody heap.

She paused and considered what to do. Trolls were incredibly difficult to kill, even with ballistae. Without them…

A figure in orange-trimmed black robes appeared, striding along the wall. Kelluon lifted his hands high and called upon his magic.

A blinding white beam of light shot from the wizard lord's hands and struck the nearest troll, knocking it backward. The light faded as the troll stumbled, a two-foot hole gaping in the monster's forehead. It fell with a tremendous crash, crushing dozens of goblins in the process

Kelluon continued past Eviara and attacked again, a bright beam of light striking the next troll, burning a hole through its body and killing it instantly.

Foulfire…

Eviara had heard of the legendary spell. Pure energy able to burn through anything.

As the man destroyed the remaining trolls, she realized he had saved them. It would be a long night, but the city would survive…at least for one more day.

1

SHIFTING TILES

Terrin Delmont, better known as Rindle, huddled behind an outcropping of rock, clutching his cloak around his chest, hood over his head. Wind whistled through the pass, the surrounding tents billowing as if they might break free of their stakes and sail off at any moment. Pale, morning light gradually gave shape to the valley below and the mountains beyond, all beneath a gray sky. It was the beginning of a miserable day, leaving Rindle colder than he had ever been before. Having lived his entire life in Fastella, he had never known winter until now.

Two long, dreary days had passed since he and the Farrowen Army had departed from Dorban, the captured Ghealdan city now under the control of Farrowen. More importantly, the fire above the Obelisk of Devotion had been converted from purple to blue, the prayers channeling to Wizard Lord Thurvin in Marquithe.

By the end of the first day of travel, they were far from the coast, steadily rising in elevation, the weather growing colder with each mile. By the end of the second, they encountered a winter storm high in the mountains, coating everything in a layer of snow. It wasn't much. Even so, it was Rindle's first experience with snow. He had stopped his horse and faced the blowing flurries, mouth open and tongue extended. The brief sense of wonder did not last, the bitter wind soon freezing such thoughts until they fell off and shattered. The ride the remainder of the day had him huddling against the weather and dreaming of shelter. An evening in the tent he shared with Lieutenant Garvin wasn't much better – tossing and turning, dozing briefly before waking to the cold again and again. Still, he must have caught some sleep, for when he opened his eyes to the predawn light, Garvin was gone.

He breathed into his hands, attempting to warm them as he paced, his gaze repeatedly going to the large, white tent of the Farrowen Army commander. Two guards stood outside the entrance, their armor covered by cloaks, hoods lowered, faces obscured by shadow. Rindle wondered if the men were cold. They stood still, silent.

Shouts arose from the tent, familiar voices, the argument lasting a full minute before Lieutenant Trey Garvin emerged. The man stomped past Rindle, toward the tent the two shared.

Rindle caught up to Garvin, still rubbing his hands for warmth. "What's happening?"

His gaze fixed straight ahead, the man said, "I am leaving."

"Of course," Rindle replied. "We are to break camp and cross the pass today."

Garvin stopped, his intense gaze turning toward Rindle. "No. I am leaving the army, heading back to Marquithe."

Rindle frowned. "Why? What happened?"

"What happened is..." He lowered his voice to a growl, "I have lost my faith in this campaign. I...cannot continue."

"What of capturing Westhold and Tangor?"

"Captain Henton's problem, not mine any longer."

"The sapphires?"

"I passed that responsibility to Henton, as well." Garvin turned and continued toward the tent, ducking in while Rindle waited outside.

Moments passed, one man busily packing, the other chewing on his lip as he considered the situation. When Garvin emerged carrying his loaded pack, Rindle made his decision.

"May I come with you?"

Garvin fixed him with a stare, eyes narrowed in thought. "What you do is your own choice."

"I would prefer to come with you. I did not come to join an army. What I search for is...purpose. I need something more from life. Something I have yet to discover."

"And you believe I am the one with the answers?" Garvin shook his head, walked over to his horse, and began strapping his pack to it. "I thought I knew my place in this world, but I have lost my way. Doubts now choke my thoughts and leave me questioning every action."

Hands gripping the saddle, he rested his forehead against his horse, his voice dropping to a hush. "A soldier is taught to follow orders unquestioned. For years, I did as commanded, believing my superiors knew the right of things. That belief came from a trust in my captain, a man named Despaldi. During my years in The Fractured Lands, he proved time and again to be a man of integrity and honor. Our post became renowned for our heroics. More importantly, our survival rate outstripped other posts by a fair margin. When he left the Murguard, I traveled with him to Farrowen and joined the Midnight Guard, where I rose in his wake. Every task assigned, I executed per my orders, never doubting the motives.

"This campaign is different. Rather than giving me satisfaction, our victories leave me hollow, my actions lacking conviction. I can do it no longer. I must go back. In Marquithe, I will either regain my faith or validate my suspicions. Until then, I find myself caught upon a stormy sea without stars to guide me."

Rindle stepped closer to Garvin and placed his hand on the man's shoulder. They stood the same height, Garvin's body muscular and athletic, Rindle's lean and lanky. "Perhaps we can navigate our doubts together. I believe there is something more for me in this world, and my instincts tell me I will find it by following you."

Garvin mirrored Rindle's action, clapping a hand to the other's shoulder. "Very well. Pack your things. We leave immediately." He frowned. "The sooner we return to the coast, the sooner we escape this blasted weather."

Roddem Despaldi, Captain of the Midnight Guard, strolled down the Marquithe Palace corridor, which was dark, save for an enchanted lantern at each end and one in the center. Urlon, the guard on duty, thumped a fist to his breastplate. Despaldi walked past the man and stopped outside the wizard lord's private chambers. Pausing, he stared down at his gloved hands, the black mitts lined with the silvery script of an enchantment. With the gloves, his hands had regained their practical uses. When removed, they held power unlike anything he had ever dreamed possible.

His gaze lifted to the door, thoughts drifting to the man waiting inside. For years, Thurvin Arnolle had a tether tied to Lord Malvorian's ear. The other end was secured to the network of thieves, smugglers, and spies – a network Thurvin had developed. At the time, Despaldi felt disdain toward the scheming wizard, never trusting him, secretly calling him a weasel.

My, how things have changed, Despaldi thought as he now found himself bound to Thurvin.

The wizard lord had demanded his loyalty when he had assumed the throne, and Despaldi did so out of duty. That requirement, his dedication to his new master, became something profoundly intrinsic and unbreakable when Thurvin had gifted him with a magic all his own.

Clenching his hand into a fist, Despaldi felt the heat rise inside the magically cooled gloves. With his power, he could burn the palace to the ground and even imagined doing so – a raging inferno of fireballs and heat hot enough to burn stone. Instead, he released the power, his fist cooling as he banged it on the door, a thumping echo carrying down the corridor.

"Who is it?" a voice came from within.

"Despaldi."

"Come in."

Opening the door, Despaldi crossed the dark sitting room and headed toward the connecting office, pale blue light streaming through the open doorway. As expected, Thurvin sat at his desk, his precious book laid out beneath the light of a lantern. The new desk still smelled of oiled oak. Despaldi had accidently destroyed the prior one.

"I am here to provide an update on our training," Despaldi said.

The man looked up from the book and sat back in his chair. "Go on."

"The extent of our abilities seems to have leveled, but our skill continues to grow, even if less than when we began. I believe we will be ready soon. I also suspect my men have more uses to discover when we combine our magic."

"Good." Thurvin nodded, his squinty eyes narrowing further. "Among the augmentations in Vanda's journal, I have discovered another that appears useful to our cause."

The wizard lord stood, the top of his head barely reaching Despaldi's shoulder. *He might be small of stature,* he thought, *but his power exceeds that of any living wizard.*

For many centuries, the magic of wizard lords had outstripped other wizards by a fair margin. Since the capture of three Ghealdan cities, Lord Thurvin's magic and the prayers feeding it had expanded greatly, perhaps double that of any other human. Ever.

The wizard lord strode to the window and looked out over the city of Marquithe, the center of his power. He spoke while staring up at the moon, full and bright in the eastern sky. "You will need to select a fifth soldier to join you. As before, choose wisely. He must be fit, strong, and a skilled warrior. More importantly, he must be loyal." Thurvin turned toward Despaldi. "With the power I have gifted you, I require unwavering fealty."

Despaldi dipped his head. "And you have it."

"Good. Select your man and bring him by tomorrow evening, prior to Devotion. I will bestow the augmentation before I recharge."

"Very well." A question lingered. "What...ability will this augmentation provide?"

Thurvin walked back to his desk, finger absently stroking a page of the open book, the parchment covered in an elaborate pattern the man had undoubtedly been memorizing. "The text speaks of power, but I believe it refers to strength. How strong exactly has yet to be determined."

Despaldi considered the statement and what he knew of the prior three augmentations. "That does seem useful to our cause."

"Agreed," Thurvin said, looking back up at Despaldi. "Once he has been gifted, you have one week to train him while continuing to train with the others."

"Seven days?"

"Yes. I will then recharge each of you with my magic before you depart."

"Where are we to go?"

"Tiamalyn."

Despaldi arched his brow. "The capital of Orenth?"

"Yes. I have reached out to Lord Horus, as we discussed, extending him the offer to work together against Pallanar in an effort to prevent Orenth from attacking my unprotected front while the armies are away." The wizard lord's expression darkened. "He declined, called me mad for believing I could expand my wizardom."

"You wish me to persuade him?"

"No. I wish you to assassinate him."

The statement struck Despaldi like a whip. He blinked in shock. Even the most skilled of wizards had little hope of surviving a confrontation with a wizard lord. If he possessed the Eye of Obscurance, things might have been different, but thus far, the amulet had evaded him.

I hate that blasted thief.

"Do you believe my men and I can do such a thing?" he asked.

Thurvin lashed out with his hand, invisible ropes tightening around Despaldi's chest and lifting him off the floor. The wizard lord then floated up until his face was level with Despaldi's, the shorter man glaring, eyes filled with fire.

"You five will become the new order – the Fist of Farrow. Through my actions, you have been gifted magic beyond what any normal wizard might wield, even if each ability is highly specific in nature. However, you possess another advantage, placing you in a position to defeat anyone you face. Unlike wizards, you were a warrior first, trained and experienced in combat. Even now, you train and test your abilities, hone your skills. Most wizards surround themselves with luxuries, more concerned with parties than confrontations. They cannot comprehend what it is to fight for their lives, something you understand well.

"Together, you can defeat Horus. Together, you will eliminate him."

In the same chamber that had once belonged to her parents, Priella Ueordlin gazed into the mirror, twisting her torso, her ice blue dress clinging to every curve. The body in the reflection was the one she had always desired – lean arms, smooth legs, thin waist, round backside, full chest. Her hair was fiery red, eyes emerald green. The face in the mirror was that of a stranger – a stunning, beautiful woman with a pale and flawless complexion. Staring at her new image had become an obsession, something she had avoided with her prior appearance.

She was not alone, for Bosinger Aedaunt, her personal bodyguard, sat in a chair across the room. The big man silently read over a report. Despite his attention on the paper, Priella knew he was watching her. He always watched her, his hand never far from his sword. A lifelong soldier, Bosinger took his duty seriously…often too much so.

The second Darkening had occurred earlier in the day, another moment of glory – the adoration of her people, the blessing of her god. Nearly a year would pass before another eclipse reached Illustan. By then, she would have the adoration of the world.

A knock sounded at the door. She considered sending whomever it was away, but the guards had been instructed to ensure she remain unbothered unless it was important. They would never dare cross her. Not now. Not with her newfound power.

"Come in," she said, just loud enough.

The door opened, a man in shining Gleam Guard armor entering, his gray hair tied back in a tail, weathered face covered in gray stubble. She had long considered Theodin Rahal handsome, the man a longtime member of her father's personal guard. There was a time she dreamed of him as a lover, despite being twice her age. Now, she set her sights higher. She could have any man she desired.

"My Queen." He bowed. "Scouts have returned from Ghealdor with a report."

She turned toward him. "Wonderful. I must know what occurs in our neighboring wizardoms – which rumors are true, which are false."

"Most of it appears true, Your Majesty." He rubbed his chin, eyes narrowed. "Farrowen has done more than invade Ghealdor. They have conquered three cities, including Fastella, and are currently marching toward Westhold."

Priella crossed her chambers and bent over the map on her desk. "Westhold is clear across the wizardom."

"Yes, Your Majesty. In addition, a mountain range divides the western cities from the east. It would require the army much time to return. They are more likely to march on Tangor. Beyond that, I fear they may continue down the coast, with Severan in their sights."

"That is my fear, as well, but I must focus on the bigger picture. Now, what of the towers?"

The man shook his head. "Somehow, the Fastella Tower of Devotion shines blue, as do the flames of the obelisks in Starmuth and Dorban. The people now pray to Farrow and add to Lord Thurvin's power."

Priella bit her lip and considered the additional power feeding the new Wizard Lord of Farrowen. Those three cities equaled three quarters of Ghealdor's population, essentially doubling Thurvin's magic. Not long ago, she had assumed her own throne, Devotion each evening since bringing her pure bliss. She tried to imagine double the prayers, but it was beyond her grasp. However, it was not beyond her desire.

"Prepare the army, Theo. They will march soon."

"In winter? You cannot be serious."

She turned toward him, anger flaring. "Do you dare question me?"

He took a step backward. "No. I just mean… It is difficult to march in the winter. It requires additional supplies and logistical considerations we could avoid if we waited until spring."

"The world is changing, Theo, and change brings opportunity. I have discovered that when opportunity presents itself, you either respond or allow it to pass by, possibly to never resurface."

"Do we march for Severan to meet the Farrowen force?"

"No. In fact, I wish to empty the Severan Garrison, as well. Fleet Commander Fuerig and every able ship are to set sail as soon as possible. His ships are to dock in Severan, load up with every soldier they can transport, and set sail for the Novecai Sea." Priella put her finger on the map and traced a route around the Ghealdan Peninsula. "They are to land outside of Fralyn, and wait until further orders."

Theodin blinked, his attention shifting toward Bosinger as the bodyguard rose to his feet. "You intend to conquer Orenth? What of Lord Thurvin and Farrowen? His lands lie between the two wizardoms."

"Our main force will move on Marquithe first, but it is only a stop along the way."

He moved closer, palms held out. "Please, My Queen. What drives this offensive? What can you hope to gain?"

Anger flared. "I needn't answer to you nor anyone else! Not any longer." She noticed Bosinger's reproving expression, took a deep breath, and continued in a more relaxed tone. "Just execute my orders, Captain."

Despite his apparent dissatisfaction with her response, Theodin nodded.

"Very well. We will begin preparations for a march. In the meantime, I will send Commander Feurig to Severan, as well as messengers to the garrison in Norstan. Those soldiers will sail to Shurick's Bay, joining our eastern fleet, and will follow Feurig to Fralyn."

Priella smiled. "Wonderful. How long before you are ready to march?"

"Ideally ten days, but we can be ready in as little as seven."

"A week it is."

"Yes, My Queen. I have one other concern."

"Which is?"

"We continue to receive reports from across Pallanar – livestock disappearing, others slaughtered, torn apart by some beast." His eyes reflected concern. "Additional reports cite winged creatures in the night. Monsters of some sort."

"You suspect the dragon that killed my father?"

He shrugged. "The description would suggest so."

"How would we track something that can fly? How can you face a creature able to slay a wizard lord?"

Theodin shook his head. "I do not know."

I cannot allow such distractions.

She turned back toward the mirror, red fingernails running down her exposed throat to her chest. "Continue to track these reports, but do not allow yourself to lose focus. You have a week to gather soldiers and prepare to march."

Hooking a finger into her neckline, she pulled it down to expose more than a hint of cleavage. *That's better.* When she saw Theodin's eyes follow and the man visibly swallow, she knew the affect her appearance caused.

It was glorious to be someone others desired, the man's reaction giving her nearly as much pleasure as his fear.

2

A THUNDERCLAP

The sleigh sped across the frozen lake, metal rails scraping across a bare section of ice. The team of ice wolves pulling it seemed unaffected, their hardened claws penetrating the slippery surface. Bright sunlight reflected off the white surroundings. Upon reaching the lake's edge, the wolves scrambled up the bank and into the forest, dark pines slipping past as they climbed toward the gap between two towering peaks.

Adyn Darro rode in the middle row of seats, Narine seated between her and Jace, a blanket across their laps. A Frostborn named Jeorgan-Ji drove the sleigh, their packs and tents filling the rear. She cast a backward glance and spotted two trailing sleighs, both driven by a Frostborn, one carrying Hadnoddon and Salvon, the other with the three dwarf Guardians.

Up the mountainside they climbed, as they had since dawn. It was midday, and she was still unable to see what waited beyond the mountain. That would soon change.

Three days had passed since leaving Kelmar. Three long, boring days. While her face was numb from the bitter wind, riding in the sleigh was a fair bit more comfortable than when in the saddle. At times, it was *too* comfortable, and she would doze off, only to be startled awake when the sleigh hit a rough patch.

The trees parted, the sleigh climbing uphill at an angle, circling a wall of exposed, gray rock. The ground leveled, the sleigh crested the ridge, and the view opened to reveal the vista beyond. The Frostborn pulled the reins, and the wolves slowed to a stop, the beasts panting, steam swirling from their snouts. Adyn sat forward and stretched her neck, her gaze sweeping the horizon.

White-capped peaks dotted the skyline as far as the eye could see, the ones to the distant east thrusting into the heavens, far above the puffy, white clouds dotting the sky. The dark green of pines covered the lower two-thirds of the surrounding mountains and ran throughout the valley below. Snow covered everything, dashing Adyn's hope for relief from the cold.

The other two sleighs stopped on the ridge, each no more than a few strides from the next. Jeorgan-Ji climbed out, stepping carefully on the snow with his odd, oversized boots, broad and flat at the base. He crossed to the middle sleigh, the three drivers converging for a conversation with Hadnoddon and Salvon.

Turning toward Narine, Adyn sighed. "It appears we are destined for another night of pitching tents in the snow."

Narine replied, "At least we can huddle together to keep each other warm."

Adyn snorted. "You mean so the thief can grope me again."

"Hey!" Jace bent forward to look past Narine. "I told you it was an accident. I was half-asleep, and you…" He shrugged, "happened to be within my reach."

"Admit you enjoyed it." Adyn grinned. "Your hand seemed to anyway. It lingered for some time before I smacked you."

Narine arched a brow at Jace, waiting for his response.

"Well…" He eyed Narine warily. "I…can't really say. I was still in a dream-state."

"I am curious about what occurred in this dream," Narine ventured.

He smiled. "It was about you, my princess. All my best dreams are about you."

"Oh no, you don't," Narine said. "I am the one stuck sleeping between you two. I woke to Adyn's startled cry, you groping her, and your *hardened sword* pressed against my hip. Besides, as you may have noticed, Adyn and I aren't exactly built the same. You expect me to believe you thought she was me?"

"Um… Of course not."

"Then why continue to grope her?"

He raised his hands in frustration. "I don't know! I was asleep!"

Adyn chuckled. In truth, she hadn't minded Jace's advances as much as she claimed. Too many weeks had passed since she had been with a man, and she wondered when she might get another chance. She had even considered Jeorgan-Ji. He was just her type – tall, brawny, masculine. However, whenever he faced her, a shiver would run down her spine.

It is his eyes, she thought. The white irises were…unsettling.

The others in their party consisted of two other white-eyed Frostborn, an old man, and the dwarf Guardians from Kelmar. The old storyteller was clearly not an option, nor was Hadnoddon. The dwarf captain was just too serious, his face drawn into a permanent scowl. With black, braided beards and thick, muscular builds, the other dwarfs warranted consideration, even if every one of them stood less than five feet tall, far shorter than Adyn's six-foot frame.

Hmm… I wonder how that would work. They are so short and stocky. Another thought occurred to her. *Can a dwarf get a human pregnant?* She pondered if Salvon knew. The old storyteller seemed to know something about everything.

The three Frostborn returned to their sleighs, each securing a fur hat onto his head, covering the white hair. The center sleigh, carrying Salvon and Hadnoddon and driven by a squat man named Ordan-Do, lurched forward. The other two sleighs plowed behind, with Adyn's settling in the middle. As they raced down the white mountainside, angling toward the forest below, she considered how she had become caught up in such a dramatic quest.

She had been only eight years old when her mother died. Her aunt, who worked at the Fastella Palace, had begged Lord Taladain to allow Adyn to live there with her. Such a request came with a price, and Adyn became the playmate of a five-year-old princess – a playmate who would train to become her protector, a job for which Captain Burrock and his men were to ensure she was prepared.

The injuries Adyn endured during the next ten years – broken bones, bruises, cuts, scrapes, and worse – had hardened her. While the Indigo Guard had taught her enough to be dangerous, their aggressive fighting style was more suitable to a man. Adyn was tall and strong for a woman, but she was no man. It wasn't until she had journeyed with Narine to the University in Tiadd that she learned the art of battle, taught by the best weapon masters in the Eight Wizardoms. Those men and women knew to how to properly adapt Adyn's fighting style to suit her physical attributes. Her standard short sword had been discarded, replaced by two lighter, curved blades. A slashing fighting style, based on quickness and agility, became her specialty, honed by eight years of intensive training. When the time came for her and Narine to leave the University, Adyn had wondered if she was destined for a quiet, boring life in Fastella.

She chuckled to herself. That certainly didn't happen.

Instead, Narine became embroiled in a tenuous situation, caught between her mad father and power-hungry brother, Prince Eldalain. During those days, Adyn had been worried. Fearing the worst for Narine while doubting her ability to stop either man. After all, Narine's brother was the most powerful wizard in Ghealdor, and her father was a wizard lord – a man with the power of a god.

Jace, Rhoa, Rawk, and Salvon had solved the problem by killing Taladain and subsequently smuggling Narine and Adyn out of Fastella. Then the real adventure began.

Eldalain pursued Narine, blaming her for Taladain's death. Adyn knew his true motive was to eliminate Narine, whom he viewed as a threat. While Jace had helped the two escape the man's wrath, he ended up leading them right into the hands of Lord Malvorian, a wizard lord who sought to expand his power by capturing the Towers of Devotion across Ghealdor.

That encounter almost led to disaster, Adyn thought. *We all could have died had things gone differently. Jace nearly did die.*

The thief had been run through by a sword during the fracas. Only with the added power of an enchanted bracelet, which Narine had stolen from a wizard named Thurvin, had she been able to heal Jace's mortal wounds.

Even then, it was obvious Narine had fallen for the rogue. Adyn grinned. *She has grown so much in such a short time. Jace, this clever thief who grew up on the streets, influences her. Somehow, he has changed her for the better, Narine evolving into the woman I knew she could become.*

Adyn would never say it out loud, but she truly liked Jace and appreciated him for his impact on Narine.

She leaned close to Narine and asked quietly, "How many times has he saved your life now?"

With a furrowed brow, Narine turned toward Adyn, the princess' long, blonde hair hidden beneath the hood of her gray, wool cloak. "Where did that come from?"

"Just wondering."

Frowning as she considered the question, Narine said, "Let's see… First, the escape from Fastella, then from the tavern in Starmuth. He played a key role during our fight with Malvorian, although I also saved him. Of course, I certainly would have died from the dragon attack in Illustan if not for him."

Adyn shook her head. "I can't believe I almost forgot about the dragon attack."

"I'll not forget. Ever. It was among the most frightening moments of my life."

Jace peered around Narine, brows furrowed. "What are you two talking about?"

Adyn couldn't resist stirring his ire. "About you. In bed. So many details… Which things you enjoy, what you do well, what leaves her disappointed…"

"*What*?!" His face darkened. "Disappointed? What... Why would you tell her stuff like that?"

Narine smacked Adyn's leg. "Don't listen to her. She's trying to get under your skin." She kissed him on the cheek. "You need not worry. I am completely happy with you and your…prowess."

With narrowed eyes flicking from Adyn to Narine, Jace asked, "You promise?"

"I do." She smirked at Adyn. "If she doesn't play nice, I'll even show you, right in front of her, in our tiny little tent."

Adyn laughed. "Oh, don't tempt me. I might test you just to see if you'll do it."

"I might, you know." Narine's grin was lecherous.

"A season ago, I would have bet anything against it." Adyn shrugged. "Now, I am not so sure."

Narine blinked. "Have I changed so much?"

Adyn put her arm around Narine's shoulders and hugged her close. "Not all change is bad. Remember, you saved Jace more than once, as well. You saved an entire city back in Illustan. As I told you before we left Kelmar, I am proud of the woman you have become."

The way Narine had behaved during the wyvern attack, then during their stay with the Seers remained keen in Adyn's mind. *With each passing day, she seems more confident, growing into a leader others respect.* Even during the goblin attack, when greatly outnumbered, Narine had acted with fierce bravery. Adyn wished the princess wouldn't place herself at such risk, but she could hardly fault her results.

The lead sleigh entered the forest, the massive wolves slowing, the Frostborn guiding them through narrow gaps among the pines. Then Adyn's own sleigh was surrounded by trees, the branches scraping against the hull and racing past far too rapidly for comfort. She doubted the wolves would run into a tree, but what of the sleigh? A turn at the wrong time could be disastrous.

Just as quickly as the forest had risen, it fell away. A white field of snow lay ahead, the vast valley beyond. The lead sleigh slowed, the Frostborn shouting urgently. Jeorgan-Ji reacted, yanking on the reins and issuing a series of guttural orders. Adyn couldn't understand the words, but it wasn't necessary. The sharp drop ahead was all she needed to know. She gripped the seat and clenched her teeth, afraid they were going too fast and would go over.

The wolves slowed, the team turning and redirecting the sleigh. When it stopped, Adyn glanced to the side, the sleigh parallel to the valley and perched atop a shelf of snow. The other two sleighs had stopped, as well, all three within strides of the deadly drop. Behind them, their tracks led back toward the trees that had obstructed the danger from view.

"That was close," Narine exhaled.

"Yeah." Adyn turned and looked toward the sleigh Salvon shared with Hadnoddon. "It was a good thing the first sleigh stopped or we–"

Salvon turned from Hadnoddon and slapped his hands together. A clap of thunder reverberated from the heavens above, causing Adyn to jump with a start.

The sleigh began to shake.

Narine frowned. "What is happening?"

Jace leapt to his feet. "We need to run!" He turned and muttered, "Too late."

Not only was their sleigh shaking, everything around them was, as well – the other sleighs, the wolves, even the surrounding snow. A gap formed near the tree line, a loud crack evolving into a rumble.

Avalanche, she realized in horror.

"Get down!" Jace pushed her and Narine's heads down as he pulled the blanket up and over them.

The entire area gave way, her heart leaping into her throat as the sleighs, and everyone on them, plummeted in a wave of white.

3

SURVIVAL

Narine Killarius fought to wake. She opened her eyes but saw only blackness. When she tried to move, weight kept her immobile. The avalanche and their plunge down the mountainside came back to her.

Panic struck, her heart racing, breath coming in gasps. Overwhelmed, she struggled to move. The tight space, the darkness, a mountain of snow on top of her… It was too much.

"Narine," Jace said. "I am here."

His words, though muffled, brought her back from the edge. She felt him against her side, Adyn against the other.

"The snow is too heavy. I can't move. Use your magic, Narine," Jace pleaded.

Magic. He needs me.

Her breathing calmed, focus returning. She twisted her hand slightly and called upon her magic. Since acquiring the object around her ankle, her power far exceeded what she could wield without it. A construct formed, the light of it sparking hope inside her. Drawing in as much as she could, she pressed her hand against the blanket above her and channeled it through the construct. A burst of hardened air sprang forth, the concussion of the blast leaving her ears ringing.

The pressure against her was gone, but snow fell, covering her face, arms, slipping inside her cloak. For a moment, she feared she was buried once again, but when she opened her eyes, she saw light. They were in a pit of snow, the lip five feet above. Jace rose to his feet and climbed up. Standing on the seat of the sleigh, he reached down, Narine gripping his hand. He pulled her up and out of her seat.

"Climb up me to get out."

She paused and looked down. "We need to save Adyn. I… I can't lose her."

Jace grasped her face and turned it toward him to look her in the eye. "Get yourself to safety, and I will pull her out. The opening is too narrow for me to do it with you in the way."

Narine nodded and did as he requested, using Jace like a human ladder as he pushed her upward.

Once on top, Narine crawled from the pit, squinting in the bright sun. One of the other sleighs was visible, tipped on its side and half-buried. Salvon and Hadnoddon knelt in the snow beside it, both alive, the dwarf bruised and scraped. Their driver lay in the snow between them, unmoving.

Spinning around, Narine peered over the edge of the pit while Jace dug Adyn free. She began to stir, blinking in the light.

"You…are…heavy," Jace grunted as he tried to lift her. "We…need…to…get…you…out."

"My leg…" Adyn grimaced. "I fear it's broken."

Jace paused, panting, while Adyn remained half-buried. "Use your other leg to push off. Do anything you can to help. Once we get you out of here, Narine can heal you."

Adyn clenched her teeth and pushed while Jace lifted, his hands beneath her arms. Haltingly, inch by inch, she moved, until finally breaking free. Unprepared, Jace fell backward against the snow, causing a tiny avalanche that buried his head and ran down the back of his cloak.

"Ugh." He regained his feet and balanced on the backs of the seats, shaking himself. "That's cold."

He bent and helped Adyn up, the bodyguard eventually rising to stand on the seat, keeping weight off her other leg.

"I am going to hoist you up." Jace locked his fingers together and prepared himself.

Adyn put her hands on his shoulders, placed her foot into his hands, and pushed up. Narine extended her arms and helped from the top, pulling while Jace pushed. The moment reminded her of the time he saved her from Charcoan's soldiers in Starmuth. She had accused him of groping her backside while he helped her onto a rooftop.

Why was I so concerned about such things? It seemed so silly. She couldn't believe only a season had passed since then. *Adyn is right. I have changed.*

While Adyn lay in the snow, gasping for breath, face twisted in pain, Narine examined her leg. Her breeches were torn and bloody, her shin bone poking through.

"Your leg is broken."

Adyn opened her eyes and lifted her head, looking down at it. "Really? I had no idea. Is the bone *not* supposed to be sticking out like that?"

Narine pressed her lips together. "I forgot how nasty you are as a patient. Too bad for you, I am going to have to set your leg before I can heal it."

The bodyguard closed her eyes and nodded, laying her head back down. "Do it."

"I'll need Jace's help."

A pack flew from the pit and landed beside Narine. A moment later, two more packs followed. He then climbed over the edge and collapsed into the snow, panting as if he had run for miles.

Narine poked him. "You need to get up."

He looked at her with a hurt expression. "I feel underappreciated at the moment."

She rolled her eyes. "I'll show you proper appreciation some other time. Right now, we need to heal Adyn and see if we can keep ourselves alive."

Groaning, he crawled to Adyn and looked at her leg. He frowned and produced his dagger, holding it before her face. Without a word, she bit down on it. Jace crawled down to her leg, positioning himself with a foot near the bone, one hand below her knee and the other gripping her boot.

"I am ready when you are," he said.

Narine gathered her magic, albeit with far more difficulty than the previous use. She was tired from the energy spell, a magic unsuited to women and something that would have been impossible without her anklet. Healing, however, was another matter.

Forming a construct of repair, which glowed with a white aura, she held it ready and nodded. Jace jerked back, his foot driving the broken bone back into place and eliciting a strangled cry from Adyn. Narine applied her magic and knitted the damaged bone and flesh back together in moments. Releasing her magic, she sat back with a sigh.

An aged voice came from behind her. "It is fortunate you three survived."

She turned and found Salvon standing over her, his long, gray beard speckled by bits of snow, as were his bushy eyebrows. While disheveled, the storyteller seemed unharmed, wearing his patchwork cloak, his lute and pack over his shoulders. Hadnoddon approached, sinking into the snow with each step, which was odd because Salvon barely sank at all. *The dwarf is armored and thickly muscled, so I guess it makes sense.* Clumps of snow clung to his thick, black beard, and he squinted in the bright sunlight before fitting his helmet over his head.

"We were buried," Narine pointed toward the pit.

"What of Jeorgan-Ji?"

Narine gasped and turned toward the hole. "I don't know…"

"I checked," Jace said. "The man is dead, his neck broken. The three of us ducked down as the avalanche swept away our sleigh. He was not as lucky."

Hadnoddon grunted. "Our driver is dead, as well. He has a nasty gash to his head. When you see brains leaking, it's a bad sign."

"What of the wolves from your sleigh?" Jace asked.

"Gone," Hadnoddon said.

Salvon pointed west, down the valley. "When the snow settled, I saw them limping into the forest. In truth, without the Frostborn to control them, ice wolves are more likely to consider us food than friends. I suggest we head in the other direction."

Jace grasped Narine's hand and helped her up, her feet sinking into the snow, the cold seeping through the long, wool socks given to her by the Seers.

The Seers… Recalling them reminded her of their mission.

"How are we going to travel in this?" She began to panic again, picturing herself freezing to death.

"Have you seen the other sleigh?" Jace asked.

Salvon shook his head. "No."

"Nor I." Hadnoddon's mouth was drawn in a deep scowl. "I fear they are buried somewhere beneath the snow and dead by now."

Jace cupped his hands to his mouth and shouted, his voice echoing in the distance. Nobody responded.

"It seems as if we are left alone, the others gone," Salvon stated. "It will get cold at night and be difficult to travel. We have two tents in our sleigh. I suggest we take them, along with anything else we can carry, and begin marching north."

"North?" Narine asked.

"Yes," Jace said, pointing toward the round moon. "That's northeast, so…" He pointed toward a gap between two peaks, "that way is north. If we can reach Orenth, we can take a boat downriver and catch a ship to Cor Cordium."

Adyn stood and tested her leg while her stomach growled angrily. "I'm starving."

"Healing comes with a cost," Narine noted.

"I know," Adyn snapped. "It doesn't change how I feel, though."

With a reproachful stare, Narine said dryly, "I am overwhelmed by your gratitude."

The bodyguard sighed. "I'm sorry. You know I get grumpy when I'm hungry. And thank you." She put a hand on Jace's shoulder. "Thank you both for saving me."

Jace put his arm around Narine. "You are welcome. Besides, if you'd died, who would keep us out of trouble?"

Narine focused on Jace, who walked directly ahead of her, following the path carved by Hadnoddon. The powerful, armored dwarf led the party through the mountains as they worked their way north. Progress was slow. After an hour of traveling, the five survivors had only made it a mile. The deep snow often buried Narine up to her knees, occasionally reaching her waist. Her furs, mitts, and heavy cloak helped, but the wool socks beneath her dress were wet, and she feared how she would fare at nightfall when it grew colder. She had other clothing in her pack, which weighed her down, but that would quickly become wet, as well, so there was no point in changing.

The ground continually sloped downhill as they tromped through the snow, between thick pines. After roughly two hours, the sun behind a peak to the west, Hadnoddon stopped, almost causing Jace to run into his back. Narine didn't notice until she crashed into Jace's pack, striking her nose.

She rubbed it as he turned toward her.

"Are you okay?"

"Yeah. Just another blow to my pride."

Adyn chuckled.

Jace turned to Hadnoddon. "Why'd you stop?"

"Listen," the dwarf grumbled.

A rush of running water came from ahead.

"A river," Salvon said. "They run along all these mountain valleys."

"Yes," Hadnoddon replied. "We can refill our waterskins. Also, where there is water, there are often caves."

Shelter, Narine thought, a kindle of hope sparking.

They continued downward at an angle, slipping between hillside pines as they descended methodically. All the while, their surroundings continued to grow darker, the rush of water growing louder. The first sighting was through the forest, whitecaps amid a stripe of darkness. Within minutes, they stood at the shore of a river.

The water was no more than a dozen strides across, but it rushed past swiftly, flowing over rocks hidden just below the surface. She pulled off a mitt and bent to fill a waterskin, the frigid water splashing on her fingers. When she took a drink, it was so cold it made her head hurt. After refilling their waterskins, they shouldered their packs and continued along the bank.

They rounded a bend, beyond which the river split a gap between two rocky cliffs. A shadowy recess lurked in the face of the rock, stirring the coals of hope simmering inside her.

Hadnoddon picked up his pace, climbing up snow-covered rocks as he headed toward the recess. Jace stopped at the rocks and set down his pack.

"Why are you stopping?" Narine asked.

"His eyes are far better than ours in the dark. I will let him investigate while we rest. He'll let us know if it's worth the climb."

Narine couldn't argue with Jace's logic, so she set down her pack, Adyn and Salvon gathering close. By then, the eastern sky was midnight blue, the full moon painted with yellow in the light of the setting sun. It would be within minutes. She prayed Hadnoddon discovered a cave large enough to fit everyone.

When the dwarf emerged, he waved them to follow, then ducked out of sight again. Encouraged, Narine lifted her pack and prepared for the climb. With a little help from Jace and Adyn, it didn't go too badly. The four of them reached the opening and peered into the dark entrance where the dwarf waited. A purple glow bloomed in Hadnoddon's palm, and he handed glowing stones to Jace, Adyn, and Salvon.

"Do you have any more?" Narine asked.

"No." The dwarf turned away.

"What about you and me?"

"I don't need one. If you can't see well enough, use your magic. Otherwise, stay close to the others and you'll be fine."

Narine grimaced at him and wondered if the effect was lost in the darkness.

Adyn whispered over her shoulder, "I can almost hear your scowl."

"I am not scowling," she said with a bit too much heat.

The bodyguard chuckled but said nothing more.

Following the glowing rock Jace held above his shoulder, Narine entered a narrow tunnel, which rounded a bend and opened to a cavern. It was ten strides across and twice as deep. Not only was it large enough to house them, but a dormant fire pit occupied the center. Jace dropped his pack and released a sigh.

"We are saved," she said in a hushed voice.

"No," Hadnoddon said from the back of the cave.

"What?" Jace asked.

"This is not where we stop. Come." The dwarf climbed up an angled, rocky surface.

Sighing, the others collected their packs and climbed up behind the dwarf. When Narine reached the top, rising to her feet with Jace's help, she noticed an oddity.

To her side was an open, circular, stone door, like a wheel made of rock, that stood taller than Adyn.

"This is Maker work," Hadnoddon said.

"It stands open," Salvon noted.

"You are amazingly observant," Jace said wryly.

Hadnoddon grunted. "You do not understand. Makers do not leave entrances open."

The thief rubbed his jaw. "Perhaps someone else left it open."

"Exactly."

Narine just wanted a warm place to rest. They had enough food to get by for a while and had just filled their skins. If they could stay somewhere to dry off and thaw out, they could attempt to travel during daylight.

"Do we go inside?" she asked. "Or do we camp here?"

Hadnoddon ran his hand across the stone door, tracing dark indentations. "This is in the old language. It says, *'Within lies the city of metal.'*"

Salvon gasped.

Narine frowned. "What does that mean?"

"It means we have found the entrance to the lost dwarven city of Oren'Tahal."

4

INTO THE DARK

Jerrell "Jace" Landish considered the rolled tents tucked against the cavern wall. It had been a restless, uncomfortable night of sleeping on the rocky cavern floor with edges digging into him, regardless of his position. All along, the wind howled outside the tunnel entrance. He woke weary and sore, longing for a soft bed and a hot meal. Neither was likely to come anytime soon.

At least we have enough trail rations to keep us alive for another four or five days.

With Hadnoddon in the lead, they climbed to the shelf at the rear of the cavern, prepared to pass through the odd Maker doorway.

Jace extended a hand to help Narine up, then turned toward the dwarf. "You are sure?"

Hadnoddon spun around and nodded. "I can find the way. It is in my blood."

"And the tunnel goes all the way through?"

A sound came from the dwarf. Something between a grunt and a growl. "Dwarfs are thorough. They would never build a city without multiple routes in and out. Everyone knows that."

Salvon put a hand on Jace's shoulder before he could retort. "According to legend, the city of Oren'Tahal is part of a larger network. The tunnels should be extensive, connecting the Frost Forest to Lake Grakal."

Part of Jace wanted to believe, but another part of him screamed for an alternative.

"Are you listening to your choice of words?" Jace argued. "Terms such as *legend* and *should be* do not instill confidence. Even if we enter these tunnels and come out the other side, by leaving the tents behind, we also leave behind shelter should it be needed once we are back outside."

Growling, Hadnoddon stepped closer to Jace, his scowl making it evident he had lost patience. "If you want to carry the tents, I won't stop you. But I am done. We have many miles to go, and I'll not be burdened by them any longer."

"What is your problem, Hadnoddon?" Adyn asked. "You seem even more surly than usual. Is it the soldiers you lost in the avalanche?"

The dwarf turned his grimace toward her. "No… Well, not mainly. I am mostly upset about my axe. It was lost during the fall down the mountainside."

Aghast, Narine asked, "Your comrades died, yet you are grumpy about an axe?"

Hadnoddon grunted as he turned toward the circular door. "I was quite fond of that axe."

The dwarf entered the tunnel, quickly consumed by darkness. Salvon followed, a glowing stone in hand, leaving Jace alone with Narine and Adyn.

Narine put her hand on his arm. "Perhaps we should trust them."

"Would you rather tromp through the snow?" Adyn asked.

He sighed. "No. I just dislike not knowing what I face."

Narine gripped his hand. "Let's go, Jace. Together."

He knew her trepidation about entering the mountain after the panic she had experienced during the journey to Kelmar. *If she is willing to do it, why are you fighting so hard?* He could not explain it, not to himself or anyone else, so he chose to give in.

With one hand holding hers, the other gripping a glowing stone, he entered the tunnel, Adyn trailing as they left the surface world behind.

Hours passed. How many, Jace wasn't sure. The walk turned out to be easy, the tunnel mostly straight and surprisingly level. He was unsure of where they were. Certainly, far below a mountain. He just had no idea which mountain. By the time they had reached the first intersection, he guessed they had traveled eight or ten miles. Without pausing, Hadnoddon chose a tunnel and continued, the others trailing.

An hour later, a smell arose. Jace wrinkled his nose, wondering if someone had soiled themselves. It grew increasingly stronger, forcing him to cover his face. The tunnel opened to a larger gallery, pointed stalactites hanging over a still pool of water. When Hadnoddon stopped and knelt beside the pool, Jace stretched, attempting to work kinks out of his neck and shoulders.

"Sleeping on the rocky cavern floor did something to my body," he grumbled.

Salvon chuckled. "You are young yet. Wait a few decades. You'll feel that way from a soft bed and three times as bad after sleeping on the ground."

Hadnoddon stood. "The water's no good. Tainted by minerals."

"Sulfur." Salvon nodded.

"Is that what stinks?" Narine asked.

"I thought it was Jace." Adyn elbowed him in the gut.

"Oof." Jace bent with the blow. "You are hilarious."

Adyn grinned. "I have always thought so."

Jace lifted his waterskin, Hadnoddon gripping his wrist.

"Ration the water. Drink as little as possible until we find a fresh source to refill."

Grimacing, Jace left the skin capped. "Where is this city? We have been walking for hours."

"We will get there. Trust me." Hadnoddon circled the pool, leading them toward another tunnel.

Jace was weary. They had stopped only three times since entering the network of tunnels. Each time was in a natural gallery, the walls sparkling with flecks of metal. During those breaks, everyone sat on rocks, eating rations and sipping water. The rests were brief compared to the travel time in between. All the while, he continually wondered if Hadnoddon really knew where he was going. They had come to intersections a dozen times, the dwarf choosing the next tunnel without hesitation. Jace worried it was merely a display of false confidence, but he had no way to tell. He only knew he was tired, hungry, and his feet hurt. By his estimation, they had traveled at least fifteen miles. Perhaps twenty. Yet the endless tunnels continued. He held back brewing complaints, refusing to express them until someone else did so first. After all, he was traveling with an old man and a spoiled princess. Surely one of them would break soon.

"Stop," Hadnoddon whispered, drawing Jace from his reverie. The dwarf held up his hand while staring in the opposite direction. "Cover the lights."

Jace tucked the glowing stone inside his coat, Adyn and Salvon doing the same. The tunnel fell dark, other than a dim light ahead. *Daylight?* Applying restraint, he denied the urge to run toward it. Narine pushed past him, evidently experiencing the same longing.

Jace grabbed her shoulders and pulled her back, whispering, "Careful. We don't know what lies ahead."

"I need to–"

He covered her mouth. Her breathing was heavy, on the verge of panic.

In a soft voice, he said, "Close your eyes. Deep breaths. I am here. Adyn is here. Everything will be all right." He spun her around and hugged her. She buried her face in his shoulder while squeezing him tightly.

When Narine let go, he kissed her forehead, then handed her his glowing rock.

"Hold this. I'll be back."

Jace slipped past her and found Hadnoddon's shoulder, whispering, "I will sneak ahead and see what is causing the light."

The dwarf said, "Why you?"

"Remember, I am the *Charlatan of Ages*. A thief. I have spent my entire life sneaking about."

Without waiting for a response, he crept ahead.

The tunnel curved, the light growing brighter as he advanced. An opening branched off to one side, sloping downhill. He continued past it and slowed at the tunnel mouth, peering out without emerging from the shadows.

A circular cavern, shaped like an inverted cone, stood before him. It was surrounded by ledges two strides deep, creating tiers, each level wider than the one below it. Dark doorways lined each tier. The chamber was over two hundred feet across at his level.

He leaned forward and peered up. A white, glowing web stretched from wall to wall, thick strands of gossamer shining, as if made of enchanted crystal. On the web, he saw no movement, but he heard noise from below.

Creeping forward, he peeked over the edge. The bottom of the cavern was easily a hundred feet below. His eyes widened when he saw a cluster of familiar, wiry forms scurrying across and disappearing down a tunnel.

Goblins…

Jace eased back and snuck back along the tunnel to where the others waited.

"Trouble ahead," he whispered.

Hadnoddon's voice came from the darkness. "What trouble?"

"Goblins."

"What are they doing here?"

Jace considered the question and found a possible answer, solving a puzzle that had bothered him for days. "When did the Dark Lord attack Xionne in the Oracle?"

"Hmm…" Salvon pulled his glowing rock from his cloak, illuminating the group. "I would say eight or nine days past. Ten at most."

"And the goblin attack came just four days ago, right?"

"Yes," Hadnoddon grunted. "What's your point?"

"The Fractured Lands are to the distant north, way up at the edge of Kyranni. That is many hundreds of miles from here, and we are easily sixty miles from Kelmar. If the goblins began at The Fractured Lands, they could never have made it to Kelmar in five or six days. Not without some sort of magical means of transport." Jace pointed toward the cavern. "What if the goblins were down here all along? What if the Dark Lord sent them from Orntalla–"

"Oren'Tahal," Salvon corrected.

"Whatever." Jace waved it off. "If they came from here, it would explain how they arrived in Kelmar in such a short time."

A growl came from Hadnoddon. "Goblins, in a dwarven city…"

Salvon put his hand on the dwarf's thick, armored shoulder. "Easy. If this is true, there are too many to fight. Remember our mission."

The dwarf captain nodded. "The goblins can wait."

"Should we turn back?" Narine asked.

Hadnoddon shook his head. "No. It will take too long." He turned to Jace. "What else did you see? What did it look like?"

Jace described the chamber and their location compared to the goblins, hesitating before he mentioned the glowing web. Judging by the size, he didn't want to meet the creature that had woven it. He worried how the girls, particularly Narine, might react.

"What?" she blurted. "Was it a spider? How big is this web?"

He put his hand on her arm. "Don't panic. I didn't see anything other than the web. For all we know, the thing that made it died centuries ago and the web has remained dormant ever since."

"Do you think it's bigger than the spider we saw in Kelmar?" she whispered.

He sighed, not able to lie to her. "Yes. The web is...*really* big."

"Forget the web," Hadnoddon said. "There will be another main tunnel opposite this one. We will circle the cavern, remain quiet while doing so, and continue on once we reach it."

Jace considered the plan. *If we remain close to the outer wall, we will be obscured from the goblins' view...assuming they are only on the bottom level.*

With Hadnoddon again in the lead, they crept down the tunnel and into the cavern. Circling to one side, hugging the outer wall, they snuck along the perimeter. At the first open doorway, Jace peered inside. It appeared to be an apartment of sorts, filled with dusty furniture made of stone and metal. In fact, each opening they passed was similar to the first. Part of him longed to explore, to see if any hidden trinkets, gold, or jewels could be found. Another part of him screamed to hurry and get away from the chamber as quickly as possible.

Noise came from below.

Hadnoddon stopped, his back pinned to the wall, everyone else doing the same. Guttural chatter drifted up, a mix of grunts and words in some ugly, foreign language. Jace recalled hearing the same thing during the goblin attack in Kelmar. The sounds faded, then all fell silent.

They continued forward, reaching the far side of the chamber minutes later. As Hadnoddon had predicted, another tunnel led deeper into the mountain. The dwarf led them into the darkness, leaving the lit cavern behind.

An hour passed before Jace's weariness returned and Hadnoddon stopped. When everyone settled into place, a sound came from ahead – soft and subtle, yet unmistakable.

"Water," he said.

"Yes." Hadnoddon resumed walking, leading them at a slower pace.

The sound of running water grew increasingly more distinct until they reached a junction, a tunnel to one side, another leading straight ahead. The dwarf led them toward the sound, the tunnel widening to a cavern with a sloped floor and a crack in the ceiling. Water fell from the crack, ran down the rock, and poured downhill before disappearing into another fissure. Hadnoddon knelt beside the rivulet, the water ankle-deep and three times the width. With a cupped hand, he lifted a scoop to his nose and smelled before hesitatingly tasting it. Jace held his breath, watching for a reaction. When a grin emerged from Hadnoddon's thick beard, a wave of relief struck.

In moments, Jace drank the remainder of his waterskin. Bending to refill it, bubbles emerged from the spout as the water displaced the air.

Hadnoddon said, "It has been a long day. We need to rest. Here seems as a good a place as any. We can refill the waterskins after we wake, then resume the trek."

Everyone drank their fill before they settled on the upper end of the cavern, the only area where the floor was level. With his back against the wall, Narine leaning against his shoulder, Jace felt a moment of peace. His stomach growled, so he dug some dried deer meat from his pack, silently thanking the Frostborn for leaving such a valuable gift. It was chewy and salty, but he didn't mind. He had an unlimited supply of water, at least for the moment. The others also ate while listening to the calming sound of the rushing water. Minutes passed, perhaps fifteen, before Jace broke the silence.

"I am surprised, Hadnoddon. The legendary city you spoke of was…underwhelming."

The dwarf frowned. "What are you talking about?"

"Back there. The city where we saw the goblins."

A rumble of laughter echoed in the chamber, the dwarf holding his hand on his stomach. "That was no city. It was simply a mining outpost."

"Outpost?"

"The downward sloping tunnel at the bottom leads to a mine. The cart the monsters pushed was filled with ore."

Jace frowned as he considered. "They are forging weapons?"

Hadnoddon shrugged. "It is what I suspect."

"The monsters pushing the carts were much bigger than the goblins. What were they?"

"Those were ogres," Salvon replied. "There are numerous types of dark-spawn – goblins the smallest and most common, rock trolls among the largest. Trust me. You would not wish to meet a rock troll. Ogres are in the middle. Stories describe them as remarkably stupid, far more so than a goblin."

"They use these ogres as beasts of burden?"

"It would appear so." The old man stroked his beard, appearing lost in thought.

Jace asked, "How far did we walk today? Twenty miles?"

Hadnoddon snorted. "I'd say twenty-five at the least. Perhaps close to thirty. The day has been long, and it is likely well past nightfall."

"I hate these caves," Narine grumbled. "I miss the sky, the open air…the sun. In the darkness, I never know what time it is. I lost track of days in Kelmar, but this is even worse."

"Time." Hadnoddon shook his head with a wry smile. "Mankind is always worried about time. No other species pays such attention to it, treating the passing of days as if they are chunks of gold being spent."

"That is easy for you to say, Captain," Salvon said. "Your kind lives twice as long as men."

Jace's eyebrows raised. "They do?"

The old man chuckled. "Of course. Have you never asked Rawk his age?"

"I never thought about it. I figured he was around my age."

"He is forty-eight."

Jace blinked at the idea. "Yet he acts so…ignorant."

Salvon shook his head. "I prefer the term *innocent*. He knows little of the world of man. No more than what he has learned since you met him."

"That might be true," Jace admitted. "Thankfully, his…innocence hasn't caused us too much trouble."

Adyn shook her head. "There were moments we would have died without his help. I would say he hasn't caused us any trouble at all."

Jace pressed his lips together, recalling moments of Rawk's surprising heroism – the escape from Fastella Palace, the battle against a wyvern, his help during the goblin battle in Kelmar. Finally, he nodded. "Fair enough."

Salvon grinned. "Now that you better understand our friend Rawk, I would like to share a story about his people. This is an old tale, occurring nearly two thousand years in the past. It is the tale of King Ghi-Blan Durrock, the last king of Oren'Tahal."

5

GONE COLD

The Mangy Dog was just as Rindle remembered, a rough and rowdy crowd already gathered in the taproom. A shout came from the corner where six men played dice. Recognizing three of them, he had to stifle an urge to join the game.

Focus, Rindle. You have more important things to do.

He led Garvin to the bar and waved down the tall, overweight barkeep. Big Herm had owned the place for as long as he could recall. Crossing him was not recommended.

The man lumbered over and cocked his head. "Haven't seen you around lately, Rindle."

"Hi, Herm. I need a room and a meal for two."

"I assume you have the coin for this?"

Rindle placed six coppers onto the bar, the man's thick fingers covering them in a flash.

"That'll earn you two ales, as well." The man walked off

"This place is aptly named," Garvin said from Rindle's shoulder, looking around.

"We need a room and a hot meal, but our funds are limited," Rindle noted. "A decent inn would cost us a silver."

"I'll not complain, as long as the beds don't come with lice or something."

Rindle blinked. He had never slept at the inn and hadn't considered lice.

Herm returned with two ales and a key. "You want to eat here or in your room?"

"We'll eat in the room." Garvin grabbed an ale and the key.

"Thanks, Herm." Rindle took a deep drink, turned, and followed Garvin up the stairs.

The room was small, consisting of nothing more than two beds and a table holding a basin of water, a bar of soap, and two towels. Garvin dropped his packs onto a bed and headed toward the table. He then set down his ale and shrugged off his cloak, coat, and tunic, revealing a muscular torso.

"I'm going to wash up before dinner." The man turned toward the wash-basin and began wetting the bar of soap.

Rindle sat on a bed and lowered his pack, his gaze landing on Garvin's pack and saddlebag, the latter lying flat with the flap open. A glance toward the lieutenant showed the man's back to him as he splashed water across his face and torso. With care, Rindle reached for the saddlebag and slipped his hand inside. His fingers found the sharp edges of a fist-sized gem. Gripping it, he pulled his hand back, a purple amethyst in his palm.

Rising to his feet, Rindle turned his back toward Garvin and downed his ale, his other hand stuffing the gem into a hidden coat pocket, the thing barely fitting. He then spoke over his shoulder while opening the door.

"It may be a long time before I return to Fastella. I wish to say goodbye to some old friends while we are here."

Garvin turned toward him while scrubbing beneath an armpit. "What about your meal?"

"Leave it on the table. I'll eat when I come back."

He pulled the door closed and headed down the corridor, muttering, "So much for a hot meal."

He sped down the stairs and out the door, into the darkening streets of Fastella. Inhaling deeply, he headed toward the heart of the city.

"It is nice to be home," he said to himself. "Even if just for an evening."

"He will wish to see me," Rindle insisted, his frustration growing. He resisted the urge to draw his rapier and run the man through.

The guard growled, "I told you to leave off." He took a step forward, hand on his sword, stopping short of drawing it when his companion put a hand against his chest.

"Easy, Kerwin." The other soldier turned to Rindle. "I suggest you leave. Return to the palace tomorrow. Perhaps High Wizard Parsec will admit you during court."

Frustrated, Rindle turned from the gate and walked along the outer wall of the palace grounds. He only had this one night, due to leave with Garvin at sunrise. His hand went to the lump in his coat, the gem still hidden there. *I need to speak with Parsec.* He didn't have time to execute a break-in.

A beam of blue light streaked across the sky from the southeast, igniting the Tower of Devotion. He turned as the guards at the gate fell to their knees. Both men joined in the chant of Devotion heard across the city. Rather than doing the same, Rindle put his back to the wall and crept back toward the gate. Just before he reached it, one of the men turned toward him.

"Stop!"

Rindle darted through, running as fast as he could, both guards rising to their feet and giving chase.

He circled the courtyard fountain and headed for the nearest door, the clatter of the armored men following, shouting. Two more soldiers rounded a corner and raced in to intercept him, but he reached the door first.

Gasping for air, his heart racing, he dashed inside and down the corridor. A guard appeared ahead to block his path. He turned and raced up the stairwell, the shouts of those chasing him growing louder.

Up and up he climbed, two stairs at a time, panting with each stride. He was tiring, the men chasing him growing closer.

Almost there, he told himself as he passed a landing.

When he reached the top, he turned and ran down the corridor. An armed guard at the far end spun around, saw him, and freed his sword from its scabbard.

The man charged. "Intruder!"

Rindle yanked his rapier out and slowed, preparing to fight. A door opened ahead, the dimly lit corridor brightening when a magic orb appeared near the ceiling. The rumble of the chasing soldiers reached the top level.

With his big bodyguard, Lang, at his side, Parsec emerged from his chambers, the bright light shining above his head. He took one look at Rindle and shouted, "Stop! Nobody move!"

Raising his hands, Rindle dropped his rapier, the weapon striking the floor with a clatter. Five guards stood behind him, weapons ready as they gasped for air. Another guard stood between him and Parsec, the man glancing back toward the wizard.

Parsec strode past the guard and stopped before Rindle, his gaze sweeping him from head to toe, finally settling on his fallen sword. "Pick up your weapon. The rest of you, return to your posts. This man reports to me. I will see him in my chambers."

He then turned and walked back down the corridor, passing the stunned guard before dousing his magic-powered light and slipping back into his room. Lang stood outside the door, a smirk on his face as he sheathed his blade.

Rindle bent to scoop up his rapier, inserting it back into his scabbard as he slipped past the scowling guard and the smiling bodyguard. Once in Parsec's chambers, he released a sigh, Lang entering behind him and closing the door.

"Your timing was fortunate," Rindle said.

Parsec turned toward him, the man's face amber in the light of the fireplace. "Did you think you could defeat six armed guards on your own? What if I had not been in my room?"

A frown pulled on Rindle's face. "I hadn't thought of that."

"What are you doing here anyway? Your position was to remain secret, which can hardly happen when you come barging in, half a dozen guards chasing after you."

"I needed to see you and didn't have much choice. I am only in Fastella for the night and must leave in the morning."

Parsec's eyes narrowed. "What are you up to, thief?"

Reaching into his pocket, he gripped the amethyst. When he held it out, firelight flickered off the glossy surfaces.

The wizard stepped closer, gaze glued to the gem in Rindle's palm. "It is amazing and must be worth a fortune."

"It is worth more than that. With it, the Tower of Devotion can return to the purple flame of Gheald."

Parsec's eyes narrowed. "How so?"

He shrugged. "I found Lieutenant Garvin, as you requested. I was at the man's side when his soldiers captured Dorban. More importantly, I was there when he converted the obelisk to Farrow. All he had to do was swap out a gem like this." He held the amethyst in his fingers and rotated it in the light. "In its place, he used a sapphire, identical in shape and size. The man called it an octahedron. Anyway, the moment the blue gem sat in the tip of the obelisk, it turned to a blue flame."

Parsec stared at the gem for a long, quiet moment, then scoffed, "It cannot be so simple."

"Can't it? Has such a thing ever been attempted? After all, who would mess with a wizard lord. Worse, who would dare cross a god?"

The wizard cautiously plucked the jewel from Rindle's hand and held it in front of the fire, gazing into it as if he could see his own future. A smile bloomed across his face, and he began to laugh.

"I knew Gheald had bigger plans for me." Parsec clapped Rindle on the back. "Come. The future begins now."

Parsec crossed the room and opened the balcony door, stepping out into the night. Rindle joined the man, his gaze drawn toward the beam of blue light over the city. Below, the chant of Devotion continued, the hum recognizable, even if the words themselves were muffled.

The wizard glared up at the light with hatred in his eyes. "This abomination ends tonight. Enough of feeding Farrow. The souls of the city, of this wizardom, belong to me and Gheald."

He turned and began climbing the ladder leaning against the palace wall, left behind by the Farrowen Army. Rindle was surprised it hadn't been removed. Then again, a portion of that army remained in Fastella. He followed Parsec onto the palace roof. Similar to the ladder, the scaffold Garvin's engineers had built remained in place, rising up the side of the Tower of Devotion. Parsec crossed the roof to the scaffold and began his ascent, Rindle close behind.

The climb took much longer than the ladder, the scaffold consisting of many levels, the two men forced to change direction many times until they reached the top. Sometime during their ascent, Devotion ended, the blue flame in the tower reducing from a bright inferno to a low simmer.

At the top, Parsec climbed off the scaffold and paused just outside the ring of fire. Rindle stopped beside the man, his gaze sweeping from the pillars supporting the roof, to the circle of blue flame, to the crystal throne in the center. It glowed with a faint blue light, a fist-sized sapphire pulsing in the back of the throne.

"It's the gem... The one we must swap out," Rindle said.

"Yes."

Curious, Rindle knelt and put his hand over the low flame, feeling no heat.

Parsec stepped over the flame and strode toward the crystal throne. "This is it. This is my true throne. The one to bolster my power once Gheald raises me to wizard lord."

"How do you know?"

Parsec looked back at him. "Know what?"

"How do you know Gheald will choose you?"

Parsec laughed. "He will undoubtedly choose me. After all, I will be the one who returns this city and its citizens to his glory."

The wizard turned back toward the throne, still gripping the amethyst in one hand, reaching his other toward the pulsing sapphire. Rindle held his breath, his stomach roiling in an odd mixture of curiosity, anticipation, and fear. Parsec's fingers drew close to the gem, pausing for a breath before he closed the last few inches.

Bright blue light flashed, forcing Rindle to turn away, arms raised over his face. A scream arose, terrible and filled with anguish. It ceased abruptly, the light dimming as quickly as it had bloomed. Rindle lowered his arms and turned back toward the throne.

Parsec was gone, his purple robes in a rumpled pile at the foot of the throne, smoke drifting from them. Rindle's gaze swept the area, searching for another sign of the wizard, but all he found was the purple amethyst resting on the dais beside the man's robes. He stared at the gem for a time, thoughts racing until they led him to a frightening conclusion.

The guards will think I killed him, caused the man's disappearance.

He leapt over the fire and scooped up the amethyst, careful to avoid the throne, suddenly fearful of it. Another thought occurred to him and he gasped.

The other gems, the ones Garvin swapped out... They were all dormant when he took them, but this one remains alive with the magic of Farrow.

Without a doubt, he knew now that a god had destroyed Parsec.

He stuffed the gem back into his pocket and turned, his toe kicking a ring with a black stone mounted in it. Squatting, he scooped up the ring, hopped over the flames, and hurried down the scaffold. The warm thoughts he had of visiting his home had turned cold. He now wanted to be as far from Fastella as possible.

Images of Parsec's last moments haunted Rindle as he hurried down the dark streets of Fastella, casting repeated glances over his shoulder. When he had returned to Parsec's chamber, his bodyguard asked why Rindle was alone. He had told him Parsec was still in the tower, contemplating how to swap out the gems. It has bought him a little time, but he feared what would happen should Lang climb the tower and find the wizard's robes. Lang was among the few men Rindle truly feared.

A fist flashed, striking Rindle's jaw. He landed on his backside and blinked at the pain. Herrod stepped out of the shadows, the hulking man glaring down at him as he lifted his cudgel. Herrod was also a man Rindle feared.

I wonder if I can draw my blade before he can hit me.

"I am disappointed, Rindle," a female voice came from the darkness. "You returned to Fastella but did not come to see me."

He scrambled to his feet, dusting himself off. "Cordelia." He struggled for the right response. With the wizardess there, he dared not attack Herrod. The pair was too much to handle. "I had no intention of returning. It is just for one night, then I'll be gone."

"Tsk, tsk, Terrin." His real name. A bad sign. "I thought I was clear about our arrangement. You rushing off to join the Farrowen Army was not part of the deal."

"Please, Cordelia. I am sure we can come to an agreement. I just wish to leave the city and promise to never return."

"You wish to leave Fastella alive? Hmm...," she said. "Well, I am a woman of business. Convince me it will benefit my situation, and you shall have your wish."

He searched for an idea, Parsec's death still on his mind. "Would it help if I told you Parsec is dead?"

"Pfft. What do I care? Another wizard will take his place and things will continue as they are."

"What if you replaced him?"

She snorted. "Unfortunately, I lack the raw ability with the gift to challenge the other wizards."

He reached inside his coat.

"Careful," Herrod growled, stepping closer.

"It's not a weapon," Rindle said. "I am reaching for a ring." He pulled it out and held it in the moonlight. "This is for you, Cordelia."

"Why would I want a ring? It's not even a diamond. Appears to be black onyx, which is basically worthless."

Rindle grinned. "This ring is worth far more than diamonds. It is enchanted. With its power, Eldalain defeated many wizards. Parsec later claimed the ring and used it to defeat Charcoan."

"What does it do exactly?"

He heard the interest in her tone, knowing he had her. "It increases your magic. Quite significantly, I believe."

After a beat, she said, "Take the ring, Herrod."

The big man reached out and plucked the ring from Rindle's palm.

"Give it to me."

He stepped back into the shadows and handed the ring to Cordelia. She slipped it on and gasped.

"While a bit large, it is amazing nonetheless." Her tone was filled with wonder. "I agree to the trade. You are free to go. If you ever return, you will report to me immediately or you will die."

"Agreed."

She turned and walked away, the hulking Herrod at her side.

Rindle sighed in relief and hurried off, fading into the night.

6

QUITE A PAIR

Blythe Dugaart crept in a crouch, snow to her knees, the pale light of dawn filtering through the trees. The tracks she followed had undoubtedly been left by a deer, but far larger than any deer she had ever encountered. She remained wary, eyes scanning her surroundings as she advanced, her breath swirling with each exhale briefly obscuring her view.

A flicker of movement appeared in her peripheral vision and she froze, holding her breath. Moving slowly, she turned her head and spotted her quarry in a small clearing three hundred feet away. A beam of sunlight streamed through, illuminating the white stag. It was huge, easily twice the size of a normal deer, perhaps three times. The antlers alone must have been six feet from tip to tip, covered in dangerous spikes. It snorted, a puff of steam rising into the morning air.

The beast then lowered its head, turning away as it nosed through the snow. With its backside facing her, Blythe crept forward. Each step was carefully placed, toe sliding in first to limit the crunch of snow. She circled around until she stood a hundred fifty feet away with a clear but narrow view of the animal between the tree trunks. Biting the end of her glove, she pulled it free and reached over her shoulder. Ever so slowly, she eased two arrows from her quiver, placed one against the string, and pulled it back. The air was still, no breeze to affect the flight. Taking aim with one eye closed, she focused on her target, all else fading away until all she saw was the buck's flank. She released, immediately nocked the second arrow, and released again.

The first missile struck the beast's neck. The stag reared, the second arrow burying in its hind quarters just before it bolted. Ready, Blythe ran after it.

Trees flew past, snow spraying through the air, her breath coming in gasps. The white backside of the deer was visible ahead, dots of crimson staining the snow as it ran. Despite its wounds, the animal steadily outdistanced her. It then burst from the trees and raced across the clearing she had crossed while tracking it.

By the time Blythe emerged into the clearing, the stag had neared the next section of forest, a quarter mile away. A shadow moved in the trees, Brogan emerging. The big man held his falchion ready, the massive deer charging directly toward him. The buck lowered its head, prepared to impale him.

"No!" she cried.

At the last moment, Brogan brought his shield around while leaping to the side. The antlers struck a glancing blow as the warrior spun, his sword coming around to graze the top of the stag's hind leg. Brogan fell backward into the snow as the stag faded into the shadows of the woods.

Blythe ran across the clearing, slowing as she came to Brogan. He sat up and shook his head, which was covered in clumps of white.

His gaze met hers and he grinned. "That was fun."

She pressed her lips together and kicked snow into his face. He wiped the flakes from his eyes and saw her glare.

"What?" he asked.

"Remember our conversation in Kelmar? You promised to stop with the unnecessary risks, stop placing yourself in the worst danger possible."

Grunting, the big man stood, snow falling from his furs and armor. "I did say that, didn't I?" He had the grace to appear guilty. "I am sorry." He turned toward the forest where the deer had disappeared. "We need food. I thought to help and– Look out!"

The charging stag burst from the forest, its antlers lowered at Blythe. She reached for an arrow, knowing it was too late. Just before the stag struck, Brogan crashed into her and sent her flying. The antlers collided with his shield in a tremendous impact. He sailed through the air, limbs flailing, landing in the snow and skidding to a stop as the charging beast barreled past him.

Blythe pushed herself up. The stag slowed, turned, and came toward them again. With haste, she grabbed an arrow, nocked it, and took aim. She would only have time for one shot. The thing lowered its head, prepared to skewer the fallen warrior – the man she loved.

She loosed, the arrow sailing toward the charging stag. It struck, burying deep in the animal's eye and knocking it off course. It roared past Brogan, just missing him with its antlers, the buck's body tilting to the side opposite the arrow until it toppled and slid across the snow in a wake of white powder. The stag did not get up.

"Brogan!" Blythe shouted as she ran over to him.

He rolled over with a groan. "That hurt."

She laughed, tears streaming down her face. "You big, brave idiot." Kneeling at his side, she wiped snow from his face, his short beard covered in clumps. "Are you hurt badly?"

The man sat up, wincing. "My ribs may be broken. Shoulder doesn't feel too great, either."

"Why do you continue to risk yourself? You promised."

"It was going to kill you. No promise can stop me from trying to prevent that."

She put her bare hand against his cheek and shook her head. "We are a pair, aren't we?"

He swallowed, eyes flicking away shyly. "I am who I am, Blythe. All I can do is my best."

Leaning forward, she kissed him, his snowy beard grazing against her face, his lips warm. She pulled back and gazed into his eyes. "And I will do my best for you."

His gaze lowered. "Your best is more than I deserve."

She lifted his chin, forcing him to look at her. "I am no prize to be awarded to someone based on merit. The heart wants what it wants, Brogan. Mine wishes only to be at your side. The longer you live, the longer that wish remains intact. It is all I ask."

He nodded. "Very well."

Glancing toward the dead buck, he said, "Let's head back to camp and get the Frostborn. We'll need a sleigh. That thing is too big to drag back on our own."

Brogan crawled out of the tent, wincing in pain as he stood. He worked his shoulder and took a deep breath, greeted by a sharp ache in his ribs. Blythe emerged from the tent and gave him a look of concern.

"Thank you for bandaging my ribs," he said.

"The bandages will help to ease the pain, but ribs take weeks to heal."

He gave her a wry smile. "I find myself missing Narine."

She snorted. "You miss her *healing* ability."

Nodding, he walked toward the campfire with her at his side. "Yes. I had grown used to it, thinking little of injuries because I knew she would heal them moments later."

A fire burned in the center of camp, their companions already seated on nearby logs. A spit had been built, a massive side of meat cooking over the fire. The smell of venison wafted toward him and made his mouth water. It had been days since his last meaningful meal. Days since anyone in the party had eaten something other than trail rations.

Rhoa stood as he came near. "How do you feel?"

Brogan shrugged. "Like a six-hundred-pound battering ram smashed into me."

"Six hundred?" Algoron scoffed from his spot on the log beside his nephew, Rawk. "I'd wager it weighed eight hundred or more."

Lythagon, the leader of their dwarf escort, added, "Solid piece of hunting. It earned us plenty to eat for the next few days." The other two dwarves from Kelmar, Drakonon and Filk, nodded eagerly.

A stocky man with white hair and white eyes squatted beside the fire, stirring coals with a stick. "More importantly, this will sate the ice wolves," Ghibli-Kai said. At the mention of the beasts, Brogan glanced across the camp where the massive, five-foot-tall wolves lay in the snow, staring intently toward the cooking deer. "If they go too many days without proper food, they become difficult to control."

"What?" Rhoa exclaimed. "Are you saying they might eat *us*?"

The Frostborn shrugged. "It is always a remote possibility but becomes a realistic one if they have gone hungry."

Brogan hadn't considered the wolves a threat, having grown used to them over the past four days. His gaze swept across his companions around the fire. Rhoa chewed on her lip, Algoron tugging on his beard, both apparently lost in thought. Rawk, who sat between them, appeared frightened. *He seems frightened of everything,* Brogan thought. *Yet when faced with danger, he rises against it.* There was a time Brogan held doubts about his companions, but no longer. Not after Kelmar. *When pressed, even that arrogant thief, Landish, stood strong and risked his life to save others.* He hated to admit he was wrong, even to himself, but Jerrell had evolved into a better person. *He calls himself Jace now. Perhaps that is part of his change.*

He sat near the end of a log, Lythagon to one side, Blythe to the other. Urla-Ri and Octan-Ti, the other two Frostborn in their party, took a steaming kettle off the fire, poured the hot liquid into pewter cups, and passed them around. The odd tea the Frostborn drank tasted of dirt and leaves, but Brogan was happy to drink something hot. He took a sip and realized it didn't taste as bad as it had the first day.

Perhaps I have grown used to it. Perhaps one can grow used to anything given enough time.

Blythe found his free hand and took it in hers. He looked down at her smooth, pale skin in his big paw – her fingers long and slender, like her body, his fingers like sausages, befitting of his hefty physique.

I remember when I was young and fit. It seemed like many lifetimes had passed since those days. Lifetimes filled with regret.

Failure. My life is a tale of failure. I am sorry, Rictor. I miss you still.

Twenty years had passed since the prince's death. Rarely did a day pass where thoughts of his friend did not cross his mind.

A punch in his sore shoulder ended his brooding in an instant. Wincing, he turned toward Blythe, who glared at him with an arched brow.

"You were scowling," she said. "You promised to let go of the past, to live for today, look toward the future."

"Sorry," Brogan grunted. "Old habit." He forced a smile. "Keep me honest, Blythe. Help me do better."

She patted his cheek. "Oh, I will. It has become my life's goal."

From the neighboring log, Rhoa chuckled. "You have your work cut out for you, Blythe. I know Brogan's type well. Lived with a man named Juliam for a decade. He thought he had to protect me from the world. Much like Brogan, he was a big, stubborn oaf. The only way to wrangle such men is to grip them by the ear and never let go." She smiled. "At least that's what Juliam's wife always said."

Blythe laughed. "I do believe you have the truth of it, Rhoa. Wise words, indeed."

"Yes. I have always thought of Sareen as wise." Rhoa's tone carried a hint of sadness, mirroring the look in her big, brown eyes. "I miss her. After my parents died, she was the closest thing I had to a mother. I even miss Juliam looking over my shoulder, his constant concern."

Rawk took Rhoa's hand, his meaty one dwarfing hers even more than Brogan's did Blythe's. "We are here, Rhoa, so you still have family. You can trust us with your life."

She gave him a smile. "Thank you, Rawk."

Blythe leaned close and whispered into Brogan's ear, "I believe there is something between them, but neither knows what to do."

His brow furrowed. "Something?"

"They like each other, silly," she said with a grin.

He looked over at the dwarf and the acrobat, the two sharing a quiet conversation. "Of course they like each other. Anyone can see they are friends."

She rolled her eyes and sighed. "You are completely blind to some things, aren't you?"

He bristled. "I notice plenty."

"You lived next to me for six years, yet you never noticed how I felt about you."

"Well… You never told me."

"*You* never told *me*, either."

"I…" He sighed. "I am a mess, Blythe. Are you sure about this?"

She narrowed her eyes. "Don't make me beat you up again."

Her menacing look, combined with the threat, was too much.

He burst out laughing, the others around the fire joining in. Aghast, she punched him. Pain flared from his injured shoulder, his eyes bulging, jaw clenching, tears forming.

"Oh, I'm sorry," she said, her eyes concerned as she gently rubbed his shoulder. "I forgot."

"It's all right. It was my fault." Brogan shook his head. "For my own health, I'll try not to goad you into more violence."

His comment stirred another round of laughter.

7

OREN'TAHAL

The tunnels seemed endless, the group walking in silence with Hadnoddon in the lead, Adyn at the rear. She held one of the glowing rocks in one palm, her other hand resting on the sword at her hip. While her eyes had grown accustomed to the darkness, the blackness beyond the aura of the three glowing stones had her constantly on edge. From time to time, she would pause and look backward, listening, watching for signs of movement, but nothing ever came of it. Still, she couldn't shake the feeling that someone, or something, was following them.

They passed another intersection, and Hadnoddon proceeded down the opposite tunnel without hesitation. Adyn slowed and eyed each path warily, expecting something to come charging out of the darkness. Seeing nothing, she hurried to catch up. Moments later, the dwarf stopped and held up his hand, indicating nobody move.

Then she heard it. A distant clang. Another. A third and a fourth. The sound of someone striking metal again and again.

Hadnoddon whispered, "We are close. Remain silent and watch for my signal."

With the dwarf in the lead, they advanced at a deliberate pace, timing their steps to the beat of the clangs, which gradually grew louder. The tunnel, which had been level for most of the day, began to slope downward, the air growing warmer and tainted by the smell of sulfur. A dim light emerged from ahead, the warm glow drawing them toward it, at the same time feeding the rising anxiety swirling in Adyn's stomach. The tunnel turned, and an opening appeared ahead.

Emerging from the tunnel, they crossed a flat rooftop made of brown stone marked with gold and silver striations, stopping when they reached the waist-high wall at the far end.

Similar to Kelmar, Oren'Tahal was built inside a mountain, the rocky ceiling hundreds of feet above them. But while Kelmar occupied the heart of a circular cavern, this dwarven city was long and narrow, as if the buildings had been built along opposing walls of a steep canyon. Half were built from rock marked by metallic striations, similar to the one they stood upon. The other buildings were crafted of metal sheets held together by silver rivets, reminding Adyn of heavy, plate armor.

Two hundred feet below, a broad street ran through the city, the street split by a daunting crevice. From the depths of the fissure came the reddish-orange glow that filtered throughout the cavern and illuminated the city.

"Is that fire rock down in that chasm?" Jace whispered.

"Lava," Salvon said, gazing down at it. "Same as what comes out of a volcano."

"Look there." Hadnoddon pointed toward the far end of the city.

A half-mile away, the wiry forms of goblins swarmed about. Among them, ogres pushed carts across an arched bridge, the only visible means over the crevice. At the far side, the monsters stopped at the top of a set of stairs surrounding a circular structure adjacent to the fissure. There, they dumped the carts into a pile of raw ore that tumbled down the stairs and settled beside a round well of molten lava. The hot glow illuminated two ogres that stood at opposite ends of a massive, black anvil. Each monster held a heavy hammer, the pair pounding on rods of glowing metal, striking them in unison.

"It is true," Hadnoddon said in wonder. "*Vis Fornax,* the Forge of Might. It exists. With it, items of power can be crafted – blades that never dull, weapons that never break. All far lighter than steel."

"Yes," Salvon said in an ominous tone. "But it is in the control of dark-spawn. How will mankind survive if the enemy holds such an advantage?"

Adyn imagined waves of darkspawn pouring over cities. Superior numbers armed with unbreakable weapons light enough for even goblins to wield without tiring.

She scowled. "We need to do something about this."

Jace turned toward her. "What can we do? There are only five of us. There are six of those big ogre things and at least a hundred goblins."

Narine put her hand on his arm, turning him toward her. "Adyn's right. We cannot just leave things as they are. Perhaps fate led us here."

"Fate," Salvon repeated with narrowed eyes. "She is a fickle mistress and rarely brings you toward what you expect. In this case, Narine may be correct."

"I agree." Hadnoddon continued to stare toward the forge. "We cannot allow darkspawn to use the sacred forge."

Jace sighed. "You people are going to get me killed with your strange compulsion to do the right thing." He turned toward Narine and gave her a slight nod. "I…may have a plan that will work. It's dangerous, but it seems danger has become our normal."

Adyn laughed and clapped him on the back. "Well said."

Jace turned toward Hadnoddon. "Can you get us to the other end of the city, somewhere close to the bridge?"

The dwarf snorted. "Of course. Follow me." He headed back into the tunnel.

After retreating to the last intersection, Hadnoddon led them down a tunnel that ran parallel to the city. Another turn brought them to a building directly across from the forge. They descended flights of stairs, eight by Adyn's count, before reaching the main level. Each floor they passed contained metal-framed furniture topped by dust-covered pillows. There was no evidence of pillaging or destruction. Rather, it gave the impression that the previous owners had left on vacation and had yet to return.

A thousand-year vacation, Adyn thought. *Not even dwarfs live that long.*

The main floor turned out to be a shop with furniture and shelves littered with trinkets, everything blanketed in dust. Jace approached a shelf, blew the dust from one object, and picked it up. Adyn and Narine stopped beside him to see what he had found.

It was a tiny dragon made of gold and emeralds, its eyes amber topaz, the crests down its back purple amethyst. It was gorgeous.

He turned and handed it to Narine. "Since we encountered the first wyvern, I have wanted to gift you a pet dragon."

She smiled, holding it in her palm, the figure mere inches from her face. "It's wonderful."

"Will you two stop your swooning?" Hadnoddon said from a door. "I am going to open it, so shut yer traps."

Curious, Adyn and Jace snuck across the room and peered over the dwarf's shoulder as he put his hand on the metal handle. The dwarf eased the door open to reveal an empty metal cart on the street outside. Beyond the cart stood the arching bridge, the glow of the forge coming from the opposite side of the chasm.

"Perfect," Jace whispered. "I have what I need."

Hadnoddon closed the door and faced Jace with a grimace. "Just what is this plan?"

He grinned and rubbed his palms together. "It's the best kind of plan. Subterfuge."

Somehow, the scowl on the dwarf's face deepened. "That sounds like sneaking and trickery."

"Exactly."

"I don't like it."

The thief bristled. "Why are you so bothered? I haven't even told you the plan yet."

"It's…dishonest."

Jace laughed. "Would you rather just walk up to the monsters and ask them to leave?"

"No."

"Listen to the plan, then tell me if you have a better idea. If not, we do as I say, and we might live to fight another day. Isn't that the most important thing? Aren't we supposed to save the world?"

The dwarf crossed his arms and glared at Jace. "Fine."

So Jace explained his plan. As it began to take shape, Adyn found herself grinning. Being devious seemed to come naturally to the thief. It was one of the reasons she had grown to like him so much…as long as he remained honest with her and Narine.

8

VIS FORNAX

Jace listened through the cracked door, the squeaking of wheels growing increasingly louder. Chatter emerged, unintelligible at first…his stomach churned as he began to doubt his plan…then he recognized a word. Other words followed, and the conversation took shape.

"…going, you worthless lumps. We have much work to do and little time," said a nasally, squawking voice. The cart came into view, pushed by two ogres, trailed by a cluster of goblins, the one talking wearing a necklace of bones. The cart moved gradually up the bridge, the goblin yelling, "Push, or you'll feel the bite of my whip."

The voice faded, the words again incomprehensible. Moments later, the cart crested the bridge and faded from view. Jace closed the door and turned toward Narine.

She stood in her shift, the thin, pale material clinging to her curves. Even in the dim light, she was gorgeous.

Unable to restrain himself, he leered at her with a smile. "The view suddenly became quite interesting."

With a hand on her hip, eyes narrowed, she asked, "Are you really going there now? In this situation?"

Adyn chuckled. "You must admit, he *is* consistent."

Jace crossed the room, the stone floor cold beneath his feet. Like her, he had stripped to only his breeches, torso and feet bare. He put his hand on her cheek and stared into her eyes. "What's wrong?"

Narine sighed. "This plan of yours… It relies so heavily on my abilities."

"True." He kissed her, his lips lingering on hers for a moment. His palm remained on her cheek while he stared into her striking blue eyes. "You can do this. I have faith in you."

She smiled, looking away. "I pray I can."

"The augmentation spell worked."

It was only the third time they had tried the spell and had yet to attempt a different augmentation. There just hadn't been an opportunity.

Her brow furrowed. "You can understand them?"

He grinned. "Yes. There was a shaman in the group that just passed through. He was berating the ogres pushing the cart, treating them as if they were mindless animals."

"Can you speak their language, as well?" she asked with an edge of excitement in her voice.

Jace replied, a guttural string of sounds emerging. To him, it made complete sense.

"What did you say?" Adyn asked.

"I said, *I wish it would rain, so I could see how a wet shift clings to your body.*" Jace had seen her in a wet shift once, the image burned into his mind. It was among the moments that had first drawn him to her.

Narine playfully slapped his shoulder. "You pervert!"

Laughing, Adyn shook her head. "It's hard not to like you, Jace."

He grinned. "I have always thought so."

The princess rolled her eyes. "What am I to do with you two?" Despite her comment, she smiled. The twinkle in her eyes left Jace eager to kiss her again.

Approaching footsteps spoiled the moment, Hadnoddon and Salvon descending the stairs and entering the room.

The dwarf stopped and gave Jace a questioning look before his gaze settled on Narine. A surge of jealousy arose, and Jace found himself wishing he could cover her with something. It was a foreign feeling, giving him pause. *When did I start caring if someone else leered at a woman?* She affected him unlike anyone else. Sometimes it caused concern. Other times, he couldn't get enough.

"Why are you two stripped of your clothing?" Salvon asked.

Adyn explained. "Narine tells us it is easier to maintain an illusion if there is less to mask. Goblins are skinny and don't wear much."

Narine added, "I have never masked this many people. It'll be worse when we are spread out. The less details I have to manage, the better."

Salvon nodded. "Makes sense."

Hadnoddon grunted. "If you say so."

Jace bent, scooped up his and Narine's clothing and shoved the bundle into Salvon's arms. "Keep this in the cart with you. Hadnoddon and Adyn will place the packs in the cart. Remember, don't start across the bridge until we reach the middle."

"Understood." Salvon nodded.

Adyn nodded firmly, the dwarf doing the same.

Jace turned toward Narine. "All right. It's up to you."

She took a deep breath, her brow furrowed in focused concentration. The hair on his arms stood on end as she used her magic. The armored, bulky form of Hadnoddon twisted, his skin turning green and covered in warts, his beard turning to a blocky jaw, mouth having an underbite with two sharp teeth jutting up over his upper lip.

Adyn underwent a similar transformation, shifting from the epitome of a lean, athletic female to a thickly built, and quite ugly, ogre.

"You need to hunch over, Adyn," Jace noted. "You're standing too tall, your posture too proper."

She did so, her hunched form and artificially long arms perfecting the illusion.

"All right," Narine said. "Our turn."

He turned toward her. "Remember, I am to be a shaman."

She nodded and pressed her lips together, her outstretched hands twisting as she wove the illusions.

First, Jace's own arms became thinner, wiry, his skin turning a pallid gray. He looked down and found himself wearing a loincloth, a disturbing chain of human bones around his neck. Then Narine's image blurred, her pale shift turning to gray, leathery skin, her curves melting to a gaunt, lean build, blue eyes turning to red, golden hair to a bald head with oversized ears.

"Do I look all right?" she asked.

He laughed. "You look horrible. It's perfect. Now, just add some blood so we appear wounded."

Streaks of crimson spread across her arms and torso, his own image acquiring similar wounds.

Jace drew the dagger at his hip, gripping it and wishing he hadn't shed his throwing knives. "Remember the plan." His gaze swept the room. Salvon's appearance remained the same, Adyn and Hadnoddon dull-eyed, green, and ugly. "Surprise is our best chance, perhaps our *only* chance."

"We will do our part." Hadnoddon grinned, a grim expression for his ogrish face. "I look forward to wielding a tool of Oren'Tahal."

Jace walked to the door with Narine at his side, gripped the handle, and cast one last backward glance. "Count to twenty and slip out. Try to block Salvon from view until he is in the cart, just in case a monster is looking in this direction."

He eased the door open and peered out, no movement in sight. The clanging of hammers echoed from the forge, the structure partially blocking the ogres there from view.

Stepping outside, he and Narine snuck along the building fronts, toward the main tunnel that led to the mining post. At the corner, he peered down the tunnel and found it dark, empty.

Thank the gods.

He turned toward Narine. "Ready?"

She nodded. "Let's go."

He took off in a loping run, back hunched and arms flailing, just like he had seen from the goblins. "Intruders! It's an attack!" he cried in goblin speak.

The two of them ran up the arching bridge, the stone beneath their feet growing warmer and warmer, heat rising in the air. Jace glanced to the side, over the low wall of the bridge. A red glow came from molten lava below, the jagged chasm splitting the city to the far wall, over a half-mile away. As they rose higher and neared the apex, the forge came into view.

Clusters of goblins stood nearby, joined by a pair of ogres with thick, muscular arms that virtually hung to the ground. Jace yelled again and waved, the goblins turning in his direction. Two goblin magic users stood among them, and a concern arose that hadn't previously crossed his mind.

What if they all know each other and don't recognize me?

Still running as they reached the downslope, he yelled one last time, his voice rising to a scream. Finally, a shaman reacted, waving its hands and issuing commands. The host broke apart, the main force charging toward the bridge, led by one of the shaman.

Faced with eighty armed monsters rushing toward them, Jace slowed, Narine slowing with him. He leaned toward her and whispered, "Have your magic ready in case we need to defend ourselves."

Her eyes widened, which was a considerable task since they were grossly oversized. "What?"

"Shh. Just be ready."

He turned toward the wave of goblins and rested against the bridge wall, acting as if he were exhausted and overcome by his wounds. As the shaman drew near, Jace said in their tongue, "The mining outpost…" *Gasp, gasp.* "Captured by dwarfs…" *Gasp.* "Their numbers…too great…"

The shaman turned and began to shout urgently while pointing toward the tunnel from whence Jace and Narine had come. In moments, the monsters raced down the far side of the bridge. As the thudding of their footsteps faded, the squeaking of wheels arose, coming from the two false ogres pushing a cart over the bridge.

Jace grinned and turned toward Narine. "That went well."

"I'm glad you think so," she said. "There are still two-dozen goblins over there, along with two ogres."

He nodded and gripped his blade. "I see only one shaman. We must kill him swiftly."

Still in his act, he limped down the bridge with her a step behind.

Adyn, with Hadnoddon by her side, grit her teeth, her thighs burning as the pair pushed the cart up the bridge. They reached the apex, her panting heavily. *The dwarf is stronger than he appears,* she thought. He hardly seemed affected, and she wondered at his stamina, although it was difficult to determine while hidden by the ugly illusion as a male ogre. *I think it's male anyway.* She then wondered if there were female ogres.

A grin crossed her face as she imagined how she must appear, all green and gross. Part of her wanted to pause and lift her loincloth to see if Narine had included certain details of the ogre anatomy.

She shook her head. *Focus, Adyn.*

The cart crested the arch and rolled down the back side of the bridge, toward the forge, which stood at the bottom of a short flight of stairs, arcing around it in a wide circle. Ahead of her, the illusion of two bloodied goblins hobbled off the bridge. Beyond Jace and Narine, a shaman stood among twenty-some monsters, including two ogres hammering metal. An array of tools, including another massive hammer, rested on top of a workbench near the anvil. The cart began to gain speed, drawn forward by gravity, providing relief as she pushed with far less energy.

"Are you ready?" she asked without looking at the dwarf.

He whispered, "Not yet. We must get closer and not allow them time to react."

From the cart, beneath the pile of cloaks, came Salvon's voice. "He's right. You only get one chance."

It took no effort to keep the cart rolling, the wheels squeaking as it descended the arcing bridge. Ahead of them, Jace and Narine reached the other goblins, the shaman leader waving his arms and jabbering in its odd, twisted language. Jace replied, shaking his head while holding his bloodied shoulder.

The goblin shaman began to shout, pointing at Jace and Narine. *Oh no.*

"Push hard!" Hadnoddon said with a grunt, the cart gaining speed.

Narine concentrated on the illusions, feeding all four of them with a steady thread of magic. Being spread out increased the complexity and required added effort.

Jace, standing beside her, was possibly engaged in an argument with the goblin shaman, but it all sounded like gibberish to her. For all she knew, the nasty tone could be a standard greeting.

She turned toward the bridge, the orgish forms of Adyn and Hadnoddon pushing the cart across it. They had crested the middle of the bridge, and the goblins seemed to pay them no attention.

Just a little longer.

The goblin shaman screeched loudly, and she spun toward him in alarm. When the surrounding goblins raised their weapons, Jace gripped her arm and pulled her backward, the pair descending the stairs to the same level as the forge.

"Get your magic ready. We are in trouble," he said in a hushed tone.

"What's wrong?" she asked as they backed down the stairs, toward the chasm.

"He asked me who I was, and he didn't care for my response."

Goblins nocked arrows, others brandishing swords and spears.

Desperate, Narine released the illusion spell and formed a construct of protection while still backing away. Putting everything she had into it, she recast the spell as a shield, and just in time. Arrows struck the shield, shattering in a spray of splinters on impact. Spears sailed toward them, several bouncing off harmlessly while one strayed to the side and skittered across the ground.

Narine felt heat against her back and looked over her shoulder, eyes going wide. They were a stride from the fissure's edge. There was nowhere to run.

Pushing as hard as possible, grunting with each step, Adyn and Hadnoddon aimed the cart toward the cluster of goblins at the top of the stairs, the monsters focused on Jace and Narine, loosing arrows and launching spears. The screeching wheels grew louder and louder as the cart gained speed.

"Let go!" Hadnoddon bellowed, the pair releasing their grip.

The shaman turned toward them, its overly large, red eyes growing even wider. It scrambled to the side, shouting something just before the cart struck, narrowly missing him as it plowed into the crowd. Goblins screeched, limbs flailing as the cart mowed them down, taking out half the monsters in the process.

Adyn gasped, realizing she had forgotten to retrieve her swords before they had released the cart. She took a step toward it, hoping to reach it before the enemy attacked.

The shaman, rising to his feet, screeched and pointed toward her, his minions reacting. They shifted between her and the cart, armed and ready. She stopped, Hadnoddon standing beside her.

"Now what?" she asked.

"Ignore them. Focus on the shaman."

A roar came from her side. She turned to find an ogre, the monster much larger than she realized, standing seven feet tall and many times her own weight, swinging a massive hammer toward her.

She dropped to the ground, the hammer sailing past, the head grazing Hadnoddon's shoulder plate. The dwarf spun as he flew across the bridge to land hard, armor skittering across the stone surface, helmet striking the bridge wall.

Adyn tensed as the ogre hefted the hammer above its head, prepared to crush her. She rolled away, the hammer striking the stone with a massive crack, sending a spray of shattered rock in all directions. The bridge beneath her shook, a section of rock crumbling and falling into the fissure.

Hastily, she scrambled to her feet.

With the goblins distracted, Jace gripped his dagger, his mind racing. An ogre came toward him, gripping a five-foot-long hammer in its massive paws, the monster snorting while the goblin shaman issued orders, instructing the ogres to kill the intruders. The shaman laughed, the sound somewhere between disturbing and comical.

"I don't think my shield can stop him," Narine said in a panicked voice. "What do we do?"

"When he is two strides away, run in the opposite direction of the bridge and get clear."

"*That's* your plan?"

The ogre rushed toward them.

"Now!"

Jace made a swipe with his blade to draw the monster's attention while Narine darted off. The monster lifted its hammer for a massive strike. Jace froze.

Timing is everything.

At the last possible moment, he dove through the monster's legs, the hammer striking the ground in an explosion of rock shards, the ground between the ogre and the chasm edge cracking from the mighty blow. He rolled, rose to his feet, and swiped his blade across the monster's back. It barely sliced though the ogre's skin, leaving only a thin, crimson streak.

The monster spun around, its long arm and even longer hammer trailing in a sweeping arc. Jace dove backward, the melon-sized head of the hammer grazing the stubble on his chin as it swept past. He landed on his back, hitting the ground hard and knocking the wind from his lungs.

His eyes bulged as he fought for breath. The ogre leapt toward him with a roar and another overhead strike. Jace rolled away, the hammer smashing down with a tremendous impact.

Rising to his feet, Jace saw the ogre turning toward him, the crack from the chasm edge now approaching fifteen feet in length.

Near the foot of the bridge, Adyn backed away from the ogre, knowing that even a glancing blow from the hammer was likely to kill her. The goblins watched, as if it were nothing more than a public duel, unaware of Salvon rising to stand in the cart beyond them. He lifted her sheathed swords and waved them above his head. She nodded eagerly.

The old man threw the swords, still in their scabbards. They sailed over the goblins and crashed to the ground just strides away from her. She took a step toward them but had to leap backward as another hammer strike fell, the ogre just missing her, the blow so close that bits of rock pelted her legs. Desperate, she dove for the blades.

The hilts in her grip, she rolled to her feet, hastily drew both swords, and tossed the scabbards aside. With a sidestep around the advancing ogre, she stood ready. It lunged with a low swing, intending to crush her knees. She leapt up, the hammer sweeping beneath her. Landing, she lunged with an overhead strike, intending to cleave through the monster's arm. Her blade struck and slid off, leaving a gouge but nothing severe.

Wow. These things are tough.

The monster reversed its swing, and she leapt backward with a yip.

Narine's eyes flicked toward Adyn, who faced one ogre, then back to Jace, who did his best to survive an attack from the other beast. *What can I do?* She was exhausted, her magic all but spent. The ogre's thunderous blows had created a massive crack in the rock, each swing of his hammer threatening to destroy the man she loved. *The ogre is too strong. The wounds from Jace's dagger don't appear to affect it.* Her gaze went to the well of molten lava beyond Jace and the ogre, an idea forming.

With a shout, she burst into a run. "This way, you stupid beast!" She darted past the ogre and Jace, not stopping until she stood beside the well. It was even hotter than when she stood beside the chasm.

Jace yelled, "What are you doing?"

"Lead him here! I have an idea."

He turned toward the monster, arms waving as he squawked something in goblin speak. The ogre roared and lunged with a sweeping strike. Jace leapt backward, the hammer flashing past just shy of his chest. The beast attacked again, stumbling when his hammer hit no resistance, and Jace dashed over to where Narine stood.

She gathered her magic, usually as easy as taking a breath, now like wading through a pit of mud, each step a struggle, but she fought through it. A construct of illusion formed, and she cast her spell.

As the monster came toward them, she solidified her illusion. Just a few inches in front of where they stood was a flat image twelve feet across and six feet tall – their exact likenesses standing before the well. It felt like she peered at a detailed tapestry.

She took Jace by the hand and pulled him to the side. "Let's get out of the way. I can only hold this for a moment."

They slid aside, keeping the illusion between them and the approaching monster. The ogre roared and charged with a downward slash, the hammer passing through the illusion and striking the side of the well in a tremendous crash. The well wall shattered, cracks spreading across it.

"Run!" Jace said, pulling her by the hand.

They ran toward the steps, reaching them just as the well wall burst.

Hot lava came rushing out, engulfing the ogre's lower legs, setting the monster ablaze in an instant, a roaring cry arising from the beast. It flooded the area and flowed into the crack created by the ogre's overhead strikes, the rocks popping and fizzling as the crack widened.

Adyn was tiring, the ogre graced with an array of lacerations from her blades, its blood practically black. *No matter how hard I strike, I can't cut deep enough to cause it damage.* If the fight lasted much longer, she feared she would make a mistake.

The monster swung again, and she leapt out of the way. A rock wall stood to one side, the stairs down to the forge to the other, leaving her trapped between the waiting goblins and the base of the bridge. A quarter of the way up the bridge, Hadnoddon stirred, the dwarf rising to his feet, his arm hanging limply at one side.

A section of the bridge between her and Hadnoddon was broken off, a ten-foot wide span remaining. *Another blow from the monster could cause the rest to crumble.* She gasped at the realization.

Adyn made a feint toward the forge, the ogre lunging to cut her off, then she bolted for the bridge.

"Hadnoddon!" she shrieked, racing toward him. "Get ready to run."

The dwarf staggered. The side of his head was covered in blood, his helmet askew, red streaks down his face, globs of it matted in his beard.

"Here it comes," the dwarf said, blinking as he stared at the ogre.

Reaching him, she turned and saw the monster lumbering toward her, circling past the gap in the bridge. "I'm going to distract it. When I do, you bolt past it. No matter what, get off the bridge."

The monster quickly closed the gap, so Adyn reacted before Hadnoddon could reply.

She launched her blades into curving strokes, each in the pattern of a figure eight, the whirr of them cutting through the air a threat to any who came too close.

The ogre stopped short of her and swung the hammer in a sweeping arc. Expecting it, she leapt backward to get clear. With the monster off balance, Hadnoddon darted past. The creature reacted swiftly, bringing a backhand strike around with surprising speed. The hammerhead just missed the back of the retreating dwarf.

Seeing her opening, Adyn raced in with a vicious slash across the monster's torso and continued past it. The wounded beast roared mightily and charged. With a prayer on her lips, Adyn tossed the dice.

Jace ran up the stairs surrounding the forge, dragging Narine with him. He turned and found the lava spreading across the floor below, a rivulet of it pouring over the chasm edge. The ogre flailed as it burned, the monster's body blackened, its warts popping from the heat. It collapsed in flames, dead.

Jace turned toward the bridge as Hadnoddon raced off, Adyn a dozen strides behind him with an angry ogre giving chase. Then she stumbled and fell, her swords skittering across the rock and off the bridge, settling behind the fleeing dwarf. She rolled over and looked up as the ogre raised its massive hammer.

Jace and Narine both gasped.

The hammer came down, but at the last instant, Adyn rolled and fell into the gap, disappearing from view.

"No!" Narine cried.

The hammer struck the bridge with a mighty crack, the entire span buckling. The ogre staggered and fell to one knee, the hammer flying from his grip, spinning to land on the ground between Hadnoddon and the shaman. The earth shook, a rumble echoing throughout the city as the bridge beneath the ogre crumbled. In a chain reaction, stone sections across the span fell into the chasm, dropping the ogre toward the lava below.

"Adyn!" Narine cried as she collapsed against Jace.

Adyn dangled from a small shelf of broken rock – all that remained of the bridge – her arms stretched above her. Heat rising from the lava below made the chasm walls too hot to touch. The sulfur was thick, her head becoming weary. Exhausted, she tried to pull herself up, unsuccessfully. Her palms began to slip. Bit by bit, she felt the stone sliding beneath her fingers.

I'm sorry, Narine.

A meaty hand gripped her wrist. Hadnoddon's bloody face appeared above her, the dwarf clenching his teeth as he lifted her from the fissure by one hand. When the lip was to her waist, she lifted her leg, caught the toe of her boot on it, and pushed. Hadnoddon stumbled backward, taking her with him, the pair landing on the ground with a grunt.

She rolled over with a sigh. "That was close."

The goblin shaman yammered something, the other goblins shrieking in reply, raising spears and swords.

"Oh no," she groaned.

Adyn rolled over, scrambled forward on her hands and knees, and grabbed her blades, gripping both hilts as she rose to her feet. Hadnoddon stood beside her, unarmed. Even if he had a weapon, they were greatly outnumbered. The shaman chanted, hopping up and down while waving its arms, prepared to unleash some dark magic.

The goblins advanced toward them.

Adyn prepared herself, swords ready, despite her weariness. Over a dozen goblins remained. Too many to face alone, but she refused to die without a fight.

For every monster I kill, Narine's chances of surviving increase.

Jace pulled Narine along the top of the forge stairs. Adyn hadn't died in the fall, but the situation had become dire, the shaman ordering the goblins to attack her and Hadnoddon. He then spotted Salvon behind the goblins, still standing in the cart, his lips moving as if talking to himself.

A terrifying screech came from the chasm. Giant, red claws crested the rim, followed by a massive, armored body. The creature climbed over the edge, seemingly oblivious to the surrounding lava, and released another screech, its claws clicking together rapidly. The goblins froze.

"A scorpion?" Narine muttered.

"Whatever it is, that thing is frightening," Jace said.

Narine cried, "Adyn! Look out!"

The scorpion launched toward the goblins, smashing into the crowd, crushing three at once. It reared back with a thrashing goblin in each claw, the monsters squealing in pain. The shaman backed away, waving its hands, still chanting, prepared to unleash some sort of spell. Focused on the scorpion, it did not see Hadnoddon sneaking toward him.

The dwarf picked up the ogre's discarded hammer with his good hand, lifted it, and smashed it down on the shaman from behind. The shaman collapsed in a heap, head smashed in, blood oozing out.

"Adyn, run!" Narine howled.

The bodyguard responded, skirting around the fracas, the goblins feebly hacking at the scorpion's armored hide. Hadnoddon ran beside her, the pair reaching the cart where Salvon stood at the same time as Jace and Narine.

"We need to get out of here," Jace said.

"Our stuff, our food and water… It's in the cart," Narine said, her voice frantic. "We'll never survive without it."

Jace looked up at Salvon standing over them. "Get down, Salvon. We need to get out of here."

No response.

He pulled on the man's cloak. Unexpectedly, Salvon stumbled backward and fell from the cart, hitting the ground, hard.

"Salvon!" Narine cried and rushed to his side. The man sat up, blinking. Narine put her hand on his head. "Are you all right?"

"I am fine, but that was close." He stood and brushed himself off while examining the situation.

The goblins, or what remained of them, were all dead, no longer a problem. The scorpion was another story, the monster turning toward them, chittering. It suddenly launched forward, curved tail arcing over its body, the giant stinger at the end of it striking Salvon in the back.

Everyone gasped, all eyes on the stinger point jutting from the man's chest. Even Jace stared in wide-eyed shock. More surprising than the sudden attack, though, was Salvon's reaction.

The old storyteller blinked and looked down at his chest. "Oh bother."

Salvon waved his hand and the stinger retracted, the monster backing away. A hole remained in his chest, light seeping through it. Everyone stared at Salvon, locked in a state of both confusion and horror.

"Perhaps the magmorius was a poor choice," Salvon said in a nonchalant tone. "They are quite stupid, functioning purely on instinct when not closely guided. Still, it was the best I could do when things took a turn and seemed beyond your control." He shook his head. "I cannot have any of you dying. Not yet anyway."

Stunned, Jace stuttered, "What… What are you?"

Salvon smiled and dragged his palm over his chest, the hole sealing in an instant. "That is a question for another day. I had hoped to remain with you a bit longer, but this is just as well. Your path is clear, and I have other seeds to sow, plans to nurture, a future to shape."

The man turned and trailed behind the retreating scorpion, both crossing the lava-covered floor without any visible effect. The monster slunk over the chasm edge and faded from view. When Salvon approached the lip, he glanced back one last time, then leapt off, his patchwork cloak trailing for an instant before it, too, disappeared.

9

GRAKAL

The circular, stone door rumbled, opening to reveal another cavern. Chilly air drifted through, colder than the tunnels of Oren'Tahal. Adyn breathed in deeply. The fresh air felt good, the cool breeze soothing after hours of carrying her pack over her cloak and clothing.

Following the others, she passed through the doorway and into a natural cave no more than twenty strides deep and half the width. Dim light emanated from the entrance, and she fought the urge to run toward it.

Thank the gods.

Hadnoddon pressed his palm against the wall, a seemingly innocuous rock sinking in slightly, the stone door rotating closed. He turned toward the others. "We can either rest here or continue onward."

"I have had enough of caves," Narine said. "I would rather see what waits outside, then decide."

The dwarf frowned. "Your eyes have grown used to the darkness. You will lose the advantage if it is bright out there."

Jace snorted. "I have never been so anxious to lose something in my entire life."

Adyn knew what he meant. For the past two days, ever since Salvon's disappearance, little had been said, nobody mentioning the man…if he truly were a man. A piece of her wondered if Salvon had merely been some sort of ghost or apparition.

After leaving Oren'Tahal, they had heard goblins in the tunnels on three separate occasions. Never did they see any of the monsters, for which Adyn was thankful. Even Hadnoddon, who had been so fiercely against the dark-spawn tainting the city of his ancestors, wished to avoid another confrontation. Adyn remained unsure if the dwarf's hesitancy was related to the nearly fatal results of the previous fight or if it were something else.

Hadnoddon grunted. "All right. Let's see what waits outside."

With Jace leading, the four of them crossed the cavern. Only Adyn was forced to duck at the entrance, walking crouched until she was in the open air, the bite of the wind seeping down her neck. She stood upright and gazed upon the surface world for the first time in five days, her breath swirling in the twilight.

The western sky was purple, while the sky to the east, below the full moon, was bright, the glow of the rising sun highlighting incredibly tall mountain peaks. A white-capped mountain loomed over them, the snow turning to gray rock just a few hundred feet above where they stood. Below their position, the rock led to pines encircling a vast lake, the far shore barely visible, despite their elevation above it.

Minutes passed, yet nobody spoke. They just took in the view as the sun slowly edged over the eastern peaks and warm light shone upon them, brightening the surrounding vista. It was peaceful and spectacular.

Breaking the silence, Jace said, "That must be Lake Grakal. The city of Grakal lies on the north bank."

"Grakal," Narine repeated. "It's an Orenthian city, known for fishing, mining, and logging. Have you been there?"

He shook his head. "No, but Tiamalyn lies downriver, which I *have* visited. More than once. Quite memorable visits actually."

Adyn frowned. The way Jace said it made her wonder if something had occurred in Tiamalyn. Something he would rather not discuss. "At least we don't have to tromp through snow," she noted.

Narine sighed. "Yes. At least we have that."

Jace took her hand. "Come on. Let's head down to the lake. We'll follow the water's edge until we find a means to cross."

The four of them began their trek down the mountainside and into the forest. The going was slow as they forged their own path through underbrush. Soon, they heard a gurgling sound, Jace angling toward it to find a rivulet trickling down the hillside. They refilled their waterskins, then continued their descent.

The sun was well into the sky when they reached the lake where waves crashed against the shore, driven by a stiff mountain breeze. In the distance, white sails dotted the water's surface.

"Those must be fishing boats," Narine said.

"Let's follow the shoreline." Jace pointed west. "Perhaps one will be close enough to flag down. My feet are killing me. I'd far rather take a boat to Grakal than walk."

The wind coming across the water was cold, but not bitterly so, which was unsurprising. Adyn knew the weather was different on this side of the mountains, the air warmed by the Novecai Sea to the west. She wondered if snow ever fell at the lower elevations. If so, she suspected it melted quickly.

In some spots, the forest ran right up against the water's edge, but for the most part, the shore was clear of anything but small shrubs and yellowed grass. On five separate occasions, they crossed water running down to the lake. Four were rivulets, easy to navigate by hopping from rock to rock. The fifth was a rushing creek, the water much too deep to cross without getting wet. A quarter-mile upstream, they found a fallen tree and crossed, balancing carefully. Jace and Adyn helped Narine for fear of her falling in. Too often, Adyn had witnessed Narine's feet betray her. While it might be funny in another situation, she couldn't allow her to get wet when they didn't know when they might reach shelter.

It was midday when they spotted a boat near the shore, tucked in a sheltered bay near the southwest corner of the lake. Jace led the party out to a small peninsula, stood upon a rock jutting up from the water, and began to shout. He called five times before someone on the boat reacted. The fishermen called in return, the words unintelligible. Jace waved his arm back and forth. A man on the boat waved back. Moments later, the three men on the vessel hauled in a net filled with fish and raised the sail. Adyn breathed a sigh of relief when the ship turned and drifted toward them.

A man named Bruno sat at the tiller, guiding the small fishing boat. He was a large man but surprisingly well-kempt, his dark hair and beard neatly trimmed, his vest and collared tunic quite stylish.

The other two fishermen were noticeably less refined – one a tall, thin man named Harp, the other a young, overweight man named Grohl. Those two sat in the middle of the boat, adjusting lines and tying them off according to Bruno's commands.

Adyn and Narine sat at the bow, cloaks cinched tight, hoods up. Narine kept her eyes on the water, likely to battle against her usual seasickness. After sailing out into the middle of the lake, Bruno set a course toward the northwest. The man had even taken the liberty to describe the concept of tacking, explaining how the boat couldn't sail directly into the wind but needed to sail at an angle to it before changing course. Accordingly, he noted that the trip back to Grakal took much longer than the trip out. Jace, who sat in the middle of the boat with Hadnoddon, expressed interest and asked a slew of questions. In fact, Jace seemed to get along well with Bruno, the thief and boat captain exchanging stories and small talk during the three-hour trip.

The sun was low in the sky by the time the boat drifted into the bay beside the city.

No wall surrounded Grakal. While similar to Tiadd in that aspect, Adyn quickly decided the two ports were just about as different as possible.

Grakal lacked any sort of pier, the city's shoreline instead lined with a slew of short, wooden docks stretching beyond the city in both directions. The buildings were all made of wood, many two stories tall, some three. Peaked roofs capped each building, dark smoke rising from many of the chimneys. The buildings were colorful, painted with reds, blues, yellows, and greens, making the city itself strikingly distinctive amid the dark green pines surrounding the lake.

When the boat drifted near shore, the sails were lowered and tied off. Harp and Grohl each dug an oar from the hull and set the pin into a mount. They then began to row, the craft lurching forward as Bruno steered toward an empty dock. Reaching it, Harp discarded his oar, grabbed a rope, and climbed out. In moments, the boat was secured.

Adyn took Harp's hand and climbed out of the boat before the man turned and helped Narine. He leered at Narine's chest the entire time, and it required a concerted effort for Adyn to resist punching the man, instead gaining a measure of satisfaction in imagining doing so, him flailing as he fell into the cold water.

Oblivious, Narine stood on the dock, smoothed her dress, and lowered her hood. "Thank you, Harp."

The man grinned, the effect spoiled by his missing teeth. "My pleasure, miss."

I'm sure, Adyn thought.

Hadnoddon climbed out, the dwarf swatting Harp's hand away rather than accepting the assistance.

Jace extended his hand toward the captain. "Thank you, Bruno. You saved us from many hours of walking."

Bruno chuckled as he shook it. "I'd not wish to walk from the south end of the lake." The man cocked his head. "Did you truly come through the mountains?"

Jace shrugged. "Why else would we be out there in the middle of nowhere?"

Bruno rubbed his jaw. "Honestly, I can't think of *any* reason to be out there. I've been fishing this lake for twelve years, since I was just fourteen years old. I've never seen anyone on the south shore."

"Well, I'm happy to have been your first." Jace grinned.

Bruno chuckled, watching Jace closely as he stood and climbed out of the boat.

Once on the dock, Jace turned back toward him. "You live here. We need food and a place to sleep. Any suggestions?"

The grin on Bruno's face widened. "I certainly do. When you clear the docks, take the main road toward the heart of the city. Look for an inn called The Randy Bull. Tell Maisy I sent you, and she'll set you up well."

With a smile and a nod, Jace replied, "Thanks again. Are you sure we can't pay you something for your trouble?"

Bruno shrugged. "No trouble. However, if you end up at the Bull, I'll find you there. You can buy me a drink."

"Fair enough." Jace turned toward Adyn, Narine, and Hadnoddon. "Let's go find this inn. I'm starving."

Adyn snorted, her stomach rumbling at the idea of food. "That's an understatement."

The last of their rations had been consumed sometime during the night, well before they had emerged from the tunnels at dawn.

No wonder I'm so blasted hungry.

They walked down an alley between two houses, crossed a quiet street, and continued down the alley. It brought them to a busy avenue, far wider than the one prior, wagons coming from one direction, people on foot from the other.

Jace pointed down the street. "Bruno said the inn is in the middle of town, so we go that way."

They passed shops of various types – a tailor, a butcher, a furniture maker, a weapon shop, and a baker. The last had the door open, the scent of fresh bread wafting out sending Adyn's stomach into a frenzy. Then came a red building with a sign over the door, depicting a grinning bull.

"This must be it," Jace said as he opened the door.

Adyn grasped his arm, stopping him. "I'll enter first."

He gave Narine a questioning look, but she merely rolled her eyes. "I'm used to it."

Stepping inside, Adyn's gaze swept the room, appraising those inside. There were twenty people, half of them men, a few visibly armed. She then realized the men were clustered together, as were the women. An odd segregation. All were well dressed for such a small city. None appeared to be wizards.

She waved Jace inside, and he walked past, Narine and Hadnoddon following. Adyn watched the patrons to see their reaction. Multiple men took note of the newcomers, their gazes following as Jace and Narine crossed the room. More than one man whispered to a companion, the action causing Adyn to slip a hand to the sword at her hip with a frown. However, nobody moved, so she allowed herself to examine the rest of the room.

Tables filled the spacious dining room, a third of which were occupied. A bar was positioned near the center, thick posts at each end, lit by enchanted lanterns. A vaulted ceiling, supported by exposed beams, stood two stories above. A hallway ran between the near end of the bar and stairs rising to the guestrooms. While the hum of conversation filling the room was a welcome sound after the quiet tunnels of Oren'Tahal, the smell was the main attraction. The scent of cooking meat left Adyn's mouth watering.

She crossed the room, eyes sweeping from side to side, watching for movement, for any signs of aggression. None came. She reached the bar and settled at Narine's side, noticing she had taken off her cloak and set it on the bar. Jace stood beside Narine, also with his cloak off, his elbows on the bar as he attempted to draw the attention of the barmaid. Hadnoddon stood with arms crossed over his barrel chest, facing the room, his grimace a challenge. Adyn sighed, fearing the dwarf might start trouble.

The woman behind the bar sauntered over, narrow hips swaying overtly. She had long, dark hair and far too much makeup, painted up like some street performer. Her bright red dress was tight at the waist, accentuating a full bust. When the woman approached, Adyn noticed they were of a height, which was uncommon. More so, the woman had broad shoulders and big hands.

What kind of barkeep is this?

"How can I help you?" Her voice was artificially high and obviously unnatural.

Adyn's eyes widened in realization.

With a straight face, Jace nodded. "You must be Maisy."

The barkeep smiled. "I am."

"Bruno recommended this place."

Her smile widened. "Bruno is such a good boy to send you my way. What can I do for you?"

Jace flashed a friendly smile. "We are seeking hot meals, cold drinks, and soft beds. Can you help us out?"

Maisy put a hand on her hip and began teasing her hair. "Depends. Do you have coin? A meal and beds for the lot of you will set you back a silver piece."

"Drinks included?" Jace asked.

"Two rounds."

The thief grinned. "Done." He turned toward Narine. "Give her a silver piece."

She shook her head. "I'm out."

Jace frowned, his gaze shifting to Adyn.

"Oh, no," she said before he could ask. "I don't have a single copper."

When he turned toward Hadnoddon, the dwarf waved him off. "Where would I get human coins?"

The thief patted himself down, brow furrowed as he shook his head. "It appears we are out of funds. We have traveled quite far, without a solid meal or a decent night's sleep in over a week. Is there another way we can pay you?"

Maisy gave them a scrutinizing stare, then waved them away. "Back away from the bar, the lot of you."

After a sidelong glance toward Narine, Jace shrugged and pulled her back from the bar, Hadnoddon and Adyn doing the same.

"Turn around for me."

They all did a slow turn.

A grin stretched across Maisy's face. "If you dance for me, I'll provide the ale, meals, and a room for free."

Adyn's brow furrowed. "Dance?"

The woman pointed toward the far wall, where a raised platform stood, waist-high, eight strides long and three strides deep. "Up there."

Jace snorted. "Do you take us for performers?"

Her eyes narrowed. "I take you for people who need a meal and room but lack funds."

Sighing, Jace said, "Fine. What does this dance entail?"

"It includes removing your clothing, slowly and with flair."

The thief blinked in surprise, pulled Narine close, and whispered. "It was bound to happen eventually. I'm not the only one who is impressed by your body."

Narine jerked her arm from his grip, her voice shrill. "I am *not* taking my clothes off in front of these people!"

"Please, Narine. Be reasonable. It's not my idea–"

"No," Maisy interrupted. "Not her." She leaned over the bar, her big finger poking Jace in the chest. "You."

Jace's eyes bulged, his jaw slack, lips moving but no words emerging.

Maisy cupped her hands around her mouth and announced to the room, "We have a dancer tonight!"

Everyone cheered, the men loudest of all.

Maisy grinned. "Word will spread, sure to fill the room. It's been a while since we've had entertainment."

Adyn couldn't hold back. She burst out laughing and slapped the bar multiple times, the noise of it mixing with the crowd chattering about the announcement.

Jace scowled at her. "What is so funny?"

Tears in her eyes, the laughter taking over, Adyn could barely breathe. This long, dull day of travel had just become the best day of her life.

10

THE RANDY BULL

Narine ate with fervor, her mouth and stomach begging for more. She finished her entire plate – the fish, the potatoes, the greens, and two fresh-baked dinner rolls. Unlike the others, she downed the food with tea while they doused themselves with ale, especially Jace. By the time they finished dinner, he was on his third mug, having said little since Maisy's announcement. When he sat back, his plate empty, she put her hand on his to draw his attention.

"Come now. It's not so bad."

He shook his head, grimacing. "It's not…normal."

"What? Stripping in a tavern? Until recently, I spent most my life either locked in a palace or studying at the University, but even *I* have heard of that."

"Those performers are women."

She glared at him, her lips pressed firmly together. "So it's acceptable for a woman to take her clothes off for money but not a man?"

He hesitated before replying, seemingly noticing her shift in mood. "It's not that." He looked around before leaning forward to whisper, "It's all men here."

Narine turned, her gaze sweeping across the room. All the tables had filled, more men than women. Many even stood, leaning against the walls, since all tables were occupied. The men were dressed in a dashing flair, many in brightly colored doublets or vests, all well-groomed.

"So?"

He rolled his eyes. "They have come to watch, too. In fact, they seem *more eager* than the women."

Her brow furrowed as she considered what he meant, then her eyes widened. "Oh. These men like…*men*?"

Adyn burst out laughing. Again. She seemed to be having the time of her life. Even Hadnoddon grinned broadly.

"Haven't you noticed?" Adyn waved around. "This place is *different*. Even Maisy is different."

"What do you mean? She seems nice to me."

The bodyguard rolled her eyes, leaned over the table, and lowered her voice. "Maisy is a man, Narine."

She jerked back in shock, her eyes going to the bar, Maisy speaking to a patron. Yes, she was tall, had broad shoulders, big hands, and an odd voice, but…

Narine gasped. "She *is* a man."

The statement sent Adyn into another fit of laughter.

"Yes," Jace groaned. "And these men… They want to watch me dance, as if I am some sort of…object."

Recovering from her shock, Narine again grew angry. "Isn't that how men perceive women all the time?" She cupped her hands beneath her breasts and lifted. "Even before we became involved, you would eye these as if they were a plate of juicy steak and you had gone a week without food."

Even after she removed her hands, his gaze remained on her chest, proving her point.

"I think it's high time our roles were reversed." She poked him in the shoulder. "Maisy fed us and promised us two rooms as payment. You *will* get up there and give them a show. If you don't, you can forget about these…" She waved her hand across her chest, "for a long, long time."

He stared at her, rubbed his jaw, and sighed. "I can't believe you are making me do this."

"Weren't *you* suggesting *I* do the same when you thought Maisy wanted me to dance?"

"Um..." His shoulders slumped. "Yeah. I guess you have a point."

Hadnoddon downed the remainder of his ale, wiped his beard clean, and flashed Jace a grin. "I, for one, will enjoy watching your arrogant little arse shaking for all these people."

Jace put his hand to his head, shaking it. "Not you, too."

Adyn laughed, grabbed Hadnoddon's and Jace's empty mugs, and stood. "This has to be among the best things ever." She walked off toward the bar, Jace scowling in her direction.

Despite the heat of the discussion, Narine was sympathetic toward Jace's predicament. She could not help but imagine herself in his place. *I don't think I could bare myself in front of all these people.* Until recent developments with Jace, nobody, other than Adyn, had seen her naked since she was a child. He frequently told her she was beautiful and clearly responded well to her body, but she lacked the self-confidence to expose herself to anyone else, particularly a room filled with strangers.

She leaned close, reaching beneath the table to place her hand on his leg, whispering into his ear, "Make a good show of it, make Maisy happy, and I'll reward you. Tonight."

His eyes widened, mouth turning up into a smirk. "It *has* been a while."

"I know." She moved her hand up his thigh, causing him to gasp. "Just think of the fun we will have."

When he nodded, she sat back and smiled, knowing he was committed.

Adyn returned to the table, set down three full mugs, and reclaimed her seat with a sigh. "If it feels this good to sit, I can only imagine how it'll be sleeping in a soft bed tonight." She lifted her mug. "To Jace, for exposing himself in the name of the greater good."

Jace lifted his mug, tapping it against Adyn's and Hadnoddon's. "The greater good?" he asked.

"Sure," Adyn said. "It feels good to consume a hot meal and cold ale, and it will be great to get a solid night of sleep."

As the three drank, Maisy emerged from behind the bar, sashayed across the room, and climbed up on the stage, which was only one table over. Adyn had insisted on sitting as close as possible. Narine wondered at the bodyguard's intent, despite her claiming it was to encourage Jace. She'd always had surprisingly open views about sex.

"Welcome, everyone," Maisy said loudly. Looking at the barkeep –

narrow hips, broad shoulders, a visible lump in the throat – Narine wondered how she had ever believed Maisy was a woman. "By the spirit of the room, I can tell you have heard we have guests, one of whom has offered to give us a show."

"Offered?" Jace mumbled.

Maisy continued. "Taggert, Jed, prepare the music. The rest of you, please welcome…" Maisy bent over and whispered, "What was your name?"

Before he could reply, Adyn said, "It's Jerrell. Jerrell Landish!"

"*What*?" he exclaimed. "Don't tell them that."

Maisy rubbed her jaw, muttering, "The name sounds familiar." Shaking her head, she raised her voice and announced, "Let's welcome Jerrell Landish."

The roar of applause was impressive, every patron cheering and clapping. Jace rose to his feet, face set in a scowl.

Narine grabbed his hand and held it to her chest. "You need to smile. It's part of the show. Just remember your reward."

Indeed, a smile bloomed on his face. "If they want a show, I'll give them a show."

Jace stepped onto his chair, onto a table occupied by three men, who all gasped, their hands to their chests, and leapt onto the platform. Turning toward the crowd, he raised his arms into the air, eliciting a wave of cheers.

"My, my," Maisy said. "This should be quite interesting." She bowed with a flourish, "Jerrell, the stage is yours."

The barkeep climbed down while gesturing toward the two men at the end of the platform, one holding a lute, the other with a drum on his lap. The duo began to play.

It was a lively tune, Jace dancing awkwardly at first, which worried Narine. Moments later, he got into it, turning and lifting the back of his coat to reveal his tight breeches, shaking his backside with the music. The crowd cheered.

Jace spun around twice while removing his coat. He swung it around his head, then tossed it toward Narine. Adyn jumped up and caught it, drawing another round of cheers when she held it above her head.

The thief drew the dagger at his hip and held it high as he marched from one end of the stage to the other. He tossed the knife into the air, the metal edge flashing as it spun, and caught it by the hilt. Strutting across the stage while waving the dagger before him, the crowd clapped to the beat of the music. Jace then stopped and tossed it up again, high above the beams. He spun around and snatched the falling dagger by the blade, throwing it in one smooth, fluid motion. The crowd gasped, the music stopping as the dagger struck the beam at the corner of the bar twenty feet away, burying deep.

A beat of shocked silence preceded roaring applause, the music resuming. Jace wore a grin as he unlaced his tunic. He pulled it up and over his head, exposing his lean, muscular torso before dropping the tunic to the stage. Narine bit her lip, appreciating his sculpted build.

Adyn leaned close and said, "The thief takes care of himself. Certainly much better than one would think."

"I have noticed." Narine flashed her a feral grin. *He is mine.*

A throwing knife was strapped to each of his wrists, now visible for all to see. He crossed his arms, gripped both blades, spun, and threw one. Reversing direction, he spun back around and released the other blade. The first struck the post just left of his dagger, the other slightly to the right. Cheers shook the room.

Reaching down, Jace slid his hands into his boots and produced two more blades, tossing them across the room in rapid succession. One struck above the dagger, the other just below, the five blades forming a perfect cross. Hoots and clapping echoed across the tavern as he pulled off his boots and set them aside.

Now, dancing in just his breeches, Jace shook his backside, turned, and made thrusting motions that left Narine's cheeks red. All eyes were focused on him, people grinning, some even laughing. *Am I the only one embarrassed by this?* She was not prepared for what came next.

His back to the crowd, Jace eased his breeches down, taking his smallclothes with them. The crowd gasped. Hadnoddon, who had been in the process of drinking his ale, burst out laughing, foam spraying across the table.

Jace's bare arse was pale for lack of sun, his legs less hairy than most men, but more so than the rest of his body. Still facing away from the crowd, he pulled one foot free from his breeches, then the other, his hands covering his crotch. Squatting, he picked up a boot and slid it over his manhood before turning toward the crowd, fully naked, save for the boot. He strutted across the stage, one hand holding his boot, swinging it about, the other waving above his head in a circle. The applause was deafening.

Adyn cheered as loudly as anyone, the bodyguard appearing to have the time of her life. Even Hadnoddon laughed heartily, his beard covered with foam, as was the table. Only Narine remained silent, bothered by her own conscience.

Despite the request coming from Maisy, it was Narine who had put Jace up to this, basically through extortion. Now that he was naked on stage in front of a roaring crowd, she realized something.

I am no better than the men who objectify women.

The music slowed, the dance coming to an end. With his boot still covering himself, Jace collected his clothing and climbed down, his face split in a broad grin as he approached the table.

"That was more fun than expected," he shouted over the cheering.

Narine shook her head. "No. I shouldn't have made you do it."

His smile faltered. "It's all right, Narine. We needed a room and food."

Rising, she snatched the coat from Adyn and wrapped it around his waist, covering him. "We could have found another way. I… I am sorry."

He dropped the boot and held the coat up while blinking, confusion abruptly shifting to concern. "Wait. You aren't rescinding your offer, are you?"

She shook her head. "Of course not." Glancing toward Adyn, she said, "You two take the other room. Also, please bring his boots up when you come to bed."

Adyn shrugged. "Fine. What about you two?"

Narine took Jace by the hand. "We have something to attend to." She dragged him across the room without waiting for a reply.

Maisy met them at the corner of the bar, smiling broadly at Jace while dangling a key from her finger. "You were wonderful. If you ever seek employment, let me know. With you on stage, we could pack this place every night. Make a real show of it."

He replied, "Thank you. I–"

"He is not interested. This will never happen again."

Narine grabbed the key and pulled him up the stairs. "Come on, Jace. I have a surprise for you."

His brow arched. "A surprise?"

She stopped at the landing and whispered, "Remember that thing you suggested back in Kelmar?"

"Um… Of course."

Narine set her jaw, resolute. "Tonight, you will get it. Twice."

She continued up the stairs, Jace in tow and grinning like a child who had just been gifted a basket full of sweets.

11

ADMIRERS

A beam of morning sun shone through the east-facing window, a bright rectangle stretching across the wooden floorboards. To Jace, its brilliance paled in comparison to the sight before him.

He reluctantly rose from the tub, but his stomach's growling was a reminder of the urgency of their mission. Grabbing a towel, he wrapped it around himself and climbed out.

Narine dipped her head beneath the water, emerging with her golden hair sopping wet. She then began to scrub at it with soapy hands while Jace toweled off. Once dried, he began to dress, his thoughts wandering to the fact they were still without coin and needed a means to travel downriver. Stealing a boat was an option and simple to execute. But, for once, he was hesitant to do so.

Fully dressed, he turned toward the copper tub as Narine poured a pitcher of clean water over her head, washing away the suds. He stood transfixed, held captive by her beauty as she wrung out her hair, her upper body exposed above the water.

She looked up at him, eyes narrowing, arm crossing over her breasts. "You are leering at me."

He shrugged. "How can I not?"

Rolling her eyes, she snorted. "After last night's events, and again this morning, haven't you had your fill?"

"Never. Besides, I prefer to savor the view, to store it away for safekeeping. Who knows when I might look upon it again?"

A smile appeared as she shook her head. "For a rogue, you can be quite charming." Standing, water pouring from her glistening curves, she extended her hand toward him. "Leer away but do so quickly. It's cold, and I would like my towel."

He scooped the towel off the table and moved as if to hand it to her, hesitating for a breath as he took one last glance.

"Thank you." Narine accepted the towel and began drying her hair. "Do be a dear and check if the hallway is clear before you step out." She shot him a smile. "This particular view is for your eyes only."

"I find those terms acceptable."

He turned toward the door and eased it open before stepping into the empty corridor. After closing it, he left the baths behind, turned a corner, and entered the dining room. Three tables were occupied, two by pairs of men, the third by Adyn and the dwarf.

As he approached, Adyn sat back and eyed him. "Your smile is telling. I assume you had a pleasant evening?"

Jace hadn't even realized he was grinning until she said it. "Yes, quite. A wonderful morning, as well."

The bodyguard sighed. "I must admit, I am jealous of you two. Not about the relationship, but about the more fun aspects. Many weeks have passed since my last tumble."

He chuckled as he sat. "We did have a room full of men last night. You could have given one of them a go."

She snorted. "I doubt I'd have had much luck with that lot. They were far more into you than me."

"Orenthians," he said knowingly. "They have…open views about sex. After visiting Tiamalyn a few years back, I shouldn't have been surprised by this place. It's not out of character for this particular wizardom."

Maisy walked into the room with two steaming plates, placing one in front of Adyn, the other before Hadnoddon. "Good morning, Jerrell. I'll be back soon with your meal." A grin spread across Maisy's face. "After last night, you deserve a breakfast fit for a wizard lord."

Jace smiled. "Thank you. Be sure to bring a plate for Narine, as well. She will be out soon."

"I will." Maisy turned and disappeared down the corridor.

Adyn and Hadnoddon began to eat, the latter scarfing down a sausage in seconds until he noticed Jace watching him.

"Sorry." The dwarf gestured toward his plate. "Would you like some?"

Jace blinked, unaccustomed to the dwarf exhibiting generosity. "No, thanks. I can wait."

Hadnoddon's gaze drifted down to his plate, pausing in thought. He looked back up at Jace. "About last night… What you did… I wanted to, um, thank you." The words sounded as if they caused him pain. "We needed food and shelter. You sacrificed yourself for the rest of us. It was…honorable."

Adyn burst out laughing, bits of egg spraying from her mouth. "I am willing to wager that, in all of history, nobody has referred to stripping before a crowded taproom as *honorable*."

Laughing with her, Jace replied to Hadnoddon, "You are welcome, but it was hardly a sacrifice. In truth, I enjoyed it."

"You were certainly into the act. The crowd loved it." Adyn wiped her mouth with her napkin. "Oh. That reminds me." She reached beneath the table and dug through her pack, producing his throwing knives and dagger. "You two left in such a rush, I thought it best if I retrieved these for you." She set them on the table before him.

"I appreciate it." He hiked up his sleeves and began replacing the blades.

"There were only five," Adyn noted. "I was sure you carried six."

He tapped the side of his nose and lowered his voice. "I didn't draw the one from the back of my tunic. I thought it best to leave one secret, just in case the wrong person was watching."

The bodyguard shook her head. "You are always scheming, aren't you?"

Jace bent and slipped a blade into his boot. "It keeps life interesting."

Narine entered the room and sat at the remaining chair, wearing her other dress, her hair still wet. "Good morning," she said with a glowing smile.

Adyn's brow arched. "I see you are all smiles today, as well. I trust you found your evening…and morning…satisfying?"

Narine blushed, her gaze flicking toward Jace. "I…um…"

Adyn laughed. "I'm just teasing."

"Food is on the way," Jace said, patting Narine's hand.

Hadnoddon paused his eating again, his thick, black brows furrowed. "I still feel bad about us forcing you to embarrass yourself like that last night. If Weaver had been here, he could have told a story instead."

"I told you, Hadnoddon, *it's fine*. In fact, it was fun. I'm not embarrassed at all."

Adyn stared into the distance, her expression contemplative. "Salvon…," she said aloud.

Jace frowned, the image of the storyteller with a hole in his chest flashing before his eyes.

The bodyguard sat back. "Nobody has mentioned the old man since…" Her voice trailed off.

"We called him Weaver," Hadnoddon said. "The name came from the Seers. He said it referred to his ability to weave stories, but I always wondered if it meant something more."

Jace rubbed his jaw, smooth and clean after a much-needed shave. "From the moment I met Salvon, I had doubts about him. Even for a storyteller, someone who has traveled the Eight Wizardoms and studied history, he seemed to know too much. The very fact the Seers knew and trusted him unlike any other outsider bothered me the entire time we were in Kelmar."

Jace then recalled the confrontation with Malvorian. "Whenever a conflict arose, the old man would disappear until it was over. He was never in danger, never involved." He frowned. "And when speaking of his health, he may have claimed to be a victim of age when the subject arose, but he never had trouble keeping up during our extensive travels." Jace shook his head. "I knew something was off about the old man, but I couldn't have guessed he was…"

Brow furrowed, he looked around the table. "What is he? Who could survive that?"

Silence fell over the table, all four of them staring into space, thoughts churning, until Adyn gasped.

"I just thought of something." She leaned over the table, speaking softly. "Remember when we were in the sleighs? We crested the mountain ridge, and Salvon gave the Frostborn directions. When we emerged from the forest, we came to the drop-off, the sleighs nearly going over the edge."

Jace shrugged. "Of course, we remember. There was an avalanche. We were lucky to survive."

Adyn's eyes widened. "Exactly. We were lucky to survive, but the Frostborn and other dwarfs were not so lucky."

A look of concentration on his face, Jace nodded. "I'm following you so far. You believe Salvon had something to do with it?"

"Right before the avalanche struck, I noticed him muttering something. He waved his hands, clapping them together a moment before the thunderclap sounded overhead and the ground gave way beneath our sleighs."

Hadnoddon gasped. "You're right. He *did* clap his hands before the avalanche struck."

Jace sat back and crossed his arms over his chest, eyes narrowed in thought. "If the avalanche was intentional, perhaps the journey through Oren'Tahal was, as well. The old man directed us down the valley leading to the tunnel entrance. What if it was all a plan?"

"To what end?" Narine asked. "Certainly not to kill us. In the end, it was his intervention that saved us."

"I don't know," he sighed. "However, the string of events following Taladain's death have seemed oddly…orchestrated." His eyes narrowed again. "Salvon wasn't with us when we sailed from Starmuth to Shear, nor during the journey from Shear to Marquithe. Yet when we arrived at the palace, Rhoa, Rawk, and Salvon were there. Looking back, it seems far too convenient for coincidence."

Hadnoddon sat back and wiped bits of egg from his beard. "Whomever, or whatever, Salvon might be is likely to remain a mystery unless we meet again. At the moment, we have bigger problems. We still have no coin and must travel far. We'll need food and transportation."

Narine put her hand on Jace's. "Can you do something about that?"

He frowned. "Like what?"

Adyn smirked. "Cut a purse or two. Steal a boat. You know. Thief stuff."

"I would rather not."

The bodyguard frowned. "Why not?"

"I…" He leaned in and lowered his voice. "Thanks to you, the people of Grakal now know my true name. However, they currently associate *Jerrell Landish* with what happened last night. I would hate to spoil it. In most cities, I am known for far less reputable exploits."

Hadnoddon laughed. "Less reputable than stripping for food and a bed?"

"Yes. Trust me. This was nothing."

Two men stepped into the inn, hovering by the door while removing their hoods. Both were dressed in green cloaks, one roughly Jace's size, the other a head taller with broad shoulders and a barrel chest.

Maisy emerged with two more plates and placed them on the table. The one before Jace contained far more food than he could eat, including an appetizing fruit-filled pastry.

"Enjoy, Jerrell." Maisy ran a big hand across Jace's shoulder. "Let me know if you need anything else."

Narine smirked as the barkeep headed toward another table. "You appear to have an admirer."

The men at the door approached the table, the smaller one asking, "Jerrell?"

Immediately, Jace was on guard, his gaze flicking around the room. Nobody else was near them. He tried to give Narine a warning, but she stared up at the strangers, so he gripped her hand beneath the table to draw her attention. When their eyes met, he squeezed tightly, hoping she would get the message. A glance toward Adyn and Hadnoddon showed both obviously on guard.

"Are you Jerrell Landish?" the man asked, his companion looming behind him.

"I have heard the name," Jace replied carefully.

The man's lips pressed together briefly. "I am Captain Dantello." He gestured toward the man behind him. "This is my first mate, Halgarth. We are seeking a man who performed here last night. I am told his name is Jerrell Landish. In the name of my master, I wish to offer him my service."

"What service would that be?"

"I captain a vessel used to travel the river. A member of my crew was here last night and returned to our craft quite impressed with your performance. If you are interested in reaching Tiamalyn, I am offering to take you there."

Jace narrowed his eyes. "How much would this trip cost me?"

The man smiled. "In coin, nothing. The wizard I work for owns an establishment in the capital, one with clientele whose tastes mirror those of The Randy Bull. He is always seeking new talent to satisfy his patrons. I will give you and your party premium accommodations, as well as unlimited food and drink during the journey, if you agree to a repeat performance."

"A repeat performance?"

Captain Dantello grinned. "Based on my shipmate's glowing report, you will be a star in Tiamalyn. Whether you remain for additional evenings is up to you, but I can assure you, my master pays his help quite handsomely."

12

DESTINY AWAITS

Priella gave the three men standing before her a flat stare, the throne room quiet, other than the tapping of her nails on the arm of her wooden throne.

"If we could have a bit more time, Your Majesty." Theodin glanced toward Captains Shellock and Iberson, both men giving him a slight nod. While Theodin wore his Gleam Guard armor, Shellock was dressed in a black coat over a pale blue doublet, the coat cinched at the waist by a golden belt, matching the stripes on his sleeve. Iberson was similarly dressed, but his thick, squat build made him appear far less regal. "We could ensure we are properly prepared. As I explained, the logistics of feeding thousands of soldiers are not insignificant, even without having to contend with winter conditions."

Six people occupied the spacious chamber, including her and the three captains. One of the others was Ariella, her mother and former Queen of Pallanar, seated to the side of the room. The other was Bosinger, the bodyguard standing beside Ariella and watching the others intently, ready to react should the need arise.

Priella kept her anger at bay, her voice even. "I gave you a week, of which two days remain."

"Yes, Your Majesty." Shellock ran his hand over his bald scalp. The man stood well over six feet, broad of shoulder and known as a fearsome warrior. "We have made every effort, but the needed supply of food will not arrive in time. Yesterday's storms off the coast caused further problems, sinking three ships loaded with vegetables we had procured for the campaign."

Priella sat forward. "Your job is to anticipate problems such as this. What contingencies have you in place?"

Theodin said, "We have four more ships arriving over the next few days and another half-dozen scheduled over the next two weeks. The wagons are ready to load once they arrive."

"Good." Priella nodded. "What is the problem then?"

"We have too many soldiers for so little food," Shellock replied. "It is not enough."

The heat inside Priella flared as she gathered her magic, the power of a god flooding in. She leapt to her feet, hand cast toward Shellock. The mental manipulation construct overwhelmed him instantly. He screamed in horror, backing away, arms swinging wildly at something only he could see. She released the spell as abruptly as she had cast it, his cries subsiding.

In an instant, the vaunted warrior had been reduced to a timid, frightened child, eyes haunted as he gasped for air, beads of sweat covering his scalp, breeches soaked from his crotch to his knee. The other two men stared at him, eyes wide, faces pale.

"Priella!" Ariella stood, Priella turning toward her. "May I have a word with you in private?"

Still holding on to her magic, Priella had the urge to cast a spell and dominate her mother's will. Although Ariella was an accomplished wizardess, she was powerless to Priella's might – something previously proven.

When Ariella turned and strode toward the antechamber door, Bosinger flashed Priella a glare of warning before following the old queen. It required a few calming breaths, but Priella tamed her anger, dismissed her magic, and crossed the dais. When she reached the antechamber, she closed the door, a hard glare on her face. Her mother and bodyguard faced her, both with resolute expressions.

Ariella spoke firmly. "You must listen to those men, Priella. They have experience and knowledge you lack. In addition, you need their support."

"I need their obedience."

Her mother's lips pressed into a thin line. "A wise ruler capitalizes on the strengths of his or her subjects."

"Don't tell me how to rule. *I* am the Queen of Pallanar, not you." Priella had briefly considered the term *lordess,* then dismissed it in favor of queen, fearing the reaction the prior term might create.

In his calm, easy manner, Bosinger said, "Your mother makes a fair point. You will be more successful if you learn to rely on those whom you can trust."

She arched a brow. "*Can* I trust them?"

His eyes narrowed in thought. "You have made the decision to rule by fear and force. Many have succeeded with such an approach, and you possess the power to back such ambition. If your captains fear you enough, you can trust them not to betray you."

Priella frowned as she considered his assessment. "Is there anything I can do to prevent betrayal?"

"Some of the most well-loved wizard lords in history eventually succumbed to betrayal, as have those who were most feared. Consider Pherelyn, for example."

She sighed. "I fear I will hear comparisons to Pherelyn throughout my rule."

"That is to be expected," her mother said. "She *was* the only female to rule a wizardom before you took the throne."

"I am aware. However, her rule, and legacy, are not well-loved."

"Neither will yours be if you continue down this path."

Priella sneered, "My people love me. Adore me."

"You *forced* them to love you."

"The ends justify the means."

She spun around, opened the door, and strode back into the throne room before her mother could reply.

Reclaiming her seat upon the throne, Priella spoke with a soft, firm voice, addressing her captains. "I will have your respect, loyalty, and most of all, obedience. In the future, do not come to me with problems if you cannot also deliver solutions…even if it requires compromise."

Silent nods came from the three soldiers as her mother and Bosinger returned to their seats.

"Time is of the essence, so you will proceed as planned," Priella continued. "If you can only feed a portion of our army at this time, leave the rest behind. They can join you when sufficient food has been procured." She sat back with a sigh. "Why must *I* think of everything?"

Theodin dipped his head. "We apologize, Your Highness."

She waved her hand. "You are excused. Report tomorrow with an update. We must also outline a plan of action before you reach Marquithe."

The three men backed away, spun, and marched up the stairs, out of the throne room. The doors clicked shut, leaving Priella alone with her mother and Bosinger.

Ariella stood and approached the throne, the bodyguard at her side. "This war you plan… What do you hope to gain?"

"Not hope, Mother. What I *will* gain."

"Which is?"

Priella debated telling the truth, but she could not explain it all without revealing secrets she preferred to keep. Instead, she gave them the answer others would presume, at least until they realized the truth.

They are not ready to learn of the future. Not yet.

"I seek power, Mother. Power for myself. Power with which to make Pallanar the greatest wizardom of all time."

"What of your people?"

"The people serve me and my needs."

Ariella shook her head. "No. You have it wrong. You serve them, akin to a shepherd ensuring the welfare of the sheep in his or her care. Only when your people thrive will you succeed."

Priella glared at her mother and fought the urge to explain, to share her vision. *Not yet.* "I will attain greater power, Mother. More than that, I will not allow Lord Thurvin to take mine away."

Her mother frowned. "Thurvin?"

"He will soon control all of Ghealdor, the prayers of two wizardoms feeding his magic. What makes you believe he won't strike Pallanar next? Even now, his army marches down the coast from Westhold to Tangor. Once finished there, Severan is only a few days' march."

Ariella asked, "You intend to strike while his army is away, to take his capital city before he can advance on to Pallanar?"

"Yes, and more."

"I still see one problem," Bosinger said.

"Which is?"

"Thurvin already wields far more magic than any wizard lord in history. Marquithe is his home. Much like you, he is bound to it in order to receive Devotion. He will use his magic to defend the city, likely at any cost." The man shook his head. "Your army cannot win such a battle."

Priella ran her hands down her face and sighed. "I know."

"Then why do it?"

She shook her head. "I…cannot say. I only know it is what I must do, but I have yet to solve this one last riddle. We will succeed. We *must* succeed. This, I know in my heart. If I can just find the answer…" Her voice drifted off as she stared into space, lost in her own thoughts.

The flickering, amber light from the fireplace illuminated the heart of Priella's chamber, the crackling of burning wood disturbing the silence. She sat alone on her sofa and stared into the flames, lost in thought. Weeks had passed since she had last received guidance, the season turning toward spring when it was all to come together. Each morning, she woke believing it was the day he would contact her, but when evening came without a visit, she would pray for it to happen the next day. Now, she had run out of tomorrows, and she lacked a solution to her greatest problem.

I can wait no longer.

Drawing upon her magic, Priella formed a construct unlike any other. A construct he had taught her. A construct unknown to the rest of the world. She still didn't know how he had discovered it, but she had promised to never teach it to another. In fact, he had made her promise to only use it in absolute privacy and when the need was greatest.

The construct split apart, a component of it sinking into herself, the remainder bending, swirling, reshaping until it matched the image in her mind's eye. To this ghostly image, she spoke.

"Vanda…" The very word was laced with magic as her voice filtered through the spell she had cast upon herself. "Vanda, I need your help."

Air wavered, a silhouette of pale white appearing, forming into an old man with a short beard, head and body covered in a hooded cloak. The ghostly image opened his eyes, the irises appearing a solid white while the rest remained translucent.

"Greetings, Priella," Vanda said with a deferential nod. "I see you now possess the power of Pallan…and the beauty of a goddess. Congratulations."

"Thank you, old friend. Thank you for answering my call. I had hoped you might reach out to me first, but I can wait no longer."

"I understand."

"The plan is in motion, my army soon to march north."

The ghostly image nodded. "Very good."

She closed her eyes for a beat before resuming. "This plan calls for us to face a wizard lord, a vastly *powerful* wizard lord, in his own city. How could we possibly defeat him?"

The man shook his head. "You cannot."

Priella blinked, anger rising. "Then why go through this charade? Do you wish me to fail just as I begin my rule?"

"You misunderstand. You cannot defeat Lord Thurvin, but that is irrelevant. Defeating him will not help you gain what you wish."

"Then what must I do?"

"You shall confront him, bend him to your will."

"How? I am bound to Illustan, tethered to the crystal throne in the Tower of Devotion. To leave would be to discard Devotion. My power would wane, leaving me unable to confront him." The thought of missing even a single day of Devotion made her ill.

"Then the solution is clear. You must bring your throne with you."

Priella was taken aback by the suggestion. "This is possible?"

"While it has never been done before, I believe so. The prophecy I spoke of, the one foretelling of your rise, mentions such a thing."

He closed his eyes and spoke, his tone shifting as he recited the ancient script by memory. "'*An inferno shall rise in the south, born of bitterness. Upon a throne of crystal, the Queen of Fire and Ice shall capture the hearts of her people and the souls of her opponents. The prayers shall follow her as she leads a storm of fury, bending even the greatest powers in the world to her will, turning her enemies into allies, opposing rulers into servants.*'"

Vanda opened his eyes, his voice returning to normal. "Your destiny awaits, Priella, but you will only achieve it if you remain upon your true throne when you face Lord Thurvin."

"What of his magic?" She recalled how difficult it had been to control her mother and those in the Wizard Council. "My influence upon anyone with the gift is brief, and his abilities far exceed those of ordinary wizards."

"You have but to touch him. Akin to healing, contact augments the spell tenfold. Only then may he fall under your spell. When he does, nothing can stop you."

The lift reached the top of the tower and stopped. Priella removed her palm from the panel and stepped through the pale blue ring of fire, the chill wind whipping her cloak, strands of bright red hair tickling her face. Eight square pillars supported the four-sided, peaked roof above her. Beyond the fire, snow fell at an angle, heavy, white flakes illuminated by the pale blue glow, blurring out the city below. Even when it wasn't snowing, it was difficult to see past the flame in the darkness.

Turning, Priella focused on the crystal throne at the center.

Only fifteen days had passed since she claimed the throne as her own. Fifteen evenings in which she had sat upon it and received the blessing of her people. She stopped before the throne, her hand caressing the arm. Despite the chill in the air, the surface was warm to the touch. The throne was always warm, the aquamarine gem embedded in it glowing with life, as it would until she died.

Many years will pass before such an occurrence. I will be remembered as the savior of the Eight Wizardoms – Queen Priella, the greatest ruler of all time.

She turned and slid into the seat, her back against the pulsing gem, its warmth running through her. Like drawing in a breath, she opened herself to Pallan's magic and the sleeping throne awoke, the surrounding fire blazing to an inferno.

Ice-blue beams of light shot across the sky – one toward Severan to the northwest, one toward Rykestan to the southwest, another toward Norstan to the east, the last connecting to Shurick's Bay to the southeast. In each of those cities, an obelisk burned with the magic of Pallan, the citizens falling to their knees as they began Devotion. The prayers of thousands rushed in, the surrounding world lost to pure bliss.

She was unsure how much time passed. It could have been seconds, minutes, or hours, but there came a point when the rapture subsided, her magic filled, the prayers no longer feeding her insatiable appetite. She released her connection with the gem, the surrounding flames dimming to the same low simmer as when she arrived in the tower.

"It is time," she told herself, still holding on to her magic. Far more magic than any mortal wizard could imagine. "I must try."

Crafting a construct, she wove a razor-thin blade of air and sliced in a single, decisive motion. The blade tore through the footings below the throne, separating it from the tower itself.

She cast a construct of physical manipulation, steeling herself. It had been among her weakest disciplines prior to her rise as queen. Even now, it would be difficult, but she was determined.

Threads of magic wound about the throne, the other end of those ropes attaching to two pillars at the rim of the tower. Squeezing her fist, the throne lifted and was drawn toward the edge, passing over the ring of ice-blue fire and out into the open. Fear snaked up her spine, twisting her innards when she looked down, the ground hundreds of feet below. The throne shook. For a moment, she worried she might fall.

Priella grit her teeth and focused, growling, "I will not fail."

The throne steadied and began to lower as she extended the tendrils of magic still wrapped around the pillars at the top. The wind buffeted her, but she held the throne steady.

I am stronger than the wind, stronger than a hurricane. I am the storm to end all storms.

The words repeated in her head as she drifted toward an open courtyard where two dozen Gleam Guard soldiers waited, every man staring up in wonder as their queen floated toward them on a glowing, crystal throne.

With care, she guided the throne to an ornate wagon with six wheels – the forward portion a sheltered cabin of a coach, the rear a flatbed for her throne. It landed with a thud, the wagon shifting, creaking under the weight. Task completed, she released her spell, the invisible ropes dispersing in an instant.

She gazed down at Theodin. "We depart the morning after tomorrow. You have until then to make the necessary alterations."

Rising to her feet, she raised her voice. "I suggest nobody touches this throne. Anyone who attempts to do so will wish they had not." Then she smiled. "You should feel blessed. For the first time in history, a wizard with the power of a god will ride at the front of an army."

Electricity crackled around her as she rose above the throne, all eyes following her, jaws dropped. "The world will soon bend to Pallanar, the greatest wizardom of all time!"

13

MIRACLE OR TRAGEDY

The great city of Marquithe crowned an expansive hilltop, the outer walls surrounded by fields of yellowed grass. The view extended for miles in all directions, farms, creeks, and copses of trees dotting the countryside.

Rindle rode beside Garvin, their horses trotting uphill toward the waiting city. It had grown colder over the past few days since leaving the seaside road and angling inland, but it remained too warm for snow. Of that, Rindle was thankful.

The journey had taken twelve long, dull days and left Rindle rethinking his plans to travel and see the world. For the first few nights after leaving the Ghealdan Army, his backside and thighs ached as he crawled into his tent and fell fast asleep. Those aches eventually evolved to a numbness, hundreds of miles in the saddle having beaten all feeling from his body.

They approached the towering city walls and slowed outside the gate. After a brief exchange between Garvin and the guards on duty, they rode into the city at an easy walk.

Marquithe seemed much like Fastella in nature, the streets crowded with the usual carts, wagons, horses, and people on foot. They passed busy squares, shops, houses, and inns. Guards with dark blue capes strolled past in pairs, a fair number of them recognizing Garvin with a wave or a fist to their breastplate.

Even within the walls, they continued uphill, toward a distinctive landmark thrusting up toward the sky. The Tower of Devotion burned with the deep blue flame of Farrow, the sight briefly reminding Rindle of Parsec's death.

I wonder if Farrow consumed him like what happens at a Darkening ceremony.

The thought passed, and his mind drifted elsewhere. After a lifetime of sighting the purple flame of Gheald, he was now growing used to the azure fire. First with the flame appearing in Fastella, then when it bloomed to life in Dorban, lastly catching glimpses of it during their journey as they passed by Starmuth and Lionne.

What if the entire world falls to Farrowen? If everyone worships Farrow, what of the other gods? What power will Wizard Lord Thurvin hold?

Such thoughts had never concerned him in the past, but he now found them disconcerting.

When they reached the palace gate, Garvin spoke with the man in charge, the sergeant ordering the gate to be opened. They passed through a courtyard and entered the palace stables. Two stable hands took their mounts, promising to feed the steeds and give them a full rubdown. Rindle grit his teeth as he stretched his legs and back, wishing he could request a rubdown for himself. Garvin, however, exuded determination as he marched off toward the palace door with his pack and saddlebag containing the three stolen gems slung over his shoulder.

They passed through the guards' barracks, where men slept in bunks. The barracks opened to a sparring yard, two pairs of guards fighting with wooden weapons, grunting at the effort. A resounding clang echoed when a wooden sword struck a helmet, one man falling to his knees, the other panting as he stood over him. The scene fell behind as he and Garvin entered another building.

The next room contained a dozen long tables, guards occupying half of them, vigorously eating bowls of stew. Only three times during their journey did Rindle and Garvin stop for a decent meal, the remainder of the time surviving on rations of nuts, dried beef, and even dryer bread as they rode. He stared longingly as a man took a hard roll from a basket on the table, tore it in half, and dunked it into his stew. The soldier shoved the entire half into his mouth, grinning at something the man across from him said.

Garvin scanned the area and crossed the room, stopping to stand over a middle-aged man with a shorn head and brown goatee, a scar across the side of his face, the lower portion of his ear missing.

"Lieutenant Kline."

The man looked up. "Lieutenant Garvin. I thought you were with Henton chasing around Ghealdor."

"I was. Clearly, things have changed." His reply was flat, emotionless. "Where is Captain Despaldi?"

Kline shrugged. "The captain has been reassigned. Some special mission for Lord Thurvin. If you seek answers, you will have to go to him."

Garvin gave him a determined nod. "I see." He spun on his heel and headed toward the door.

Rindle caught up and grabbed the man's shoulder. "Don't you wish to eat?"

"Food can wait." Garvin turned away and headed for the door.

Rindle's stomach rumbled, disagreeing with his assessment.

With purposeful strides, Garvin led him down a long corridor, up a short flight of stairs, and to a spacious receiving hall. Two dozen others occupied the space, guards stationed here and there, servants bustling across the room, and a cluster of men in wizard robes conversing with a clergyman of Farrow. Garvin headed toward the far end of the room where two guards stood beside a pair of closed doors. As he drew close, he announced himself.

"Lieutenant Garvin to see Lord Thurvin. Is he in the throne room?"

One of the men nodded. "Welcome back, Lieutenant. Yes, the wizard lord is present but currently occupied."

"I am here to report on Henton's campaign. I suspect he will understand the interruption."

"You may be correct, but I cannot make that decision."

"I will accept the responsibility."

The man gripped the handle and opened the door. "As you wish."

Garvin strode past, Rindle hurrying to keep up with the man, thoughts of food lingering, his stomach unsated.

The throne room was impressive, with an arched ceiling four stories above and colored light shining in through stained-glass windows. Benches lined the chamber, split by an aisle carpeted in dark blue. At the far end of the room, a man in silver-trimmed blue robes sat upon a throne, the dais illuminated by torches burning with blue flames. Another man stood before him, the two in quiet conversation.

The man standing stopped talking and looked over his shoulder as Garvin and Rindle strode down the aisle.

The wizard lord scowled and sat forward. "What is the meaning of this intrusion? I was to be left undisturbed. I'll have those guards lashed for this."

"It was my decision, Your Majesty. The guards informed me of your wish to be left alone. I believe my report takes precedence."

Garvin reached the front of the room and stopped beside the other man, who stood not much taller than Garvin's shoulder. He was dressed in a black coat, his clothing more appropriate for a thieves' den than a palace throne room. The man had dark, unkempt hair and a mustache below an overly large nose. His shifty eyes flicked from Garvin to Rindle and back.

This man is a thief…or close to it.

"Lieutenant Garvin, returned from Ghealdor." Thurvin sat back in his throne, his scowl turning to a smirk. "Yes. I would very much like to hear this report."

The lieutenant glanced toward the other man. "I request privacy so I may give you a full report."

The wizard lord waved his hand. "Jezeron, you may leave. Continue as planned. Alert me if anything changes."

The man bowed. "Yes, Your Majesty."

He then turned narrowed eyes upon Rindle, measuring him as he walked past and headed toward the exit. The room remained silent until the door opened and closed again.

"Who is this?" Lord Thurvin gestured toward Rindle.

"He is my man," Garvin replied.

The wizard lord's measuring gaze sent a chill up Rindle's spine. He ached to squirm but remained still.

"He appears more of a thief than a soldier."

"Funny," Garvin said. "I was thinking the same of the man you just dismissed."

Thurvin ignored the comment. "You trust him?"

"Rindle has proven himself more than you might suspect." Garvin grinned. "This thief killed Eldalain, saving my life in the process. Later, in Dorban, he displayed similar heroics. We would not have taken the city without him."

Thurvin rubbed his hands together, grinning. "So, we *have* captured Dorban. I knew it. Two weeks past, I felt my power increase. Not as much as when Fastella was claimed, but enough to make a difference. I would like to hear details behind our campaign in Ghealdor."

Garvin then dove into the full report, describing how Charcoan gave up Starmuth for the opportunity to rule in Eldalain's stead. The taking of Fastella took more time to describe. A series of events Rindle did not even know had occurred until the end, after he stabbed Eldalain in the back with his rapier. Of course, Dorban came next, the city proving a challenge equal to Fastella. Once captured, with High Wizard Heldain dead, the prayers of Dorban's citizens had been diverted to Farrow.

Garvin then wrapped up his report. "By now, I suspect the army is through the mountains, preparing an assault of Westhold. The garrison located there is half of what we faced in Dorban, the terrain far less challenging. I believe Henton will capture the city in short order, then advance to Tangor."

The wizard lord stroked his dark mustache. "So, you left Henton to his own devices? It sounds as if he relied on you heavily."

"Western Ghealdor is a shadow of the east, neither city even the size of Starmuth. I am confident he will succeed."

Garvin paused for breath. "That completes my report, sire. Now, where is Captain Despaldi? I wish to give him a full report and receive my new orders."

"Despaldi is away, likely in Tiamalyn by now."

Garvin's brow furrowed. "The capital of Orenth? Whatever for?"

"He and his team are going to make Horus wish he had agreed to side with me."

The wizard lord waved his hand, dismissing the topic. "Never mind Despaldi. You now report to me, for I have use of someone with your capabilities."

He put his finger to his lips, eyes narrowed. "What of the other octahedron sapphires? Were they not in your care? Ghealdan cities falling without the tower flames burning blue will do nothing for my cause."

"The remaining two sapphires are in Henton's possession."

Thurvin grinned. "Good." He rubbed his palms together. "Tell me, what of the Ghealdan amethyst? Three jewels should have been claimed when you captured Ghealdor's eastern cities."

"Those..." Garvin patted the bag hanging from his shoulder, "remain with me."

The wizard lord bolted to stand, and Rindle feared he might attack with his magic. Instead, he burst out laughing. When Garvin cast a glance over his shoulder, Rindle just shrugged. Thurvin collapsed back into his throne, crown askew, still chortling.

"Excuse me, sire," Garvin said. "I fail to see what is so funny."

"You have just solved a problem," Thurvin said. "When the dwarf disappeared, I had no source for additional sapphires. However, some very...useful information was recently revealed to me – a book of magic unlike any other, enabling me to extend my magic in new ways. One recent discovery includes an augmentation of conversion. With it and the magic of Farrow, I can continue my campaign even without that blasted dwarf."

Rindle had no idea what the man was talking about.

"Which means?" Garvin inquired.

The wizard lord stood. "Follow me. It is time to test my theory."

Rindle trailed behind Garvin and Lord Thurvin, the trio crossing a private chamber with lush furniture and a spectacular view of the city. It reminded him of Parsec's chamber in Fastella, leaving him wondering who now ruled in the wizard's absence. They passed through a doorway into a study, bookshelves covering the wall behind an oak desk stained a dark, red-brown color. Lord Thurvin circled the desk and opened a black book filled with strange patterns and elegant text.

"Place one of the gems on the desk," the wizard lord said as he paged through the tome.

Garvin removed an amethyst and set it on the desk between him and the book. "Just what are we doing here?"

Lord Thurvin stopped flipping pages. "Ah. Here it is." He tapped the page with a grin. "You two are about to witness a miracle…assuming this spell works as I suspect."

"A miracle?" Rindle muttered.

The wizard lord arched a brow. "Do you not perceive our ability to redirect the prayers meant for another god to Farrow as a miracle?"

He shrugged and held his comment to himself. *A miracle or a tragedy?*

Lord Thurvin lifted the gem, eyeing it in the afternoon sun streaming through the window. The gem seemed to glow as it captured the sunlight. "Some incredible process taking thousands, even millions of years turned this stone to a sparkling jewel, imbuing it with the hue you see now. Imagine if I could alter its nature in moments, turning it into something else."

Rindle could only think of the gem's worth. "Why would you risk it? That rock is worth a fortune. What if you destroy it?"

The wizard lord shrugged. "Risks are inevitable when striving for greatness." He set the jewel down and stood over the book, gaze firmly locked on the pages. "Remain silent and watch. You just might witness another miracle."

Weaving his hands before him, the man whispered under his breath, eyes focused on the pages. His hands twisted, cupped palms facing each other and coming together. Finally, he lowered his hands toward the amethyst. A glow came to life in the heart of the gem, growing brighter and brighter until Rindle was forced to squint and look away. The entire room glowed with a swirling, bright purple light. The color altered until the purple was gone, replaced by blue.

Light fading, Rindle turned back toward the gem, finding a dark blue sapphire on the desk where the amethyst had been. The glow inside the sapphire died, the wizard relaxing, his mouth turning up into a grin.

Lord Thurvin lifted the jewel and turned toward the sunlight, gazing upon the prize in his hand as if he had the entire world in his possession. "Behold, the magic of Farrow has altered the very nature of this stone." He twisted it in the light, the blue inside the gem shining brilliantly.

"I suggest you two relax and enjoy yourself tonight. Tomorrow, you will gather what you need and prepare for your next mission."

"Our next mission?"

"You are to head to Tiamalyn." The wizard lord turned toward Garvin. His smile slipped away, gaze becoming intense. "I made a mistake in sending the army to take Ghealdor. I do not need to capture the cities, merely their prayers. You two are the next step in taking Orenth. Despaldi was the first. If his mission proves successful, you will find the light in the Tower of Devotion dormant." He held the sapphire out and reverently placed it into Garvin's palm. "With this sapphire, you will claim the tower in the name of Farrow, guaranteeing the prayers of Orenth's largest city. More importantly, with my ability to alter the gems, nothing can stop me from ruling the world."

14

SPECIAL TREATMENT

Captain Dantello's boat turned out to be a barge, but built to appear like an elegant, floating inn. It was easily the most luxurious craft Narine had ever stepped foot upon. Rather than having a pointed bow, the vessel was rectangular, and most of it stood high up out of the water. Its two, narrow hulls were occupied by crew members manning oars, used to augment the speed of the slow-moving river.

A two-story, rectangular building rose from the deck, the main level consisting of four moderate-sized cabins and the galley. The upper story housed the navigation platform and the captain's cabin at the front, a spacious suite with observation deck at the rear. After declaring Jerrell and his companions special guests, Captain Dantello gave them the premium upper-level room. It held four beds, a sofa, a table and chairs, four enchanted lamps, and a washbasin, all finely crafted.

While Narine's companions were impressed by the initial sight of the watercraft – the comfort, the special treatment, the spacious quarters – she feared her stomach might rebel as it had so often during past water voyages. At first, she endured a light bout of nausea, but it soon faded. In fact, the journey was so smooth, she would periodically forget they were moving, reminded only by the passing scenery – yellow meadows occupied by grazing cattle, plowed fields ready for spring planting, and rolling hills covered by green pines and gray trees bare of their leaves.

She and Jace spent much time upon the observation deck, watching the countryside slip past. It was still cool, but she was comfortably wrapped in her wool cloak. Not to mention the weather grew noticeably warmer with each passing day.

The quiet time during the journey allowed Jace and Narine to study the book of magic they had pilfered from the library beneath the Oracle. Their first opportunity to do so since leaving Kelmar. With Narine applying the translation augmentation to Jace, he would recite text while she recorded it in her journal. The long, quiet days with little interruption greatly improved their progress, revealing details behind three new augmentations. The first was interesting, but also gave Narine pause. Something called Ignacious could charge living flesh with intense heat and transform the recipient into a weapon. The second was similar in nature but in reverse, freezing anything with just a touch. Again, she was reluctant to cast such a dangerous spell, at least upon anyone she cared for. The third augmentation, however, intrigued her tremendously, and she set her mind toward mastering it.

It was mid-afternoon on the second day when Captain Dantello announced they approached the city, drawing Narine away from her studies. Her eyes ran over the eight-sectioned construct again, affixing it in her mind. While she had cast it a dozen times, drawing the sections together into a sphere and rotating it as she searched for imperfections, she had yet to apply the augmentation to anyone. Although eager to test it, she sighed and realized it would have to wait. She stuffed the book and her journal into her pack and gathered her things.

With their packs over their shoulders, Narine, Jace, Adyn, and Hadnoddon left their quarters and descended to the main deck.

When the barge rounded a bend, the river widened, the banks a mile apart. The high walls of Tiamalyn stood to the right side, a gray spire jutting above the wall capped by the emerald flame of Oren. Along the water's edge, a curved wall protected a few dozen docks. Downriver from the docks, the water rushed over submerged boulders, foam streaming along the surface. The river then dropped suddenly, the view beyond revealing the river as a narrow strip in the distance, curving through the countryside.

From the front deck, Narine stared at the river ahead, frowning. "Do you hear that?"

Jace explained, "The noise is from the falls."

Hadnoddon asked, "Falls?"

"Tiamalyn Falls. It's quite beautiful, the drop hundreds of feet down."

When the craft angled toward the docks, Narine wondered if any boats had been caught in the rapids and pulled over the edge. *Is it even possible to survive such a fall?* She shuddered. *I wouldn't want to find out.*

As they neared the docks, the boat turned, the oars from one side withdrawn. Lines were thrown, dockworkers drawing the craft in and tying it off. Since there were no rails around the deck and the height matched that of the dock, disembarking would be a simple step off – difficult even for Narine's clumsiness to mess up.

The four others who had traveled with them, three of whom were wizards from Grakal, the fourth a wealthy landholder from Tiamalyn, exited the boat. When Narine and Jace attempted to follow, they were intercepted by Captain Dantello and his first mate, the big man looming over him.

"Wait up, Landish," the captain said, his palm up. "Halgarth and I will escort you to your carriage. We must ensure you head straight to my master's property."

Jace appeared worried. "A carriage? How did you arrange that?"

"A carriage is always sent for special guests," Dantello said. "Someone watches from the city walls and sends it when they see our approach."

Jace nodded. "Makes sense." Then he frowned. "You still haven't told me the name of this master of yours."

Dantello glanced from side to side, leaned close, and whispered. "He prefers to remain anonymous. While Tiamalyn is an open-minded city, some of what transpires in his bordello would be considered unacceptable to some of the…less progressive wizards."

Jace rubbed his jaw, eyes narrowed. "So he *is* a wizard."

Dantello frowned. "Um… Yes. Of course." He turned toward shore, his eyes brightening. "Ah. Here comes your carriage now." He stepped off and gestured. "Come along. We will send you off to the city."

Following Dantello, his first mate at the rear, they headed down the dock, up the stairs, and to a paved square. A warehouse stood at one end, wagons being loaded and unloaded. At the other end was a long building containing numerous shops, people going in and out. The carriage circled and stopped before them, the sides painted white, the wheel spokes gilded. It was an extravagant coach even from Narine's perspective, and she had grown up in a palace.

Two armored guards gripping crossbows, expressions grim, bracketed the driver.

"Hand your packs to Halgarth. He will store them in the rear." Dantello opened the carriage door and gestured inside. "Please, have a seat."

With a grunt, Hadnoddon climbed in.

"What's with the armed guards?" Adyn asked.

"They are simply here to keep you safe." The captain grinned. "After all, you are special guests."

Narine followed Adyn into the carriage, the two sharing a seat across from Hadnoddon. The interior was opulent – green velvet cushions and padded walls, the door handles gold. Jace climbed in and sat beside her, scowling, which grew deeper when Halgarth climbed inside.

Jace turned toward Dantello. "I doubt we need a first mate on this vessel."

"Not a first mate," the captain admitted. "Halgarth will ensure you receive proper treatment when you arrive at the manor."

"Manor?" Jace asked as the door closed.

The coach lurched into motion, heading toward the city. Hadnoddon gazed toward the window, the hammer he had acquired in Oren'Tahal sitting on the floor between his feet. While the dwarf seemed at ease, Narine felt the tension in both Adyn and Jace sitting on either side of her. Her gaze shifted toward Halgarth, who stared in her direction. Self-conscious, she pulled her cloak together, covering herself. He did not respond.

A few minutes later, the carriage slowed as the driver called out. A call answered, and the carriage passed through the city gates.

The spacious streets of Tiamalyn were paved by red bricks, the buildings white with red clay tile roofs. Various shops slipped past – a tailor with elegant gowns and ornate robes in the window, a jeweler displaying a gold necklace with a ruby the size of a cherry, a furniture maker, a gilder, and others that gave Narine pause.

Who can afford all this?

As if reading her mind, Jace spoke. "This part of the city, the entire portion on the bluff, is called Highmount. The palace is up here, beside the falls. Most of the wizards live in this part of the city. Those who don't scheme to make it so. More than any city I have visited, Tiamalyn is a city of haves and have-nots."

"The lower portion of the city… I assume it's far less opulent?"

Jace chuckled, but it seemed forced. "Not even close."

Through the window, the palace came into view – white buildings surrounded by narrow spires, the Tower of Devotion at the center, topped by a green flame.

The carriage turned away from the palace, the view replaced by white mansions with guarded gates. Here and there, gaps between the walls revealed a view of the city below, stretching toward the west. *With such a view, the estates along the bluff must be highly sought after*. She wondered if those estates were purchased or acquired by some other means.

She felt Jace tense up when a particularly large estate came into view. The carriage turned, and Jace reached for the door. Halgarth's thick paw gripped his wrist.

"Sorry," the big man grumbled. "I cannot allow you to exit. Not until we are inside. You wouldn't wish any harm to come to your lady friend."

Narine realized the man referred to her, the humorless smile on his face giving her pause.

The carriage rolled through a pair of iron gates, a handful of armed guards standing to each side as they passed. A creaking came from behind the coach as the gates were closed.

Jace sat back, gaze fixed out the window, eyes filled with worry.

"What is wrong, Jace?" she whispered. "What is this place? I can tell you recognize it."

A sprawling lawn filled with trimmed hedges and alabaster statues eased past as the coach slowed. It then turned, rounding a white fountain with the statue of a wizard in the center, water pouring from the man's hands.

The frown on Jace's face deepened. "When did he buy that?" He turned toward Narine. "You must admit, it is a ridiculous display of vanity."

"The wizard in the fountain? Who is he?"

The carriage stopped, and Halgarth climbed out, holding the door open as he waited.

Jace whispered, "I fear where this may lead. Play along with whatever

I do."

Adyn sighed. "Who did you piss off now?"

Narine ignored her. "Why aren't you telling me what's happening, Jace? What are you planning?"

He sighed. "I don't know yet. I usually figure these things out as they go along." Ducking through the door, he climbed out of the carriage.

Narine rolled her eyes. "He is so frustrating when he keeps secrets."

Adyn placed a hand on her shoulder. "He's a thief, Narine. Secrets are in his blood." She climbed past and stopped just inside the door, looking back at her. "I'll watch your back, you watch his. I have a bad feeling about this."

Adyn stepped out just before Hadnoddon, the dwarf holding his weapon. Steeling herself…for what, she had no idea…Narine climbed out.

The manor was immense, white and pristine, standing four stories tall with red tiles on the roof and a circular tower at one end. A carriage house with an open door stood to one side, the interior large enough to house several families.

Who owns this place? Narine wondered.

A door opened, a man in shimmering green robes emerging, along with a host of guards. He was tall with dark hair, tawny skin, and dark eyes. Although probably twice Narine's age, she was immediately drawn to his handsome face, square jaw, broad shoulders. He seemed familiar somehow. Then she saw another robed figure emerge. A man resembling the first but much younger.

"Kollin?" she muttered.

The guards arranged themselves in an arc around Narine and her companions, the older wizard crossing his arms over his chest while glaring at Jace. The grin on his face did not seem friendly.

"Chancellor Mor," Jace said.

"Jerrell Landish," the man replied.

"I would say it is good to see you, Kylar, but I am not in the mood for lying at the moment."

The wizard's eyes narrowed. "Tales of your exploits are still mentioned in taprooms across the city, claiming your cleverness unmatched. I thought you were too intelligent to ever return to Tiamalyn. Obviously, I was wrong." The grin returned, oozing malevolence. "Too bad for you." He waved toward the guards. "Confiscate their weapons and lock them up."

15

BITTER REUNIONS

Jace woke to complete darkness. He sat up with a groan and worked his shoulders. The kink in his neck popped, causing him to wince. It had been a long night, but morning had to have arrived by now.

"Why are these cells always so dark?" His echoing voice was the only sound in the surrounding void. "Would it hurt to include a window?"

Silence.

He was alone and had heard nothing of Narine or the others since he had been thrown into the cell. Repeated shouts had yielded no response. From his companions or anyone else. He wondered if he would get to eat before Kylar had him executed. The answer came more swiftly than anticipated.

Noise came from outside the cell – a key slipping into the lock, the click of it releasing. The door opened, indirect sunlight streaming in. He blinked and squinted, holding up his free hand to block the light. The other wrist remained shackled to a metal ring embedded in the stone floor. Jace had tried to pull it free, to no avail. His wrist was still raw from the effort.

Four silhouettes stood outside the cell, one robed, one the overweight jailor, the other two with swords drawn.

"Good morning, Jerrell," Kylar said. "I trust you found your accommodations acceptable."

"Except for the smell. I assume you are used to it, but I prefer my room not smell of feces."

"How droll," the wizard growled. "I see your wise-arse mouth remains as irritating as ever."

"Are you going to kill me now, or do you plan to bore me to death with your whining?"

"Don't worry. You'll be dead by sunset. However, it will be a memorable death."

"I'm sure I'll remember it for as long as I live."

The wizard's face turned red. "Shut up!"

An invisible force struck Jace in the face, snapping his head to the side. The hair on his arms stood on end. *Magic.* He stifled a groan. *I forgot to put the amulet back on when we left the boat.* He had removed it early in the journey so Narine could apply the translation augmentation to him. Over recent weeks, he had grown used to her casting spells upon him, illusions and otherwise. Attacks from vengeful wizards were another story.

Working his jaw, Jace squinted into the light.

The wizard grinned at Jace's pain. "I have sent word out, inviting the entire city to the Bowl of Oren. You see, a contest will take place today. A battle of one man against many."

"Yet you extended me no invitation?"

"Oh, you will be there, thief. In fact, you are the guest of honor."

Jace's skin prickled as he was lifted into the air, his body rotating when the shackle connecting him to the floor pulled tight. The lifting stopped with his feet just below the ceiling, arm extended downward, the tight shackle biting into his wrist.

The wizard entered the cell and glared at Jace from a stride away. "You stole my property. Property I had paid dearly to acquire. For such a violation, I would execute you. However, you publicly embarrassed me, as well, and for that, I will do the same to you. You will die today, but not until every person in the city is laughing at your pitiful expense."

Cocking his fist back, Kyler punched Jace in the groin. Pain seared down his thighs and into his chest, forcing out a grunt, his face turning red as he coughed. The wizard stepped back, wincing while holding his wrist. Jace would have laughed if he hadn't been in so much pain. With a wave of

Kylar's hand, the magic released and Jace fell, tucking in just in time to avoid landing on his head. His shoulder struck hard, a crack echoing as he sprawled across the cell floor, groaning in pain

"Unlock him and carry him out. He goes to the Bowl now. We will hold him there until the event begins."

The man spun around, his robes twirling dramatically before fading from view. The jailor stepped forward and grinned at Jerrell. The big man's fist flying toward his face was the last thing Jace saw.

Narine glared at Sadie, who held a spoon full of steaming porridge to her mouth. The maid was an older woman with gray hair and lines at the edges of her kind eyes.

"Open up, miss," the maid said. "Your breakfast is growing cold, and you need a good meal in you."

"Untie my hands."

The woman sighed, lowering the spoon. "You know I cannot."

Fidgeting, Narine attempted to find a comfortable position upon the sofa. Her hands ached to stretch after being bound into tight balls by strips of black cloth. With them secured together behind her back, her shoulders were sore, as well.

"What if I promise not to try anything?"

Sadie reeled back in her chair, aghast. "I was warned. You are a wizardess who trained at the University, capable of unknown magic. If your hands were free…" She shook her head. "I cannot."

Narine stuck out her jaw. "Then I cannot eat."

The maid stood and walked toward the door. "I will be back later. Perhaps you will find lunch more to your liking."

The woman stepped out, closed the door, and locked it behind her.

Alone, Narine sat back with a sigh, her gaze going toward the window, the morning sun streaming through. *I pray Jace is all right.* Adyn and Hadnoddon were tied up in rooms down the hall from her own, but Jace had been taken elsewhere. Judging by Chancellor Mor's threatening tone during their capture, she was frightened for his safety. As a result, she had hardly slept, her twisted insides spoiling her appetite.

She sat in silence, racking her brain in search of a way out of her predicament and how to save Jace from the wizard's wrath. *Without the use of my hands, I have no way of creating a construct.* If magic could not be used, she needed another answer.

A knock came from the door.

"You'll have to allow yourself in," she said in a loud voice. "I am a bit…indisposed."

The door was unlocked and eased open. A familiar face peered inside.

"Hello, Narine."

She exhaled, nostrils flaring. "I was wondering if you would continue to avoid me. I thought perhaps it had become such a habit over the years, it was one you could not overcome."

Kollin stepped inside and closed the door behind him, brown eyes glued to her, gaze intense. He was just as she remembered – tall with dark hair, tanned skin, broad shoulders, and far too handsome for his own good. As always, his robes were the green of Orenth. His long hair had been cut and styled, perhaps the only change to his appearance.

He stopped a stride away, his gaze sweeping her from head to toe, lingering on her chest, which was thrust out because of her hands bound behind her back. For a moment, she feared he sought to extract a bit of pleasure while gaining a modicum of revenge for what she had done to him.

Instead, he said, "I heard about your father…and your brother. I am sorry."

Narine snorted. "I am not. Little humanity remained in my father, the man too hardened to care about anyone or anything, save his own power. My brother was no better and saw me as a liability rather than a sister."

So, Eldalain is dead. I wonder who rules Fastella.

Kollin rubbed his square jaw, eyes narrowed in thought. "How did you end up here, Narine? Why are you with a miscreant like Landish?"

Frustrated, she gave a heated retort. "That *miscreant* is the best man I have ever known. He has saved the lives of thousands, mine included, more than once."

He blinked, brow furrowed. "Your description of Landish sounds nothing like the stories my father tells."

"Your father is consumed by revenge, his opinion skewed by some past slight against him." She sat forward, staring up at him. "What happened? Why does your father hate him so?"

Kollin strolled across the floor, running his hand through his dark hair, gazing through the open window. "I don't know. Landish stole something and…embarrassed my father in the process. Nobody here speaks of it. The subject is forbidden. It happened while I…we were away at the University."

Narine sighed. "I am sorry for what happened between us, Kollin. It was a misunderstanding. I was young and didn't know what I was doing. I… I never meant to hurt you."

He spun toward her, lips white, eyes filled with anger. "Hurt me? You *destroyed* me!" He pointed out the window, which faced west, toward Tiadd. "I spent my entire eight years at the University with my head down, haunted by taunts, being the butt of jokes. Who would want to befriend me after…" He stopped, swallowing, apparently unable to say it aloud.

"As I said, I am sorry. However, you were not the only victim from that event. I also spent those years alone. No boy would do more than glance at me. No girl wanted to get close, unwilling to pay the cost of associating with me." She sat back and sighed. "I just wasn't ready for your advances. Not after my sheltered childhood. My reaction had been programmed into me by a madman. I know that now, better than ever before. You were only reacting to urges you barely understood yourself. It is…what most teens do. Unfortunately for you, I was not most teens. In truth, I have only kissed two men in my entire life. You were the first, and the next didn't come until eight years later, once I was far from the University."

She lifted her gaze and saw him again staring out the window, his anger spent. Instead, he seemed sad.

He ran his hand down his face and turned toward her. "I often wonder what it would have been like had things gone differently. Me…with you."

His eyes, filled with longing, traveled the length of her body again.

Sighing inwardly, Narine gentled her tone. "Our time, if there ever was one, passed long ago. Our paths crossed briefly and diverged. My heart now belongs to another."

Kollin stared at her in silence before walking toward the door, pausing with his hand on the knob. Over his shoulder, he said, "Landish is to fight in the Bowl of Oren in two hours." Even Narine had heard about the gladiator fights. Duels to the death before thousands of blood-thirsty spectators. "My father intends to embarrass him in front of the entire city. He will die there, Narine. I came to rub it in your face, but now..." His voice trailed off. "I, too, am sorry."

He opened the door, slipped out, and locked Narine inside, alone.

She began to cry.

16

THE BOWL OF OREN

Narine, Adyn, and Hadnoddon sat across from two unarmed guards, who looked imposing in their armor, grim scowls on their faces. The bodyguard and dwarf were also weaponless, their confiscated belongings somewhere at Kylar Mor's estate. Narine's weapon was her magic, but she remained unable to use it, her hands bound behind her back.

The carriage in which they rode was far less opulent than the coach they had taken into the city. This was to be a short ride down the street to the fabled stadium known as the Bowl of Oren. Narine had first heard tales of the gladiator duels when she was still a child. Back then, she had dreamed of someday witnessing such a battle herself – mighty warriors in a fierce fight to the death. That dream had somehow been twisted into a waking nightmare.

The carriage stopped, the door opening, the guards waving for her to exit. Adyn helped her out, the bodyguard gripping Narine's arm to keep her from falling. A dozen armed guards surrounded them and the carriage. Beyond the circle, people by the thousands poured into the Bowl.

She gazed up at the imposing structure – five stories tall and circular in shape, the alabaster exterior lined by tall pillars. The hum of thousands of eager spectators came from inside.

Kollin climbed out of his coach, bracketed by two Orenthian soldiers. As he drew close, the circle of guards surrounding Narine parted. She kept her face emotionless, her gaze defiant, although her shoulders ached.

"Untie her," Kollin said, pointing toward Narine.

A guard produced a dagger and cut at her bonds, severing them before unwrapping the cloth wrapped about her hands. Once freed, she released a sigh and held her hands together, working the cramps away.

"What are you going to do with us?" Narine asked.

"We have space reserved for you in Lord Horus' section." He gestured toward the building. "Shall we go inside?"

Kollin gripped Narine's upper arm and ushered her forward with Adyn and Hadnoddon a step behind, half his guards leading, the other half trailing. Rather than follow the spectators, they headed for an entrance guarded by soldiers wearing dyed green leather armor, covered in gold-tinted plates, gold helmets sporting green plumes. The guards parted, and the procession entered the building.

A set of ascending stairs led into the heart of the stadium. Narine stopped short of the stairs and jerked her arm free. Kollin turned toward her, his face drawn in anger.

"I must see him," Narine blurted.

Kollin's expression relaxed, but he shook his head. "He is to fight and die, Narine."

"You don't understand." She took his hand and held it to her chest. "I love him."

He opened his mouth to retort.

"*Please,* Kollin. The man I love is about to die. Can I not say goodbye to him?" Tears emerged, her brave façade shattering. "Please. You can send as many guards along as you wish."

Kollin took a deep breath and nodded. "Fine." He turned to the guards. "Six of you, take the short one and princess' bodyguard to their seats. The rest of you, follow me to the gladiator chambers."

Gripping Narine's arm, he led her to a stairwell and descended, the rumble of armored guards trailing. The stairs led to a curved corridor lit by torches beside doors lining the outer wall. The first door stood open, a man inside sitting on a bench, elbows resting on his legs, seemingly lost in thought. He wore a metal helmet, bracers, boots, and little else. Some sort of short, leather skirt covered his groin and buttocks. The man was scarred but built like a god…lean with bulging muscles.

They passed another room, this one filled with gladiators, the men joking and laughing. Not one of them stood less than six feet in height, some thickly built, all fit and athletic.

The third door was closed and bracketed by two guards. Kollin stopped outside it.

"Is Landish in there?" he asked.

"He is," one guard said.

"Changing," said the other. "Or at least attempting to do so." He laughed.

"She wishes to say goodbye before he dies." Kollin gestured toward the door. "Open it."

The guards looked at each other. "We were told no one was to–"

Kollin cast his magic, a thread of energy wrapping around the guard's chest. The man was lifted off the floor, the band of magic constricting until his eyes bulged and he gasped for air, his feet kicking. Just as quickly, Kollin released the spell, the guard dropping and stumbling back against the wall, hand to his chest as he panted.

"I said, open it."

Wide-eyed, the other guard used a key to unlock the door and stepped back.

Without waiting, Narine opened it and burst inside.

Jace sat on a bench, shirtless, one arm hanging limply, the opposite hand gripping his elbow. When he looked up at her, she gasped. His eye was swollen shut, face puffy and bruised, dried blood down the side of his head.

He smiled. "You are the best thing I have seen since arriving in this wretched city."

Tears returned as she rushed to his side, kneeling in front of him and gently grasping his face. "What did they do to you?"

"It turns out Kylar Mor holds grudges."

Kollin said, "You need to dress, Landish. Your bout will come soon."

Jace was still in his breeches and feet bare, gladiator helmet, bracers, and clothing lying on the bench beside him. He looked up at the wizard. "I tried, but cannot. Not with my shoulder as it is."

Narine stood, tears still tracking down her cheeks, and turned toward Kollin. "I will help him dress. Please, can you give us some privacy?"

He swallowed visibly, eyes flicking back and forth as he considered her request. "All right, but I will sense any attempt to use magic."

Anger flaring, Narine stepped toward him. "Look at him! He is injured! You expect him to fight when he can't even get dressed?" She continued forward, her finger thrusting into the tall wizard's chest, forcing him backward. "I will heal him, and you will allow me to do so. It is the least you can do." Her anger cooling, she took a deep breath. "Besides, what will the crowd think if he comes out in this condition? Your father desires a spectacle and for…Jerrell to be embarrassed. Wouldn't it be more effective if he began the fight whole and healthy?"

Tension hung over the room, Narine wondering if she had gone too far.

Eventually, he nodded. "Fine. I will leave you two alone but will remain in the corridor with my men. You have five minutes."

He exited the room and pulled the door closed. Narine spun around and rushed over to Jace. Again, she knelt, embracing her magic. Using a construct of repair, first as a probe to determine his injuries, then as a tool, she healed his wounds. He gasped, shuddering as the magic healed him. When finished, he worked his shoulder and grinned, his stunning, brown eyes again whole and gazing at her. He smiled, warming her heart.

"Thanks."

"Hush." She put a finger to his lips, whispering, "I'm not done."

Still holding to her magic, careful not to draw too much at once and attract unwanted attention, she formed a new construct, one she had never tested. The eight oval patterns materialized before her, just as she had memorized them. She wrapped the patterns into a loop, connecting the end sections together before folding in each axis to create a sphere. She then pressed her hand against his bare chest, embedding the construct inside him, leaving an opening at one axis.

Gripping his head, she pulled it toward hers and kissed him, lips intertwining as she channeled her magic into the construct. Passion rose from within, requiring concentrated effort on her part not to lose focus on the spell. As her own magic began to wane, she channeled additional power through her enchanted anklet. Her head spun with the rush of magic and the kiss, their lips pressed together for many heartbeats before she pulled away and released her power.

He blinked and looked down at his hands, opening and clenching them, eyes gaping in wonder. "What did you do to me?"

"How do you feel?" she whispered.

"I feel…wonderful. Amazing actually."

She sighed in relief. "It's the latest augmentation we discovered. Perhaps it will be enough."

"Celeritas?"

"Yes. Please remember, the augmentation is temporary. Do what needs doing to end the fight early, before it fails. Now, let's get you dressed."

With Kollin and a pair of guards escorting her, Narine climbed the stairs and entered the arena for the first time. It vaguely reminded her of the interior of the Oracle in Kelmar, but on a far larger scale.

A circular field of dirt occupied the center, surrounded by walls twenty feet high and separating the spectators from the combatants. Thousands occupied the stands, many forced to stand. The lowest level was tiered-off from the rest, those seats belonging to wizards in robes, wealthy merchants in fancy doublets, and women in brightly colored gowns.

"This way," Kollin said, leading her toward two open seats.

She paused when she spotted two thrones nearby. The larger one was occupied by a tanned, bald wizard with angled eyes, a hook nose, and a crown of golden leaves upon his head. An emerald the size of a large grape graced the front of the crown. His robes were shimmery gold, his sash and lapel emerald green. She knew in an instant this was Horus, Wizard Lord of Orenth.

Beside the man sat a voluptuous woman with long, dark hair and perfect, tawny skin. Her dress was dark green and far too revealing to be appropriate, the neckline plunging to expose an abundance of cleavage. The woman's gaze settled on Narine, her dark eyes measuring, red lips pursed in a smirk. Narine blushed and turned away. Wizardess Grenda might have been twice Narine's age, but she was still stunning – the type of woman who made others feel inferior without saying a word.

When Narine looked back, Grenda was again watching the fight below.

She then realized Kollin's father, Kylar Mor, sat to the wizard lord's other side.

"Sit," Kollin said.

Narine did as requested, Adyn and Hadnoddon seated behind her. There were two dozen guards in the section, along with a handful of wizards. She knew there was little chance of escape, so she turned her attention toward the arena floor.

Two men fought, one with a sword and shield, the other with a staff of some sort, a blade at the end. Each had shallow cuts on their arms. The man with the staff moved like the wind, darting around, staff spinning and whirling, blade and butt ends striking the other man's shield repeatedly. The fighter with the sword seemed to be watching, waiting for a clean strike. One never came.

With an impressive leap over his opponent's sword, the man with the staff spun and struck the other gladiator in the helmet, the clang of it resounding. The fighter toppled, sword skittering across the dirt. In a flash, the other man was over him, the blade end of his staff against his throat. The crowd stilled in anticipation, everyone looking toward Horus. The wizard lord stood, arms spread out, and brought one hand in, his thumb turning down.

The victor slashed the downed fighter's throat. The vanquished attempted to cover the wound, but blood spurted from between his fingers, staining the dirt. His feet stopped kicking, dead in seconds.

Staff held high, the winning gladiator bowed toward Horus and crossed the arena, pumping his weapon upward again and again as the crowd cheered. A door opened, and he faded from view. Four men in black ran out, lifted the dead combatant, and carried him away.

Narine's gaze remained on the dirt where the man had died, a crimson stain as a reminder. *Dear Gheald, Farrow, Oren…someone, please keep Jace safe.*

17

SPECTACLE

The door to his dressing room opened and Jace stood, ready. His heart raced, as it had since Narine first applied the augmentation. His mind also seemed to be racing, thoughts coming and going in moments, as if he had no time to dwell upon them. He remained unsure of what, exactly, the augmentation had done to him. All he knew was he felt good, healthy, and startingly awake.

Three guards stood in the corridor. "It's time, Landish," one said, his words coming out with exaggerated slowness.

"The time comes for us all at some point," Jace replied. "Whether mine is now or not has yet to be determined."

The guard snorted, Jace watching specs of spittle drift toward him slowly and arc toward the floor. The man's companions in the corridor chuckled. "Keep up the attitude. You'll need it."

Jace followed the lead soldier at an easy pace, while the two others trailed behind him, both with swords brandished and ready. With the number of guards he had seen in the building, attempting to escape would be risky, but he suspected he could outrun them. It didn't matter. He had been warned. If he did not appear for his fight, Narine and the others would die.

The guard in the lead stopped before a door, slid a bolt back, opened it, and stood back. "In here."

It was a small, dark room.

When Jace stepped inside, the man closed the door and slid the bolt in place. It was pitch black, save for a slice of light through a crack beneath the door.

His mind continued to race, flitting from one thought to another. He sought to tame it by mentally retracing the events of the past weeks, beginning with the assassination of Taladain, the same day he met Narine. With her in his thoughts, he felt more grounded, so he clung to those memories.

Horns blew, the crowd in the Bowl cheering. The squeak of pulleys came from above him, and the wall opposite the door moved, easing up and outward, light streaming in. As it opened, a field of dirt came into view, hundreds of feet across and surrounded by a wall too tall to climb. Jace strolled out, as if he were simply a visitor touring the city, curiously examining his surroundings.

Large doors similar to the one he had just come through were spaced evenly along the wall surrounding him. The doors were all solid wood, except for the three farthest across the arena. Those were made of metal bars, the sunlight reflecting off weapon racks inside filled with shields, blades, and other weapons, all placed too deep in those rooms to reach without the doors opening. Jace wondered if and when it might happen.

He stopped in the middle of the arena and turned, his gaze sweeping the crowd. Cheers and jeers filled the air. Ignoring them, he spun slowly until he spotted the throne.

Walking toward it, his eyes met those of Lord Horus. The man's hawk-like gaze was fixed on him, appearing curious but not angry. *That's a good sign. Maybe there is a way out of this after all.* If Horus had been out for his blood…

His gaze then shifted to the woman beside the wizard lord. Grenda smiled, her finger running across her lips, down her neck, and deep into her neckline. While Jace's pride inflamed by the woman's obvious recollection of him, he also worried she might let something slip. Something that could send Horus into a rage.

Grenda is as gorgeous as ever and likely just as conniving.

He then spotted Narine seated near the wizard lord's throne. Their eyes met – hers filled with concern, his intense and defiant.

Don't give up on me, he mouthed, knowing she could not hear him over the crowd.

Horns blew again and he spun around, alarmed. Eight of the big, wooden doors opened. A warrior emerged from each, the men striding toward him at an oddly slow gait. Similar to Jace, each wore a metal helmet, metal bracers, boots, and a short skirt made of leather strips. Unlike Jace, every one of them was tall and thickly muscled. The plumes on their helmets were the green of Orenth, while his own was red like blood.

He stood still, watching the warriors' deliberate approach, the epitome of hunters stalking prey. Yet something was off, as if time itself had been thrown out of whack. He wondered if it could be a side-effect of Narine's augmentation. Alternatively, he might have been drugged.

Would Mor drug me in addition to all this? Wouldn't Narine have noticed something wrong when she healed me?

He looked down. *I wonder how much blood has been spilled on this dirt. Oh, what is that shiny thing on the ground?*

Jace bent and scooped it up, realizing it was a gold tooth. *I wonder if the man who lost this is dead. I wish I had a pocket. I could sell this. We could use some coin…if I ever get out of here. Slim chance of that. Oh well.* He tossed it over his shoulder.

The men continued toward him, ever so slowly.

"Will you hurry up?" he shouted, losing his patience. "This is going to take all day at this rate!"

None reacted to his comment as they stalked toward him. He sighed, his thoughts drifting again, wondering what Rhoa, Rawk, Algoron, Brogan, and Blythe were doing.

Have they found the Cultivators? Are they really elves? What kind of magic can they do? Is it anything like the dwarf's magic?

More questions flitted past, his mind going down one path after another.

A gong sounded, the gladiators all coming to a stop, none more than ten strides away. The crowd fell silent. Confused, Jace spun around and saw Horus standing before his throne.

The wizard lord spoke, his voice somehow augmented by his magic, filling the immense stadium. "Welcome, citizens of Tiamalyn and beyond. Welcome to the Bowl of Oren. Here, men are judged before our god, his justice executed in the ring of battle. You have just witnessed one such judgment – a man accused of murder given the opportunity to prove himself worthy against one of our gladiators." Horus grinned and gestured toward the blood-stained ground just strides in front of Jace. "Clearly, he was unworthy.

The audience laughed, quieting when Horus raised his arms.

"The man standing before you is named Jerrell Landish, a reputed thief accused of not one crime, but *eight* different crimes in total. He is doubtless guilty of many more. Rather than pay for his crimes one duel at a time, our esteemed Chancellor Mor has decided Landish will face all eight gladiators at once."

The crowd stirred at the news. Jace frowned and turned toward his opponents, some scowling, some with arms crossed over their chests, a few with narrowed eyes, as if measuring him. He sighed. *Perhaps I went a bit too far with Mor,* he admitted to himself. Still, it remained among his more spectacular exploits.

The wizard lord continued. "Per tradition, the duel will begin without weapons."

Chancellor Mor stood and lifted an hourglass filled with white sand. It was by far the largest one Jace had ever seen.

I wonder how much sand is in there. Where did the sand come from? It must be from a beach. I would love to visit a beach with such fine, white sand. Are mermaids real?

Horus' voice boomed. "The weapon racks will open when the sand stops, assuming it lasts that long. I suspect otherwise." He raised his hands. "Begin!"

The wizard lord sat as Kylar Mor flipped the hourglass over. The gladiators surrounding Jace ran toward him. Even their running was oddly slow, each stride taking multiple breaths. He backed away, his heart racing as he mentally scrambled for a way to survive a fight against eight skilled warriors.

I am not ready to die.

A fighter to his right, a big, dark-skinned Kyranni, closed in first, fist cocked. Jace yipped and ran.

Narine sat at the edge of her seat, listening to Wizard Lord Horus' proclamation. When he finished and Mor flipped the hourglass, she could take it no longer.

She pulled away from Kollin and pushed past a pair of guards. It only took a moment for them to grab her, but by then, she stood in front of Kylar Mor.

"What if he wins?" she blurted. "What if Landish wins?"

Mor laughed. "He will not win."

"*If* he wins, the judgment is in his favor?"

Horus nodded. "If Landish were to win, it would be only by the grace of Oren. He would be acquitted."

Narine felt a spike of hope but wanted assurances. She turned toward Kollin's father. "If he wins, not only does he go free, we all go free?"

The man waved it off. "Yes, of course. But it doesn't matter. It will never happen."

Down on the arena floor, the gladiators surrounded Jace as he backed away. When one lunged for him, he dodged and bolted. In a sweeping arc, keeping clear of his enemies, Jace sped around the arena perimeter, running like a jackrabbit. Raucous laughter came from the crowd as the gladiators gave chase. In comparison to Jace, they moved as if wading through molasses. The thin hope Narine had clutched inside became a shade more solid.

The augmentation works.

She turned back toward Kylar Mor. "You must promise us transport to Cor Cordium."

"What?" He furrowed his brows.

She took a breath, steeling herself while turning toward Kollin. "If Jerrell loses, I will agree to marry your son." Kollin's wide-eyed gaze went to her body, his eyes filled with hunger. She recoiled at the thought of being with him, but lacking coin, she had nothing else of value to offer. Looking back at Kylar Mor, she continued. "If Landish wins, you will arrange us transportation, food and shelter included, to the Enchanter's Isle."

Kylar turned toward his son, and Kollin nodded. Eagerly. The wizard took a deep breath before responding. "Fine, but you will honor this wager, even if you must be forced into it."

The guards pulled her back and ushered her to the seat beside Kollin. She felt his eyes on her but refused to look in his direction. Instead, she gazed toward the arena where eight angry bears chased a much smaller, much faster rabbit.

Jace paused and leaned against the wall, having looped around the arena numerous times. Three of the gladiators had stopped giving chase, exhausted, while the other five rushed toward him. The men slowed as they converged, arms spread out to snare him, chests rising and falling as they gasped for air. Yet Jace wasn't tired. In fact, he felt great. He had merely jogged to outrun them.

When they were a dozen strides away, he lunged to the right, the gladiators leaning that direction. He reversed and went left, three gladiators doing the same, the others caught off-balance. With a burst of speed, he darted between two men leaning in opposite directions. Both turned and dove, but far too late, striking each other with a grunt instead.

He jogged away, careful to avoid the three warriors waiting near the middle. Two chased after him. A zig and a zag had them stumbling and crashing into one another. The crowd laughed.

Biting her lip, her stomach in knots, Narine watched Jace race around like a fool, the gladiators appearing twice as foolish. She would have laughed along with the crowd if she hadn't been so concerned.

Kylar Mor's face was red with anger, the man clenching his fist and gathering magic. Horus clamped his hand around Mor's wrist, his hawk-like eyes piercing, his withering look saying more than words. The other wizard released his magic and lifted the hourglass, staring at it, plainly wishing the sand to fall faster.

The last of the gladiators had given up the chase, joining the others in a huddle near the center of the ring. They appeared to be arguing, at least those who were not bent over, gasping for air. Jace stopped and shouted something, waving his arms to attract their attention. The gladiators ignored him, so he began skipping along the perimeter of the arena, leather skirt held out, swishing back and forth with each hop. He looked ridiculous. The crowd howled in laughter.

Jace stopped at the far end of the arena, his back toward the fighters. He waved to the crowd as Chancellor Mor stood and held the hourglass high. The last grain of sand fell. The barred doors below rose, the weapons inside ready to be claimed. At once, the gladiators raced toward the two nearest weapon racks.

Turn around, Jace. Stop behaving like an idiot.

Jace had the crowd in the palm of his hands. It had taken little effort for him to avoid the other men. The last three to give up the chase seemed exhausted, yet he felt fresh. *This enchantment is wonderful,* he thought. Waving as he strolled along the wall, staring up into the crowd, he realized he was having fun.

When he turned and looked across the arena, the floor was empty. Movement from the shadows caught his attention as his opponents emerged from the rooms where the weapons were stored. They held swords, shields, spears, and other instruments of death. His grin fell away, melting into a frown. Narine's warning replayed in his head.

"Remember, the augmentation is temporary. Do what needs doing to end the fight early, before it fails."

"Oh no," he said aloud, then bolted.

As fast as he could, he raced across the arena, toward the only unguarded weapon rack. The two warriors nearest the rack ran toward it, attempting to cut him off. He was far faster, yet needed to travel ten times the distance. His gaze flicked from the two men to the shadowy cell where the weapons waited.

It's going to be close.

One gladiator stopped a dozen strides before the bay, sword and shield ready. Jace slowed slightly, faking toward the man's shield side. His opponent brought his sword around, and Jace altered his path, racing past the man's sword side. Unable to stop his momentum, Jace crashed into the weapon rack. It wobbled mightily, weapons clanging as he caught his balance. Knowing he had little time to react, he grabbed the first weapon he could find. With the wooden shaft in his hands, he spun around, the blade at the end of it striking the wrist of the attacking gladiator, lopping off his hand before he could land an overhead strike.

Blood spurted from the wound. Screaming, he backed away, clutching his forearm, eyes bulging in horror. Jace lunged and drove the blade through the man's throat. The fighter fell backward, gagging on his own blood, while Jace paused to examine his weapon.

The wooden shaft was five feet long, much like a quarterstaff, a weapon Jace had trained with in the past. A blade was strapped to the end of the shaft, the metal edge covered in blood. *It's a naginata.* Jace recalled facing a man with a similar weapon years earlier. A deadly tool in the hands of the right person.

All this went through his mind before the dying gladiator's body hit the ground.

The other nearby gladiator turned toward Jace as the other six rushed toward him, spreading out in an arc. Jace set his jaw, gripped his weapon, and took their measure.

Narine's magic could fade at any moment. No more running. Let's end this.

He launched forward, closing the gap to the nearest warrior in a flash, the man bringing his shield around. Too late. A broad sweep of the naginata cut a streak across the man's stomach. A twist and another stroke left a diagonal slice across his chest. Before blood could even seep from the man's wounds, Jace was past him.

His next opponent held a flail in each hand, spiked metal balls twirling about, his mouth drawn in a grimace. To an average fighter, the flails might appear like spinning wheels of death, certain to cause damage to anyone who drew near. To Jace, the flails were inconsequential, simple to track as they seemingly gradually revolved around the man's fists.

Jace twirled the shaft of his naginata from hand to hand and sliced low, carving a deep gouge through the man's inner thigh. Knowing it was a killing blow, the man destined to bleed out, he stepped back. Narine's voice echoed inside his head.

"Bleeding out takes time, even after you slice his artery. Don't make him suffer."

He sighed. "Fine."

Releasing one hand from the naginata, Jace reached between the rotating spiked balls, snatched one from the man's hand and spun around, his arm outstretched. The spiked ball smashed into the man's helmet, denting it. Jace tossed the weapon aside. It seemed to float, drifting downward like a feather rather than a chunk of metal, even as his opponent's eyes rolled up in his head.

Pleased with his work, knowing the man would soon be unconscious, he spun and charged toward the gladiator standing farthest away, figuring it would be more entertaining for the spectators.

Narine stood, unable to sit any longer. Her breath caught in her throat, the entire crowd silent, watching.

Jace expeditiously dispatched the two warriors who had cornered him in the weapon bay. He then darted out and began laying waste to the others, moving with inhuman quickness, his weapon too swift to follow. One by one, the gladiators fell, Jace darting around too quickly for them to react. It was as if death had taken on a persona, claiming each of the vaunted warriors with a mere touch, all occurring within the span of a few breaths.

The blur that was Jace then stopped beyond the arc of gladiators, the men stumbling, blood emerging from their wounds, long streaks of crimson gracing their legs, arms, and torsos. One man's head fell off and rolled to a stop, his body collapsing. Two had missing hands, one feebly attempting to hold in his entrails with his remaining hand. The last of the warriors collapsed and lay still. Stunned silence gripped the crowd.

"No!" Chancellor Mor cried out as he bolted up and gathered his magic.

Again, Lord Horus stopped the wizard before he could strike, clamping his fist around Kylar Mor's wrist. "Get hold of yourself, Chancellor," he growled.

Jace strode toward the throne, faced his accuser, and lifted his weapon high, pumping it victoriously. The crowd broke from their stasis, cheers rising to deafening levels. Kylar Mor jerked his wrist free from Horus, lifted the hourglass, and smashed it to the floor, before stomping off and fading down the stairwell, his robes a whirl.

Kollin slipped past Narine, mumbling, "I had better go after my father."

She ignored him, watching Jace, who now had his helmet off, the red-plumed object spinning on the tip of his weapon. He circled the arena while waving his weapon and helmet in the air like a pennant. Everyone but Narine cheered, even Adyn and Hadnoddon. Instead, she remained still, her hand covering her mouth, tears running down her face.

He did it. Thank the gods, he did it.

Jace suddenly stiffened, staggered, and collapsed in a heap.

As one, Narine and the crowd released a stunned gasp.

18

PARDONED

Adyn stood near the antechamber door, absently caressing the hilts of her swords. It felt good to have them at her hips again. She suspected Hadnoddon felt the same about his hammer, despite how he stared into space with a scowl, his arms crossed over his chest as he leaned against the wall. When Jace entered the room, now dressed in his own clothing, Narine rushed into his arms. With her head on his shoulder, she hugged him tightly, his cheeks puffing, eyes bulging.

"Oof," the thief choked out. "I am happy to see you, as well, but it's difficult to breathe."

Narine released him, gripped his chin and gave him a kiss. "Sorry. I was just so–" She stopped in mid-sentence and stared toward the figure standing in the doorway. "Kollin."

He stepped into the room. "Hello, Narine." He approached her and Jace, nodding to the latter before his gaze returned to her. "I wanted you to know, despite our troubled past and the missed opportunity from my father's lost wager, I never wished to see the man you loved dead."

Jace arched a brow and turned toward Narine. "Love?"

She blushed and smoothed her dress, ignoring Jace as she spoke to Kollin. "Thank you. As I said before, I never wished ill for you. Our past…is better left there. We were both young and naïve."

"Agreed." He nodded. "I wish my father felt the same way. He refuses to forget what happened between him and Jerrell, even after he survived his trial in the Bowl of Oren."

He turned his gaze toward Jace. "I was far away in Tiadd when the incident between you and my father occurred. He won't talk about it, and the entire staff is forbidden to speak of it. Perhaps you could shed some light?"

Jace rubbed his jaw, eyes narrowed. "I don't think so. I do not wish to poke the bear when I am about to escape."

Through the door Adyn stood beside, shouts arose. It was Kylar Mor's voice. A loud boom sounded – a thunderclap preceding silence.

Adyn smirked. "I believe Chancellor Mor was just put in his place."

The door opened, a guard entering, followed by Lord Horus and Chancellor Mor, the latter frowning, eyes seething hatred as he glared at Jace.

Horus approached the thief. "Mister Landish, per Orenthian tradition, you have earned your freedom by a trial of combat."

"You cheated," Kylar Mor blurted, hands clenching into fists. "You and this...*wizardess*," he sneered at Narine. "How did you do it? What witchery did you perform?"

Narine stiffened and set her chin. "I don't know what you mean, Chancellor. I was seated behind you and could hardly have cast a spell without your knowledge."

Horus turned toward Mor. "She is correct, Kylar." He gestured toward Jace. "This man was stripped of his belongings and alone on the arena floor. He had no enchanted weapons, nor could she have performed a spell in our presence."

"How do you explain what we saw?" Mor sounded incredulous.

Jace shook his head. "I don't understand it, either." His eyes grew wide in an exaggerated expression of wonder. "Perhaps it was the will of Oren. I believe it was your god's desire for me to survive. I *do* have important things to accomplish." He shrugged. "After all, who can question the will of a god?"

The Chancellor's eyes narrowed, his lips and knuckles turning white.

"Without another explanation," Horus said, "I accept this reasoning."

A man in a green doublet with white ruffles stood in the doorway to the throne room. "Your Majesty." He paused as Horus turned toward him. "An embassy has arrived from Marquithe – five men led by Captain Despaldi of the Midnight Guard."

Adyn held in a gasp, her gaze meeting Narine's, whose own expression reflected alarm.

"I am starving, and my meal awaits," Horus said. "Tell the captain I will meet with him after lunch."

"Yes, Your Majesty," The man bowed and faded into the throne room.

Horus put a hand on Jace's shoulder, his intense gaze upon the thief. "Jerrell Landish, I acquit you of all past charges. You are free to go." He fixed a stern gaze on the wizard beside him. "In addition, there was a wager placed prior to the battle. With your victory, Chancellor Mor has agreed to arrange and fund your transportation to the Enchanter's Isle." Horus turned toward Jace. "I believe it is your intended destination?"

Jace gave Narine a questioning glance before replying, "Yes. That would be wonderful."

The wizard lord nodded. "You heard him, Chancellor. See it done. I want them on your private barge within the hour."

Horus and his guards exited the room, leaving Kollin and his frustrated father behind.

The coach ride was circuitous, looping around the northern edge of the city before the road turned sharply and began a series of switchbacks in a descent to the lower district. The street leveled, and the coach took them through a market, along narrow streets with small, slender houses, and eventually stopped at a gate along the river. They climbed out, passed through the gate, and descended to the docks. All eyes were drawn to the spectacle less than a thousand feet upriver.

The waterfall roared, white spray swirling in the sunlit afternoon air, refracting into a multi-hued rainbow. It was a majestic sight, the falls hundreds of feet tall and twice as wide. Adyn had never seen anything like it. She stared, transfixed, until a call captured her attention.

Turning toward the voice, she saw Captain Dantello approaching. "I never thought I'd see you again." The captain shook his head, lifting his hat to scratch behind his ear. "I figured the lot of you were dead by now." He nodded toward Jace. "Especially you. Chancellor Mor has had a bounty out on you for years."

"Hello, Captain." Narine gestured toward the barge. "Tell me, how did you get your barge down here? Just yesterday, it was up there." She pointed toward the top of the falls.

The man grinned. "You have it wrong. Chancellor Mor owns *two* barges – one for the upper river and another for the lower. I swapped with Captain Yarrick, who usually commands this craft, since I have...history with you people. He is taking my barge back upstream to Grakal the day after tomorrow."

Dantello moved closer to Jace, his voice dropping. "Did you really face eight men in the Bowl?"

"He did," Adyn said. "Eight gladiators, each at least twice his size. Just like that..." She snapped her fingers, "they were all dead."

Hadnoddon said in his low, grumbling voice, "It was a massacre."

The captain's face grew pale as he stepped back. "Oh, um... Well then, I'm glad no confrontation took place when we last met."

"You should be. Otherwise, you'd be dead." Adyn's tone carried a threat.

"Yes." He kneaded his hands and backed away, noticeably uncomfortable. "Please, come aboard. Your things have been brought to your rooms, and we are ready to depart."

Jace gave Adyn a questioning look as the captain walked away.

She smirked and shrugged. "May as well use the story to our advantage. We should now encounter little trouble on the trip. Perhaps not until we reach Cor Cordium."

He snickered. "Good thinking." A broad grin spread across his face. "I'm not used to others fearing me. It'll be a nice change."

Narine took his arm. "Rather than them trying to capture or kill you?"

The thief shrugged. "My line of work offers all sorts of perks."

She laughed, the pair stepping onto the barge, Adyn and Hodnoddon following.

The moment they stepped on deck, the ropes were untied, and the barge pushed off, oars carrying it from the small bay to the heart of the river. This time, there were no other passengers, allowing Adyn and Hadnoddon to each choose their own room. Jace and Narine took the upstairs suite, closing the door behind them and drawing the curtain.

Adyn rested her elbows on the rail at the rear of the barge as the great city of Tiamalyn faded into the distance. They had only spent twenty-four hours there, but she suspected the visit left a lasting impression.

The view was impressive – the tall, white walls, the raging waterfall, the palace and Tower of Devotion looming over it all. Her gaze affixed to the top of the tower, the green flame of Oren visible, despite the afternoon sun. The fire suddenly faded.

She startled and gripped the rail, staring at the tower, trying to determine if it was a trick of the sunlight.

Hadnoddon stepped beside her and grunted. "Nice view, eh?"

"Do you see the tower up there?" She pointed toward it.

"Yeah. Of course."

"Can you see the green flame at the top?"

He frowned. "Are you daft? There is no green flame. Not like the one we saw when we arrived yesterday."

A lump tightened Adyn's throat. "Oh no. Not again."

19

TRUE POWER

Outside the window, the sun shone over the city of Tiamalyn. It had been years since Despaldi last visited. Nothing had changed. Not in the city. Not in the palace where he now stood.

The room where Despaldi and his men waited was filled with ornate furniture – a hand-crafted table and chairs made of a dark, lacquered wood, a glass cabinet filled with cups, plates, and vases from around the world, a sofa covered in green velvet, and a long lounge chair to match. He had no time to waste on such frivolities, the objective before him too monumental.

In his mind, he went over the plan. Again.

The other four members of the Fist of Farrow were spread throughout the room – one pacing, one on a sofa, two at the table, all expressions fixed with a fierce intensity.

No relaxing today. Not until we finish our business...assuming we survive.

His gaze went to Vlad, a lean warrior, thirty years of age. The man flexed his fingers while eyeing his insulated gloves, likely anxious to remove them. Despaldi understood. The power he had been gifted with was intoxicating. So much so, it never left his mind, even while he slept.

Like Vlad and Despaldi, Ferris wore enchanted gloves, each pair of mitts imbued with a different, very specific enchantment. The man stared into the distance as he grappled with his thoughts. By his blond hair and blue eyes, one would think him Pallanese or even Ghealdan, but he was Farrowen through and through. Of the bunch, Ferris seemed the most at ease, which was nothing new. His calmness under pressure was among the primary reasons Despaldi had recruited him. His cold demeanor fitting for his new abilities.

Next came Garek, the biggest of the bunch, a muscular man who stood as tall as Despaldi but with a much thicker build. The thirty-year-old's bald scalp gleamed in the afternoon sun. Despaldi had never seen the man with hair, even before his elevation to the Midnight Guard four years earlier. Garek's personality was opposite of Ferris', often ruled by his emotions, displayed by his tendency to rush into battle. However, he had shown enough strength and skill to overwhelm his opponents, which made him ideal for his new role. More importantly, he was loyal.

Lastly, Despaldi looked over at Zeph pacing the room. While a brilliant strategist and skilled with his knives, Zeph had always been a worrier. Today was no different.

"Will you just relax, Zeph?" He allowed his irritation to seep into his voice. "Your pacing is distracting me."

The man walked closer and spoke in a hushed tone. "I'm sorry, but what do you expect when I am about to face a god?"

Garek snorted. "Horus is no god. He is a wizard. A powerful one." The man sat back on the sofa. "Don't believe me, just look at what happened to Taladain and Malvorian."

"True," Vlad added. "When faced by something unexpected, they lost. The same could happen here."

"*Could*?" Zeph shook his head. "Could is not good enough. I prefer to win by design."

Despaldi put a hand on Zeph's shoulder. "We have a plan. A good plan. Stick to it for now but be prepared to adjust tactics on the fly should something go sideways."

"You just described every single enemy we have faced."

"Exactly. Wizard lords are not immortal, Zeph. Just difficult to kill." Despaldi looked back out the window. "Besides, we have surprise on our side. They confiscated our weapons. Since we are not wizards, we couldn't possibly utilize magic. What threat could we pose?"

He sensed, rather than saw, the man nodding. "Surprise offers an advantage, albeit brief."

A knock came from the door.

Despaldi turned toward it. "Come in."

The same guard who had escorted them to the room stuck his head in. "The Wizard Lord will see you now."

Without uttering a word, Despaldi exited the room, trailed by the other four men. Seven more guards waited in the corridor, four leading, four trailing as the procession walked down a corridor, into a receiving hall, then to the guarded doors leading to the throne room.

The rectangular throne room was made of alabaster stone, a high ceiling supported by fluted columns. White marble tiles with green striations covered rows of steps running from wall to wall, a dark green carpet down the center. Despaldi followed the lead guards down to the main floor, before which was a dais. A throne carved of white marble and covered with emerald cushions rested on the dais. Upon the throne sat Lord Horus, Wizard Lord of Orenth.

Draped in golden robes with emerald green trim and sash, Horus struck an imposing figure. The wizard lord's bald, tanned head was polished, eyes angled, hooked nose giving him the appearance of a bird of prey. A gold circlet, graced by a large emerald, sat upon his head. From his appearance, one might think him forty years of age. Despaldi knew the man's true age was three or four times that number.

The four lead Orenthian guards split up, two positioning themselves to each side of the dais. Despaldi stopped ten strides from the throne, two of his men settling to his left, the other two on his right. He ached to remove his gloves, but it was not yet time.

Soon. Very soon.

"Welcome, Captain," Horus said. "It is an odd coincidence for you to appear in my court today. One of your very own countrymen just pulled off the greatest upset the Bowl of Oren has ever seen."

"Not such a great coincidence. Many valiant warriors call Farrowen home."

"This was no warrior, but rather an undersized thief named Landish."

Anger rushed in, but Despaldi kept it hidden and fought off a scowl. "I have heard the name," he said evenly. *Landish must wait. Horus comes first.*

The wizard lord tented his fingers before his lips, eyes narrowed, the room silent for a few beats. He then said, "I understand you have come from Marquithe with a message from your new wizard lord. I do hope he has given up on his plan to coerce me into siding with him against Pallanar."

Despaldi bowed. "Do not worry, Your Majesty. Lord Thurvin understands your position and has no intention of pursuing it further."

Horus nodded. "I am glad we understand each other."

"Rather, I have come here with a message of a different sort. One I believe you will find enlightening." Despaldi glanced backward. The other four guards in their escort stood ready in an arc behind them. Other than the wizard lord and his eight guards, there was nobody else in the room. He turned back toward Horus. "I suspect you are aware of Lord Thurvin's campaign in Ghealdor?"

"Of course. Such news has shaken the world." The wizard lord cocked his brow. "Is it true the Towers of Devotion have been converted to Farrow?"

"Yes, Your Majesty. Three cities by now, perhaps four. Soon, the entire wizardom will be under our control, the prayers feeding Lord Thurvin. You understand what that means."

Horus frowned. "Thurvin's hunger for power is obvious, but at what cost? What of Gheald? What of the other wizardoms?"

"As for Gheald, I have no idea. What becomes of a god without worshipers?" Despaldi shrugged. "Regarding the other wizardoms, we are prepared to accept their surrender, beginning with Orenth."

"What?" Lord Horus stood, his voice rising. "You dare to step into my court and demand surrender?" He sneered. "I could destroy you here and now, as quick as a breath. What would your precious little wizard lord do about that? His army is two wizardoms away, his own magic bound to Marquithe."

"There is more," Despaldi said in an even tone. "Lord Thurvin recently discovered how to extend his magic, to gift unique abilities to those he trusts."

The wizard lord scoffed, "What nonsense is this?"

Despaldi grinned. "Behold."

He pulled off one enchanted glove, then the other, revealing hands that glowed orange with the heat of a forge. To his left, Vlad removed his gloves, fingers crackling with electricity. To the right, Ferris' hands were covered in frost, steam rising from them.

Horus gaped. "How is this possible?"

Despaldi sneered. "Lord Thurvin's magic is unequaled, exceeding that of any wizard lord in history." He held his hands before his face, eyeing them as the heat increased in intensity. "With this power, he is prepared to change the world."

Horus growled, "You mean *rule* the world."

"Exactly." Despaldi urged the magic to ignite, heat from his hands rising to an inferno. "Attack!"

Thrusting his hands forward, a burst of flames shot out. As expected, they did not touch Horus, the wizard lord protected behind a shield of magic. Despaldi turned and directed his attack toward the two soldiers to the wizard lord's left. The men screamed as they burst into flames.

At the same moment, Vlad blasted the two soldiers to the other side with a bolt of lightning, frying the men in their own armor, bodies twitching violently as they fell to the floor.

The singing of drawn swords rang out from behind. Despaldi spun, fireball in hand, and tossed it at the nearest guard. It struck the man in the face, chunks of fire splattering as the man screamed and fell backward.

Ferris extended his hand, a layer of ice coating the three remaining Orenthian soldiers, slowing the men, their armor cracking in the cold. A sword of ice materialized in his hand. With a thrust beneath an exposed armpit, he skewered the nearest soldier.

Coated in ice and unable to move, the last two soldiers were helpless when Vlad released another bolt of lightning, the bright blue electricity arcing from his fingertips to their frozen armor, smoke rising from their helmets as they collapsed, blackened, smoldering sockets where eyes once existed.

On a current of air, Zeph rose above the fracas, hands circling as a horizontal tornado blasted at the wizard lord, lifting Horus off the floor and slamming him against the throne in a bone-shattering collision.

Horus fell to the floor, body broken. However, his bones instantly realigned, wounds sealing as he floated up and cast a new shield. It blasted out and up, striking Zeph and launching him across the room, the man striking the wall.

"This is where you all die!" Horus shouted, the wizard floating five feet above the dais as he prepared for a mighty attack.

However, Zeph's efforts had not been in vain. His blatant attack had distracted the wizard lord, as had the magic of the others. What Horus did not expect was Garek, who had darted to the side of the room at the onset, seemingly fleeing the battle. The big man then circled around a thick pillar and rushed the dais from behind.

Garek slammed into the throne with tremendous power, his magic-enhanced push launching it into the wizard lord's back, striking Horus before he could release his magic. The heavy throne knocked him to the floor with a crack, landing on him before bouncing and colliding into the marble benches, breaking into pieces.

Despaldi strode over to Horus and looked down at the wizard lord. Vlad and Ferris stood beside him, magic ready. The fallen wizard was conscious, but the back of his head was covered in blood, arm bent in an unnatural manner. Horus clenched a fist, arm rapidly healing with his magic, the gash in his head sealing. Despaldi could not allow him to fully recover.

"This is where you die, Horus," he said, mimicking the man's statement.

Ferris drove his ice sword into the wizard lord's back, and Horus' mouth opened in a gaping, silent scream. Vlad unleashed a bolt of electricity through the blade and into the man, the discharge lasting for a few breaths before he released it.

Still, with the use of his magic, Horus remained alive.

Clenching his fists, Despaldi squeezed tightly, concentrating as he made them hotter and hotter. When they glowed with the white light of the sun, he thrust them downward, bathing Horus in intense flames, the blast continuing for a short span, requiring utmost concentration, the heat forcing the others to back away. Despaldi then released the magic, the flames from his fists fading.

The wizard lord's robes had disintegrated to wisps of blackened thread, prone body still burning and blackened beyond recognition. Despaldi kicked, the burnt corpse shattering to embers that spread across the floor.

"Wizard lords are not gods," he said, turning to find Zeph across the chamber, staggering to his feet, the man's head bloody.

The door burst open and guards charged in, trailed by a man in green robes.

Ferris flung his hands in a broad arc, tiny shards of ice filling the air, the sharp points striking the attackers in the face and eyes, the blinded men screaming as they crashed into each other and fell down the stairs. Vlad launched a lightning strike, electricity arcing across the mass of armored soldiers.

Despaldi crafted a fireball and threw, just as a white-hot beam of magic shot from the enemy wizard. The blast struck Zeph, who screamed and fell, a hole through his chest. The fireball struck the wizard in the side, setting his robes aflame. Garek lifted a dead soldier and launched the corpse across the room. The wizard waved his hands, his magic snuffing out the fire. Before he could cast another spell, however, the thrown soldier smashed into him and knocked him against the wall. Both collapsed into a heap.

With a single, magic-powered leap, Garek flew over the rows of benches and landed at Zeph's side. It took but a moment for him to look up. "Zeph is dead."

Despaldi growled and climbed the stairs, angry about losing one of his men to a simple wizard who had happened upon the scene. He reached the top and pulled the dead soldier's broken body off the wizard. The man stirred, his eyes flickering open. Despaldi reached down and gripped the man's hands, the smell of burnt flesh rising as the wizard screamed, his skin charred in an instant. Satisfied, Despaldi stood and turned toward Ferris.

"Freeze his hands. Cut off his pain."

Ferris knelt and gripped the distraught wizard's hands, the scarred, angry flesh instantly coating in frost. The wizard's cries stopped, his head dropping to the floor as he gasped for air.

"Who are you?" Despaldi asked.

"Chancellor Kylar Mor," he whimpered.

Despaldi remembered hearing the name in a story. The victim of one of Landish's exploits. "Horus is dead. Orenth is without a wizard lord. Nobody can save you, but you can save yourself."

"What do you want?" The man's eyes were clenched as he spoke, tears running down his face.

"I simply seek the truth. Answer a question. Nothing more."

"You will have it."

"Horus mentioned the name of a thief. He was here today, fought in the Bowl of Oren."

Mor started laughing. It was not a laughter of joy, but one of madness. When he stopped, he said, "Landish. Jerrell Landish."

"I have a score to settle with Landish," Despaldi said. "Where is he?"

"He took my barge downriver to Shear. From there, he was guaranteed passage to Cor Cordium."

Despaldi frowned. "The Enchanter's Isle? Why?"

"I have no idea." Mor opened his eyes. They bulged as he lifted his head. "Do you intend to kill him?"

"Yes. Him and his companions. I have a debt to settle and an item to recover."

The wizard began to laugh again, hysterical and unceasing. He was still laughing as Despaldi led his remaining men from the room and out of the building.

20

HIDDEN IN PLAIN SIGHT

The sleigh climbed the mountainside, the sun edging over the mountain to the east. Rhoa Sulikani sat in the second seat beside Rawk and Algoron. She pulled Salvon's journal from her coat and opened it to a marked page. She read the passage again, the words remaining the same as the prior twenty times she had read it. Shock had gripped her the first few times, but her state of mind now teetered between disbelief and betrayal.

Today, I located the offspring I had labored so long to bring into this world. Her name is Rhoa. Remarkably, she was in Fastella this entire time, her parents having left Hassakan after she was born. With her located, I can initiate other portions of my scheme. While elaborate, requiring decades to plan and many years to come to fruition, the child's existence must remain unknown to the enemy. Without her, the shift in power is impossible.

She paged through the book and located the next passage she had marked, one dated ten years ago.

The fee has been paid, the thief certain to alter the lottery. I was careful to plant the seed, a gentle nudge in the right direction. Tomorrow, her parents will be claimed for sacrifice, and I will be there to protect her. When relying on me alone, I will set her on the path, placing the blades in her possession and lighting a fire in her heart. Time will surely lead her back to the man who destroyed her family, toppling the first tile of fate. Yet, to ensure the future I require, I must also send the thief to claim the amulet.

A tear formed at the corner of her eye, and she turned away from Rawk beside her. She didn't want him to see her cry. She knew the questions he would ask, and she wasn't prepared to discuss the subject. Not yet. Not until she could confront Salvon herself.

He caused my parents' deaths. How could he do such a thing? She wished it to be false, just her misinterpreting the old man's notes. At the same time, she wondered if Jace could be the thief mentioned. *If so, what does he know of Salvon's plans?*

The sleigh slowed and the ground leveled as they crested a pass between two peaks. When they came to a stop, Rhoa stuffed the journal into her coat. She had yet to read it in full. Those early passages continued to draw her in, tugging on her emotions, leaving her wondering how much of her life had been a victim of the old man's machinations.

She climbed out of the sleigh, stepping lightly onto the snow, the surface a hardened crust able to bear her weight. The others were not so lucky, sinking to their knees…or farther. She held a mitted hand up to shield her eyes from the sun and gazed upon the snow-covered valley. It looked no different than the nine prior valleys they had crossed. The mountains, trees, and snow seemed endless.

"Are you sure the forest we seek will have no snow?" she asked.

Lythagon tugged on his braided black beard, eyes hidden behind the tinted glass on his helmet, snow practically reaching his waist. "Yes. Xionne's instructions were quite clear. Cultivator magic is unique, the cold unable to penetrate a forest they call home."

She sighed. "Ten days have passed since we left Kelmar, yet the scenery remains nothing but endless snow-covered mountains and forests firmly in the grip of winter. How many mountains must we climb before we reach this forest? Are we even traveling in the right direction?"

Ghibli-Kai, who stood to her other side, shrugged. "We were to head east, and I have maintained that course, straying only when the terrain required it."

Brogan waded through the snow, holding his hand over his eyes as he scanned the horizon. "The Great Peaks are now northwest of us."

To their north, mountains obscured the horizon, but none were as tall as the Great Peaks, the impossibly tall mountains down the spine of the continent.

"What if we now turn north?" Rhoa suggested.

"And go where?" Lythagon asked.

She pointed between the two nearest peaks. "Just to the next pass, to see what lies beyond."

Lythagon looked at Ghibli-Kai.

The Frostborn shrugged. "At this point, I am willing to try anything." He pointed east. "Snow-capped mountains are visible for many, many miles in that direction, which does not inspire hope. It will cost us only a day to reach the saddle to the north."

The dwarf nodded. "Very well."

Mixed feelings stirred inside of Rhoa, part of her thankful to try something different, anything different, to locate their destination. Another part worried her suggestion would lead them farther off course.

How many days can this last? How long can we *last?*

The sleigh continued uphill as it had for much of the day. The trees parted, the incline leveling slightly, the saddle ahead bracketed by two towering peaks covered in white, patches of gray rock visible. Rhoa bit her lip as the sleigh neared the top of the saddle, stomach churning in anxiety. The sleigh ahead of theirs slowed to a stop. Ghibli-Kai shouted to his team, the ice wolves slowing until their sleigh stopped beside the first. Brogan, Blythe, and Lythagon climbed out of the other sleigh and trudged off through the snow.

Ghibli-Kai climbed out and glanced back, looking at Rhoa. "We will get a view of the next valley. Do you wish to join us?" He turned and waded through the deep snow before she could reply.

Rawk must have sensed her hesitation. "I will come with you, Rhoa."

She turned toward him, the dwarf's eyes hidden behind his dark spectacles. With the bright, snow-covered surroundings, she again found herself wishing she had similar spectacles of her own.

"I...," she stammered. "I would like that."

"I will remain here," Algoron said. "I have had enough of tromping through the snow for no good reason."

Rhoa knew what he meant, having seen it again and again. When she stepped out of the sleigh, the crust of the snow supported her once again. In contrast, Rawk broke through with each step, sinking to his crotch. It looked ridiculous from her position, standing on top of the snow with her head high above his.

When she laughed, he looked at her in feigned consternation. "This is not easy, you know. Not all of us weigh so little."

Still chuckling, she walked beside him, stepping with care in order to not break though the hardened surface. "I am sorry. It just struck me as funny. I am not used to being so tall."

Rawk smiled in response.

The two circled around the ice wolves lounging in the snow, the monstrous animals watching them. Even after a week, Rhoa couldn't bring herself to trust the wolves. With their size, should anything go wrong, it might be a quick end for any of them.

As they neared the others, she heard them speaking.

"...nothing but snow-capped mountains as far as we can see," Brogan said, exasperated. "Perhaps over the next range?"

The hope Rhoa had harbored was crushed in an instant.

"I don't know," Lythagon said. "We were instructed to head east, not north. For all we know, this turn has already put us off course." The dwarf's gaze settled on Rhoa as she stopped a few strides shy of where they stood.

Rawk glared at the other dwarf. "Do not blame Rhoa. This is not her fault."

"I said nothing of the sort," Lythagon said.

Ghibli-Kai removed his fur hat and ran his hand though his white hair. "I just don't know what to do. Soon, we will have to turn back. We are already many miles beyond any route known to the Frostborn. I fear we may not make it back if we continue much farther."

Sighing, Rhoa walked past her companions as they discussed what to do next. Her gaze drifted across the horizon – towering peaks to the northwest, lower peaks before her, the mountains continuing as her gaze drifted east. She then looked down at the mountainside and gasped.

The valley floor was covered in varied greens of leaf trees amid pines and grass-covered meadows. A river ran through the valley, flowing into an open lake surrounded by trees. Beyond the lake and forest, she saw nothing but scrub-covered, barren land. However, her attention was drawn to the heart of the forest below. There, a cluster of trees with leaves of gold shone in the afternoon sunlight.

She stared toward it, her heart filling with hope. "It's beautiful."

Rawk stopped beside her and grunted. "I thought so at first, as well, but after seeing a similar sight day after day, I long for warmer weather. I am done looking upon snow."

Rhoa frowned down at him, his lower body still buried in snow while she stood upon it. "I'm speaking of the forest down there. The green valley, the golden trees, the lake… Isn't it wonderful?"

He frowned. "I see a frozen lake, but I am tired of ice, as well."

"Frozen?" She frowned and turned. "Blythe! Would you come here for a moment?"

The tall redhead walked over, taking the path Rawk had forged. "Yes?"

Rhoa pointed toward the heart of the valley. "What do you see?"

Blythe peered down for a moment and shrugged. "I see a valley of pines and dormant leaf trees. A frozen lake at one end and snow-covered land beyond."

Rhoa stared at the golden trees and felt as if she could feel a warmth coming from the area. "Am I going crazy?"

Looking at her, Rawk tilted his head. "What do *you* see, Rhoa?"

After a moment's hesitation, she described the forest as she saw it.

The dwarf looked down at the valley and muttered, "Magic."

"Magic?" Blythe asked.

He clapped his hands together and began laughing. Jumping, he let out a loud whoop.

"Are you all right?" Rhoa asked in concern.

Rawk reached up and took her hand. "It is magic, Rhoa. Cultivator magic. It masks their forest in an illusion."

She turned from him and peered down at the valley, realizing what he meant. "Magic doesn't affect me, so I can see through the illusion while the others cannot."

"Yes!" he said excitedly.

"I forget that about you." Blythe grinned. "We should have guessed the elves would hide themselves somehow." The woman spun around and shouted, "Rhoa found it!" She pointed toward the valley. "It's right there, hidden in an illusion."

They all rushed through the snow and stared down at the valley with stunned expressions.

Rawkobon Kragmor sat wedged between Rhoa and his uncle, Algoron, as he had for the past eleven days. Today was different. Today, hope filled his belly.

Trees sped past the sleigh driven by Ghibli-Kai and drawn by four massive ice wolves. Each wolf had a name – Ilko, Betch, Frolla, and Drakka. While the Frostborn addressed each without pause, they all were the same to Rawk. Terrifying. Enormous with long, gray fur, a mouth full of white teeth, fangs sharp, and yellow eyes that made him believe they considered him dinner rather than a companion.

Ghibli-Kai is nice enough, but I will be glad to be done with the wolves.

The trees parted, the scene opening to a snow-packed clearing. The Frostborn driver pulled the reins and shouted at the wolves. When the sleigh came to a stop, Rawk stood to get a better view.

Mere strides ahead of the wolves was a black chasm, fifty strides across and the bottom too distant to see. *We almost drove over the edge.* He shuddered, imagining a fall that never ended. The thought was worse than striking the ground and dying on impact. He looked up at the sky, recalling the same fear when he first emerged from his underground home of Ghen Aeldor. Back then, the open, endlessness of the sky had him frightened of a fall up. To think back on it now, he realized it was ridiculous. Nobody ever fell up. At least not that he had ever seen.

"Come on." Rhoa climbed out as the other two sleighs came to a stop. "We can walk from here."

Rawk climbed out, head sweeping from east to west, the chasm extending in both directions. "How are we going to cross it?"

She pulled her pack from the rear of the sleigh and frowned. "Cross what?"

"The chasm," Algoron said. "It appears to go on for miles."

Rhoa peered ahead. "I see no chasm. Just a bunch of flowers leading to the forest's edge not far from where the snow ends."

Rawk's eyes narrowed. "Magic again. The chasm is an illusion, discouraging anyone from passing."

Algoron chuckled as he picked up his pack. "Clever. Even monsters would be deterred by such a ruse."

While Rawk dug his pack out and threw it over his shoulder, Rhoa walked over to the other sleighs and explained the situation. The others climbed out and gathered their gear before saying their goodbyes to the Frostborn, thanking the men for the transportation.

With packs, waterskins, and weapons gathered, they trudged across the snow and stopped at the chasm's edge. Rawk leaned forward to peer down. The bottom, if one existed, was beyond his view.

Rawk turned to Rhoa. "Are you sure?"

She frowned. "I think so. Where does the chasm start?"

"Just a few feet in front of us."

She gripped his hand. "Allow me to lead. If anything happens, don't let go."

"Never."

"I hope you know what you are doing," Brogan muttered. "You would not survive the fall. I can't even see the bottom."

"Hush." Blythe elbowed the big man in the ribs, his eyes bulging as he released a long groan. "Oh, sorry," she said, rubbing his arm. "I am just not used to you being so brittle."

"Yeah. Age, I guess." He winced and rubbed his side.

Rawk gripped Rhoa's hand and they took a step, her foot stopping just shy of the edge. Rawk gripped her hand as tightly as he dared. She took another step, her foot hovering over the drop for a moment, the front half of it vanishing. When Rhoa completed her stride, half her leg had disappeared.

She turned back toward Rawk. "Am I to the chasm yet?"

"Your leg… It disappeared, right over the drop."

Grinning, she pulled him forward. "Come on."

Rhoa took another step, her entire body fading from view. Placing his faith in her, Rawk lifted his foot and stepped out into the chasm, his breath held tightly, stomach twisting. The air shimmered. A wave of heat washed over him as the view changed dramatically.

It was suddenly a sunny, summer afternoon, massive oaks, maples, and pines standing fifty strides away. Between him and the forest itself was a clearing filled with flowers – reds, oranges, purples, and whites blanketing the area where the chasm had been moments earlier. Butterflies flitted past him and Rhoa, dancing from flower to flower, the scent of the blossoms tickling his nose. Birdsong filled the air, joining a distant trickle of flowing water.

Rhoa smiled and turned toward Rawk. Despite the gorgeous surroundings, she was the most amazing aspect of his view. "Can you see it now?"

He nodded numbly. "Yes."

"Isn't it wonderful?"

"Beautiful."

The others emerged into the flower patch, starting with Brogan and Blythe, then Algoron, and lastly came Lythagon, Drakonon, and Filk.

Brogan blinked in surprise, Blythe grinned in wonder, and Algoron scratched his head while muttering, "Impressive trick."

The other three dwarfs began to joke amongst themselves, laughing and punching one another in the shoulder. Rawk turned toward his uncle, the two of them exchanging knowing looks. As usual, they both felt like outsiders amid dwarf companions. Neither had ever fit in among their own kind, Algoron burdened with his secret longing for precious gems, Rawk labeled a hairless freak among a race whose men took pride in their long, groomed beards. Long before his exile, even before he began to hear the gemsongs, Rawk had felt like an outcast.

"We made it," Brogan said. "Now what?"

"Now," Rhoa replied, "we find the elves."

Brogan grimaced. "I hope they are nothing like the stories told in Pallanar."

Blythe chuckled. "I highly doubt they steal human children."

"Luckily, we have no human children among us."

She gave him a sidelong smile. "Only some adults who behave like children."

He snickered. "Fair enough. Let's go find these forest devils."

Blythe nudged him again. "Don't say that when we see them. They might become upset."

A female stepped from the shadow of the trees. "Forest devils?" She stood of average height, if she were a human, slender build, arms crossed over her chest, blonde hair tied back to expose pointed ears. Her eyes were angular in an exotic way, irises yellow and piercing. A longbow and quiver were strapped to her back, while an odd, curved dagger rested on her hip. Her clothing was brown and green, a vest over a tunic, tight breeches tucked into tall boots.

Rawk muttered, "A Cultivator... They do exist."

"Of course, we exist," the elf replied. "I am Chi-Ara, daughter of Bri-Ara and Tyrilus, next in line for the throne of Silvaurum. You are intruding on our lands. Turn back, or you will suffer the consequences."

Brogan laughed. "Listen, woman. You have a fine bow there, but you are outnumbered and in no position to make threats."

The female elf whistled, shrill and brief. Two dozen elves emerged from the forest, male and female, armed with bows and spears. Another half-dozen rose up from the flowers, three to one side, three to the other.

"This is no threat," Chi-Ara said. "It is a demand. Leave or die."

21

THE SILVAN

When elves appeared mere strides away, Blythe anticipated Brogan's reaction, her hand gripping his wrist as he reached for his sword. "There are too many," she whispered. "Besides, we are not here to fight."

Despite his scowl, he nodded, the tension in his arm easing slightly.

She stepped forward, hands held up to show she meant no harm. "We have come seeking the Cultivators. We intend no harm."

Chi-Ara approached, shaking her head. "I don't know how you discovered our location, but we have no interaction with humans. Haven't for many centuries."

Rhoa asked, "If the Dark Lord wins, what happens to the elves?"

The elves stirred at the mention of the Dark Lord but stopped when Chi-Ara held up her hand.

"The Silvan remain loyal to Vandasal, as we have for millennia. We are safe in our forest, beyond Urvadan's reach."

Blythe gave Lythagon a questioning stare. "The Seers sent us here. Did they give any instruction as to how we convince the elves to cooperate?"

Chi-Ara moved a few strides closer. "Seers?"

"Yes," the dwarf said. "My name is Lythagon Bundigg, a Maker. My clan once called the great dwarven city of Oren'Tahal home, before it was abandoned. We eventually settled in Paehl Lanor and became the Guardians for the Seers. By that time, you were gone, the Frost Forest occupied only by ghosts.

"Although many centuries have passed, we never forgot our distant cousins, the Cultivators. I had never thought I might see one, until the Seers sent us on a quest of great importance."

"Why would the Seers have you seek us out?"

Blythe replied, "The sisters sent us here in search of an object of power. Something called the Arc of Radiance."

A few elves gasped, others stirring, until Chi-Ara slashed through the air with her hand.

"The Arc is sacred," she sneered. "Humans would never be allowed near it."

"You don't understand." Rhoa held her open hands out in supplication. "Darkspawn stalk the Eight Wizardoms, creatures of legend have returned, and magic is no longer in balance. According to the Seers, Urvadan is behind it all. Our entire world is at risk."

Chi-Ara stared into the distance, brow furrowed in thought. Ultimately, she shook her head. "It does not matter. You will leave–"

"Chi!" Another elf stepped from the forest, his long, blond hair held by a headband similar to Chi-Ara's. In fact, his appearance was nearly identical to hers, features slightly more masculine, lean body lacking her curves. "You cannot!"

She turned toward the newcomer. "They are intruders, Ty. They cannot be allowed to enter."

The male elf stepped closer and put his hand on her shoulder. "The Seers and Makers are servants of Vandasal, no different than us Silvan. If they seek our assistance, it cannot be dismissed. If Urvadan truly is attempting to extend his reach into the world, how much time would pass before Silvaurum is at risk?"

"I will not listen to their–"

"*Chi*!" he shouted. "You are not queen. Not yet. Mother will decide where their path next leads."

She stared at him for a long moment, her face drawn in a grimace until she turned and stalked off into the forest.

He sighed, shook his head, and turned to face Blythe and her companions. "Forgive my sister. She is young, just approaching the end of her first century. The brashness of youth pervades…" His face turned into a wry smirk, "as does a stubborn streak she inherited from our mother."

First century? Blythe had heard legends of elves living many times longer than humans, but she would have guessed the female to be in her early twenties at the oldest.

"My name is Tygalas. Once you have surrendered your weapons, we will escort you to meet my mother."

"Your mother?" Rhoa asked.

"Yes. Bri-Ara, Queen of Silvaurum, the Golden Forest."

Stripped of her bow, quiver, and even her belt knife, Blythe felt naked. If being weaponless bothered her, Brogan downright hated it. The man stomped through the forest as if each pounding step was him fighting back at the elves who had taken Augur from him. She tugged on his arm and arched a brow when he turned toward her. The scowl on his face eased somewhat, his stride containing less obvious anger.

Rhoa had unstrapped her fulgur blades, sheath and all, from her thighs, knowing she could not hand the bare weapons to anyone else. Neither Rawk nor Algoron ever carried a weapon, so neither had to surrender a thing. Lythagon and the other Guardians didn't seem bothered about giving up their battle axe, sword, and hammer, the three of them joking as they strolled through the forest surrounded by armed elves. Blythe wished she felt so at ease.

There was something to the wood, a feeling not too dissimilar to how she had felt while in the Frost Forest. Yet the latter had been cold, dormant, the presence subtle. These trees were healthy, thriving, and gave her the impression a branch could reach out and twist around her at any moment.

The trunks of the leaf trees were enormous, requiring four people with arms extended to encircle one. The pines were even larger, tall, bare trunks reaching up forty feet before dark branches stretched out. More than anything, the presence of the forest felt old – the passing of a man's life but only a moment to the ancient beings surrounding her.

After an hour's walk, the spacing between the trees grew wider, rays of sunlight streaming through. They climbed a slope that eventually leveled, the late-day sun shining upon ruins of an ancient city. Crumbled stone walls, broken pillars, and partially intact buildings surrounded them. Vines covered much of the stone, trees thrusting up into the sky here and there, some coming from what was once a building, others broken through the stonework of a plaza. It was as if nature had defeated civilization, reclaiming the ground but leaving the ruins as a reminder of what once existed.

Then they came to the largest trees she had ever seen sprouting from the ruins. Something changed, the presence Blythe had sensed since entering the wood growing far more intense. Without a doubt, she knew the forest was somehow sentient. Most amazingly, the canopy above was covered in leaves of glittering gold with long, arcing branches connecting one tree to another.

The elves led them to the largest of the trees, its trunk twenty strides in diameter. Tygalas made a gesture with his hand, and a creaking sound arose. An opening appeared in the tree trunk, soft, golden light streaming from the arched doorway.

Tygalas stepped inside. "Follow but be respectful. My mother is fair but possesses a temper, which is easily stoked."

With the elf in the lead, Blythe and her companions stepped through the doorway, only Brogan having to duck. The wood of the tree itself shone with a golden-hued aura, lighting a curved stairwell leading up. They ascended numerous stories, the effort leaving Brogan grunting and huffing with each step. Even Blythe gasped for air by the time the stairs ended. They crossed through an arched doorway and into a world of wonder.

The trees themselves had woven into a city of wood, high above the forest floor. Circular platforms twenty, thirty, even fifty feet in diameter were everywhere, often at different elevations. Wooden furniture, shelving, and eating ware were visible through gaps in the golden leaves, elves moving about or lounging in quiet discussion. Hammocks made of vines were strung along the rear portion of some of the platforms. Wide, flat branches arced from one tree to another, connecting platforms in a twisting maze of rising paths. Golden leaves surrounded the city and masked the view of the ruins and the ground below. A soft, sweet aria whispered in Blythe's ears, as if the wind had discovered a voice too beautiful to fully exist.

"Careful while crossing," Tygalas said as he began up one of the arcing bridges. "The fall is quite deadly, and I am unsure if the trees will catch you."

Rhoa whispered to Blythe, "The trees would catch us?"

"I can feel it. The trees are…alive."

"Of course, they are alive. Look at the leaves."

"No." Blythe considered how to explain herself. "I mean, they *know* we are here. I believe they can think, perhaps even act."

Rhoa frowned. "Sometimes I wish magic *did* affect me. At times like this, I feel like I am missing something awe-inspiring." She sighed, gazing up at the golden leaves. "At least it is still pretty."

By then, Tygalas was twenty strides ahead. Rhoa rushed up the branch, balancing easily as she caught up to the elf. Blythe crossed haltingly, careful to remain in the center, arms extended to her sides for balance. She couldn't help worrying about how far she was above the ground, even if she could not see it. At the top of the arc, she paused and looked over her shoulder. Brogan was a dozen strides behind her, crossing in careful steps, arms also spread out. Rawk and Algoron trailed directly behind him in a crouch, and the three dwarfs from Kelmar had yet to begin crossing. The other elves in their escort waited in the doorway.

When she reached the other side, she stood beside Tygalas and Rhoa, waiting for the others to cross, which took time. When the last of the dwarfs reached them, Tygalas put his hand against the tree trunk, a door opening to reveal another set of ascending stairs. He began the climb, leading them up the spiraling staircase. This time, Blythe counted fifty stairs before they reached the top. Less than the previous climb, but it still placed them hundreds of feet above the ground. She followed the elf and Rhoa through the arched doorway and gasped.

The sun was low in the sky, just above the peaks to the west. Golden trees surrounded them, the tops of which were no more than twenty feet above. Here, above the forest canopy, sat a sprawling, circular platform made of thin branches woven together. Along the rim of the platform was a thick branch, a few dozen elves sitting upon it, as if it were a simple bench. Group by group, they stopped in mid-conversation, startled eyes turning toward the newcomers.

At the far end of the circle were two thrones made of living wood. A male elf with silver hair and green eyes sat on the smaller of the two. He had a circlet of golden leaves upon his head, his gaze intense. A female elf with striking eyes of gold occupied the larger throne. A crown of wood and golden leaves lay nestled in her long, auburn hair. Other than her hair color, her resemblance to Chi-Ara was striking. A wooden staff with a gnarled end sat in her hand, the butt resting against the floor, the entire shaft glowing with a pale golden light.

Tygalas whispered, "This is my mother's court, a place known as the Crown of Silvaurum. Follow and do as I do. No matter what, remain silent unless my mother tells you otherwise."

He walked toward the thrones, Blythe and her companions doing the same, trailed by their armed escort. Each step on the woven floor gave a little, springing up when relieved of her weight. Angled, elven eyes stared as they crossed the floor, expressions ranging from curiosity to fear to undisguised hatred.

Tygalas stopped a few strides before the thrones and bowed, Blythe and the others mimicking him.

The female elf scowled, eyes measuring them. "Humans," she spat the word as if it tasted foul. "How dare you bring humans to Silvaurum, Tygalas. It is forbidden."

"Greetings, Mother." He dipped his head. "I know our laws as well as anyone. However, circumstances have given me the inclination to make an exception."

Her face twisted in anger and she appeared ready to retort when the man beside her put a hand on her arm.

"Peace, Bri-Ara," he said in a quiet, yet strong tone. "We have raised him well. Perhaps we should listen before we react."

The queen inhaled deeply, eyes narrowing before she nodded. "Very well. Explain yourself, Tygalas."

"I shadowed Chi as you requested, monitoring the interaction between her and the intruders. I remained hidden until I could wait no longer. Chi meant to send them away, but I fear what may occur if we do not consider otherwise." He rubbed his smooth jaw. "They have been sent here by the Seers, on a mission linked to prophecy."

"The Seers still exist?" the queen asked.

"According to the intruders, the Seers remain hidden in Paehl Lanor."

She frowned. "My grandmother spoke well of the Seers. They were once our neighbors, before the Cataclysm, before the world went mad and we fled Silvacris."

Tygalas looked over his shoulder, his gaze briefly meeting Blythe's before he spoke. "According to these humans, Urvadan's power has grown, his influence extending beyond the borders of the Murlands."

The queen waved it off. "We have heard such nonsense many times over the past two thousand years, yet nothing changes. What proof can they offer? Without validation, we will remain safe in our forest, away from the destructive nature of humans. I will not risk my people for nothing."

"There is more, Mother." His gaze was intense. "They have come for the Arc of Radiance."

The woman stood, the surrounding elves gasping. "The Arc is sacred. It could never be wielded by a human. Never!"

Tygalas held his hands out, his tone pleading. "Centuries have passed since Grandmother died, yet the Arc remains unclaimed. Perhaps we should allow them to try. There is the prophecy–"

"Do not quote the prophecy to me, boy. It has been read to me thousands of times over the past four hundred years. I know every word of it."

"Then you know there will come a time when we have no choice."

"The Dark Lord's influence cannot touch us. Our magic has kept his minions at bay for millennia." She frowned. "However, I would be interested to know how these humans discovered us. Even if the Seers sent them, they should not have been able to locate our forest."

Tygalas shook his head. "I do not know. May one of the humans respond?"

"Yes, but be brief." Her gaze swept across the group until it settled on Blythe. "Tell me, humans. How did you find Silvaurum?"

Blythe looked at Rhoa and gave her a nod, as did Tygalas.

The short acrobat took a step forward. "It was me, Your Highness."

"Majesty." The male elf beside the queen gave Rhoa a subtle smile.

"Sorry, Your Majesty. I..." Rhoa hesitated to share her secret. "Well, I can see through magic."

The queen tilted her head. "What do you mean?"

"A man once told me magic was nothing but an illusion. Apparently, such illusion does not affect me."

Bri-Ara stared at Rhoa, her golden eyes narrowed. "So, rather than viewing a chasm and a dead forest, you saw Silvaurum as it truly is, even before crossing the barrier?"

Rhoa nodded. "Yes."

The queen rubbed her jaw, brow furrowed. "This is distressing news." She waved her arm. "Take them away. Hold them in one of the buildings below. Feed them but keep them guarded. They will remain our prisoners until morning when I can meet with the Elders." She sat back in her throne. "Tomorrow, we will decide their fate."

Elves armed with spears and bows surrounded them, prodding them back toward the stairwell.

Blythe and her companions complied, a cloud of melancholy over them. She wondered what fate would bring come morning.

22

LIGHT IN THE DARKNESS

The ruins were dark, the shadows thickening, the sun below the horizon. Tygalas remained quiet, the elf appearing sullen as he led them past a broken pillar, fallen and shattered into six sections. A dozen armed elves trailed behind the group, spears ready, longbows in hand.

Rawk felt unsettled after the brief meeting with the elven queen. He hadn't been sure how the elves might receive them, but he hadn't expected hostility. *They treat us like we have done something wrong. Worse, they behave as if humans are evil by nature.* He had met enough humans to know some deserved such a label, but not his companions, and certainly not Rhoa.

They passed through the arched doorway of an intact wall and the view changed.

In the dark shadows beneath a cluster of trees was a pulsing, golden-hued aura. A soft hum whispered from the light. Blythe changed course, angling toward the aura as if bewitched.

"Blythe," Rhoa said. "Where are you going?"

"Stop!" Tygalas shouted. "You mustn't."

Elves reacted, several nocking bows.

"No! Don't shoot!" Rhoa shouted and hurried after her.

Fearing what might happen, Rawk chased down the two women, positioning himself behind Rhoa as a shield from the elves.

The shadowy trees parted to reveal a clearing, the forest floor covered in stone tiles, a pedestal in the middle. Above the pedestal hovered the source of the golden light – an ornate longbow, pulsing and rotating, held in the air by some unseen magic.

"It's spectacular," Blythe muttered.

"What is it?" Rawk asked.

"Don't touch it!" Tygalas stopped between Blythe and Rawk to stare at the object above the pedestal. "For an outsider to soil the bow with their touch… It is forbidden."

"Why?" Blythe asked.

"It has belonged to the queen of my people for millennia, at least until my mother took the throne." He shook his head. "The bow will not accept her, nor will it accept any living member of our tribe. My sister, like all queens before her, was born with golden eyes and thought she might earn the right to carry the bow." Tygalas sighed. "Still, we wait for an elf who proves worthy. Unfortunately, our births are…rare."

Rhoa frowned in thought. "That's odd. I don't recall seeing any children."

A shadow seemed to come over the elf, his expression darkening. "We have no children at this time."

"None?" Rhoa asked, eyes wide. "There must be hundreds of elves here. Surely some must have recently borne children."

Rawk knew elves lived much longer than dwarfs, many times longer than humans. Yet to have no children was a frightening thought. *What can it mean?* he wondered.

Rather than reply, Tygalas turned from the pedestal. "Come. I must get you to your quarters. Once you are there, I will request food. I suspect you are hungry."

The four of them left the glade to rejoin the others, but Blythe continued to glance over her shoulder and toward the golden light of the magical bow. Rawk recognized the look in her eyes. The longing, like an obsession beyond her control.

She is drawn to its beauty like I am to a gem.

Rawk's own weakness had led to his exile. He feared what might happen should she bend to hers.

The elves sequestered Rawk and his companions inside the only intact building amid the ruins. The structure had no windows, the only way in or out through the doorway. The roof was strangely missing, no evidence of it having caved in, while the floor was made of stone pavers, many of which were cracked. Although the sun had set, a pale light emanated from the golden leaves overhead, illuminating the area in a warm glow. The light was subtle, allowing Rawk to remove his spectacles without squinting, yet bright enough to allow the humans to see.

The elves gave them water and brought them food – apples, nuts, berries, some sort of poultry meat roasted to perfection. They ate in silence, alone inside the building, leaning against the walls. The elves remained outside. How many, Rawk was unsure.

When finished eating, he whispered to Rhoa sitting beside him, "We could escape. It would be easy for my uncle and I to craft a doorway."

She shook her head. "Our situation is not so dire. Not yet anyway. Besides, if we escaped, where would we go? This was our destination."

He sighed. "I suspected you might feel that way."

Through the open doorway, he spotted a pair of elves in quiet discussion beside a fallen wall no more than twenty paces from the building. "I dislike being held captive. I also fear the queen's intentions. She seemed…"

"Angry?" Rhoa asked.

"Yes, and more. She harbors hatred toward humans. I believe many of the other elves do, as well."

"I recognize what drives her. It is vengeance, something I lived with for many years." Rhoa stared into space as she spoke. "I hadn't realized it, but the darkness of it had begun to stain my heart. It is an emotion that clouds reasoning, as if anything contrary to achieving it must be invalid."

Rawk took her hand. "He is dead, Rhoa. Taladain can no longer destroy families as he did yours."

She looked down at their joined hands. "Yes, but at what cost? I thought I would feel free after his death. Instead, it left me…empty. My need for revenge was sated, but it had become so much of me, only a void remains."

"That is not true, Rhoa. You now have companions who care for you. Then there is this mission, our quest to stop the Dark Lord. It has given you a new purpose. I should know, for in that purpose, we are alike."

Rhoa sighed. "I suppose you are right. I just... I cannot help but feel as though this is all our fault."

"What is our fault?"

"The entire sequence of events that led us here. It began when we...when *I* killed Taladain."

"You cannot blame yourself." He shook his head. "It is the Dark Lord who is to blame."

She looked at him, her large, brown eyes staring into his. "Did the Dark Lord stab Taladain in the heart? Did he confront Malvorian and kill him?"

"You can't be sure we killed Malvorian. He was alive when we left the throne room. Also, we had nothing to do with Lord Raskor's death."

"Yet we were there at the time."

They both fell silent. Her last statement carried a sadness that made his heart ache, but he didn't know what else to say. Lost for ideas, he closed his eyes and began to pray for guidance.

Please, Vandasal. We are at a crossroads, in dire need of something to set us on the right path. If not for me, do something for Rhoa and the others. They do not deserve to die.

Somehow, just reciting the brief prayer made him feel better.

A horn reverberated in the night, the elves responding with shouts and cries of surprise.

Rawk's eyes popped open and he stood, as did his companions. Through the open doorway, he saw elves running, ducking, leaping, and loosing arrows, all with inhuman quickness. Flaming arrows flew in and landed among the ruins, igniting the grass.

Tygalas ran in, stopping at the doorway. "We are under attack. Remain here where you are safe."

"Under attack?" Brogan asked.

A grim scowl crossed the elf's face. "Darkspawn."

A massive fireball landed just beyond the doorway in a blinding explosion, Rawk staggering back from the heat. When he lowered his arm, Tygalas was on the ground, unconscious, clothing on fire, head bloody.

Brogan tore off his cloak as he rushed toward the fallen elf, using it to pat out the flames. When he rolled Tygalas over, he did not move. Blood ran down his face, eyes closed, cheek blackened and raw.

A fire, hot and impassible, burned just outside the building.

"We are trapped," Blythe said. "Without weapons, we are trapped and helpless."

Rhoa turned toward Rawk. "Rawk, Algoron, get us out of here."

Rawk spun toward the wall and stood two strides from his uncle. "Ready?"

When Algoron nodded, Rawk began.

He ran his hand down the wall, pressing his fingers into it, urging cracks to form, to widen, to break. When he reached the ground, he stood up, arm extended above his head, and moved his hand across until it met Algoron's path. The two stepped back from the rectangle they had crafted and gave it a shove, Rawk commanding the stone to give, to break free from the neighboring blocks. As one solid piece, the door fell outward and crashed to the ground in a cloud of dust.

Rhoa ran out the opening in the wall and into pandemonium.

Elves darted about, ducking, twisting, loosing arrows with frightening speed and accuracy, felling goblins. Their movements were fluid – leaps, dives, twists that left the acrobat in her mesmerized. The moment of wonder was forgotten when she saw hundreds of goblins rushing through the forest, the monsters in a frenzy.

A goblin burst from between two broken pillars and came at her with a spear. She twisted, the point just missing her stomach. Rawk picked the goblin up, hoisted it above his head, and threw it into two others rushing toward them. The three monsters went down in a heap, but three more appeared to take their place. Rhoa scooped up the fallen spear, pointing it toward the onrushing attackers as she backed away.

With Blythe at his side, Brogan emerged from the building and barreled toward a goblin rushing at an elf engaged with another monster. Just before the goblin's sword found the elf's back, Brogan kicked the monster's hand and knocked the weapon from its grip. When the goblin turned toward him, he gripped the monster by its over-sized head and gave a hard twist, snapping the scrawny creature's neck. The elf gave him a nod of thanks before turning to intercept another goblin.

Brogan scooped up the fallen sword and noticed another dead monster with a quiver still strapped to its back, a short bow on the ground beside it. He picked up the bow and tore the quiver free before turning toward Blythe, tossing them to her.

"Take these and start loosing."

She caught the quiver and bow, frowning at the latter. "I haven't used a short bow in years."

"I'm sure you'll make it work." With a growl, he swung the sword in a sweeping arc, cleaving into the side of a charging goblin.

Blythe released arrow after arrow, striking goblins with efficiency, albeit with less power than when she used a longbow. Eleven arrows later, the string snapped. She frowned at the bow in disgust and tossed it aside.

Horns blew, and another wave of goblins came rushing through the ruins.

I wish I had my longbow. Frustrated, she turned in search of another weapon.

Just strides away, the three dwarfs from Kelmar fought in a triangle formation, their backs to one another. Two had acquired weapons, one a spear, the other a sword. Beyond the dwarfs, she spotted a golden light through the trees. *The magic bow*. It was worth a try. Anything was better than dying without a fight.

She bolted toward it, ducking beneath a goblin thrown by Lythagon.

Rhoa thrust her spear into a goblin's stomach, the monster twisting as it fell. The spear snapped, half remaining in the dying darkspawn. She tossed the other half aside as a fireball flew overhead, arching toward a cluster of three elves standing on a pile of rubble, rapidly loosing arrows at the surrounding goblins. One dove out of the way just before the fireball struck, the other two caught in an explosion of flames and shattered stone.

"We need to stop the magic users," Rhoa shouted to Rawk, pointing in the direction where the fireball originated. "Their magic won't harm me."

Rawk nodded. "Come along, Uncle. We must help Rhoa."

The two dwarfs bent, scooped up handfuls of stone, and began launching them at rushing goblins. One was struck in the face and collapsed. Another was hit in the shoulder and spun around, stumbling while it shrieked. A third ducked, the stone missing, and continued its charge. Rhoa rushed toward it, the monster lifting a sword high, preparing for a downward chop. Just before it attacked, she dove sideways, rolled, and came to her feet in a run, heading straight toward the goblin magic users.

The two magic-wielding goblins faced her and began chanting, waving their arms around.

Rawk and Algoron chased after Rhoa, both with disks of stone in each hand, felling any goblin who came near.

A goblin rushed in from one side, intent on intercepting Rhoa. With a heave, Rawk launched his stone disk. It struck the goblin in the back, knocking it off its feet, sword clattering across stone tiles. Another goblin lunged, a spear aimed at his face. Just in time, he swung his other hand, the stone disk knocking the spear tip aside. His uncle stepped in with a similar stone weapon and cracked the monster in the head. It collapsed in a heap.

By then, Rhoa was almost to the shaman. A ball of red, sizzling magic burst forth, striking her in the chest. Rawk's eyes grew wide, fearing for her, but the magic dissipated, bits of crackling, red energy spinning off her and striking him and Algoron instead.

His legs locked up, the stones falling from his grip. His muscles cramped into tight knots, leaving him unable to move. Out of the corner of his eye, he spotted Algoron similarly frozen. The dwarf tipped toward him. Like a pair of tiles lined up on end, they both toppled to the ground, helpless to stop themselves. Rawk's head struck a broken block of stone with a crack. Darkness caved in.

Brogan tossed the hilt aside in disgust, the blade remaining in the fallen goblin. *Who made these worthless weapons?*

Another monster rushed him, its spear aimed at his midriff. He knocked it aside, reached out, and gripped the monster's neck, lifting the spindly goblin off the ground with one hand. The monster's red eyes bulged, legs kicking as it tried to pry his hand open. With a mighty heave, he smashed the goblin into two others, all three going down in a heap.

He claimed the fallen spear and made ready, grinning as another cluster of monsters charged toward him.

Blythe leapt over a broken wall and darted through the trees. Three goblins came from her right, one pausing to aim its bow. She dove to the ground, the arrow passing over her as she rolled. Leaping to her feet, she raced toward the pedestal in a flight for her life, never considering she might not be able to use the bow. Urgent need crushed such thoughts before they could materialize. She reached the pedestal and thrust her hand into the golden light.

She gripped the bow, the wood warm to the touch and pulsing, as if alive. The rhythm shifted, syncing with her heartbeat, the bow becoming an extension of her being. She spun around and the world opened to her, the surrounding forest becoming something far more than a bunch of trees. The smell of the damp soil, sweet flowers, and the earthiness of wood greeted her. Her vision sharpened, the shadows receding, rushing enemies no longer obscured by the gloom of night.

She drew an arrow from the quiver on her back, placed it on the string, and pulled back. Another arrow materialized beside it, one made of golden light. She released, both arrows finding the same target. The goblin jerked backward, eyes bulging. Its body shimmered with a golden aura, becoming brighter and brighter. When the light faded, so had the goblin. Vanished. The other attacker gaped at Blythe, backed away, turned, and fled.

In the grip of curiosity and awe, she held the bow up and pulled the string back. As before, an arrow of light appeared. She aimed and loosed, the arrow striking the fleeing goblin in the back, as she knew it would. The goblin turned to light and vanished.

Instilled with hope, she raced out into the fracas and began loosing with fury, arrows of light appearing each time she drew the bowstring back. Darkspawn shrieked in horror as the tide shifted.

When the shaman magic failed, Rhoa rushed toward them, the two goblins backing away and chittering urgently. She scooped up a fallen spear and lunged, skewering one shaman in the shoulder. It shrieked while the other waved its arms, preparing some sort of magic.

Pulling the spear free, she stepped back, ready to impale the monster, when sharp pain came from her leg. She looked down to find a spear tip drawing back, blood coming from the wound. Her leg gave out and she stumbled to her hands and knees. She never saw the butt of the spear coming. It struck her head with frightening force and she collapsed.

Dead goblins surrounded Brogan and the two remaining dwarf Guardians. Lythagon's arm dangled at his side, blood oozing from the dreadful wound on his shoulder, white bone visible. Drakonon lay dead, the dwarf trading killing blows with a goblin moments earlier. Filk remained upright but leaned heavily on a spear, an arrow protruding from his thigh.

Somehow, Brogan remained uninjured but was starting to slow, breaths coming in deep gasps. Another wave of goblins raced toward him. Too many for the three of them to face at once.

"Get ready. Here come another bunch of the blasted monsters," he said, the two dwarfs turning to face the attackers.

The monsters rushed toward them with madness in their eyes, weapons in hand but not held as if prepared to attack.

Something has them scared, he thought.

A silhouette stood on a broken wall, illuminated by a golden bow. Arrows of light burst forward in rapid succession, felling eight goblins in a flash, their bodies glowing before fading away. Another burst took five more, leaving just four.

Brogan lunged out as the goblins ran past, his spear low. The lead monster tripped, squealing as it tumbled in a ball of flailing limbs. Those following fell over the first, one impaling its companion in the process. Lythagon leapt forward and smashed one on the head with a rock. Filk thrust his spear, taking another in the stomach. Sword in hand, Brogan sliced the last goblin across the back, it falling with a scream.

As swiftly as the battle had begun, the area grew quiet.

Shrieks continued in the distance, heard above the crackling of the nearby fires. Whimpers of the wounded, elves and darkspawn alike, came from the surrounding ruins.

He turned as Blythe jogged toward them, the golden bow in her hand. She slowed and looked around, searching her surroundings. All the while, he gaped at her.

"It looks like the worst is over," she said, then noticed his expression. "What's wrong?"

He stammered to say something, the words crumbling to grunts and groans.

Lythagon had no such trouble. "Your eyes, Blythe… They are golden, like the bow in your hand."

23

DESPERATION

"Rawk… Rawk. Wake up."

The voice was distant, lost in the murk. He swam through the gloom, struggling to the surface. His eyes opened to a blur. He blinked, the blur solidifying.

"Brogan," he muttered.

The big man smiled. "I'm glad you are still with us. Your head is covered in blood, but head wounds bleed heavily and often appear worse than they are in reality."

Brogan helped Rawk sit upright. Broken walls, fallen columns, and piles of rubble surrounded him. *The ruins in the forest.* The memory of the elves came rushing in.

Algoron sat on a nearby wall, holding his head. Blythe, the shimmering, golden bow on her shoulder, eyes now a golden hue and glowing slightly, bandaged Lythagon's arm. Filk sat nearby, grimacing, an arrow sticking out of his leg. That was when Rawk saw the dead goblins surrounding them and recalled the attack.

"Where is Rhoa?" he asked.

Brogan shook his head. "I don't know. Haven't found her yet."

"What of the goblins?"

"Dead or gone. The elves chased after those remaining, likely to be sure the darkspawn don't return. Perhaps she is with them."

Rawk frowned at the thought. Rhoa was fierce and brave, but lacked the weapons required. She didn't even have her fulgur blades. *That doesn't sound right.*

"Rhoa!" Rawk called out as he stood, then groaned, staggering to steady himself. It hurt his head to shout. Hearing no reply, he tried again.

Blythe finished bandaging Lythagon and knelt on the ground beside the still form of an elf.

"Is Tygalas all right?" Brogan asked.

"He is breathing but will not wake." Blythe stood. "Carry him again. We will make for the big tree with the stairs."

Brogan squatted beside the unconscious elf, slipping his arms beneath him. "At least he isn't heavy."

A hand holding his head, Rawk followed Blythe and Brogan through the ruins. Algoron groaned as he trailed them. Filk walked with a heavy limp and leaned on Lythagon's good shoulder with every step.

The scene was surreal. Dead goblins were everywhere, many with arrows sticking from their bodies. Here and there, elves lay among the dead. A group of elves rushed by, carrying buckets and shovels, racing toward the burning undergrowth. Rawk suddenly recognized the risk. Should the fire spread to the trees, all would be lost.

They drew near the tree with the stairs. Eight elves stood at the base, all armed with bows, expressions ranging from anger to sorrow. Chi-Ara was among them.

"What have you done?" she exclaimed, stomping toward Blythe, her face twisted in horror. "The Arc is sacred!"

"The Arc?" Lythagon asked.

Chi-Ara pointed. "She carries the bow on her–" She gasped and stepped closer, peering at Blythe. "It cannot be," she breathed out. "Your eyes..."

Blythe shook her head. "I did not know. We were under attack and–"

Brogan interrupted. "Your brother needs a healer. He is alive, but his body is covered in burns, a nasty gash on his head."

Chi-Ara tore her gaze from Blythe, expression shifting to concern. "What happened?"

Rawk replied, "Goblin shaman fireball. It exploded close to Tygalas.

Brogan pulled him free and doused the flames, but he has been unconscious ever since."

Resolute, Chi-Ara nodded. "Follow me." She turned toward the tree, muttered something illegible, and the doorway opened.

Rawk sat on the floor of the pod, what the elves called their homes high in the trees. He leaned against the tree, a dome of glowing, golden leaves overhead. Brogan, Lythagon, and Filk lay in hammocks, sleeping, noisy snores coming from the two dwarfs in an alternating sequence. Even Algoron slept, the dwarf's head leaning against Rawk's shoulder. Blythe paced along the edge of the platform, periodically stopping to stare into space. Her fingers continued to caress the golden bowstring across her chest, the longbow on her back pulsing, as if with a heartbeat.

Is she worried for Rhoa, as well? he wondered.

Troubled thoughts had plagued him throughout the night, only allowing him to drift off for short periods before waking with a start. Each time, he would look around in search of Rhoa's face, hoping the attack and her disappearance were nothing more than a bad dream. Hope did not change the truth.

When light began to filter through gaps in the trees, he dug out his spectacles. Slipping them on, he winced, the frames grazing the wound on his head, still caked with dried blood. He needed a wash, and perhaps a healer, but such thoughts slipped away, overshadowed by his concern for Rhoa.

Motion through the leaves caught his attention, Chi-Ara and eight armed elves approaching over the arched bridgeway. She stepped into the pod, her gaze on Blythe, scowling in silence for a moment. She then clapped her hands.

"Time to wake."

Brogan stirred, as did the two dwarfs, hammocks swaying as they sat up.

"The healers have done what they can for my brother. He will live, but his scars persist." She dipped her head toward Brogan. "I… Thank you for saving him."

The big man rubbed his eyes, groaning as he slid from the hammock and to the floor. "I couldn't let him burn to death. It wouldn't have been right."

"As it was, we lost too many last night." Chi-Ara's voice was filled with sorrow. "Twenty-nine Silvan in total. Most in the ruins below and another while pursuing the monsters last night. They now drink with our ancestors in the Halls of Vandasal."

Despite her sadness at the loss of her people, Rawk was focused on his friend.

"What of Rhoa?" He rose to his feet, staggering, setting a hand on the tree to steady himself. "Have you found her?"

Chi-Ara stared at him, her lips pressed firmly together. "I have already said too much. I am to escort you to the Crown of Silvaurum. There, my mother and the elders will receive you. What answers you will be gifted will be at their mercy." She turned and climbed back onto the bridge. "Come."

They all stood and climbed out of the pod, Lythagon helping Filk as the dwarf limped along, his leg bandaged by strips of cloth. After crossing two bridges, they entered the tree with the upper staircase. The going was slow, the spiral stairwell filled with grunts and groans. They emerged into sunlight, the edge of the sun a halo along the top of the trees to the east.

Again, Queen Bri-Ara and her husband, Tyrilus, occupied the two thrones at the far end of the ring. In addition, seven chairs had been added beside the thrones. Seven elves sat within those chairs. Four were males with long, white hair tied back in a braid. The other three were females, two with white hair, one with gray-streaked brown. All wore a circlet of twisted twigs upon their head.

Chi-Ara led them across the springy floor, the almond-shaped eyes of the elders watching. They stopped a few strides before the arc of chairs, Chi-Ara waiting until all had settled and were silent.

She bowed. "I have brought the prisoners as requested, Mother."

The queen's eyes never left Blythe, her golden-eyed stare like hardened steel. A long, still tension hung in the air. Rawk ached to ask about Rhoa but bit his tongue, intent on waiting for the proper moment. Eventually, the queen broke the silence.

"Much occurred over the past day, beginning with your intrusion upon our forest. It seems an unlikely coincidence that darkspawn attack the evening of your arrival. Never in two thousand years have darkspawn tread upon our sacred soil. For an army to attack and claim twenty-nine Silvan lives is beyond disconcerting."

She sat forward and shouted, "Why must you humans destroy everything you touch?!"

Brogan growled, "Listen, lady. We had nothing to do with the attack. Without us fighting back, it would have been far worse."

Bri-Ara's face grew red, ready to retort, until Tyrilus put his hand on hers. "At ease, Bri. These people are not the enemy."

The queen sighed, her posture relaxing as she turned toward him. "We have lost so much. Our tribe is contracting. I fear what the future brings…if our time is nearing its end. Even our trees begin to fail." She pointed toward Blythe. "And then this outsider, this *human*, claims the Arc of Radiance. How is it possible? Why would the bow not choose me or another of our people?"

An elf woman with white hair said, "The legend of the Arc says its magic is based on need. Each generation, it chooses the one individual who might best serve the Silvan. It cannot otherwise be wielded."

"Look at her eyes," another elder said. "There can be no doubt."

Blythe stepped forward and knelt, head bowed. "I apologize if I did something to offend you, Your Majesty. We were under attack, the situation desperate. I simply sought a weapon to defend myself. I…did not understand what would happen."

Bri-Ara spoke softly, her tone gentle. "Please, rise." Blythe stood and backed up to stand beside Brogan. "Your actions saved many lives, including that of my son. For his life alone, I am grateful. For the welfare of my people, we *all* are grateful." She glanced to the left, then the right, the elders nodding before she continued. "The council and I discussed the situation for most of the night. The Seers sending you here could not have been by chance, nor could the darkspawn attack last night. It is now apparent the Dark Lord seeks to expand his dominion, and the Seers, much like the Silvan, oppose him.

"We will support you in any way we can."

Rawk could wait no longer. He stepped forward. "What of Rhoa? Have you found her?"

The queen frowned. "The short woman from your party?"

He nodded. "Yes. We haven't seen her since last night."

Bri-Ara turned toward her daughter. "Tell them."

Rawk spun toward Chi-Ara, a lump in his throat, fearing what she might say.

"A squad harried the retreating monsters last night, felling as many as possible. Among them was a prisoner, bound and unconscious. I fear they have taken your friend."

Brogan groaned. "Oh no."

Panicking, Rawk turned toward the man. "What? What do you know?"

The big warrior's eyes were pained as he spoke. "While fighting in The Fractured Lands, the darkspawn would sometimes steal off with captives. There is a short period where they might be saved, but it is exceedingly rare."

Rawk gripped the man by his coat and pulled him down to his level. "Say it, Brogan. What will they do to Rhoa?

"I fear they intend to sacrifice her to the Dark Lord."

"Sacrifice? How?"

Brogan swallowed, his eyes flicking toward Blythe. "They remove all the skin and feed what remains to a magic-fed fire, burning them alive."

24

BURNED ALIVE

The world was obscured by a fog of pain. Rhoa's eyes flickered open, only to immediately squeeze shut again. Her head hurt, a pounding in her temple. At the same time, her leg throbbed and shoulders ached.

She tried again. In the moonlight, she saw the ground slipping past just below her face. Shadows surrounded her, the movement of thin, distorted silhouettes. Turning her head, she saw stretched, bare feet, toes clawed, skin gray. The feet were attached to scrawny legs, dozens and dozens of them, all walking in fits and bursts, jostling her repeatedly.

Goblins...

Her hands were tied behind her back, her torso and legs strapped to some sort of log. She tried to move, but the ropes around her wrists were tied too tightly.

The scrub-covered ground became an incline covered in rocks. The goblins climbed upward, her body tilting with them. The top of her head struck a rock. Pain flared, Rhoa crying out with her eyes clenched tightly. When she opened them again, the world swirled, her stomach recoiling as spots blotted her vision, churning and contracting until she saw nothing but darkness.

Something poked Rhoa in the side and she stirred. Her chin rested against her shoulder, head heavy and neck aching. Lifting her head, she winced. The top of her scalp hurt, as did the lump on the side. Worse, though, was her thigh. It felt as if it were on fire.

She opened her eyes. A goblin stood no more than a foot away, its red eyes burrowing into her. Cackling laughter burst from the monster, startling her before it turned toward its brethren. Fighting through the fog in her head, she took stock of the situation.

Now upright, she remained strapped to the post, her bonds too tight to allow more than shallow breaths. The goblins had taken her to a spacious cavern, her position near the rear of the cave, hundreds of goblins between her and the opening at the far end. A fire burned near the center, four shaman goblins standing around it, chanting in unison. Rhoa had no idea what was happening, but she feared what they had planned for her.

Her memories of the fight in the ruins were hazy – a series of images that meant little. She had no idea if her friends, or any of the elves, had survived. *I am in trouble.* Yet she could only think of her dry mouth and parched throat.

"Please," she pleaded in a horse, cracked voice. "Water. I need water."

A pair of goblins turned toward her as they chittered and squawked in their disturbing, guttural language.

She swallowed and tried again, slightly louder. "Water. To drink. Please."

A clawed hand flashed out, her head snapping to the side from the slap. She blinked, tears in her eyes, blood starting to drip down her cheek. The goblins laughed.

One shaman shouted something unintelligible. The others drew close, hundreds of them clustering around the fire. They all began to chant. Rhoa could not understand the words, but she could guess at their intentions. Fears she had harbored since she was ten years old surfaced, images of innocent citizens being sacrificed for Taladain flashing before her eyes. She had made it her life's mission to stop Taladain, but the wizard lord's death hadn't stopped her nightmares.

Sacrifice. They intend to sacrifice me. The only question was how.

By the time the chanting stopped, Rhoa was panting with fear, her forehead, palms, and ribs damp with sweat. The crowd of monsters parted. One of the goblin magic users shuffled toward her, its necklace making noise as the bones knocked against one another. It held an ominous, curved dagger, the blade blackened. As the darkspawn came near, dagger pointed toward her, she tried to shy away. It was no use. Her bonds held fast.

The goblin grinned and began cutting at her sleeve, slicing it open from her shoulder to elbow. It pulled and tore the sleeve away, exposing her arm. All grew quiet, the goblin horde watching in anticipation as the blade inched closer to her flesh. Rhoa had never known such terror, the depths of it causing her to seize up.

I am going to die.

A teeth-rattling roar shook the cavern. The darkspawn spun toward the entrance, deep shadows surrounding glowing, amber eyes split by black, slitted pupils. The eyes were massive.

With a roar, a monster burst into the cave – a towering, green dragon with iridescent purple scales on its head and neck. Its head reared back, inhaling with a deep hiss. A tremendous blast of fire erupted from its mouth, the dragon's head sweeping from side to side, the roaring flames engulfing the horde of goblins. Horrified shrieks filled the cavern, the darkspawn flailing as they were burned alive.

When the flames came toward Rhoa, she winced and turned away, unable to move. The roar from the fire mixed with the agonizing cries of dying goblins. It was terrifying. Yet she felt nothing.

The sound died out, the cave falling silent, other than the crackling of flames. She slowly opened her eyes and turned forward, the goblin shaman lying on the ground before her, blackened body still burning. In fact, every single goblin was on fire, some still moving, most lying still. Smoke, tainted by the stink of burnt flesh, filled the air, and she began to cough. The dragon jerked with a start, its slitted eyes turning toward her. It rushed forward and another blast erupted from its maw, the blaze surrounding Rhoa and blotting out all else. Again, she felt nothing. The flame faded.

"How curious," said a deep, yet distinctly female voice.

With fervor, Rhoa scooped water from the spring and drank. Much of it splashed onto her face, ran down her chin, and splattered all over her clothes. She did not care. It was cold, refreshing, quenching her vicious thirst.

She looked up toward the dragon, its disturbing eyes watching her every move. "Thank you for cutting my bonds."

The dragon lifted a front foot and eyed a black talon longer than Rhoa's fulgur blades. "Seemed better than leaving you to rot."

Rhoa splashed water onto her leg, attempting to wash out the wound. The open gash looked bad. She gripped the spear she had taken from a dead goblin and leaned on it as she stood. The pain brought tears to her eyes. She wiped them dry with the back of her hand and turned toward the dragon. The light from the fire in the neighboring cavern had dwindled, the dragon's amber eyes glowing in the darkness.

Rhoa asked, "You aren't planning to eat me, are you?"

"In truth, I haven't decided what do to with you." The dragon's tone sounded as if it were honestly reflecting on the situation.

"Well, thank you for saving me from those…darkspawn."

It released a low growl. "Filthy monsters. They should not have entered my domain."

She considered what to say. Having a conversation with a dragon was a little disorienting. "Are you… Is your name Zyordican?"

The dragon huffed, a swirl of smoke coming from its snout. "Where did you hear that name?"

"A friend. A storyteller. He spoke of the last remaining dragon. A female named Zyordican."

Its eyes narrowed. "After all this time, a human knows my name? I haven't been among humans in many centuries."

Rhoa thought back to the attack on Illustan. "Did you attack a city west of here? A…human city?"

Zyordican strode closer. Rhoa fought the urge to back away. *The fire might not affect me, but those teeth would.* She wondered if dragons ate humans, then pondered if she would be a filling meal.

"I was enraged. Acted in haste. Something of an anomaly for my kind."

"Why were you angry at the humans?"

"In truth, I was not. I just attacked the first enemy I could find."

"That city must be eight hundred miles away."

"I can travel quite swiftly. Distance means little to a dragon."

"What happened? Why were you so angry?"

The dragon turned its head, eyes narrowed, as if lost in distant thought.

"Your friend is correct. I am the last of my kind. At least the last alive."

"What do you mean?"

"Much time passed while I waited for my egg to hatch. The moment was drawing near when I woke to find it missing. I searched and searched these caverns, but it was gone."

Rhoa frowned. "If the last male died thousands of years ago, how do you still have an egg?"

The dragon chuckled, puffs of smoke emerging. "Time means even less than distance to a dragon. To us, even the lives of elves pass in rapid fashion. Yours will have passed in a blink to me. Our eggs take many centuries to gestate. We mothers keep them warm the entire time to ensure proper development."

Shaking her head, Rhoa said, "I am sorry someone stole your egg. If it were me, I would have been enraged, as well. I myself was burdened for many years with a desire for vengeance against the man who murdered my parents."

"What happened to this man?"

"I killed him. Drove a blade right through his heart."

"It sounds as if he deserved it."

"In truth, my parents were merely two among hundreds, even thousands, of lives the man had destroyed."

"Then it is good he is dead."

"Yes. I just wish I felt better about being the one who ended him."

"If he was so evil, why did someone else not do it before you?"

Rhoa sighed. "Because he was a wizard lord. Nobody else could kill him because of his magic."

"Ahh…" The dragon nodded. "You are immune. Magic cannot harm you. This is unique?"

Frowning, unsure of how she should respond, Rhoa decided on truth. "Yes."

The cavern fell silent, the light fading as the fires in the other cavern slowly died out.

In a nonchalant tone, the dragon said, "I have decided not to kill you."

Rhoa responded cautiously. "Th-thank you?"

"Follow. It is growing dark here, and I doubt you can see without light."

"I cannot."

The dragon turned, its massive, spiked tail slithering past Rhoa as it stomped off. She limped after it, moving with care, arm extended before her since she could not see. Amber light flashed ahead, the dragon blowing out a burst of flames.

Zyordican said, "Memorize your surroundings each time my flame appears. You can advance in the darkness until I do so again."

They continued through the caves, the dragon leading, illuminating the surroundings briefly, and Rhoa following, leaning heavily on the spear with each step. After many minutes, Rhoa covered in sweat from the effort of walking with her wounded leg, a soft, warm glow came from ahead. The cavern floor sloped down, the dragon slithering off to the side as Rhoa entered. It was hot. Far hotter than the other caverns. The air smelled of sulfur, growing more intense the deeper she advanced.

At the far end of the room, a pool of molten lava surrounded a flat outcropping of rock. The peninsula was quite large, easily large enough for the dragon's body. An odd boulder five times Rhoa's height occupied the center of the peninsula. It was black as night, the polished surface like a mirror, edges rounded. Rhoa, driven by curiosity, forced herself into the heat. As she reached toward the boulder, her distorted reflection extended a hand toward her, fingertips meeting. The smooth surface was warm to the touch. From within, she felt a *thump, thump*. Again…*thump, thump*.

Turning around, she faced the dragon. Zyordican stared at her intently. "Is something wrong?" the dragon asked.

"What is it?" Rhoa asked.

"What?"

"This shiny, black boulder. It feels as if…as if it is alive."

The dragon's eyes widened as it rushed forward. Rhoa backed away in fear, right into the boulder. The warm rock against her back, the dragon arched its head above her, eyes angry.

"Do not toy with me, human."

"I… I am not." She patted the boulder with her palm. "It does feel as if it is alive."

The dragon stretched its neck out above Rhoa, until its snout struck the boulder. It pulled back and tilted its head. "You have found it. My egg remains. It was here the entire time, masked by illusion.

"How curious."

25

HEALING

It was midday when Rhoa limped out of the caves, emerging from the shadows to squint at the bright sun. The weather was cool, but nothing like the snow-covered mountains to the south and west. She stood on a hillside, the rocky terrain dotted by scrub – a shrub here, a patch of dry grass there. Miles in the distance, at the bottom of a valley, sat a thriving, green forest surrounding a small cluster of gold.

She pointed toward the forest. "My friends are there."

"With the Silvan?" Zyordican asked, peering out from the tunnel mouth.

"Yes. We were sent there on a quest."

The dragon snorted, a burst of smoke billowing from its snout. "Since when do the elves care about the concerns of humans?"

Rhoa sighed. "It appears they do not, even after we informed them of Urvadan's rise. Perhaps now that their home has been attacked by darkspawn, they will listen."

She turned toward the dragon. "Thank you again for freeing me from those monsters. I fear…" A shudder shook her frame. "Whatever the darkspawn had planned, I'm sure it would have gone poorly for me." She smiled. "Also, I appreciate you not eating me."

"Why do humans always believe we dragons wish to eat them? Have you ever *tasted* a human?"

Rhoa laughed. "Not that I can recall."

The dragon shook its head. "They are not the tastiest of creatures. Besides, dragons do not need to eat. We are made of magic, our energy coming from within. We require no food or water to survive, unlike you lesser beings."

"Well, thank you anyway," Rhoa said. "I need to leave. My friends must be worried, and it will take me the rest of the day to make the journey."

Limping, Rhoa began down the hillside. She estimated the distance at ten miles, a journey that would normally take four hours. Her injuries would make the trip take at least twice as long. It would be well past nightfall when she reached the forest's edge.

"Wait," Zyordican rumbled from behind.

Rhoa turned as the dragon stepped from the shadows and stomped toward her.

"It is too painful to watch you hobble down the hillside." Zyordican turned sideways, the dragon arching its neck toward Rhoa, its giant wing above her like a canopy, blocking the sun. "Climb on. I will transport you to the elf queen."

Stunned, Rhoa's gaze swept over the beast. Body as broad as a ship, wings reminding her of the largest of sails, rear legs as thick as a tree, long, sinuous tail curving around her.

"I… How do I do that?"

"Begin at my tail and climb onto my back. Take care for my crests. Some are quite sharp."

She limped over to the dragon's tail, diameter too large at the base for her arms to reach around, and easily twenty feet in length. Discarding the spear she had used as a crutch, she gripped the edge of a crest, lifted her uninjured leg, and climbed up. The crawl took some time, her leg throbbing mightily while she decided which crests to grab and which to avoid. Once on the dragon's back, the surface leveled, making her climb easier. She stepped between the two outstretched wings, feeling the dragon's muscles through its scaly hide. Beyond the wings, at the base of the neck, she found a two-foot gap in the crests. There, Rhoa sat, a leg to each side of Zyordican's neck, where the iridescent purple scales began.

"Hold on and don't let go," the dragon warned.

Rhoa gripped the large, rounded crest before her. The dragon pumped its wings and leapt, Rhoa's stomach lurching with it.

The dragon flew up and out, over the hillside, then shot forward with a burst, the ground below speeding past. With a few more pumps of its wings, the dragon rose higher, the view expanding in all directions. Zyordican leveled, wings outstretched, as it glided toward the elven forest. The dragon then banked, while Rhoa held on tightly. Her heart soared with the thrill, the experience a thousand times more spectacular than performing on the trapeze. She whooped and smiled so hard it hurt her face.

It was the most amazing moment of her life.

Vines sprouted from the woven, wooden floor and climbed up Rawk's body, twisting around his legs, up his torso, over his shoulders, finally encircling his head. He held his breath, fighting back panic, resisting the urge to break free from his bonds. From the vines came a warmth – pulsing, soothing, coaxing him to relax. His eyes drifted shut, time growing distant. He might have fallen asleep. It was difficult to tell.

The vines withdrew, the soothing sensation ceasing. He opened his eyes, and the healer stepped back, her hand on Rawk's shoulder as she gazed at him with her green, almond-shaped eyes.

"How do you feel?" the elven woman asked.

His head no longer ached. He touched the wound. No longer tender. Nodding, he said, "Much better. Thank you."

The elven woman stepped back, her brown robes and white hair billowing in the breeze upon the Crown. She turned toward the throne and bowed. "He is the last of the injured, My Queen. They have all been healed. I should now return to my pod to check on your son."

Bri-Ara nodded. "Thank you, Grislana. I know you have done everything possible for him."

"He is near full health." The healer frowned. "I only regret I can do nothing for his scars."

In a firm but gentle tone, the queen replied, "You could not prevent the burns. Only treat them within the limits of your magic."

The healer bowed again and crossed the court toward the exit. Rawk turned toward his friends, seated in a shaded area along the rim of the platform. He walked toward them, noting that Lythagon and Filk had removed their bandages. Their gear remained damaged, gaps torn open where the wounds had been, but their flesh was now intact. Both had been healed before him, their wounds certainly more serious than his or Algoron's, the last two in the party to receive the healer's attention. However, Grislana could not heal the wound to Rawk's heart.

It had been almost a full day since Rhoa's disappearance. She was never far from his thoughts as he grappled with helpless worry. Part of him ached to go off in search of her, but he had no idea where to look. He was no tracker and could not do it on his own.

"We need to go find Rhoa," Rawk said aloud. "Blythe, you are a hunter. Surely you can find her."

Brogan grunted. "If she was captured by the darkspawn, there are far too many of them for us to face alone. We need help."

"Perhaps I can convince Bri-Ara," Rawk ventured.

Algoron snorted. "The elf queen possesses little love for humans and is unlikely to risk her own people to save one human."

Frustrated, Rawk looked across the court, toward the queen. "Why does she hate them so anyway? What have humans ever done to her?"

"We have a history, humans and my people."

Turning, Rawk found the queen's husband standing behind him, his sad gaze fixed on his wife.

"She does not hate them. She fears them."

"Why?" Rawk asked.

"Many centuries ago, humans, elves, and dwarfs coexisted. We even worshiped the same god."

Algoron asked, "Vandasal?"

"Yes." Tyrilus nodded. "While there were battles and small disputes, war was uncommon, until the Cataclysm. When Urvadan captured the moon, the root of his power, and locked it in the heavens above Murvaran, it did far more than break the world.

"When things settled, new gods had risen – gods of man. With the gods came wizard lords. I do not believe mankind was meant to harness such power. It soon corrupted the men who had been gifted with the power of their gods. Wars were fought, many thousands slaughtered. The struggle lasted for years. In the end, my people were reduced to a fraction of our former selves, no more than a few dozen remaining when we abandoned our prior home, Silvacris.

"We came here, to the ruins of an ancient city where elves and humans once coexisted. With our combined magic, we transformed the forest surrounding the ruins, eventually creating what you see now – Silvaurum. It has been our home for two thousand years."

"It is a wondrous place," Blythe said.

"You might believe so, but much has changed over recent decades." His arm swept toward the horizon. "When I was a youth, the leaves were golden throughout the forest. It thrived as we thrived, our magic and the forest as one. As our numbers wither, so does our magic. Even these trees we call home, among the oldest trees in existence, suffer." He stepped to the rim, reached out, and pulled a leaf-covered branch close. "Look closely. The leaf edges are curled, wilting. The gold turns to brown, our magic dying. It continues to grow worse.

"I fear… We all fear the Silvan will soon pass from this world. It is a concern that never leaves our minds. Such fears are worse for my wife. As Silvan Queen, responsibility for the welfare or our people is a weighted yoke upon her shoulders. None, including our soothsayers, can identify the cause of our problem or how to shift the tide."

Tyrilus fell silent. His story left Rawk with a sense of sadness, as much for his own people as for the Cultivators. Both races had suffered greatly during the rise of humans – one fleeing to a remote forest, the other hiding deep underground. The separation had saved the elves for a time, but something had changed. Would the same happen in Ghen Aeldor?

Perhaps Algoron is right. Perhaps it is time for the Makers to return to the surface world. He wondered how it might come to pass and at what cost.

Shouts arose, drawing Rawk from his reverie. He spun around to find elves pointing toward the sky. Raising his hand to shield the sun, he squinted and searched until spotting something that made him gasp.

"A dragon!" Brogan shouted.

Blythe slid the golden bow from her shoulder and held it ready. None of the others had weapons. Rawk felt panic arising. He was at the top of a forest, the nearest source of stone many feet below. Such disconnection from the ground made him feel helpless.

Elves rushed from the stairwell, armed with spears and bows, watching as the dragon banked, turned, and drew closer. The beast flew low, briefly blocked by the golden leaves, until it reemerged just above the court, wings flapping as it slowed and drifted down, rear legs outstretched toward the open space in the heart of the Crown.

"It is going to land!" someone shouted.

A dozen elf warriors raced to the throne, positioning themselves in front of the queen, weapons ready. Everyone else backed to the rim of the Crown, eyes wide, mouths gaping.

Someone rode on the green dragon – a familiar form clinging to the monster's back. The dragon landed, wings folding in, a puff of smoke stirring from its massive snout.

"We have arrived, child," the dragon said in a deep, female voice.

Rhoa patted the dragon's neck, her face stretched in a glorious grin. "Thank you, Zyordican. That was *fantastic*."

Climbing to her feet, Rhoa turned and crept across the dragon's back before sitting and sliding off. She landed on the woven floor with a grunt and fell to her knees, teeth clenched in pain, hand gripping her bloody thigh.

The bonds of shock holding Rawk captive shattered. He rushed over to her. "You are hurt." He gripped her by the arm and helped her up. "Your leg. Are you all right?"

Rhoa grinned at Rawk, chuckling. "I just flew on a dragon. A...*dragon*!" Her eyes lit with excitement. "Yet all you worry about is my wounded leg?"

The dragon swung its neck around and peered toward the throne. "Greetings, Elf Queen. We have not met, but I did once spend time with your ancestor. Ori-Ara, the grandmother of your grandmother. She and I shared a bond for a time, a common need in a time of trouble. The elves have never been unkind to me or my brethren, so I harbor no ill will toward yours."

Twisting its neck in the other direction, the dragon looked upon Rawk and Rhoa. "Your friend is a Maker?"

"Yes. His name is Rawkobon."

"Strange times, indeed."

The dragon reached for its foreleg, talons pinching the small claw on its elbow. It snapped the claw off and extended a foreleg toward Rhoa, massive palm open, the broken, black talon in the center. "Take it."

Rhoa reached out and picked up the talon, which was the size of a dagger. Oddly, it seemed hollow.

"I owe you a debt, child. The rent in my heart now healed," the dragon said. "If you ever find yourself in dire need, blow upon this horn. I will hear it and will come. I just pray you do not do so until my…duty is complete. The time is near, but I fear the world is changing. Even I am at risk should the Dark Lord rise unchallenged."

With a slight nod, the creature said, "Farewell."

The dragon lifted its head toward the sky, arched its wings, and leapt. With two mighty flaps, it lifted higher, banked, and soared off to the north.

26

SONG OF SORROW

Blythe sat in silence, eyes closed, essence bound to the pulse of the bow on her back. Since the moment she had first gripped the Arc, she had felt different. It wasn't just her connection to the bow, but to the trees surrounding her. Their song had been soft and unknowable before, but now it was clear. The song held such sorrow, it countered any joy she received from the spirit of the bow.

She sensed a presence draw near and opened her eyes as Brogan sat across from her.

He stared at her, expression reflecting concern. "You are sad. What's wrong? Not something I have done, is it?"

Blythe gave him a sorrowful smile. "No. This is not about you. It is...this forest. Even before Tyrilus told us, I knew it was dying. The forest itself knows it is dying. Even now, it sings of the past."

"You can hear the trees?" He looked up at the branches above the pod, the same pod where they had slept.

She shook her head, a tear falling. "It's so sad, Brogan. These trees are thousands of years old."

He took her hand and held it in both of his. "I don't understand, but I would do anything you ask if there is something I can do to help."

With her knuckle, she rubbed the tear away. "No. It just feels...as if it is their time. I believe the trees would have died long ago had the elves not used their magic to keep them alive."

His mouth twisted into a scowl, something he did well. "If that is true, maybe the trees are sad because they want to die but the elves won't let them."

She blinked, taken aback by his assessment. "You might be right." Something about the idea gnawed at her, but she couldn't quite figure out what it was. He stared at her, brows furrowed. "What is it?"

"I miss your green eyes."

Her heart fluttered. "Do I look so terrible?" She had yet to see her own reflection since the change and feared doing so.

"No." He shook his head, turning her hand over in his while looking down at it. "You are as beautiful as ever. It's just that your eyes now… They appear alien." His gaze lifted to meet hers. "It's as if I see someone else peering back at me from deep inside you."

Blythe could not deny she felt different…was different. Yet her thoughts remained her own, as did her feelings toward Brogan.

Movement was visible through the branches, Rhoa appearing over the arched bridge. She walked with ease, her limp far less noticeable, a smile on her face.

Rawk stood and crossed the pod to meet her. "You look well."

"I feel much better. The healer could not use her magic on me. She tried, but it failed, as I told her it might. Instead, she cleaned the wound, sewed it closed, and applied a fresh bandage while I ate and drank my fill. After all that, and the fact I rode on a dragon…" She grinned broadly. "I could not ask for more."

"What happened, Rhoa?" Brogan asked, still seated across from Blythe. "You disappeared. Nobody could find you, not even the elves. Rawk was just about to tear the forest apart to search for you when the dragon showed up."

Rhoa smiled and put a hand on Rawk's thick arm. The dwarf's cheeks turned red, and he looked away. She recited her story, how she had been stabbed in the leg and knocked out during the battle. Rawk's face reflected concern when she described the events – her tied to a post, the goblins taking her to a cave, the shaman with the curved blade about to harm her when the dragon burst in.

If the first half of her story was terrifying, the second half was nothing short of incredible, although it was clear Rhoa hid something.

Once finished, Algoron shook his head. "I still don't understand why the dragon flew you here or why it said it owed you a debt."

Rhoa's smile faded, her jaw clamping shut. After a brief pause, she shook her head. "I cannot say. I promised I would not, and I never break my promises. If you don't believe me, ask Taladain."

The dwarf held up his hands. "Easy. It was just a question."

"One I cannot answer."

Rhoa crossed the pod and sat down. "My question is, what's next?" She looked at Blythe. "I understand you now have the Arc of Radiance. In fact, the way Grislana explained it made it sound as if you are...bound to the bow?"

Blythe nodded. "It is as good a description as any. I cannot explain it, but when I first touched the bow, I immediately felt more...alive. It is as if everything leading to that point had been nothing but a dull dream, the bow waking me to a world filled with song, light, and magic."

She glanced toward Brogan, his scowl returning. Reaching out, she took his hand. "This is about *me*, Brogan. The bow has nothing to do with *us*."

"There is still an us?"

She leaned forward and kissed him, smiling when she sat back. "Of course, you silly man."

The sound of someone clearing their throat caught everyone's attention.

Tygalas stood at the edge of the pod where it met the bridge. "Pardon my interruption."

As one, they all stood.

"You are walking," Brogan said.

"We were worried," Blythe added.

The elf stepped into the pod, facing Brogan and Blythe as he walked to the middle. The side of his face had splotches of pale, glossy skin – a remnant of his burns. "Thanks to you, I live, as do many more of my people than if you hadn't acted as you did." He took Brogan's hand and placed it upon his heart, doing the same to the big warrior. "I am in debt for your bravery."

"Um, well..." Brogan shrugged. "I have a habit of doing stupid, brave things." He smirked at Blythe's arched brow. "I am trying to cut back, so you were lucky. I...just acted."

Blythe laughed. "At ease, dear. I could hardly fault what you did. After all, I am as guilty as you in this matter." Her hand went to the pulsing, golden bow on her shoulder.

Tygalas released Brogan and turned to Blythe, taking her hand and putting it to his heart. As he reached to do the same to her, Brogan's hand shot out, snatching Tygalas by the wrist, stopping him just shy of her left breast.

She shook her head. "It's just a form of greeting, Brogan. He meant nothing improper."

Abashed, Brogan released the elf's hand and stepped back. "Sorry. I didn't…"

"I meant no offense," Tygalas said. "Our ways differ. You are unfamiliar with our culture, as we are with yours." He turned toward Blythe, looking her in the eyes. "I was told the Arc claimed a human and how it altered your eyes. Still, I had to see it myself to believe."

She frowned. "You said the Arc claimed me? I think you got that backward."

The elf shook his head. "Not so. The Arc is like these trees – alive and knowing. You could not have touched it, let alone used it, without the Arc giving itself to you, bonding with you."

Despite the odd nature of his statement, in her heart, she knew it to be true.

Tygalas rubbed his chin, golden eyes narrowed. "Humans and Makers appear on our lands for the first time in many centuries. Darkspawn attack, killing dozens. A human bonds with the Arc of Radiance and chases them off. A dragon appears, returning one of the humans after freeing her from the darkspawn…" He shook his head. "A bewildering series of events in such a short period. It cannot be coincidence." Tygalas turned and crossed the pod, speaking over his shoulder. "I hope the council sees the truth of it."

He paused at the bridge and looked backward. "Come along. We shall discover what my people intend to do with you."

Brogan asked, "What does that mean?"

"The council has been in discussion these past few hours, ever since the dragon's appearance. I was instructed to present you to them at sunset. I only hope my mother and the elders have agreed to do what must be done."

The Crown was bathed in amber light from the setting sun. Unlike the morning meeting, when only the elven elders and royal family were present, the entire platform was crowded and most had to stand, the seating around the rim occupied.

There must be three hundred elves here, Brogan thought as his gaze swept the area.

He stood beside Blythe and Rhoa with Rawk, Algoron, Lythagon, and Filk clustered to Rhoa's other side. The space between them and the two thrones was empty, save for Tygalas and his sister, both facing the queen, waiting. Just as earlier in the day, the seven elders occupied the chairs arranged to the side of the thrones. Finally, the queen stood and thumped her staff against the wooden floor, the knob at the top of the staff flaring with a golden aura. The crowd quieted as the glow from the staff dimmed.

"For the first time in centuries, our entire tribe assembles in the Crown of Silvaurum. Such a rare event would not occur without just cause." The queen's voice boomed, easily heard by everyone present. "We suffered a tragedy last night, losing twenty-nine of our people to a darkspawn attack. That count would be higher if not for the actions of our visitors. Even so, I fear much more is at stake, for the very future of our people remains in doubt."

A rustle ran through the crowd, worried mutters and words of prayer slipping from the tongues of the surrounding elves.

"The council has discussed this topic many times over recent decades. Debates filled with concern and ideas, but never action. Today, after all that has occurred, we agree it is time for a change." The queen paused for a breath. "Today, we have decided to leave Silvaurum for good."

Gasps and exclamations erupted, the elves noticeably upset. Brogan feared where it might lead until the queen lifted her staff, a golden brilliance coming from it as the trees began to shake, the woven floor beneath his feet wobbling with fury. Everyone staggered. Some fell, many crying out in surprise. The queen lowered her staff, and the trees stilled.

"Listen," she demanded. "Only a handful of births have occurred in the past century, none in decades. Our magic wanes, and the trees beyond the ruins lost their golden leaves long ago. Even those at the heart of the forest, the blessed trees we call home, are dying. You have heard their song of sorrow. The spirits of the trees are ready to pass and would have done so long ago without our magic, which also diminishes. The situation is no longer tenable. We must leave."

"Where will we go, Mother?" Chi-Ara blurted.

"Ah…" The queen nodded. "That is the question. The answer lies not in our future, but in our past." Her gaze swept over the crowd, golden eyes as hard as steel. "We shall return to Silvacris and reclaim our former home."

The queen's husband stood and stepped to her side, his jaw firmly set. "Silvacris remains dormant, awaiting our return," Tyrilus said. "With our magic, we shall bring the forest back to life. If the trees can be reborn and thrive, so may the Silvan."

Anger in her voice, Chi-Ara asked, "What of the humans? What of their lust for destruction? Our people abandoned those lands long ago to escape persecution, to escape the humans' desire for conquest."

Queen Bri-Ara nodded. "This was true, daughter. For a time, we made Silvaurum our home, and for most of those years, it was the best choice for our people. However, we can no longer deny the facts. If we remain here, we will eventually die out."

"You would rather have us risk ourselves to the whims and wars of mankind?"

"We risk worse if we remain!" Bri-Ara stepped forward, her face a scowl as she glared at her daughter. "Did you forget what happened last night? Did you not see darkspawn within our very home?" She pointed to the north. "The Murlands are not so far from here. Our scouts have warned us time and again about the deadly monsters and twisted darkspawn that live there. We have known this since we first arrived two thousand years ago. Only our magic, and that of our forest, has kept those creatures from invading. After last night's attack, we must assume this forest no longer possesses the magic required to protect us."

Chi-Ara crossed her arms over her chest but remained quiet.

The queen stepped back and announced, "We have six days to prepare. Do so well. On the seventh day, we leave at dawn."

27

COR CORDIUM

The island nation of Cordium lay ahead, green and brown mountain peaks rising above the sea. Narine hugged the rail – the ship's deck tilted from the force of the wind on the sails, the bow rising and falling to the rhythm of the sea – and stared toward the shimmering, silver walls of Cor Cordium, the capital city and center of Enchanter operations. All said, it had been a pleasant journey from Tiamalyn, particularly the three days on the barge to reach Shear. From there, Narine and her companions had boarded a ship, sailed down the channel past Yor's Point, then made the short sea crossing to Cordium. Only during the last stretch had she been ill. Even then, it had been a short bout of nausea, the seas pleasantly calm.

She wore her cloak but barely required it, the cold weather of the mountains to the south now far behind, the wind lacking the bite of winter. Similar to Tiadd, Cordium remained warm throughout the seasons, likely hot and humid during summer months.

Jace appeared at her side, snaking one arm around her waist. "The walls aren't really made of silver, you know."

She gave him a wry look. "You are aware I was trained at the University, right?"

"Of course."

"Don't you think they teach us about each wizardom and its capital?"

"I guess so. What else do you know about the Enchanters and their city?"

She tilted her head in thought. "Cor Cordium is the central hub of the Eight Wizardoms, located at the heart of the Novecai Sea. The walls appear silver but are simply built of rock containing reflective flecks that aren't even metallic in nature. It is two cities in one. Regular citizens and visitors occupy Mundial, the outer district, while Cor Meum, the inner sector, was built on a higher section of the island and is reserved for Enchanters. They are a secretive lot, very protective of the details and methods behind enchantments. Unlike the other seven wizardoms, Enchanters do not train at the University, but only practice in Cor Meum and their satellite towers located in Marquithe and Balmor."

"Interesting," Jace said, staring toward the city.

Beyond the outer wall, the inner wall, separating Cor Meum from the outer portion, was now visible, gray towers peering above it, the highest of which burned with a silvery flame that flickered in the morning sunlight.

Jace pointed toward the high tower. "Why does the flame brighten like that?"

She gave him a knowing smile. "Do you not know how Lord Belzacanth gathers his magic?"

He gave her a level look. "I get the feeling you know and wish to hold it over me."

She pressed her finger against his chest and pushed him away. "You keep information from me all the time – your past digressions, your schemes, your secrets."

Jace blinked, his expression aghast. "I would never!"

She laughed, placed her hand on his chest, and gave him a kiss. When she pulled away, she bit her lip. "Would you like to know?"

He rolled his eyes. "You are so frustrating."

She chuckled. "All right." When she turned toward the tower, her gaze settled on the shimmering flame. "Unlike the other wizardoms, there is no Devotion held here. Rather than harvesting the power of prayers, Lord Belzacanth and his god, Cora, gather bits of magic from each use of an enchanted object. Not just from here, but from anywhere in the world."

He clutched the amulet hidden beneath his tunic. "How does that work? Take the Eye, for instance. I don't actually use it. The thing just works when someone attempts to use magic against me."

"I suppose that is when it happens. The way I understand it, with each use, a tiny slice of the bearer's essence is consumed and sent to the Enchanter's Tower of Devotion. In this case, the amulet reacts to the action of another, but it is likely your own essence feeding Belzacanth."

He rubbed his jaw, eyes narrowed toward the city as the ship drifted closer. "Think of the enchanted lanterns alone. There must be thousands of enchanted objects in each major city."

"True." A realization struck Narine, drawing a worried frown. "There is a theory that the more powerful the object, the more of the user's essence is consumed." She looked down and lifted her skirts to her knee, revealing the golden object around her ankle. "I wonder how much of my soul is lost with each use of this bracelet."

Jace stared down at her calf, grinning. "I do love your legs. Perhaps you could wear shorter skirts so I could see them more often?"

Her mouth dropped and she swatted him. "That would be scandalous!"

He chuckled.

"Set your perversions aside and listen. I am serious." She put her hands on her hips. "Aren't you concerned? The object you wear is at least as potent as mine."

He shrugged. "What of it? After using it, I don't feel like I have lost anything."

"They say… They say years of your life can be expended with excessive use."

He slipped his arm around her again, drawing her close. "Listen." With one hand, he swept stray strands of golden hair from her face. "I told you before. I never expected to live to an old age. It is rare in my profession, and given the nature of our quest, the odds haven't improved. I just want to be with you and see this through, even if I have my doubts about the Seers. If it means I shave decades off my life, so be it. If I…we don't do what must be done, the Dark Lord wins and the world is doomed. What choice do we have?"

She smiled and shook her head in wonder. "You seem to know just what to say to reel me in. I swear, you are far too smooth for your own good."

He grinned. "I *am* quite lovable when given the chance."

Narine laughed. "You are incorrigible!"

"I do my best."

"Too well if you ask me."

"Yet you remain with me when I have given you numerous opportunities to run away."

"You forget. I am stubborn. You'll not be rid of me so easily."

Their gazes locked, each with a glowing smile. Jace leaned in, his grin falling away, their lips meeting. His embrace was warm and strong, lips soft against hers. Her heart began to race, worries distant and forgotten for a moment.

"Ugh… Will you two stop?" Adyn said, interrupting.

Narine pulled away and smoothed her dress when she noticed the sailors on board staring at her, grins on their faces. Adyn stood two strides away, arms crossed over her chest, Hadnoddon at her side in a mirrored stance.

"Um, ah… Sorry," Narine sputtered. "We were just–"

"You would have thought they had enough of each other after three nights on the barge," Hadnoddon said. "We hardly saw them, even in daylight."

"I know," Adyn replied. "I suspect Narine is making up for lost time. Until recently, she had never–"

"*Adyn*!" Narine barked, her teeth clenching. "You needn't tell everyone you meet."

"Hadnoddon is hardly everyone." The bodyguard grinned. "Besides, given your recent adventures in the bedroom, I thought you were past your prudish ways."

Narine's back stiffened. "I was never a prude. Merely sheltered. It wasn't my fault. You know what happened when we arrived at the University."

Jace arched a brow. "What *did* happen? It had something to do with Kollin, right?"

Despite herself, Narine blushed. "Yes. I'll tell you about it later…in private."

"Well, you may have to wait a bit." Adyn turned and spoke over her shoulder. "We are about to dock, so come below and get your things."

Narine turned toward Jace, disappointed their moment had passed. "I guess we had better go."

He nodded. "Once we settle in the city, I will work on a plan."

Narine arched a brow. "*You* will work on a plan? What about the rest of us?"

Jace grew serious. "Retrieving the item we seek will require a well-executed heist. This is what I do, Narine. Trust me. I will think of something. Just give me some time."

He took her arm and led her toward the stairwell. "Let's get our stuff and find an inn. It's been weeks since we left Kelmar. It will be good to settle in one place, if just for a few days."

Jace led Narine, Adyn, and Hadnoddon down the pier, all curiously watching the activity on shore. Dockworkers pushed loaded carts onto metal rails, then connected them together. The carts were made of wood, reinforced by metal frames, rolling on odd, metal wheels.

His gaze followed the track where it ran up at an angle until it reached the top of the city wall, a hundred feet up. The track then faded from view as the wall curved.

They reached the end of the pier and climbed a rise leading to the open city gates. There, men in silver and black armor waited below a black and gray standard with an open eye at the center – the emblem of the Enchanters. With a friendly wave to the guards at the gate, Jace led the party into the Cor Cordium.

He paused inside the gate and examined the busy square, taking a deep breath of salty sea air tainted by the aroma of fish and refuse. A fountain occupied the heart of the square, children playing beside it. Carts and wagons were positioned along the perimeter, merchants selling produce, crab, lobster, and fresh fish.

At first glance, the city reminded him of Fastella – the ancient, Maker-built buildings made of gray stone, the busy square, the docks, all surrounded by aqua and cerulean waters. But there were clear differences.

A squat, square tower stood just inside the gate, guards loitering beside the open entrance. Two stories up, an arched opening faced the heart of the city. A metal rail mounted to stone beams, supported every ten strides by a stone column, ran through the opening and down the center of the main street.

"Curious," Jace said, eyeing the odd track. "It's like the one rising up to the top of the outer wall."

At that moment, two men in silver and black robes entered the city, bracketed by four armed guards. Jace immediately knew them as Enchanters. The two men entered the tower, one removing a hidden charm from his robes and pressing it against a metal plate in the wall. A humming sound arose, and a platform appeared inside the building, lowering gradually until it met the ground. The two men and a guard climbed onto the platform, placed the charm against another panel, and the platform began to rise.

The group watched curiously, none saying a word as they waited to see what happened next. Another hum arose, distant and faint at first, soon growing louder and louder. Two full minutes passed before a cart came speeding down the rail. It slowed as it reached the tower, then disappeared inside.

Narine said, "It reminds me of an enchanted lift." She pointed through the open tower door. "Except this one runs horizontally."

"So what do you call a horizontal lift?" Adyn asked. "It certainly isn't doing any lifting."

"A mover…," Hadnoddon muttered. "It just moves stuff, so I'd call it a mover."

Jace remained silent as he examined the single-rail track. It was an oddity to be sure, the cart unlike anything he had seen before – metal wheels turned at an angle, the body made from rounded, wooden slats, like the hull of a ship, and much wider than the rail itself. Moments later, the hum returned, the cart reappearing with the two enchanters and a guard upon it as it gained speed and raced toward the upper city.

Once the cart faded from view, Jace waved them along and led them down the central street, walking through the shadows cast by the rail overhead and the pillars supporting it.

It was a bustling, thriving city with shops lining the street, citizens going about their daily business, and guards in metal-studded black leather armor watching for trouble. When they passed a bakery, the aroma of freshly baked bread called to him, teasing his mouth and stomach, but he ignored it and continued onward.

A filthy beggar sat at the next street corner, calling out to passersby, holding out a dented pewter cup. At the following intersection, a voluptuous woman in a low-cut bodice stood in an open doorway. When his eyes met hers, she called out to him. He flashed her a grin, and she beckoned with her finger.

Jace turned toward Narine. "Remain here. I'll be right back."

He crossed the road and climbed the stairs, the woman backing into the building. She had brown hair, green eyes, and tanned skin. Her dark blue skirts were ruffled and tailored to be uneven, reaching her ankle on one side, exposing her calf on the other. Turning, she hiked the higher side up farther while biting her lip.

"My name is Mandy," she said in a sultry tone, batting her long lashes, lips pursed.

The sitting room was empty, the building quiet.

"Where are the other girls?"

"Sleeping. We often work late, you know." She bit her lip, her expression demure. "Why? Don't you see something you like?"

Jace closed the door behind him while leering at her exposed leg, his gaze rising past the curve of her hips to those of her breasts, on the verge of bursting from her bodice. "I see quite a bit I like."

He dug into his coat and fished out a couple coppers, among the winnings he had gained playing dice with the sailors. Extending his hand, he held the coppers out to the woman.

She gave him a flat look, one hand on her hip, the other gesturing toward her body. "You don't believe this is worth more than two coppers?"

"I'd wager a tumble with you is worth gold."

Her expression softened. "Well then…"

"But I am not after a tumble. I only seek information."

After a brief pause, she sighed and snatched the two coppers. "What do you need?"

"I am interested in getting into Cor Meum."

She snorted. "Whatever for? The Enchanters are a stuffy lot."

"Have you been there?"

"Not I, but some of the other girls have had the misfortune. The men there have…odd perversions. Disturbing even." She shook her head. "No, thank you. I do well enough down here. It's not worth the extra silver." Her voice dropped to a whisper. "Lately, girls have disappeared."

His eyes narrowed. "You suspect something…nefarious?"

Her gazed flicked from side to side, the woman obviously nervous. "Two of our own have been gone for weeks, both after leaving to visit the Enchanters. I heard another house, one near the Cor Meum gate, lost four girls at once. They were summoned, promised one gold piece each, but never returned."

Rubbing his jaw in thought, he asked, "These disappearances… When did they start?"

Even her shrug was sensual, but Jace did his best to ignore it. "The first was perhaps six or eight weeks past. At the time, we thought nothing of it. Sometimes girls leave with a man or choose another path. This time… There have been too many, all after heading into the Enchanter's Den."

The recent timing struck a chord with Jace. He suspected the disappearances were connected to other events going on in the world, but he couldn't see how. Not yet anyway. At the same time, they stirred a memory from his past. One he preferred to forget.

"I happen to be a professional myself, specializing in…acquisitions." He winked. "In the past, I was part of a guild, but have operated on my own for years now, most recently based in Marquithe. I need information about Cor Meum. Is there a guild in the city, or someone I can talk to for information?"

Mandy tilted her head, eyes narrowed in thought. "There are items that come and go from the city. Items people pay to keep secret. Word is, these people have a contact who frequents The Frightened Cat Tavern on Briar Street, four blocks to the north. When you get there, ask for Binder."

"Thank you."

She shook her head. "I should have known you had other business on your mind. It's too bad, really. I like the look of you and had hoped I might change your mind about spending a few more coins." She toyed with her hair. "Are you sure information is all you're after?"

Chuckling, he dug into his coat pocket. "Yes. The two women waiting outside would have my hide if I…accepted your offer." He pulled out two more coppers and placed them into her palm. "This is for the information. It was more helpful than you might think."

Jace opened the door and hurried down the stairs. Narine, Adyn, and Hadnoddon stood across the street, watching his approach. Adyn stared with an arched brow, Hadnoddon with his usual scowl. The princess had her arms crossed over her chest, her lips pressed together, foot tapping the ground impatiently.

Jace sighed to himself. *I am in trouble.*

"That was quick," Adyn commented.

From the open doorway behind him, Mandy called out, "Be sure to come back if you would like something more."

When he turned back toward her, she blew him a kiss, her other hand caressing her bodice, her smile mischievous.

"More?" Narine growled.

"It was nothing, Narine. I merely paid her for some information." He waved for them to follow. "Come along."

"Where are we going?" she asked.

"If you must know…" Jace considered how much he wished to reveal. Narine's lack of trust irritated him, so he chose to irritate her back, knowing how much she hated when he kept his schemes to himself. "We are seeking another cathouse. One of a different sort." *She will just have to keep guessing.*

Adyn snickered as he turned and headed down the street.

Nostrils flared as she huffed, Narine gave Adyn a sidelong glance. The bodyguard had the audacity to grin, which made her even angrier. The scantily clad whore Jace had visited was beautiful. The thought of donning something like the woman's outfit made Narine blush. In the back of her head, she knew her jealousy was misplaced, but she just couldn't help it. *He was in there for too short a time to do anything.* Still, the woman had captured his attention, and for that alone, she wanted to go back and set the woman's skirt ablaze. She clenched her fists tightly, barely resisting drawing upon her magic.

The farther they walked from the central street, the more rundown their surroundings became. Jace eventually turned down a narrow street, his gaze searching the buildings they passed. Refuse-filled wooden crates sat beside one of the buildings, a heap of clothing resting between them. Narine jumped when the pile moved, and she realized someone slept there. She then saw two men talking in a recessed doorway, both dressed in dark, worn clothing, hair unkempt, faces unshaven. The men stopped their whispers, dark eyes following Narine, grins forming to reveal gaps of missing teeth. She realized she had fallen behind a few strides, so she rushed ahead, eager to place herself between Adyn and Hadnoddon.

Jace stopped and stared up at a sign depicting a black cat, back arched, tail straight up, eyes wide. "This is it," he said and reached for the door.

As the door opened, a gray, striped cat burst past him and into the street. It raced to the corner and disappeared down an alley.

Jace laughed. "This alehouse appears to be aptly named."

Narine glanced down the street to see if the two men followed. "Will you tell us what this is about?"

He rolled his eyes. "Information. Just play along and don't cause trouble."

Adyn led Jace inside, hand on the hilt at her hip, eyes flicking around the room. Narine entered next, Hadnoddon a step behind her.

The interior was dark, an enchanted lantern dangling above each end of the bar, the area where the tables were located dim, other than light seeping through the curtains. Shadowy forms sat huddled over a few of the tables. The place reeked of stale ale and unwashed bodies.

Jace approached the bar and claimed an empty stool. Three other patrons sat along the bar, each focused on the tankard before them, all quiet, as if attempting to forget the world outside. A heavyset man waddled along the back of the bar. He had bags beneath his eyes and a heavy brow beneath a head of thinning, black hair, wisps of it combed over the top.

"Ale?" the barkeep asked.

"Yes. Three, please." Jace slid three coppers toward the man.

With a grunt, the bartender scooped up the coins and headed toward the barrel at the other end of the bar.

Narine gripped Jace by the elbow. "This place is disgusting. Do you really want to drink something from here?"

He shrugged. "I've seen worse. Besides, I need information. Buying a drink is a courtesy. I can hardly ask anything of him if I don't buy something."

The man two stools down from Jace turned, his gaze settling on Narine. He was a big man, brawny, with a broad face and brown goatee. His beady eyes made Narine uncomfortable, particularly when they leered, the man grinning.

She pulled Jace close again. "I think we should go."

"Please, Narine. Just give me a few minutes."

The barkeep returned with the three mugs, slid them across the bar, and made to turn away.

"Pardon me," Jace said, placing another two coppers on the bar. "This is for you."

The man frowned. "What for?"

Jace grinned. "For being helpful. I am seeking assistance…a way to get something into another part of the city." He leaned over the bar and lowered his voice. "I was told to ask for Binder."

The man's gaze flicked toward Adyn, Hadnoddon, then back to Jace. "I may know the name."

"Where might I find him?"

"You don't find him. He finds you."

"What do you suggest?"

"Return here after sunset. Sit in the same spot. Come alone." The man walked off and began speaking with another patron.

Jace turned, mug lifted toward Adyn. "A toast for making it this far."

They tapped mugs, the dwarf joining in, all three taking a long drink.

Narine put her hands on her hips. "Why are you three toasting?"

"Not very good ale, but certainly better than nothing," Jace noted, wiping the foam from his upper lip. He then turned to Narine. "You heard the man. I am to be back tonight. Until then, we can relax."

"Aren't we going to get a room?"

"Of course, just not here. Let me enjoy my ale, then we will go find a nice inn. Something more suitable for someone like you."

She bristled. "Like me?"

He cocked his head. "You wouldn't wish to sleep *here*, would you?"

Another glance around the room reinforced her earlier assessment. "Not in the least."

28

CONUNDRUM

Night had fallen, the streets in the poor quarter of Mundial dimly lit by enchanted lanterns at every other street corner. As a result, the alleyways in between remained pitch black, an environment suitable for a thief. Despite his relaxed appearance, Jace kept himself alert, watching and listening for any movement as he crossed the city. He reached The Frightened Cat, pausing outside with a casual backward glance. Nobody had followed.

He entered the tavern, the interior just as dark as the street, the building now filled with four times the people as earlier in the day. A barmaid walked past, a large woman who didn't bother to return his smile. Jace shook his head.

Now that's just poor manners.

The barstool he had occupied earlier in the day was open. He doubted it was a coincidence. Claiming it, he waved for the big barkeep and exchanged a copper for an ale. It tasted fresher than the drink he had purchased hours earlier.

The man has tapped a new barrel. Perhaps this is my lucky night.

A hand clamped on his shoulder. He turned, following the arm attached to the hand. It belonged to the tallest man he had ever seen. Far too tall to pass through a doorway without ducking. The stranger stood even taller than Brogan. He had wavy brown hair, broad shoulders, and a chin too large for his face. Dressed in a simple tan tunic, he seemed innocuous, other than his height and the cudgel on his hip.

Beside the towering giant was a wiry man with dark hair and a curled mustache. He stood no taller than Jace and was roughly ten years his senior. He wore a black vest over a dark brown tunic, his shoulders covered by a black cloak.

"They call me Binder. I heard you were seeking my services." With two fingers, the smaller man twisted the end of his mustache, his gaze measuring. "Let's discuss this in my office."

He turned and walked deeper into the room. Jace stood to follow, and the big man pushed him from behind, causing him to spill some of his ale.

"Watch it," Jace said over his shoulder. "There is no need to be rude."

The giant grunted in response.

Jace crossed the room and joined Binder in the back corner, the surrounding tables all empty. The man claimed an open seat, and Jace sat across from him.

Binder leaned over the table, dark gaze intense. "Where did you get my name?"

"A woman," Jace said nonchalantly. "I paid her for information. She is used to giving far more than that."

"I see. However, it gives me little reason to trust you."

Jace sat forward and said in a hushed voice, "I am a thief, formerly of the guild in Fastella but am now an independent contractor."

"A thief? We have no guild here, and I have no need for thieves."

"I do not seek employment. I seek a means into Cor Meum."

Binder snorted. "Gaining entrance to the Enchanter's Den is no easy task, even for a thief."

Jace shrugged. "I have often done what others believe impossible. What makes this place so special?"

Sitting back, Binder smoothed his mustache. "Information has value. I hardly see why I should share for nothing."

Reaching into his coat, Jace withdrew a single silver. He was almost out, his winnings spent in less than a day, but he would worry about that later.

He slid the sliver across the table. "This had better be worth the investment."

Binder took the coin and grinned. "It depends on how clever a thief you are."

"I assure you, I am the best."

The man snorted. "Do you consider yourself the likes of Jerrell Landish or something?"

Grinning, Jace said, "Actually, that is exactly what I believe. You see, I *am* Jerrell Landish."

Binder narrowed his eyes, stared at Jace for a long pause, and burst out laughing. He looked up at the big man towering over him. "Did you hear him, Crusher? He thinks he's Jerrell Landish." Still laughing, the man shook his head. "I have heard stories of Landish. He is much taller than you. More handsome, too. They say he is the most skilled thief of all time, able to steal the smallclothes right off a man without him knowing."

Jace groaned at the reference. *I wish I had never done that.*

"Claiming yourself as Landish…" Binder's laughter calmed. "I doubt you could carry his lockpick."

Jace sighed. Rather than argue, he let it pass. "Listen, I need the information. Surely a silver is sufficient compensation."

The other man shrugged. "I'll tell you all I know. If it's of use to you, so be it."

With that, he began to describe what Jace faced and why entering Cor Meum was such a challenge. The conversation went on for roughly an hour, Jace growing more worried with each new piece of information.

When finished, he left The Frightened Cat and wandered down the street, lost in thought. The Enchanter's Den, also known as Cor Meum, posed a bewildering challenge. For the first time in many years, Jerrell "Jace" Landish worried he might fail.

The Lunartide Inn was, in many ways, the inverse of The Frightened Cat. It was bright, airy, and the innkeeper, a woman named Willow, seemed friendly enough to make Jace wish she were his mother. Despite her blocky build, the woman was constantly on the move – filling glasses, running to the kitchen, serving tables. Renita, the woman's niece, helped in the dining room, while Renita's husband, Ricardo, worked in the kitchen.

Jace finished his breakfast and sat back, hand on his stomach, feeling as if it might burst. Hadnoddon was still eating, as was Adyn. Narine had given up long ago, her plate still containing an uneaten sausage, a biscuit, and bits of fruit covered in some sort of sweet sauce. He contemplated wrapping her remaining food up to save for later, but the idea flitted away in a flash, replaced by his worry about getting into Cor Meum.

The group exchanged small talk, Jace disinterested and barely a participant. He hadn't explained to them why he was so worried, preferring to come up with an answer to the problem before frightening them too much. Schemes were his thing and breaking into places he didn't belong his specialty. He had always come up with a solution before and was sure it would come to him, given enough time and thought.

Willow entered the dining room and bustled over to their table, the woman placing her fists on her broad hips as she glared at Narine's plate. "Are you feeling well, young lady? You didn't eat much. No wonder you are undernourished."

Jace snorted and reached for his glass of water, wondering what the woman was thinking. Narine's body was filled out quite well from his point of view. Clearly Adyn agreed, the bodyguard covering her mouth to keep her food from spraying across the table as she laughed.

Narine glared at Adyn before turning toward Willow. "The food was wonderful, and I am feeling well enough. I guess my stomach just cannot handle so much at one time right now."

The woman bent down and whispered, "You are not with child, are you?"

Caught in mid-drink, water sprayed from Jace's mouth, dousing Narine and the table. She gasped, eyes wide, her dress covered in water droplets.

Jace coughed several times before he choked out, "I'm sorry. I… It was an accident."

He picked up his napkin and reached across the table to wipe her chest dry. Willow's eyes bulged, the woman obviously shocked.

Narine caught his wrist and took the napkin from him. "It's all right," she said, her look warning him away. "I've got it, Jace."

Rising to his feet, he ran his hand through his hair, feeling like a ship thrown off course. The question echoed in his head. *"You are not with child, are you?"* His heart raced, a lump in his throat.

Stepping away from the table, he said, "I need to get some air. I'll be back later."

He rushed outside and closed his eyes for a moment, taking a deep breath to calm his racing heart.

The street was busy with foot traffic, the bulk of which headed toward the upper city. Turning in that direction, he trailed a cluster of finely dressed merchants. Three were men, wearing vests over colorful doublets, and the fourth was a woman with a black shawl over a dark red dress, a black hat on her head, wispy veil covering her face. He overheard them talking.

"…client is seeking a cane that sends tiny jolts of electricity into the user each time it is leaned upon," one of the men said. "This man's acquaintance possesses one and swears by it."

The woman looked at the man. "It shocks the user? Whatever for?"

"It is supposed to relieve pain by stimulating sore muscles." The man shrugged. "Sounds fishy to me, but if I can secure one, this client is willing to pay handsomely."

Another man said, "I believe I saw a cane listed on today's auction schedule."

The original speaker nodded as they reached the end of the street. "And it is among my primary targets for…"

Not finding anything interesting in that conversation, Jace stopped and gazed at his surroundings, the view opening to an expansive plaza.

From the top of a low bluff, the towering walls of Cor Meum stood over the plaza, silver flakes sparkling in the bright morning light. Two-story houses stood along the bluff, below the wall and separated from the plaza by a ten-foot-tall wrought-iron fence. Every hundred feet, a sign reading *Warning* graced the bars, leaving Jace curious.

In the center of the area, tucked against the bluff wall, was a five-story-tall structure, arcing out in a half-circle, the center of the arc split by an open archway. The doorframe was made of black metal, squiggling silver lines running up it and shining in the sun. Above the arch, a track ran through an opening in the wall, the same track connecting to the tower inside the harbor gate.

So, this is where the people mover goes.

Two dozen guards in black leather armor stood near the arch, half inside, half outside, weapons ready, all watching as people gathered outside. Additional guards paced the roof of the building, passing silhouettes visible between the gray merlons.

Jace headed toward the arch, driven by curiosity. He had, of course, heard of the Enchanter's Auction. Everyone had. It was the source of stories, the items purchased there ranging from mundane to legendary.

The crowd funneled through without incident, until the couple before Jace passed through the arch. The black metal doorway glowed red, a humming buzz rising. Guards rushed the couple and hauled them back outside while Jace entered, the archway still buzzing angrily. Stopping just past the doorway, Jace waited while the couple was pulled aside, the guards beginning to search them.

He turned toward a guard. "What did they do?"

The man snorted. "Tried to sneak in with an enchanted item."

Jace recalled the amulet beneath his shirt. "So, the archway detects enchanted objects?"

"Yeah. The magic in them sets off the alarm."

"But isn't this place filled with enchanted items?"

"Approved ones, yes. Once sold and paid for, the winners pick them up at the warehouse next door."

Jace's eyes narrowed. "Will those two be allowed in?"

"Yes, once we have identified and confiscated whatever triggered the archway. If it's not among our list of stolen objects, they will get it back when they leave."

"Thank you for the information," Jace said and turned away, lost in thought.

His hand went to his tunic and gripped the amulet hidden beneath it. *The Eye set off the alarm, as well. It was luck of the gods that they passed through the arch first. This is another complication – one Binder did not mention.* As far as Jace could see, the only way to reach the lift to the gate was through the auction. He wondered if the path to the warehouse beside the building had an alarm, as well.

Inside, he discovered the building had no roof, the guards he had seen above pacing the top of the outer wall, not a rooftop as he had assumed. The interior had elevated benches arranged in an arc, all seats facing a dais at the center. The horizontal lift rail ran along the interior of the wall, above the seating and adjacent to where the guards walked. His gaze followed it to an open platform beside a lift rising to the Cor Meum entrance a hundred feet up.

A man in gray robes approached. "Would you like a bidding chip?"

Jace looked at the man's hand, his palm occupied by a metal disk with the number 1,043 etched on the surface. *Best to appear as if you belong*. "Yes. Thank you." He accepted the disk with no intention of bidding.

He climbed the stairs and found a seat at the top of the riser, preferring to keep everyone in front of him. People continued to enter, the building filling rapidly. Although much smaller, it reminded him of the Bowl of Oren – the circular structure, the elevated seating, the anticipation from the crowd. However, the contest here was not one of blood, but one of possession. Jace was unsure which he considered higher stakes.

An old Enchanter wearing silver-trimmed black robes climbed upon the dais. His long beard was black with gray streaks, face weathered. He had an odd, cone-shaped black hat upon his head, another cone-shaped object on a pole in front of his face. A younger man standing beside him placed a ledger upon the podium. The old Enchanter held a pen, capped by a bright red feather. There was no inkwell visible.

The old man lifted his hand high, and steam billowed from small openings at the front of the dais below his feet, the ports emitting a screeching whistle as if a hundred teapots had gone off at once. Jace's mind flashed back to his first encounter with Rhoa atop the Enchanter's Tower in Marquithe. A similar alarm had triggered at the time, the room filling with steam. It had been a tense encounter, ending with Rhoa leaping out the tower window.

The little acrobat beat me to the Eye, yet I now possess it. She has no need for it anyway. I wonder how she and the others fare.

The whistle stopped, the crowd silent. The old man spoke into the cone on the pole, his booming voice easily heard by Jace sitting in the back.

"Welcome to the Enchanter's Auction. I am Auction Master Pelquath. This is our final auction of the week and promises to be special, numerous, rare items joining those already in high demand."

He faced the man with the ledger, the two having a brief exchange before he turned back toward the crowd.

"The first item up for bid is a set of ten enchanted lanterns, guaranteed to function for a hundred years."

Two women in form-hugging, black dresses circled the floor before the dais, each holding a platter with five pewter lanterns shining with a blue glow.

Pelquath said, "The bid opens at five silvers."

Hands popped up, each holding a glowing, circular disk. The man upped the bid, continuing higher and higher until he reached a price of one gold and seven silver pieces. The winning bidder's number was recorded, and the old man announced the second item.

"Next, we have a pair of spectacles. Very unique in nature," Pelquath said as a young woman walked out, the spectacles on a silver platter, lenses tinted in a purple hue, reminding Jace of Rawk's. "This enchanted item enables the wearer to see through fabric – *any* fabric."

Jace sat upright, clutching his bidding disk. He hadn't intended to buy anything, but the possibilities of such spectacles stirred his imagination. Yes, they could be used for voyeurism, but he considered what a wonderful tool they could be for a thief, able to spot hidden valuables on any person.

Sadly, the bid shot up far beyond the two silver pieces remaining in his pocket. By the end, the spectacles were sold to an old man in fancy clothing for the exorbitant price of eight gold pieces.

The next item was an enchanted chest able to keep the contents cold at all times. The auctioneer claimed it was among their greatest achievements, certain to change food storage forever. Jace wasn't so sure, but the item sold for twelve gold pieces.

Apparently, someone believes in the idea.

And so, the auction continued – items described, bids issued, money exchanging hands. In the back of Jace's mind, he began to track the totals, realizing stealing from the auction could be his next great caper…if the future allowed for him to return to his old profession.

The breeze tossed Jace's hair, salt spray swirling above the water and obscuring the sea beyond the bay. A lone ship drifted in from the southwest, white sails tinted with the warm hue of the setting sun. The ship, likely the last of the day, eased toward the pier.

I wonder where it came from, he thought. *Judging by the direction, it could be Starmuth or Fastella, or from somewhere much farther away.*

He sat on a post, legs dangling over the water, waves rolling in as he watched men pushing carts loaded with ore, tools, cloth, and other supplies. The carts rolled down the pier and were loaded onto the metal rails before being connected together.

Now that he had the chance to watch, Jace understood how the carts and track worked. Each wheel was cast with an inner hub that ran on top of the rail, another piece of a larger diameter inside the track, the weight of the cart holding it between the rails.

When finished, there were twenty carts in total. The man overseeing the workers, an Enchanter dressed in black and silver robes, held a charm to a panel at one end of the rail, and the carts began to move.

The wheels squeaked as they rolled forward and climbed the long incline to the top of the wall. The movement was slow, much slower than the single, boat-shaped cart he had seen conveying the two Enchanters across the city. Minutes passed before it reached the top and leveled, riding along the wall, then disappearing from view.

The cart faded from his thoughts, immediately replaced by concern about getting into Cor Meum. It had been a long day, although interesting and informative. Yet he was no closer to solving his conundrum.

With a sigh, he spun around and dropped off the post to land on the pier. The ship he had seen drifting into port was tied off, the plank in place, two Enchanters crossing it to the dock. One was young and overweight, likely a clerk rather than a master. The other… Jace gasped.

"Olberon," he whispered to himself, recalling the lecherous old man in a flash.

The wheels turning inside Jace's head stopped and locked into place, a plan forming instantly.

He turned and ran toward the city gate, waving at the startled guards as he sped past.

Jace had spent his entire life navigating busy streets, eyes tracking the traffic flow, watching for openings and darting through them. Such skill became an asset in moments such as this. He raced as fast as he dared, slipping through gaps as they opened, leaving startled cries in his wake.

The Lunartide Inn was over a mile from the gate, just blocks away from the Enchanter's Auction. The timing would be close, but he had to try. This one idea was all he had.

Reaching the inn, he ran inside, scanned the dining room, and rushed up the stairs to the third floor. He burst into the large room they had rented, his hope rising when all three of his companions were inside, startled looks on their faces.

"Adyn," he panted. "With me. Now."

He spun from the room and rushed down the corridor, opening the window at the end of the hallway. The neighboring roof peak was just below the window, an easy step through. His boots firmly on the roof, he ran along the peak just as Adyn came through the window. He reached the building next door, gripped the downspout, and climbed up. This one had a flat roof, of which he was thankful. He would only get one shot.

Crouching, he snuck toward the edge and peered over the central street just as the sun slipped behind the horizon.

In the distance, he saw the horizontal lift speeding toward him from the harbor.

Adyn appeared at his side. "What are we doing?"

"We are jumping onto that cart," he said, pointing toward it.

"I assume this is not just for fun."

"Grand Master Enchanter Olberon is on it. We need him." He gave her a resolute nod, tone serious. "Alive. The others, we can kill if necessary."

"How will I know which one he is?"

"You'll know. He's an old man who gets awfully handsy with women."

Jace backed up a few strides, watching as the cart came down the track. To his side, Adyn waited, mirroring his stance. As the vehicle sped toward him, he said a brief prayer to the gods, then burst into a run.

At the rooftop's edge, he leaped, sailed through the air, and fell toward the track. The cart charged ahead and rolled beneath him just in time. He landed with a grunt, the air blasting from his lungs as he struck the rounded, wooden nose, gripping the edge just in time to prevent himself from falling off.

He pulled himself up to find two startled men gaping at him, the pudgy one a few years younger than himself. Jace knew him to be Berrold, an acolyte in the Marquithe Enchanter's Guild. The other was Grand Master Olberon, his gray beard and wispy hair fluttering in the breeze. Behind them was a single armored guard, the man fighting with Adyn after she had landed on him in the rear of the cart.

The old man thrust a rod at Jace, red sparks of energy blasting forth. The magic scattered off Jace, falling away in sizzling sparks across the surface of the cart.

Olberon recoiled, his eyes round with shock. "What?" he exclaimed.

Jace reached down for the panel and pulled the circular metal seal off, the cart slowing rapidly. The motion caused him to drop the disk and he fell backward, legs dangling and kicking as he hung above the city streets. Grunting, he pulled himself back up as Olberon placed the disk back onto the panel. The cart again darted forward.

With a lunge, Jace kicked his leg over the edge, his boot smashing the younger Enchanter in the face, Berrold's head snapping back, eyes rolling up as he fell limp. Jace then climbed onto the cart, pulled the seal off the panel, and turned to the old man, gripping the front of his robes while lifting him from his seat.

"Don't move."

Jace drew the dagger at his hip and pressed it against the man's neck, the tip drawing blood when the cart lurched to a stop. At the same moment, Adyn knocked the guard out of the cart. He flipped and fell the two stories to the street, striking the ground with a clatter when he landed helmet-first.

The old man's eyes were wide, his mouth gaping. "Please, don't kill me."

"Tell me how to reverse this cart," Jace growled.

"I… I can't."

Adyn leaned past the unconscious young Enchanter. Her nose was bleeding, lip split. She grinned at Olberon, the blood on her teeth painting a malevolent smile in the fading light.

She licked his cheek. "There's a bit of my blood to mix with yours when he slices you from ear to ear."

"Ah… Ah…," the old man stammered. "Flip the activation seal. Insert it into the panel with the black side up."

His dagger still in place, Jace did as the man instructed. The cart began to roll backward.

Jace lifted his knife away, the man relaxing in relief. He flipped the dagger around and struck Olberon's temple with the pommel. Olberon's eyes rolled up, and he crumpled in his seat. Jace pulled the old man down to the floor, on top of his unconscious acolyte.

He sat with a sigh.

"What now?" Adyn asked.

"I spied on the tower and gate last night before I met with Binder. Both closed at sunset, the day guards meandering off to some tavern. Only a skeleton crew remained, and they were focused on what occurred outside the walls." The buildings sped past as the cart raced toward the harbor gate. "We wait until dark, sneak out of the lift tower, and carry these two back to the inn."

"What do you plan to do with them?"

He grinned. "This old man is our ticket into the Enchanter's Den."

29

INTERROGATION

Narine was relieved to see both Jace and Adyn alive, even if the latter had clearly been in a scuffle. However, the two unconscious Enchanters were cause for concern, both slumped in wooden chairs, bound and gagged. She was particularly worried about the old man, the side of his head bloody, skin pale.

"Is there no other way to do this?" she asked.

"Not as far I as I can tell." Jace sat on a bed across from the two captives.

"What about the supply carts we saw at the dock?" Hadnoddon rested against the wall, thick arms crossed over his barrel chest. "Couldn't we stow away in those and just ride in?"

The thief shook his head. "I asked Binder the same thing when he told me it was how he smuggled goods into Cor Meum. The carts pass through an enchanted gate just prior to entering the upper city. Anything with a heart-beat passing through the gate triggers some sort of defense and trips an alarm. Others have tried in the past. None survived."

Adyn suggested, "We could steal a set of armor and go in as guards."

"No good." He shook his head. "The armor is enchanted to a specific host. Anyone else attempting to don it acquires a horrible, unbearable rash. I'd rather not endure such a thing if I have another option. Besides, Binder says a Master Enchanter is required for others to gain entrance past the Sentinel."

"Sentinel?" Narine asked.

"Yeah. It's some sort of imposing guardian designed to destroy anyone who attempts to enter uninvited. Binder was afraid of it, whatever it is."

She asked, "What about the auction? You said you went there today. Did you not learn anything?"

"Oh, I learned plenty, the first being that there's an alarm that is triggered when an enchanted item passes through it." He ran his hand through his hair. "We can't go that route unless we leave your anklet and the Eye behind."

Adyn snorted. "There is little chance of Narine taking that thing off. She might be more addicted to the bracelet than she is to you, thief."

Narine shot Adyn a look. "You are not being helpful." The bodyguard grinned, her face still bloody. "You look horrible. Wet a cloth and clean your face."

"I thought it might help to intimidate them."

"They are about to wake up tied to a chair, held captive by four strangers. I doubt they need further intimidation."

With a sigh, Adyn turned toward the washbasin. "Fine."

Jace continued to stare at the two Enchanters, eyes narrowed as they had been since he and Adyn first returned with the hostages. Finally, he nodded.

"Heal the old man, Narine. Then see if you can wake him."

"All right." She crossed the room.

"Once he wakes, nobody speaks except for me." Jace stood, his gaze sweeping the room. "Got it?"

The others nodded, while Narine prepared her magic. A construct of repair formed around her outstretched hand. She held it beside his head and extended her awareness, delving into the wound and weaving it back together, doing her best to ease the swelling against his brain. The man shivered, the healing complete, but did not wake. A construct of mental manipulation resolved the issue, the old man jumping with a start, eyes wide as he gasped for air around the gag in his mouth.

Jace loomed over the elderly Enchanter, the tip of his dagger brushing against the front of his robes. "Exercise caution before you act, Olberon. A scream will get you killed. Complying will not."

The man nodded, eyes filled with fear.

Gripping the Enchanter's gag, Jace slid his blade beneath it and sliced with a jerk, the cloth splitting instantly.

The old man coughed and worked his tongue, his gray beard matted with drool. "How do you know my name?"

"We are glad to have you with us," the thief said with a smile. "Janice says hello."

The Enchanter blinked. "Janice? The maid who…" His eyes grew wide again. "It was *you*."

Jace pulled the Eye of Obscurance from his tunic, the amulet falling against his chest. "Yes, I possess the amulet. It is rightfully mine since I was the one who claimed it from Shadowmar seven years ago."

"You don't understand… The Eye is dangerous."

"I understand the Eye quite well. However, the amulet is not why you are here." He leaned close to the man, his glare intense. "How do we get inside Cor Meum?"

Olberon blinked, his gaze sweeping the room. "You cannot."

"Listen, old man. We are going inside with or without your help. One of those options allows you to live. I'll let you guess which." Jace hefted the seal he had taken from Olberon. "I can use this to reach the gate. I need you to get me inside, past the Sentinel."

"Impossible. There are safeguards."

"Explain."

"Upon achieving Master, each Enchanter's likeness is recorded and stored in a vault. The Sentinel is connected to this vault and requires my presence to pass."

"Seems easy enough to fool with an illusion."

The man shook his head. "It is not just my appearance. I speak of my essence."

Jace turned toward Narine. "Do you know what this man is talking about?"

She nodded. "Each living being carries an essence, unique to themselves. It is not something we can see."

"We could make him come with us," Adyn offered.

Jace shook his head again. "I have had bad luck with uncontrolled members in my party. Too unpredictable." He looked at Narine. "Can you copy it, like you do with your illusions?"

Without replying, Narine cast an inverted energy construct, one that revealed energy rather than produced it. She held the construct up and peered through it, toward the old man. A pulsing pattern surrounded him, intersecting lines of energy undetectable to the human eye. While elaborate, the pattern consisted of many small sections repeated again and again, forcing her to learn only a portion of it to apply the entire field.

"I believe I can replicate it," she said.

"Can you do that and mask the four of us with an illusion at the same time?"

"It will be difficult, but I can manage. I will need time to memorize his essence, though."

"We have all night." He pointed toward both captives, the younger one with a string of drool hanging from his open mouth, still fast asleep. "Be sure to memorize both of their faces, as well."

An idea struck Narine. Still holding to her magic, she altered the construct to one of mental manipulation. Gently, she laid it upon Olberon, hoping the Master Enchanter hadn't been trained to notice such things.

The old man's gaze swept the room, first landing on Adyn, to whom he flashed a grin. He then turned to Narine with an undisguised leer. "My, my. You are delicious. Perhaps you would enjoy giving this dirty old man a spanking?"

Adyn burst out laughing, covering her mouth when Narine frowned at her.

Jace said, "Don't feel bad, Narine. He treated me much the same when he thought I was Janice."

He prodded Olberon to reclaim his attention. "Do you know anything about the Band of Amalgamation?"

The old man's bushy, gray eyebrows rose, his smile fading. "Where did you hear that name?"

"A group of witches told me about it. Asked me to fetch it."

"It cannot leave the Cor Meum. The armband is dangerous, the effect permanent."

Jace sighed. "Of course, it is. I suppose the thing is hidden away someplace exotic, as well?"

Without hesitation, Olberon said, "It's in the Repository beneath Belzacanth's tower, same as any other precious..." The old man's eyes grew wide. "Why did I say that?"

He looked at Narine, his face turning red. "You did something to me with your perverted magic, you…you…*witch*," he sneered.

Narine stepped close the man, whipped her hand back, and slapped him. It stung her palm, the violence an uncharacteristic reaction. Jace grinned at her.

"I am a *wizardess*," she said evenly as she sat on the bed, glaring at the old man as he blinked and worked his jaw. "Now, sit still while I memorize your face. We are visiting the Repository tomorrow morning with your doppelgänger as our escort."

30

SENTINEL

Dressed in Acolyte Berrold's robes, Narine walked at Jace's side as they headed toward the harbor. They were both masked in elaborate illusion – her as Berrold, him as Olberon. With the Sentinel waiting, she dared not miss any detail.

Accordingly, much to her embarrassment, Jace and Adyn had stripped the two hostages of all clothing, allowing Narine to examine them closely and craft the illusions to perfection – every visible scar, hair, or wrinkle. Her cheeks warmed again as she recalled the shriveled old man sitting naked and helpless while she cast a mirror image over Jace, who joked continuously about the situation. Adyn, of course, thought it was great fun and made numerous comments that had Jace and Hadnoddon chuckling.

Narine looked over her shoulder. Adyn and Hadnoddon walked behind them, both in the image of city guards dressed in full armor, the silver studs on their black leather armor shimmering in the morning sunlight. Despite herself, she felt a moment of pride. The illusions were flawless, even with her having to add inches to the dwarf's stocky frame so he didn't appear so short.

They reached the end of the street, the harbor gate and lift tower now visible across the square. As before, two dozen guards were near the gate, another half-dozen standing outside the tower.

Stomping angrily, his robes swirling, Jace headed directly toward the lift tower. His face drawn into a scowl, he did not slow when a guard moved to intercept him. "Out of my way," he grumbled, his voice a startingly good impression of Olberon's.

One of the guards addressed him. "Master Olberon. It is good to see you. We were concerned when we discovered the magnavessel back in the tower. Danlin, the guard who had accompanied you, was found dead in the street."

Cold sweat began to track down Narine's ribs, and she found herself holding her breath. *I hope you know what you are doing, Jace.*

"Good. The idiot tried to steal my seal. Tore it off the panel right in front of me. He lost his balance when the vessel stopped, so I gave him a shove." Jace shook his head. "Got what he deserved if you ask me."

"Why would Danlin do such a thing?" one of the guards asked.

Another said, "I thought he had been behaving odd lately. Maybe he took a bribe from someone who wanted the seal for themselves."

Jace glanced around, eyes narrowed in suspicion. He leaned toward the men and whispered, "We have had troubles lately. Could be related. You know… The disappearances?"

The guards' eyes widened, some nodding.

The man who had first approached Jace asked, "If Danlin stole the seal, how did you get back?"

Jace snorted and shook his head, a stellar act of irritation as he grumbled, "We were stuck up on the track above the street until an hour past nightfall before we caught someone's attention. A young lad was kind enough to throw the seal back up to us. By then, it was too late to enter Cor Meum, so we returned to the harbor gate and found an inn for the evening."

The guard then pointed toward Hadnoddon and Adyn. "Who are these two? I don't recognize them."

Jace stepped closer to the guard and glared up at him menacingly. The image of the wizened old man staring down the burly, armed guard almost caused Narine to laugh, especially when the guard backed away.

"Do you pass me for a fool?"

"Um…no."

"Good. Because I'd have to be a fool to allow any unknown guards to escort me after what occurred last night." He gestured toward Adyn and

Hadnoddon. "These two came with us from Marquithe. I've known them for years. They will ride with us and ensure we reach Cor Meum without any further trouble."

Without waiting on a response, Jace stomped into the building, climbed aboard the lift, and produced the seal he had stolen from Olberon. Narine, Adyn, and Hadnoddon joined him just before he planted the seal in the panel. It began to rise.

The guards faded from sight, and Narine sighed in relief. The sides of her shift, the only thing she wore beneath the robes, were damp, her stomach tied in a knot.

The lift stopped, allowing her to get a good look at the magnavessel. Made of wooden slats, it was much like a boat, both the front and back ends rounded. A cavity with a wooden floor and a pair of back-to-back benches completed the craft. Mounted to the front was a black, metal panel covered in silvery script.

Jace climbed into the front of the vessel and sat on the forward-facing bench. Narine settled beside him, while Adyn and Hadnoddon sat in the rear, facing backward. Lifting the seal, Jace twisted it. One surface was black, the other silver, both covered in runes unfamiliar to Narine, but obviously magical in nature. He pressed the black side into the panel, silver side up, and the vessel began to hum.

It shot forward, rapidly reaching top speed, the city below racing past.

Narine grinned. "This is actually…fun."

Jace nodded. "It is an interesting mode of travel. Even a galloping horse doesn't go faster than this." He turned and spoke over his shoulder. "Remember, I do all the talking. Just follow my lead."

He then put a hand on Narine's leg, his face drawn in a frown. "I will be happy when this is finished. I dislike the use of illusion when it deprives me of your beauty."

She shook her head. "You are far too devious and much too charming for your own good." Still, she could not resist smiling at the warmth she felt inside.

The cart sped past the Lunartide Inn and continued toward the opening in the wall above the Enchanter's Auction. Once inside, the track turned and ran along the curved wall, the vessel slowing as it neared the platform where the track ended. A cluster of guards stood between the platform and a lift station, three stories above the auction floor.

Everyone climbed out, Jace leading the way with Narine just behind him. He spoke to the guards briefly, complaining about how he was late, and headed toward the lift. Inserting the seal into a panel, he called the lift down to their level, climbed on, and when all four of them were ready, placed the seal into the activation slot. The lift began to move.

As it rose, Narine gazed over the lower city, already bustling, the streets full, although the sun had just crested the outer wall, much of the area still in shadow. Up and up they went, the lift not stopping until it reached a dark opening high above the lower city. Rather than a gate, it was a simple corridor with an arched ceiling. Enchanted lanterns mounted to the walls lit the way. Thirty strides in, the corridor ended at a drop, frighteningly dark and unknowingly deep. In the distance, far across the pit, sunlight shone through another arched doorway.

To one side of the tunnel, just a few feet from the pit's edge, was an activation panel. Jace pressed the seal into it and a hum arose. A series of oversized doorframes between them and the opposite tunnel came to life, each pulsing with a crimson hue, illuminating the building and allowing Narine to examine the interior.

The doorframes were made of some sort of metal, suspended from the tall, arched ceiling above the pit, the ceiling curving down to walls a hundred feet apart and made of stone blocks coated with a green slime. It smelled horrible. Narine was unsure if the smell came from the slime or from something in the pit. She bent over and peered down, thinking the pulsing red light might reveal the bottom. She was wrong.

Movement appeared in the distance, a platform coming toward them, suspended from a track along the peak of the arched ceiling. The humming grew increasingly louder as the platform closed the distance. It reached the end, stopping with an echoing clang. When Jace removed the seal, the doorways over the pit dimmed to black, the building falling silent.

"I believe we have discovered the Sentinel." He put his hand on Narine's shoulder. "Use your magic and do it well. I fear what this…thing will do should it not believe I am Olberon."

Narine cast a backward glance, the corridor empty. She called upon her magic, formed an energy construct, and began to weave. It was a difficult, painstaking process, requiring complete concentration. When she had the core of Olberon's energy pattern constructed, she replicated it again and again until it encased Jace completely.

Finished, she panted as if she had run for miles, her forehead wet, hair sticking to it, shift and robe damp from the effort.

"Are you all right?" Jace asked.

She nodded, blowing out a breath. "It is done." *I just pray I got it right.*

"Good." He climbed onto the lift, his weight causing it to rock. He turned toward them. "What are you waiting for? Let's see if this monstrosity will let us past."

Carefully, Narine stepped onto the platform. It swayed, and she gripped Jace by the hand, him pulling her close.

The image of Olberon grinned in the darkness. "Don't worry. I've got you."

When Adyn and Hadnoddon climbed on, the platform again wobbled. Jace gripped the seal and placed it into the control panel at the center of the lift. The frames once again came to life, the red glow illuminating their surroundings. Humming, the platform began across the gap.

Before they reached the first frame, Jace shifted to the front edge of the platform. "I hope this works," he muttered.

The angry, red glow filled Narine with dread. Instinctively, she knew something insidious was connected to the aura. She held her breath in anticipation. Just as the platform met the first threshold, the glow turned from red to white. The platform passed through the opening, Narine cringing. Nothing happened. She released her breath but continued to watch the frame, the white glow gradually returning to red.

They passed through seven more frames, each aura turning white just prior to their arrival, returning to crimson shortly after passing. The platform stopped, and Jace led them down another corridor, bright sunlight beckoning at the end. Just before they emerged, Narine released the energy spell, hoping there was no need to maintain it any longer. Even if there were, she had quickly neared the last of her reserves. Illusions required very little of her magic. Energy spells were another matter.

Stepping outside, they stopped and gazed at the surroundings, setting their eyes upon Cor Meum, a city within a city, for the first time.

The buildings glittered in the morning sunlight, same as the walls surrounding the city. Rather than streets with rows of housing, the area was simply a massive plaza littered with short towers – some round, some square, some with bridges connecting one to another. Fountains and open forges sat among clusters of towers, smoke rising from the forges and into the morning sky. At the heart of it all was a massive tower. Not in height, but in girth. It had to be hundreds of feet in diameter but rose only ten stories before reducing to a narrow, silvery spire jutting up toward the heavens. The top of the spire glimmered like a tiny, silver-white star.

When she spotted two young men in black robes rushing toward them, Narine gripped Jace by the arm and whispered, "We have company. I hope you know what you are doing."

The visage of Olberon gave her a sidelong smile. "Have I not gotten us this far?"

"Master Olberon!" one of the approaching men called out. He was probably in his twenties, stick-thin with long, black hair to match his robes. "Master Olberon," he panted, slowing. "You are late. The Conclave of Masters has already begun."

Angrily, Jace countered, "You don't think I know that? I would have been here last night, but Berrold and I were accosted. We were lucky to escape with our lives."

The other acolyte, a pudgy man with a thin, brown mustache and brown bangs, his hair appearing as if it had been cut beneath a bowl, kneaded his hands together worriedly. "I had feared that word of our troubles might reach the lower city. If citizens in Mundial are brave enough to attack Master Enchanters, what of us?"

"Calm down, Dowman," the taller acolyte said. "We still have the Silver Soldiers to protect us. Besides, when was the last time you visited the lower city?"

Jace interrupted. "I don't have time for this."

"You are correct, Master. Come. We will escort you to the Conclave."

Without waiting for a reply, the two acolytes hurried across the plaza. Jace turned toward Narine, rolled his eyes, and followed. She surveyed the upper city as they hurried between two towers and past a forge where a man pounded glowing metal with a massive hammer. The area was quiet, other than acolytes here and there, always traveling in pairs.

She then realized the two men led them toward the massive building in the center. It was undoubtedly home of Belzacanth, Wizard Lord of Cordium, the most powerful Enchanter alive. The fear in her stomach resurfaced, rising with each step. After their recent past with wizard lords, she feared another encounter.

31

CONCLAVE

The Conclave was a circular chamber in the heart of Cor Cordium Palace. When Jace passed through the doors, a man in white announced Olberon's name, interrupting an Enchanter who had been speaking. All fell silent, everyone in the crowded room turning toward him.

Jace led Narine down a set of stairs bracketed by seats filled with men in black robes. The illuminated floor was marked by an eight-pointed star outlined in silver. An ornate chair sat at each of the star points, one of which remained unoccupied. Bearded Master Enchanters, two of whom were as old as Olberon, sat in the other chairs, watching him with judging glares. One chair was taller than the others and gilded in silver. A wizened old man in silver-trimmed white robes occupied the throne, a glittering cone-shaped hat on his head. He held a black scepter covered in silver script, the top capped with a bulb of silver, polished to reflect its surroundings.

Belzacanth, Jace thought.

He glanced up into the hollow core of the Tower of Devotion, the glimmering light of the silver flame streaming down through a crystal panel at the distant top. *It must never grow dark in this room.*

Instinctively, he knew the empty chair on the floor was Olberon's and headed toward it, gesturing for Narine to claim a seat in the triangle-shaped seating section behind the chair. Maintaining a sour expression, he sat and cast a challenging glare toward each of the other masters before he gave a deferential nod toward Belzacanth.

"You are late, Olberon," the old wizard lord said, giving him a withering glare.

"I apologize, Your…" Jace's mind raced, trying to decide what term to use, "Majesty." He held his hands out in supplication. "Berrold and I were attacked last night and were lucky to escape with our lives."

"Attacked? Here in Cor Cordium?"

"Yes. Our escort on the magnavessel. He sought to steal my seal. For what purpose, I have no idea."

"This is an interesting revelation." The wizard lord stroked his long, white beard. "I wonder if it is related to our current dilemma."

Jace continued. "While late, I am here now. Please, what did I miss?"

A master with a short, black beard said, "In truth, very little." Jace estimated the man to be in his forties, decades younger than any of the other masters.

"True, Ghenton. However, the facts are worth knowing," said one of the older Enchanters. He turned toward Jace. "Over the past season, there have been disappearances. Most have been…working women who vanished during a visit in Cor Meum. It was a curious oddity at first, but after the tenth disappearance, women stopped coming. That was three weeks past.

"More recently, and of more concern, this plague, whatever the cause, has claimed our own."

"Just how many are we talking about?" Jace asked.

"Three masters and eleven acolytes."

Jace blinked. "Fourteen in just three weeks?"

"As far as we can tell, yes."

Another Enchanter added, "Perhaps an enemy has infiltrated our ranks and attempts to dismantle the Enchanters by killing us one at a time."

Belzacanth scoffed. "How would an enemy enter Cor Meum? Without the assistance of a Master Enchanter, it is impossible."

Ghenton nodded. "Precisely. What if one of our own is in league with this enemy?"

Worried mutters passed through the crowd.

Belzacanth clenched his scepter, and the bulbous top shone with a brilliant light, drawing all attention. "Silence!" he roared.

The bright light dimmed, a stillness settling over the room.

In a firm but quiet voice, the wizard lord said, "Thus far, I hear conjecture but see little to support your theories."

Jace had hoped to finish in short order so he could complete his quest for the Band of Amalgamation. According to Olberon, it was in the Repository somewhere in this building, but he did not know exactly what he searched for or where to find it. Somehow worse, he had an inclination as to what the Enchanters faced. It matched a pattern he had seen before – an ugly series of events leading to a dark discovery. In a flash, he committed to boldness.

Why stop now?

"I believe I know what is occurring in Cor Meum," he announced.

All eyes turned toward him, many sets of bushy eyebrows furrowing.

"Please, Master Olberon," Belzacanth intoned. "Enlighten us."

Rising to his feet, Jace strolled into the center of the floor and began turning calmly, watching the crowd as he spoke. "The pattern of events occurring here matches a problem I encountered some years ago in Eleighton. Disappearances had plagued the city for a year before I arrived." It was Jace's own past he spoke of. A contract he would never forget.

"Our tower is in Marquithe. Why were you in Eleighton?" asked a Master Enchanter with wispy, gray hair and long mustache.

Inwardly, Jace recoiled, fearing where such questions might lead. To counter, he snapped in reply, "I have the floor and will not suffer interruptions!"

The old man blinked, taken aback.

"Olberon is correct," Belzacanth warned. "Let him speak."

Jace nodded toward the wizard lord and resumed his story. "What I discovered in Eleighton was the stuff of nightmares. The man who had committed these crimes drained his victims of blood, treating humans as nothing more than vessels to feed his dark magic. I speak of sorcery."

A collective gasp swept over the room, the mention of sorcery causing a stir of mutters. Even Belzacanth seemed disturbed.

But Jace was not finished. He raised his hand high, turning as he waited for the crowd to quiet.

"Ask yourself, why would an Enchanter resort to the forbidden dark arts?"

The wizard lord nodded and sat forward in his chair. "Why, indeed."

Jace turned toward him. "You are old, Belzacanth, even by wizard lord standards. Perhaps a member of this very Conclave seeks an advantage in the hopes of boosting his abilities enough to topple his own wizard lord."

Another stir ran through the room. The masters stared at Jace, three with narrowed eyes, one rubbed his chin in thought, two appeared frightened.

"You have spent too long away, holed up in your tower in Marquithe, Olberon," Ghenton scoffed. "Black magic is a myth. You don't expect us to believe this nonsense."

Belzacanth sat back in his throne and stared into space as he spoke. "I recall the rise of a sorcerer when I was a child. A man who came close to destroying Orenth with his black magic."

"Why have we never heard of this?" another master asked.

"You are old, Thandellon. Approaching ninety years, I believe."

The old master nodded.

"Yet the man of whom I speak died two centuries before you were born. Even back then, details of his rise and demise were scarce, the years burying what memories remained." The old wizard lord exhaled dramatically. "Believe me when I tell you, sorcery is real and poses a dire threat if one of our brethren has embraced this dark art."

The ominous statement led to hollow silence. It was the perfect setup for what Jace had planned.

"With such a threat looming, we dare not delay," he said to Belzacanth. "It must be settled here and now."

The old man nodded. "Agreed. But how?"

Jace rotated as he spoke to the audience. "Sorcery requires sacrifice – both from the victims and the man who wields it. The power can only be employed by a man whose skin is covered in the twisted runes of the dark arts." His gaze met Narine's, still masked as Berrold. *Please, Narine. I hope you have maintained the entire illusion.* Gritting his teeth, he brought his hands to the front of his robes. "To determine the guilty party, we need but bare ourselves."

With a flourish, he tore open his robes, exposing himself to the entire room, drawing startled gasps. His gaze lowered to the sagging, weathered body of Olberon, wearing nothing but his smallclothes. Of course, no ink marked his body. Turning around, he measured the reactions, seeking out the perpetrator.

"You expect the lot of us to expose ourselves in this sacred forum?" Ghenton asked, incredulous. "You make a mockery of the Conclave." His words were thick with disdain.

Belzacanth slid off his throne, shuffled to Jace, and gave him a nod. "Cover yourself, old friend."

Jace pulled his robes back on, cinching them at the waist.

"Sit." The wizard lord directed Jace back toward his seat, then faced the crowd. "If sorcery is at the root of the evil lurking within the Cor Meum walls, I would know now. One section at a time, you will do as Olberon has done, exposing yourself to your brethren to prove your innocence." He nodded toward the seats behind Jace. "We will begin with Olberon's section. Rise and open your robes!"

The command left no room for doubt. Jace turned and waited while men ranging from their late twenties to eighties stood and opened their robes. His gaze shifted to Narine, breath held as he prayed her illusion masked her shift and curves. Among the last to do so, she pulled her robes open, exposing the portly body of Berrold, unmarked by runes, her shift invisible behind the illusion.

"Very good." Belzacanth nodded. "Cover yourselves, and we will move on to Hadlogue's section."

The old Master Enchanter at the front bared himself, as did every man seated behind him. None bore the marks of sorcery.

The wizard lord turned again, facing the next master wizard. "Ghenton, you and your section are next."

Everyone sitting behind the young, dark-haired Master Enchanter did as requested. However, Ghenton glared at Belzacanth with a sour expression, not doing as requested. Instead, he removed a vial from his robes and held it up. It was filled with dark liquid.

Ghenton turned the vial, examining it as he spoke. "I had hoped to wait until we neared the next Darkening. Given time, I could have claimed as many as thirty souls, making my power unstoppable." He undid the silver sash at his waist, his robes falling open. He pulled one side off his shoulder, then the other, the robes falling to the floor in a heap as he stood wearing nothing but his smallclothes.

His body was covered in twisting lines, shapes and symbols most sinister. The crowd gasped.

"What have you done?" Belzacanth breathed.

"I have done what was necessary. I'll not wait until I am old and wizened for you to die. Not when I might achieve immortality before my body decays." Ghenton unstoppered the vial and poured it onto his chest, dragging it from shoulder to shoulder while crimson streaks ran down and stained his smallclothes. Once empty, he tossed the vial aside, the glass shattering on the floor. He then began smearing the blood across his torso and arms, body glistening in a most disturbing fashion. All anyone could do was stare, jaws gaping, eyes widened in horror.

Ghenton stepped toward Belzacanth, eyes wild, a malevolent grin on his face. "Time to die, old man!"

The wizard lord raised his scepter, the bulb at the top radiating a silvery light, and thrust it toward Ghenton. Silver lightning arced, striking the mad Enchanter in the chest, the room shaking with a thunderclap, Ghenton's body twitching mightily. However, he did not fall.

Belzacanth gripped the scepter with both hands, power surging as the lightning continued to pour into Ghenton.

Jace spun away, gripped Narine's hand, and rushed up the stairs, forgetting his role as the feeble, old Enchanter.

He reached the top, just before the door, and looked over his shoulder as the lightning ceased.

Belzacanth leaned against his throne, panting, appearing worn. Sparks sizzled across Ghenton's body, the man's arms spread, back arched as he screamed. For a moment, it seemed as if he might collapse.

Then his screaming ceased and head lowered, an evil grin returning as he glared at the wizard lord. Ghenton lunged forward and clapped his hands together, a blast of angry, red energy bursting forth and striking Belzacanth in the chest, launching the old man into his throne with a terrible crack.

The mightiest Enchanter in the world, a man three centuries old, lay crumpled in the throne, open, empty eyes staring at nothing, a gaping hole in his chest, white robes smoldering. The shimmering light coming from the tower above flickered and faded, the room falling dark.

Dead. Another wizard lord dead, Jace thought as he ran out the door.

32

MAGICAL NATURE

Adyn paced, fingers caressing the hilts of the swords at her hips. She hated being separated from Narine and Jace, unable to protect her, fearing what crazy scheme he might hatch next. *He cares for Narine and would never allow harm to come to her… Well, not intentionally.* It was not his intent she worried about, but rather his reckless nature. Worse, he didn't have the Eye to protect him, the amulet safe in their room at the Lunartide Inn.

"Will you sit still?" Hadnoddon chided, the dwarf leaning against the wall with his arms crossed. "You're making me anxious."

"Good," she snapped. "There is plenty enough anxiety to go around."

It was just the two of them in the room where they were to wait while the Conclave took place.

Still masked behind Narine's illusion, the dwarf said, "You are normally so calm, confident. What's got you so bothered?"

She sighed. "This entire plot, this strange city, these illusions… We have woven a tapestry to hide behind and are one snag away from the entire thing unraveling. Worse, those two are locked up in a chamber filled with Enchanters, and I have no idea what is happening–"

A massive *boom* shook the room, making them both flinch. Adyn drew her sword, went to the door, and eased it open. She peered down the curved corridor, hearing shouts and another crash. A door opened, footsteps running toward her.

The illusions of Olberon and Berrold came around the corner, the pair running faster than anyone might imagine when seeing them.

Adyn stepped out, sword in hand, the dwarf just behind her. "What's going on?"

"You don't want to know," Jace said as he slowed. "We need to find a way downstairs…now."

"Another wizard lord is dead," Narine said, the statement weighted by a sense of finality.

"That's why we need to hurry." Jace continued down the corridor, eyeing each closed door but not opening any of them. "The Enchanters are distracted. We only have a short time to find the Band and get out of here."

Adyn and Hadnoddon stalked after them. "How much longer can you maintain these illusions?"

Narine's response was firm, determined. "As long as I must."

Jace stopped outside a closed door, the panel beside it containing a circular recess. He pulled out Olberon's seal and snapped it into the panel. A click sounded. He tentatively reached for the handle, gripped it, and opened the door, exposing a dark, curved stairwell.

"We passed six other identical doors with panels like this one," Adyn noted. "How did you know?"

He pointed toward the inside of the door, which was covered in silver script. "This door was protected with an enchantment. The hair on my arms stood on end when I got close to it, so I figured it must be protecting something of value."

As he entered the stairwell, he said, "Close it behind you. We don't need anyone following."

Adyn trailed behind Jace, leading Narine and Hadnoddon downward, the dwarf closing the door, darkness closing in. Dim light bloomed when Hadnoddon produced one of the glowing stones they had used in the tunnels of Oren'Tahal.

Jace stopped, freezing for a moment. He squatted, holding his hand over the stair just below where he stood.

"Magic. I can feel it." He extended his leg past the stair to the one below it. Nothing happened. He stepped over the suspect stair and turned back. "Step over this one. Do not, by any means, touch it."

Adyn moved closer to it, examining the stair. It looked no different than any other, but she was careful to do as he instructed, reaching backward to help Narine navigate past it.

A dozen steps later, the stairwell brought them to a short corridor, a closed door at the end. The wood was charcoal in color, blackened metal bolts lining each panel. A seal opening sat in the heart of the door's center panel. Jace held his seal up to it, prepared to insert it, then stopped. Frowning at the object in his hand, he turned it over, silver surface down, black side facing him. He then pushed it into the panel, a click sounding, the door swinging open with a low, ominous creak. Light bloomed, enchanted lanterns within coming to life.

His hand extended in front of him, he eased through the doorway. Adyn, Narine, and Hadnoddon entered and examined their surroundings.

They stood on a landing at the top of a short flight of stairs. A circular-shaped room stretched out before them, a tall ceiling supported by a ring of pillars halfway between the outer wall and the center of the room. It was filled with objects and oddities. Treasures of a magical nature to be sure, but Adyn had no idea what type of effect accompanied the objects.

Jace said, "Olberon described the object as an armband, so look for something matching such a description." He descended the stairs, pointing. "Spread out and search, but don't touch anything. Enchanted objects can be deadly."

Adyn paused as the others fanned out. When nobody turned left, she chose that direction, walking between shelves, tables, and crates filled with strange objects. She passed curiosities ranging from a sword made of glass to a corset laced with tiny, sharp blades. Some things were encased in glass cubes, others resting upon pedestals as if on display. As she neared a table where an open book rested, it began to glow with a golden light. Music came from the book, calling to her, the lure irresistible. It was a song of everlasting happiness, bliss unequaled. She reached for it, her hand mere inches away when someone pushed her aside.

Stumbling, Adyn spun around, prepared to draw her blade.

Hadnoddon said, "Remember. Don't touch anything."

"You don't understand…"

He pulled an apple from his pocket and held it up. "It was to be a snack. Shall we see what happens?"

The dwarf tossed the fruit toward the book. When it touched the pages, the golden light flashed, forcing Adyn to shield her eyes. She lowered her hand as the apple rolled across the table and fell to the floor with a metallic thud. It had turned to solid gold.

"Neat trick." Hadnoddon turned toward her. "I like gold as much as anyone but would rather not have you turn to metal."

Adyn nodded numbly, realizing how close she had come to death. "I… I'll go this way and keep looking." She turned from him, embarrassed.

Control yourself, she thought.

Scanning her surroundings as she walked, she continued looking for something one might call an armband. She passed through a narrow gap between two shelves and came to an open area with a singular pedestal in the middle.

A golden coil sat upon the pedestal, the diameter a bit larger than her upper arm. Moving closer, Adyn examined the squiggly script of enchantment on the inside of the coil. She unsheathed a sword and slid the blade through the coil, using it to lift the object off the pedestal. Noticing an old rag resting on a nearby table, she picked it up, placed the band into the rag, and wrapped it up.

"I found it," she called out, slipping between the shelving as she headed back toward the entrance. "Let's get out of here."

Adyn gripped the cloth-wrapped object as Jace and Narine led the way across the plaza, toward the Sentinel entrance. Enchanters in black scurried about the plaza and disappeared into various towers, the men clearly distraught, their reality having been altered by the revelation of a sorcerer among them, as well as the death of their wizard lord.

A Master Enchanter, bracketed by two acolytes and a compliment of six armed guards, angled across the plaza and intercepted Jace mere strides from their goal.

"Where do you think you are going, Olberon?"

Jace put his fists on his hips and replied in his grating voice, "I'll not be part of this, Pelquath. The use of sorcery is against our tenets, regardless of what happened to Belzacanth."

The old man narrowed his eyes. "You are not our god, Olberon. Regardless of the means, Ghenton defeated Belzacanth. Only Cora can decide his worth. If selected by Cora, he will become wizard lord. If not…it could be you. Do you intend to join as an applicant?"

Jace frowned. "The Darkening is weeks away. I don't have to decide now."

"True. However, you should consider it. Of the others, I believe you offer the best chance of success against Ghenton."

Jace arched a brow. "You will not apply?"

The old Enchanter shook his head. "Not I. This is as far as I go, my ambition sated. When my time comes, I prefer a quiet, peaceful death. Being consumed by a god… Not so much."

Jace clamped a hand on the old man's shoulder. "I will think on it."

"That is the most I could ask." The old man stepped aside, he and his two acolytes walking toward a distant tower, guards trailing behind.

"Come on." Jace resumed marching toward the waiting Sentinel.

Adyn caught up to him, glancing backward before asking, "How did you know his name?"

"He announced himself at the auction yesterday."

"All right." She was impressed. "But how do you always know what to say during these random encounters?"

Jace shrugged. "I didn't. I just made up the thing about tenets. I don't even know what a tenet is, but I've heard men like that speak of them as something sacred. From there, he led the conversation. I just behaved like a crabby old man talking to someone I had known for decades."

She laughed, despite the realization of how tenuous the situation had been.

33

SACRIFICE

Their illusions discarded, Narine and Jace again wearing their normal clothes, they gathered in their room at the Lunartide Inn to pack their things. Jace informed Olberon and Berrold of what had occurred, leaving both men distraught. Narine and Adyn fed the bound men leftovers from lunch and gave them some water before reapplying their gags. After locking the door, they descended to the dining room, where Jace gave Willow specific instructions to hold his room until nightfall. If he did not return, she could rent it out to another party. Olberon and Berrold would then be discovered and freed as a reward for their compliance.

As one might expect, the dining room, and likely the entire city, was abuzz regarding the lack of flame atop the Tower of Devotion. Belzacanth had held the position for centuries, not one living person ever having seen the flame doused. It was mid-afternoon when the four travelers departed and headed toward the harbor in search of a ship, eager to be away from the city.

As they walked down the street, Adyn considered all that had happened since leaving Kelmar – the tragic avalanche, a dangerous journey through Oren'Tahal, Salvon's disturbing disappearance, Jace's incarceration and trial by arms in Tiamalyn, the journey to Cor Cordium, the eventual recovery of the object of power. Nothing had been easy, the quest filled with twists, close calls, and near-death moments. Somehow, two more wizard lords had died in the process.

We did not kill either man, but their deaths occurred while we were in the city. Five of eight wizard lords have died in our presence within the passing of a season.

She didn't understand why, but bizarre events continued to follow wherever they went. Despite all this, Adyn and her companions had somehow succeeded in their mission. The Band of Amalgamation was in their possession.

But what of the object's nature? Why did Olberon call it dangerous, the effect permanent? What effect?

Those questions and more ran through her head until reaching one she chose to voice aloud.

"Where will we go?" Adyn asked, glancing toward Hadnoddon. "Xionne never told us what to do once we found this thing." She thumbed toward the pack on her shoulder where the band lay hidden. "Where do we head to next?"

The dwarf frowned and tugged on his beard. "I don't know exactly. She inferred that destiny would guide us." He gave her a sidelong look. "You may have noticed the Seers can be somewhat cryptic."

Jace burst out laughing. "That is akin to saying water can be somewhat wet."

The four of them laughed. It was a pleasant, relaxed moment after a day of tension.

They entered the square near the harbor gate and found it oddly quiet, lacking the vendors and citizens who occupied the area the day they had arrived. *I wonder if it has something to do with Belzacanth's death.* As before, two dozen soldiers in silver-studded black leather armor clustered near the entrance to the city, intense gazes watching those coming and going. Also as before, Jace waved to the guards and flashed a friendly smile. It was a small gesture, but it gave Adyn the sense their visit had come full circle.

They passed through the gate, the chilly sea breeze hitting them as they descended the short hill to the docks.

Jace suddenly stopped. "Oh no."

Adyn followed his gaze, her eyes widening when she saw Roddem Despaldi striding toward them, bracketed by three others.

Despaldi stopped ten strides away and gave a grim smile. "My, my. If it isn't our little thief and his band of misfits. Where are Reisner, the old man, and the acrobat? Did you have casualties along the way?"

In a nonchalant tone, Jace said, "Oh, they are about, causing mischief, upsetting plans laid by you and your power-hungry wizard lord."

The man sneered. "You have caused me far too much trouble, Landish. I will have the Eye in my possession and will end you in the process." He glanced toward his men. "To prove I am reasonable, I will allow you to decide if you die quickly or in a long, lingering fashion."

"I have become quite attached to the Eye and prefer to retain it." Jace shrugged. "As for my life, many others have tried to end it, yet I persist. You see, I can be frustratingly stubborn in that regard."

"I had hoped you might feel that way."

Despaldi held his hands before his face, both covered in long, black gloves. He tugged on one glove and pulled it free. His hand glowed like the hot coals of a fire. The other hand came free, appearing the same.

"What have you done?" Narine breathed.

"I have discovered the true meaning of power." The Captain of the Midnight Guard gestured toward the three men beside him. "And I am not the only one."

The man to Despaldi's left tore similar gloves off, his hands glistening and white, as if made of ice, swirling white steam rising from them. The two men to his right uncrossed their arms. One punched the cart beside him, his fist smashing through the wood, splinters spraying through the air. The other man removed his black gloves, arcs of pale blue electricity sparking between his fingers.

"We are the Fist of Farrow, deliverers of death," Despaldi said. "Lord Horus thought to stop us. He thought wrong. How can you hope to succeed where a wizard lord has failed?"

Jace whispered, "Be ready to run back into the city as fast as you can." He then raised his voice. "Only one wizard lord? Surely you can do better than that."

Despaldi frowned. "What do you mean?"

"We ourselves have seen the end of four wizard lords, including your own Lord Malvorian."

"Four?"

"Get ready," Jace whispered as he held up a hand with four fingers extended. Louder, he said, "Taladain." One finger folded. "Malvorian." Another. "Raskor." A third. "And, most recently, Belzacanth."

With the last finger still up, Jace pointed toward Cor Cordium, the tower spire just above the city wall. Despaldi and his men all turned to peer in that direction.

Jace spun, gripped Narine's hand, and rushed off. "Run!"

All four of them rushed past startled dockworkers and up the hill, toward the gate. Despaldi and his men ran after them.

"Help!" Jace bawled. "Attack! Guards, help!"

A cluster of city guards armed with halberds and swords rushed out of the gate. Archers on the wall above loosed arrows. Despaldi waved his hands. A blast of heat flared, incinerating the arrows in mid-flight, as Adyn and her companions ran through the gaps between the guards. A blast of frigid air struck from behind, and she looked back to find the guards in the front coated in ice, the men slowing and stumbling. Lightning struck the guards, arcing from man to man, frying the soldiers in an instant. All twenty guards collapsed, eyes gone, sockets black and smoldering.

"Close the gates!" Adyn shouted as she and Hadnoddon ran through, a stride behind Jace and Narine.

A guard repeated the order, chains clanking as the massive, black, iron portcullis slammed down. The remaining four guards stood inside the gate, ready. Archers continued to loose arrows from the top of the wall, to no avail. One of them toppled and fell in a streak of flames. Another was struck by a thrown halberd, the impact so hard he flew twenty feet across the square before he fell to the ground.

"What do we do?" Narine asked as the four of them huddled beside the gate.

"If we run, they will tear up the city. Hundreds of innocents could die." Hadnoddon pulled his massive hammer off his back. "I say we fight."

"What?" Jace exclaimed. "Did you see what they can do?"

"He's right, Jace," Narine replied.

Adyn nodded. "I agree." She dropped her pack and began to dig through it. "We have our own weapons."

Jace rolled his eyes. "Fine. Maybe they won't get through the gate anyway."

A city guard's flaming body smashed into the gate with enough force to crack the surrounding walls.

"I don't think the gate will last," Adyn said, removing a bundle from the pack.

"I get the same feeling." Jace looked down at her. "What are you doing?"

Adyn rose to her feet and dropped the rag to reveal the golden coil in her hand. She gripped it and pulled, the coil resisting as it straightened. "I am using this thing."

Narine gripped Adyn's wrist. "It's dangerous. You heard Olberon."

Adyn stared at Narine, who flinched when another flaming body struck the gate. "Sacrifices must be made, Narine. Others have done so already. It is my turn."

Nodding, Narine released her grip. Adyn placed one end of the coil around her bicep. It clung to her skin, the band tearing from her grip and wrapping around her arm like a snake come alive. Constricting, the coil grew tighter and tighter, causing Adyn to gasp. Then the magic struck.

Her entire body stiffened and grew hot. The skin on her arm began to peel off and fall to the ground, the effect spreading rapidly. The heat grew into a raging fever, causing her to swoon and stumble to her hands and knees. Her clothing burst into flames, and she screamed in fear.

I am dying!

34

THE FIST OF FARROW

Despaldi's hands flared with heat, igniting the guard Garek held above his head. The powerful warrior then turned and launched the flaming soldier at the gate. The impact was thunderous, bits of flaming, leather armor passing through the bars as the corpse fell to the ground. Two guards with bows emerged from the guard tower at the top of the wall.

Pointing toward them, Despaldi shouted, "Vlad! Ferris! Archers!"

Ferris crafted a shield of ice and held it up before Despaldi, an arrow striking it immediately, bouncing off. Vlad clapped his hands together, a bolt of lightning blasting forth and striking the merlon between the two archers, their arrows loosing far off the mark as shattered rock pummeled them. One stumbled and fell out of sight. The other reappeared with a nocked arrow. The next lightning burst shattered the merlon to the man's other side, chunks of stone pelting the man, a section of the wall breaking free. He tumbled through the opening, arms flailing as he plummeted and smashed to the ground, dead.

"Lift another one, Garek," Despaldi said in an even tone. "The gate won't hold much longer."

At last, I will see the end of Jerrell Landish, he thought. *I will then return to Marquithe with the amulet, labeled a hero for defeating Horus and reclaiming the Eye of Obscurance, the final threat to our plan.*

Garek lifted a guard above his head and turned toward Despaldi, who placed his glowing, orange hands on the dead soldier's armor. His hands flared with heat, the corpse bursting into flames. Garek turned and launched the burning soldier with a mighty heave.

Narine clung to her magic, ready for anything should the gate fail. Her fear turned to horror when Adyn fell to the ground and burst into flames, screaming. She cast a construct of frigid energy and loosed a blast of cold air, dousing Adyn with it and choking off the flames. As the steam swirled, her throat constricted in fear for her best friend. The air cleared, revealing a sight difficult to comprehend.

Still on her hands and knees, Adyn's hair had burned away, head bald and splotchy, covered by peeling sections of dead skin, dark areas beneath. Bits of her remaining clothing fell off and drifted to the ground – cloth and leather blackened and smoldering. Charcoal-colored patches spread across Adyn's body. At first, Narine feared they were burn marks, but as skin fell away, the patches grew larger and larger, giving her the impression of an incredibly fast-spreading disease washing over the bodyguard.

Mere breaths passed before Adyn was naked and skinless. Her entire body seemed to be made from bands of dark metal, thin lines covering her still form. When Adyn remained unmoving, Narine feared her dead, turned into a statue. She, Jace, and Hadnoddon stood staring at Adyn in silence, transfixed, in a state of horror and shock.

Then Adyn moved, lifting her hands off the ground as she sat back on her knees. Her metallic face turned up toward Narine, silver eyes like beads of liquid metal, mouth opening and closing, as if she wished to say something. With everything else burnt away, the only thing remaining on her body was the golden coil around her bicep.

The Band of Amalgamation, Narine thought. *It has done something to her.*

"By the gods," Jace breathed. "Are you still alive?"

The transformed bodyguard gazed down at her hands, twisting them, fingers covered with seams, as if wrapped in narrow strips of metal. "What has become of me?"

Narine reached out and tentatively touched Adyn's arm. It felt like metal, but not cold like a sword or shield. This metal was warm. It felt…alive.

A thud shook the square, men shouting as another flaming guard struck the gate. Bars were bent, some broken, half of them smoking from the pile of burning corpses at the base.

Gripping Adyn's metal arm, Narine pulled herself closer, her hand going to Adyn's head. It felt warm, as well. "Do you need healing?"

Adyn grasped Narine's wrist, removing the hand from her forehead. "Don't. Save your energy for the fight. I feel well enough."

"What if we cannot reverse…this?" Narine choked out, a tear tracking down her cheek.

Adyn gave her a sad smile. "It is so like you to worry about others." Reaching out, Adyn scooped up her swords. The belt and sheaths had melted away, blades blackened. "Years ago, I swore to protect you. In line with that duty, I made the decision to use the Band. Even if I didn't understand where the path might lead, it is the path I chose. Let us survive today before we concern ourselves with tomorrow."

Wiping the tear from her cheek, Narine nodded numbly. *I must be as brave as her. I must make Adyn proud.*

Adyn felt oddly hollow, her emotions flattened, yet her body seemed stronger than ever before. Her movements felt odd, joints resisting. She tapped a sword blade against her arm. It clanged off, arm undamaged.

How curious.

A hole suddenly burst through the gate, a flaming, armored body flying through it. The guard and broken iron bars struck the paved street in a clatter as another cluster of city guards emerged from a street across the square

With resolve, Adyn stood. "Let's fight."

The four city guards nearest the gate rushed forward, prepared to engage. Another dead soldier flew through the opening and collided with three of the guards, toppling them in a twist of limbs and armor.

Two of Despaldi's men ran through the broken gate, one launching a bolt of lightning at the fountain in the middle of the square. Water burst from it and poured out. The other extended his icy hands and released a blast of frigid air, instantly freezing the water and coating the cobblestones in a layer of ice. The first stood ready, waiting for the newly arrived guards to advance, electricity crackling across his open palms. The guards charged forward, some slipping on the ice. A crackling bolt of lightning struck the ice, every man upon it jerking violently, fried inside his own armor.

When another cluster of soldiers rushed in from a side street, the man with icy hands flung his arm in a broad arc, sending sharp shards of ice toward the soldiers, pelting those in the front. The men screamed, blood running down their faces as they fell to their knees, some with icicles jutting from their eye sockets. A crystalline sword of ice then materialized in the attacker's hand as he chased after those who remained standing.

All this took place as Adyn rushed in, swords in hand, ready to attack the electricity-wielding man. When she was two strides away, a ball of fire struck her in the side and launched her off her feet. She hit the ground, rolled, and came up in a crouch, the bits of burning energy surrounding her on the ground. Steam came from her side, but no fire burned, nothing melted. The strike had stung, but not as badly as she expected. She rose from a crouch and glared at Despaldi and another man approaching the broken gate.

"What is this?" Despaldi sneered as he lifted his leg to step through the broken bars.

Narine stood beside Jace, him gripping a throwing blade in each hand, both watching Adyn charge into the fracas. Just strides away, Hadnoddon pressed his back against the wall and gripped his massive hammer.

A fireball struck Adyn, knocking her down. Narine gasped, fearing for her friend. Yet Adyn's metallic body seemed unaffected. The bodyguard rose to her feet, prepared to face Despaldi. As the enemy captain walked through the gate, Hadnoddon lunged, hammer coming around in a sweeping arc. Before the hammer struck the intended target, the man at Despaldi's side reached out and stopped the hammer, his meaty fist gripping the handle and tearing the weapon free from the dwarf's grip.

"Kill him, Garek," Despaldi growled.

"With pleasure." The other man grinned, hefted the hammer, and swung.

Narine channeled her magic and drove a wedge of air into the man. The strike knocked him backward, the man staggering as the hammer came around. It missed Hadnoddon and smashed into the gate with a tremendous clang. The broken portcullis wobbled, the remaining bars falling outward, chunks of stone blocks crumbling from the wall.

Despaldi gestured toward the man with Hadnoddon's hammer. "Take care of the dwarf." He grinned, eyes filled with malice. "I'll handle the other two."

In a hushed voice, Jace said, "When I attack, create an illusion like at the forge in the dwarven city."

She immediately knew what he meant. Twisting her construct, she wove a curtain of illusion in the likeness of the square, placing it just behind them.

As Despaldi advanced, Jace cocked and threw his knives in a flash, blades spinning. Despaldi waved his hands outward, a wall of flames obscuring the man, the air between them wavering from the heat.

At the same time, Narine created false versions of her and Jace mere inches in front of them. She tugged on his coat as she backed away.

Hidden behind their own likenesses, they passed through the curtain of illusion, masking them. She then sent their doppelgängers running across the square. Despaldi chased after them, his glowing hands swirling as a ball of fire came to life. He threw, launching the fireball like a streaking comet. It passed harmlessly through the illusion of Jace and struck a building in an explosion of flames and shattered rock.

From the side, Adyn charged with a roar.

With Despaldi distracted, Jace pulled the knives from his boots and threw.

When Adyn saw Despaldi chasing Narine and Jace across the square with a fireball in his hands, she went after him, her swords ready. Before she could reach him, an enemy attacked from the side, arms lashing toward her. Pale blue electricity struck. She shook violently, her muscles seizing up and leaving her unable to move while her body burned hotter and hotter. A scream slipped from her constricted throat, weak and feeble. Her heart stopped beating.

Her attacker stiffened, his back arching, eyes gaping. The flow of electricity ceased, releasing her. She fell to her hands and knees, heartbeat resuming as she gasped for air. The man who had attacked her staggered, turning, trying to reach over his shoulder. Lightning crackled from his fingers to the two blades buried in his back, but he could not reach them.

Still on her knees, Adyn slashed with her sword, her blade cutting deep gouges across the man's hamstrings. He stumbled and twisted, falling onto his back and driving the two knives even deeper. She slid her sword across his throat to finish him before climbing to her feet.

Despaldi stopped and turned around, his gaze sweeping the square as the illusions of Jace and Narine ran right through two people emerging from a side street. "Where are you, princess? You can hide behind your illusions for only so long."

With a growl, Adyn rushed toward the man.

Narine turned as Hadnoddon was thrown fifteen feet through the air and smashed into the guard tower. Even wearing his helmet, the impact was dreadful. Still hidden within her curtain of illusion, she prepared another spell, masking Hadnoddon's still form from view, a false version of him rising to his feet and drawing a knife. The soldier gripped the dwarf's hammer as he stalked toward the illusion. The fake Hadnoddon burst into a run along the city wall, toward the broken gate. With a mighty lunge, the man swung. The hammer passed right through the illusion and struck the wall with a tremendous impact. A section of the wall, five strides across, cracked and crumbled. Heavy stone blocks and debris poured down onto the man, a deadly avalanche falling, spreading, and racing directly toward Jace and Narine.

"Run!" Jace pulled her along, the pair running clear of the falling wall as it buried the enemy soldier. Unfortunately, they abandoned the curtain of illusion in the process.

"There you are." Despaldi grinned from a dozen strides away, his burning hands radiating heat. The man lunged, holding his hands toward them.

"Sorry," Jace said as he shoved Narine aside.

She tried to catch her balance, but was unable, taking two stumbling steps before she fell face-first and slid across the cobblestones, bruising her knees, scraping her hands and elbows. When she looked back, a cone of flames shot from Despaldi and engulfed Jace.

"No!" she screamed.

"No!" Adyn cried as she raced toward Despaldi, too late.

A fiery inferno swirled in the air, obscuring Jace completely, the heat forcing Adyn to slow and cover her face. She circled behind Despaldi and came at him with a sword strike intended to take his head off.

At the same moment, his attack ceased, and he spun, ducking beneath her blade. The man's outstretched hand slapped against her thigh, her metallic skin glowing orange, heating immediately, searing her. She screamed and stumbled backward, limping and gasping in pain. Her leg was barely functional, unable to bear her weight.

Despaldi grinned and strode toward her. "So, your metal body is *not* invincible. Good." The orange glow of his hands grew brighter and brighter, nearly white, incredible heat coming from them.

Then she saw movement behind the man.

Jace was alive. He patted his body, finding it intact, one hand eventually gripping the amulet beneath his tunic. *The Eye. It stopped Despaldi's magic from harming me*. Yet it hadn't stopped the attacker, who turned his attention on Adyn.

Drawing the dagger on his hip, Jace crept up behind Despaldi. The man's hands glowed brightly as he prepared to attack her. Jace burst forward, closing the last five strides in a breath, and rammed his blade into the base of Despaldi's neck, burying it to the hilt. He let go and stumbled backward as the man spun toward him, eyes gaping in shock. White-hot hands reached for Jace, but he scurried backward, out of the way. The man took a stride, then lurched, his gaze lowering to his chest, the tip of Adyn's sword sticking out, slick with his own blood. She yanked the sword free, and Despaldi fell…dead.

Jace exhaled and shook his head while staring down at the man. "Too bad. He was beginning to grow on me."

Dusting herself off, Narine stood wearily. She had used too much magic over the course of the day and was exhausted. Her hands and elbows were bloody, dress torn and stained. None of it mattered. Jace and Adyn had survived. She could ask for little else.

The two of them, her best friend and the man she loved, stood over the downed Captain of the Midnight Guard, exchanging words. They did not see the man approaching from behind, his hands covered in ice, face red with fury as he gathered his magic.

Desperate, Narine gathered every bit of magic she could hold, formed a construct of mental manipulation, and cast it upon the man just before he attacked.

He lurched backward, eyes rolling up in his head, and collapsed into a heap.

Jace turned, saw the man on the ground, and looked back at Narine. "What did you do?"

Narine exhaled and released her magic, exhaustion washing over her. She staggered, legs giving out. Jace leapt forward and gathered her in his arms. Spots of light danced before her eyes, and she feared she might faint.

"I've got you, Narine," he whispered.

It was the last thing she heard.

35

SWOON

With Narine's limp form draped over his shoulder, Jace lumbered through the destroyed gate. Adyn limped beside him as she supported Hadnoddon, the dwarf's helmet discarded after being dented beyond use, his black hair matted with blood. He had been difficult to wake and staggered with each step, but there was little choice and no time to waste. The last of their attackers turned out to be fast asleep, the man's frozen hands thawed. Whatever Narine had done to him had proven effective, but they all agreed. It would be best to be gone from Cor Cordium before the man woke.

Dockworkers and sailors stood in clusters upon the docks, staring toward the broken wall and destroyed city gate, watching the wounded party come toward them.

"What happened?" a man shouted.

"Is it safe?" another asked.

"Is that woman made of *armor*?"

"It is dark magic, I tell you."

"Sorcery, most foul!"

Jace glowered at them, the men backing away. He then continued past, down to the nearest pier.

A sailor with coppery skin and a red turban on his head rushed toward him. "We witnessed what happened. To have survived, you must be blessed with the luck of the gods."

"Yeah." Jace gestured toward Adyn and Hadnoddon – a woman made of metal and a dwarf with a bloody head. "Don't we appear the lucky lot?"

The man walked beside them. He stood a half-head taller than Jace and wore a curved scimitar on his hip. Jace assumed he was Hassakani.

"My name is Quiarre, First Mate on Hassaka's Breath." He pointed. "The big ship at the end of the pier."

"Great. I am so happy for you," Jace grunted. Narine was getting heavy.

"Times have been difficult of late. We could use some luck on our ship. My captain wishes to offer you free passage, your luck certain to better our fortunes."

Stopping, Jace turned toward the man. "Where are you heading?"

He shook his head. "We have no cargo at this time. Any destination will do. With your luck, we hope to reach a port with cargo of high demand, which we will bring elsewhere."

Eyes narrowed, Jace asked, "You are offering free transportation to the port of our choosing?"

"Yes." He nodded. "Your quick wit is a good sign. Clearly, the gods watch over us."

While Jace was suspect of the offer, he was too exhausted to worry about it. Turning toward Adyn and Hadnoddon, he asked. "Where to?"

The dwarf grimaced as he looked up at him. "We must meet up with the others. Perhaps back to Orenth?"

"You heard what Kylar Mor said. My life is forfeit if I ever return. However, Shear seems a safe enough destination, particularly since we no longer have to worry about Despaldi."

Adyn nodded. "Shear it is."

Quiarre rubbed his hands together. "Very good." He hurried ahead, waving them to follow. "Come along. We set sail as soon as you board."

The walk down the pier was longer than Jace had hoped, and he found himself wishing they had found a ship moored closer to shore. He carried Narine up the plank and onto the deck.

Men scurried about, preparing to set sail – reeling in lines, securing nets over barrels, storing items into holds. A man in white came up the stairs from the cabins, holding bedding in his arms. He walked over to Quiarre and said something in Hassakani. Quiarre then approached Jace as Adyn and Hadnoddon gripped the rail.

"Captain Harlequin is in her cabin, looking over charts for the passage to Shear. It is a near port, and we should be there in the morning."

"*Her* cabin? Your captain is a woman?" Jace asked.

"Is that a problem?" Adyn asked in a weary voice.

"No." He shook his head. "Just unusual." He turned toward Quiarre. "Do you have a place for us to rest? We are a bit worn, and she…" He pointed toward Narine's backside, "is not getting any lighter."

Quiarre nodded. "Yes. Of course. Follow me."

They descended a set of narrow stairs, Jace doing all he could to not fall on the way down. It didn't help that his balance was thrown off by Narine's weight and the swaying ship. The first mate opened a door and waved Jace in. Two sets of bunks lined the walls, so he set Narine down in one of the lower beds and sat beside her with a sigh.

Adyn and Hadnoddon stumbled in, him falling onto the other bottom bunk while Adyn sat on a wooden chair, the legs snapping. Chair pieces scattered as Adyn fell to the floor with a thud.

Jace chuckled at the surprised look on her face. "Perhaps you have gained weight with your…new condition?"

She sighed and climbed to her feet. "You might have a point."

"Do not worry," Quiarre said. "I will have a new chair supplied. We shall reinforce it, make it strong. Also, a meal will be here shortly. You must be hungry after what just transpired ashore."

Jace nodded. "I could eat."

"Wonderful. But first, I will return with some genuine Hassakani swoon." The man bowed and ducked out the door, leaving them alone.

"Swoon?" Hadnoddon muttered from his bed.

"Alcohol," Jace replied.

"Strong alcohol," Adyn added. "Sounds perfect. A little something to dull the pain."

She looked at Narine, expression on her metal face unreadable. "I have only seen her like this once before. She pushed herself too far, used too much magic in a short period. I suspect she will sleep the remainder of the day and will be recovered tomorrow. Until then, we will have to live with our wounds."

A knock sounded at the door.

"Come in," Jace said.

It opened, revealing Quiarre's smiling face. He held a decanter in one hand, four pewter cups in the other. "Swoon, from the best distillery in Hassakan." The man set it on the table and left.

Adyn opened the decanter and poured three glasses, handing one to Jace, one to Hadnoddon, and grabbing the last for herself. "A toast. We survived again…somehow. Perhaps we will all live to see this thing through, whatever the outcome."

Jace lifted his glass, downed the entire thing, and released an "Ahh."

They had retrieved the Band of Amalgamation, but it had changed Adyn with its magic. Olberon's words replayed in his head. *"The armband is dangerous, the effect permanent."* True or not, he tried to imagine being in her situation, the sacrifice required to don it in the first place. It was a frightening thought.

She is a brave woman, and a good friend.

Still, possessing the object of power was but a stop on their journey. The problem was they had no idea where to go next or where the journey might end. The thought was disconcerting, and he found himself wishing for more information once again.

Why must those blasted Seers be so cryptic?

With a sigh, he stood. The world twisted, and he stumbled to the table, landing stomach-first on top of it, his cup rolling off and onto the floor. He fell to his knees, upper body still on the table as he looked up at Adyn, her face twisting, head bobbing. Suddenly, she collapsed toward him. He let go and fell to his backside as she smashed into the table. A crack sounded, legs breaking, tabletop and Adyn crashing to the floor.

Jace's eyes grew heavy as he lay on his back in the middle of the cabin.

The door opened, Quiarre peering in. The first mate smiled down at Jace. "Sleep well, Master Landish. We will be in Hassakan soon. There, you will meet your destiny."

Jace attempted to reply, but his lips were too heavy, eyes impossible to keep open as darkness invaded.

36

THE RETURN

Morning sunlight streamed through gaps in the trees, shining down upon the surrounding ruins below Silvaurum. Elves with full arms and bulging packs over their shoulders continued to emerge from the central tree, the Silvan people gathering in clusters among the ruins.

Brogan stared longingly as a group of elves approached from the opposite direction, led by Chi-Ara. Some held furs and cloaks in their arms, while others held weapons. Among them, a female elf warrior carried a familiar baldric, the scabbard housing a weapon Brogan had known for twenty years. Yes, there had been a fifteen-year gap in that relationship, but it had been forced upon him as a penance for one of his many regrets. Even now, he ached to run up and tear the weapon from the elf's grasp.

Chi-Ara stopped a few strides away, feet shoulder width apart, posture proud. "As promised, your weapons are returned. Use them wisely, but beware. We will not hesitate to kill you should the need arise...despite what my mother says."

Striding past Chi-Ara, Brogan gripped the hilt with one hand, scabbard with the other, and drew the sword with a flourish. The massive trees surrounding him lit up with an aura of magic, something he had been unable to see without the enchanted weapon. To hold Augur again felt glorious.

We are one again.

He turned toward the elf princess and flashed a grin past his gleaming blade. "Attempting to kill me is one thing. Succeeding is another altogether. I have lived a dangerous life, often surrounded by monsters, magic, and death. Thus far, I remain breathing, while those who faced me are long gone from this world."

Chi-Ara grimaced, and her brother put a hand on her arm.

"At peace, Chi. They have proven themselves allies, not enemies."

Her narrowed eyes remained on Brogan as he slid Augur back into its sheath. "Your sword is not an ordinary weapon, is it?"

He slipped the baldric over his shoulder, rotating it so the sword was at his hip. "It is not." He glanced toward Blythe, the golden bow strapped to her back. His gaze then shifted toward Rhoa, who was busily strapping her fulgur blades to her thighs. "Objects of power. Three members of this small group now possess them. Somewhere far from here, our companions have additional enchanted items, perhaps three others by now."

He gave Chi-Ara a sidelong glance. A sudden revelation struck him, a truth he had not acknowledged until that moment. "We are no random party who stumbled upon your forest. This group has been brought together by fate. Every obstacle thrown in our path – and there have been many – shatters when we face it together. I just wish I knew what, exactly, destiny has planned for us."

Chi-Ara gave him a measured look, saying nothing.

Elves stopped emerging from the tree. There were hundreds in total, all adults, which felt strange. He then observed something else out of place.

"These people are not dressed for travel." He turned toward Chi-Ara. "You are aware winter waits beyond this forest, right? It's cold, the ground covered in snow. They will freeze."

"We do not travel as you expect, human. The weather will not affect us."

Brogan frowned at Blythe, who shrugged. "These people are as bad as the Seers," he whispered to her, eliciting a smirk.

The seven Elders walked out of the massive tree, their white hair easy to pick out in the crowd. Despite their lack of wrinkles, they moved with the slow care of someone whose body neared the end. They dispersed, each heading in a different direction. The elf queen and her husband emerged last, her face resolute, his reflecting sadness. Bri-Ara turned back toward the tree, put her hands upon the thick trunk, and closed her eyes. The other Elders all did the same, each selecting their own, unique tree. Incredibly, each of those elves began to glow with a golden hue.

The bark of the trees shifted in color, fading from a red-tinted brown to a dull gray. Leaves of gold then began to drift down like heavy flakes of snow, soon covering everything. Brogan looked up, mouth agape as every tree in the grove shed its golden leaves. As leaves fell, bits of blue sky appeared through the branches, beams of sunlight filtering through, growing brighter and brighter while the leaves piled higher. Even for him, it was a moment of profound sadness – a thing of magic and majesty coming to an abrupt end after thousands of years of existence.

"The trees," Blythe whispered. "They go peacefully. I believe they are…relieved."

He looked at her. "What do you mean?"

"This grove survived on elven magic. The trees were ready to die long ago. This is what they wanted."

What the trees wanted? Brogan resisted telling Blythe the statement sounded ridiculous. The moment was too solemn, and the comment felt…insensitive.

He shook his head. *These odd people are getting to me, as well. Trees wanting to die… Since when have I ever considered the feelings of trees?*

When the last of the golden leaves had fallen, waist-deep piles covering the ground, Bri-Ara addressed her people.

"Silvaurum is no longer. Let us depart and allow our grove to rest peacefully." She then turned and waded through leaves shimmering in the morning sun.

The elves all followed, Brogan and his companions among them. Once beyond the grove, they came to a clearing in the forest, the ruins here more intact than what Brogan had seen prior. It gave him a sense of the city that had once existed, the marker of a civilization long gone and forgotten. Empty shells of buildings, open holes once occupied by windows and doors, stood on both sides of the street. Everything was made of the same tan stone as the ruins within the forest.

They crossed an open area and passed through a standing archway in the middle of a partially crumbled wall. The walls surrounded a plaza of cracked tiles, a waist-high dais in the middle, a hundred strides in diameter, the rim made of stone blocks. Eight thick, stone columns with runes etched in their surfaces surrounded the dais, spaced in even intervals.

Queen Bri-Ara ascended a set of narrow steps leading to the dais, the elves following as she walked to the center. As Brogan climbed the stairs, he examined the dais floor. It was paved with a mosaic of colored tiles forming an elaborate pattern, all surrounded by a ring of scrawling, golden script reflecting the morning sunlight.

When everyone had gathered on the dais, Bri-Ara lifted her staff, eyes closed as she faced the sun. The dull glow at the top of the staff flared, the golden light growing in intensity until it was too bright to look upon directly. She opened her eyes, lowered the staff, and inserted the butt end into a circular slot at the hub of the dais.

The golden script encircling the ring began to glow, the shine rising until it obscured the surrounding city from view. A humming arose, pulsing loud enough that Brogan considered covering his ears. Many of the elves around him did just that. Beneath his feet, the mosaic transformed, tiles changing in color, the elaborate pattern shifting to become another, distinctly different design. The golden glow from the staff and the outer ring subsided, the humming drifting to silence.

Somehow, everything around them had changed.

Cold air rushed in, breath visibly swirling. It was darker, still morning, but the sun was below the horizon. The eight columns had been replaced by massive, ancient trees covered in frost. Brogan looked up and saw branches arcing from tree to tree, dormant pods visible above. In all directions beyond the eight trees was a forest covered in ice, the forest floor blanketed in snow.

"We are in the Frost Forest," Blythe muttered.

Brogan nodded. "We just traveled hundreds of miles in seconds. How is it possible?"

The queen and seven elders climbed off the dais, each walking toward one of the towering trees. As before, they each pressed a palm against the tree and closed their eyes. A hum arose, joined by a golden aura. It began slowly, emanating from the base of each tree and working upward as the frost-coated bark warmed. From a dull gray, the bark turned a warm red, the frost thawing to beads of water, a crackling sound climbing the tree as it came to life. Bits of frost popped and broke free from the branches above, golden leaves sprouting in moments and quickly obscuring everything above from view.

The snow on the ground melted, steam rising, billowing outward toward the surrounding forest. As the steam expanded, the trees came to life, shattering their frozen shell, green leaves sprouting, dark green pines shedding snow.

"It is a miracle," Brogan muttered in wonder.

Bri-Ara approached and stopped at the edge of the dais, facing her people, arms stretched toward the golden canopy above. "Silvacris is reborn, and with it, I pray the Silvan will thrive."

A small, female figure in a white dress emerged from the dark forest, hair jet-black, eyes covered by a blindfold. At her side was a dwarf in heavy chainmail, a sword on his hip, shield strapped to his arm.

"Greetings, Elf Queen," Xionne said. "Welcome home."

37

CHOICES

Elves funneled into one of the towering trees, a golden light shining through the arched doorway to an ascending stairwell. The visual similarity to the recently abandoned tree city was striking, but the song coming from the trees sounded quite different. The forest sang into Blythe's ear – a song of hope, joy, and persistence.

Xionne and Bri-Ara stood off to the side, the Seer and elf queen in quiet conversation. Blythe watched the two women and wondered what they discussed. They seemed to treat each other with respect, which was a good sign. After the brief conversation, Bri-Ara entered the doorway and disappeared into the tree.

Xionne, her dwarf Guardian at her side, approached Blythe and her companions, her hands clasped at her waist. The short Seer, eyes hidden behind a black strip of cloth, faced Blythe as she spoke.

"Your success in retrieving the Arc was foretold centuries ago. Even the Cultivators are aware of the prophecy and the events to follow."

"What events follow?" Brogan asked. "We have the thing you told us to get. So now what?"

The Seer pressed her lips together in a long pause. Brogan squirmed, seeming unnerved by the small woman's glare through her blindfold.

"The prophecy turns, and forks lie in wait. It is difficult to know which path to take, for the choices of man are many at this stage. Most of the possible results point toward the end of all things." She unfolded a piece of paper, holding it while speaking in an odd tone. *"And lo, with the Arc of Radiance in hand, those bound by destiny tread a path shifting from the bizarre to shattered darkness. The Queen of Fire and Ice sweeps over the lands, all bending to her will, her gathering host unlike any in history, her lust for power certain to doom her race. The spawns of darkness extend toward the land of Bal, where the past meets the future. There, the servants of light shall confront the Dark Lord's minions. Beware, the true enemy lurks in the heart of darkness, beneath the light of the moon. Only when all players converge, objects of power in hand, may the fate of the world be decided."*

Brogan turned to Blythe, then Rhoa and the dwarfs. Nobody said a word. Ultimately, he threw up his hands and shouted at the Seer, "Why can't you speak plainly? I have done my best to show you respect, Xionne, because that is how we Pallanese are taught to behave toward you. I can't do it any longer. Not when our lives and thousands more are at stake."

He bent over until his face was level with hers, no more than a foot away. "In plain words, tell us. What…do…we…do?"

Xionne's nostrils flared, lips white. "I share the words of prophecy, but I cannot do more than that." The small woman reached toward Brogan, finger prodding his chest and forcing him backward. "Your choices will determine the future, *Jaded Warrior*, but I cannot make them for you."

She slapped the paper into Brogan's hand and spun on her heel, her escort trailing as they faded into the woods. Nobody spoke until the pair was consumed by shadows.

Brogan muttered, "I think I found a sore spot. She was actually angry."

Rhoa laughed. "If someone among our group was supposed to goad Xionne, you did a fine job. Jace would be proud."

The big man grinned, then sobered again. "I just find it exhausting the way everything is so cryptic, those women pulling at strings as if we were puppets, always expecting us to blindly follow along."

Blythe took the paper from his hand and looked it over. After a moment, she said, "At least she told us where to go next."

Brogan's brow furrowed. "She did?"

"The prophecy mentioned the land of Bal. It also mentions our path and the Bizarre."

Brogan blinked. "The Great Bizarre?"

Blythe nodded while folding the sheet of paper. "It appears we head to Balmor. A long journey and one best taken by ship."

"What of this Queen of Fire and Ice?" he asked.

"One thing at a time," Rhoa said. "Let's focus on reaching Balmor, then things will work themselves out. They have thus far."

Brogan sighed. "Fine. So, we head back to Growler's Rock and find a ship?"

"Yes."

"Agreed."

Blythe considered the journey. Even after taking the magical gateway from Silvaurum to the Frost Forest, reducing their journey by hundreds of miles, Growler's Rock remained a good distance away.

"We should get going," Rhoa said. "We have far to travel and must do so on foot, at least until we reach the coast." She shouldered her pack and looked up, the sun blotted out by the thick canopy of leaves above. "Which way do we go?"

Blythe pointed west without hesitation. As an expert in woodcraft, she had long possessed an innate sense of direction. In addition, something had changed inside her since acquiring the bow, her connection and awareness of the surrounding forest far greater than ever before. She closed her eyes, able to feel the sun shining upon the trees, the leaves drinking in the light, feeding the limbs, branches, and trunk of each tree. She also felt another presence nearby, one she suspected remained hidden for a reason.

Opening her eyes, she released a sigh, resigned for the journey ahead. When she lifted her pack off the ground, it felt lighter than before.

Blythe frowned at Brogan. "Did you remove some items from my pack again?"

He shrugged. "No sense in you carrying all that weight. It's better if I bear the burden for you."

"Brogan..."

He placed a hand on her hip and looked her in the eye. "Let me do this for you. It is a small thing, but it makes me feel better." His gaze flicked toward the golden bow. "You are burdened enough as it stands."

Rhoa threw her pack over her shoulder and headed in the direction Blythe had pointed, walking with a slight limp, the four dwarves following.

When Blythe's gaze met Brogan's, he gave her a smile. "How are you?"

She shook her head. "I feel well, but different. It is...difficult to articulate."

Brogan jerked in surprise, hand gripping his hilt when an elf stepped out from the tree he had been hiding behind.

"You are the first human to wield the Arc of Radiance." Tygalas approached with a pack over his shoulder, a staff made of golden wood in his hand. "The bow is of our magic, and our magic is of the forest. I suspect...there is more affecting you than a shift in eye color."

"I suppose that makes sense." Blythe considered her altered appearance and began to worry about returning to the world of humans. *Will I fit in? Will they see me as a freak?* "Is the bond...permanent?"

Tygalas must have noted the concern in her tone. He put a hand on her shoulder, responding in a gentle tone. "I believe so. According to our historians, the connection with the bow is for life, impossible to break once established."

She suddenly felt trapped. "Would it also be true for a human?"

"I do not know." The elf shrugged. "Attempt to discard the bow. See what happens."

Even as she considered it, a stab of pain shot through her stomach. Doubling over, she clutched her midriff and fell to one knee. She discarded the thought, huffing quick breaths as the pain slowly subsided.

Brogan knelt in front of her, his hand on her shoulder. "What's wrong? Are you all right?"

She nodded, rising to her feet and blowing out a breath. "I am fine now."

"As I suspected," Tygalas said. "You cannot even think of abandoning the bow without inflicting pain upon yourself."

Blythe wiped beads of sweat from her brow. Her furs were too much for the warm weather in the forest. "Well, I will not attempt that again."

She forced her thoughts to turn elsewhere, her gaze shifting to the tree city above.

"Why aren't you up there with your people?"

"I owe you my life, a debt I must strive to repay. In fact, I carry the burden of the other lives you saved. I can only make it right by accompanying you on your journey."

"Great," Brogan muttered. "Another one."

Blythe nudged Brogan with her elbow, forcing a grunt from him.

"What of your mother?" she asked.

He smiled. "I first posed the request three days past, asking again and again, much to my mother's irritation. Each time, she refused...until minutes ago. It appears the Seer said something to change her mind. So, if you will have me, I will join you."

Brogan was about to reply, but Blythe gave him another nudge.

She smiled at Tygalas, taking Brogan by the arm. "We would be happy to have you join us. Come along. Let's catch up to the others."

"No need to run. Their legs are very short," Brogan noted, his face then twisting in question. "How many steps do you think each of them must take to reach the coast? Could be millions!" He laughed heartily.

She gave him a curious look. "Why is that funny?"

"Honestly, I don't know." He gave her a big grin. "It just is."

They passed beyond the golden grove and entered the forest, alive and thriving, so different than when they had passed through on the way to Kelmar. At the time, the future had been in question, the answer coming in the form of a prophecy – a prophecy that created more questions than answers.

Xionne's statement replayed in Blythe's head. *"Your choices will determine the future."*

She prayed they would make wise choices, for she dreaded what future awaited should they choose poorly.

EPILOGUE

Lord Thurvin Arnolle strode out of Marquithe Palace and into a courtyard filled with Midnight Guard soldiers. Their armor was wet, dark blue capes hanging limply, eyes squinting against the mist. He glowered up at the gray skies and cast a shield against moisture, draping it over himself like an umbrella.

I cannot be defeated. Not by a wizard, not by an army, not even by nature.

A short, stocky soldier with dark hair and a thick mustache approached, thumping a fist to his breastplate.

"Captain Quiam," Thurvin said. "What is the latest report?"

"The Pallanese Army approaches from the south. They will reach the hilltop soon."

"How many?"

"Two thousand at the vanguard, another four thousand lagging a few days behind. They have supply wagons with them, but not enough to support a siege." Quiam stroked beads of water from his mustache. "The rumors appear true. The queen rides with her troops."

Thurvin pressed his lips together, brow furrowed. "What is she up to? She cannot hope to challenge my power. Not now, and certainly not after she has suffered two weeks without Devotion." Leaving Marquithe for even a day had become unthinkable. Thurvin could not imagine skipping a single Devotion.

"Perhaps she is unaware of what has occurred in Ghealdor."

He considered the idea. "She is young but was trained at the University. She must have scouts in Ghealdor to keep her informed." He shook his head. "It doesn't matter. I will face her regardless. If it turns to aggression, her campaign, and rule, will be short-lived."

He strode past Quiam and climbed into a waiting carriage, pausing before he closed the door. "Meet me at the south gate."

The soldiers mounted their horses as his carriage pulled out of the palace grounds. As he rode, Thurvin considered the situation.

While the young were prone to rash decisions, Queen Priella undoubtedly had an experienced staff to guide her. They would never agree to assault a city held by another wizard lord. It would be suicide. Yet she had an army with her. Two thousand men were too many for a mere escort. Four thousand marching behind her could be nothing less than an act of aggression. It was a conundrum.

What motivates this woman?

He then considered what his spies had told him of Priella. The Pallanese were odd by nature – prim and proud, stoic and intolerably honorable. As Raskor's daughter, she had been groomed to be a leader, guided by the finest tutors prior to her stint at the University. Reports about her out of Tiadd were slim at best, the princess largely behaving as a recluse, focused on her studies and noticeably absent from social activities.

Somehow, she was the last surviving child of Raskor and Ariella, the five boys dying in a variety of interesting and sometimes mysterious manners. Unbelievably, the citizens of Pallanar whispered of a curse tied to the girl, many blaming her for the troubles plaguing the royal family. It was a preposterous notion to be sure, but uneducated citizens often grasped for superstition rather than more logical causes for their problems.

No, the curse could not be true.

What interested him was the public's shift in perspective after she assumed the throne. Once gifted with the power of Pallan, she had gained the love of her people, seemingly in an instant. *Perhaps they finally perceive her as Raskor's daughter, the rightful ruler after his death.* The man had also been well-loved.

The carriage stopped in the square near the south gate, and Thurvin still hadn't reached a firm conclusion regarding the queen's visit. He climbed out, recasting his shield against the drizzle.

Soldiers filled the square, some on horseback, most on foot, all armed. Archers lined the top of the city wall as far as he could see, bows in hand, ready to rain death upon enemy soldiers.

Quiam dismounted and met Thurvin, walking at his side as they headed toward the wall. "I left orders for the gate to remain closed, sire. Only you, I, or Adderly may call for it to open."

"Good," Thurvin replied as he circumvented a puddle. "Where is Adderly?"

Quiam pointed toward the wall. "Up there, in charge of the archers."

Thurvin nodded, still striding toward the wall. "Very well. I will meet with him and get a look at this army."

He reached the wall and cast a construct, forming a platform of solidified air beneath his feet. With a twist of his wrist and the raising of his hand, the platform lifted him up along the wall. To the ungifted, he would appear to float up of his own volition, another display of his power. *Watch me. Believe in my magic.* He hoped it might inspire confidence in his men. The same confidence he held firmly within himself.

The rising, magical platform stopped when even with the top of the wall, a hundred feet in the air, and Thurvin stepped off.

The top of the wall was six feet deep, the outer section lined with merlons that stood higher than Thurvin's head. He spotted Adderly twenty feet away, past a half-dozen archers, and approached the man.

"Adderly. Please report."

The sergeant turned toward him. He was tall and thin with a pointed, brown beard and a scar across one cheek. "It is wonderful to see you, Lord Thurvin." Adderly pointed toward the gap between two merlons. "Have a look, sire."

Thurvin settled beside the man and gazed out into the morning mist.

Long, yellowed grass surrounded the hilltop city of Marquithe, split down the center by a road paved with rectangular stones. A distant rumble could be heard, the unmistakable sound of many feet and horses approaching. It was difficult to see with all the moisture in the air, but at the edge of his vision, he spotted the marching army.

The vanguard consisted of a few dozen horses, ridden by soldiers in polished Gleam Guard armor. At the lead, a standard-bearer waved the Pallanese flag – a blue diamond on a field of white. In the heart of the riders was someone in a gray cloak, hood up.

Soldiers on foot trailed behind the cavalry, a line of armored men fading into the gloom. While he could not see them all, he knew there were two thousand, roughly equal to how many soldiers he had remaining in Marquithe. If it came to a siege, the Pallanese could not hope to win. They would need to outnumber him by five or six times to sway the odds in their favor…assuming they could breach the gate.

I wonder why she did not bring a larger force.

The horses stopped just beyond bow range, save for a cluster of three, including the cloaked rider. The trio rode toward the gate at an easy walk.

Thurvin turned toward Adderly. "Have your men ready but be prepared for treachery. Do not attack unless the enemy does first. I will meet this queen myself. It is time to find out why she brings a foreign army upon my lands."

Casting a construct as he stepped off the wall, Thurvin fell toward the square a hundred feet below. The thrill of the drop tickled his stomach, bringing an adrenaline rush he had come to crave. Even as he plummeted, a thread of magic wrapped around him, tendrils lashing out to his left and right, spanning the gap between the two guard towers. The ends anchored to each tower, lengthening as he eased into a soft landing. Once his feet touched down, he dismissed the magic.

"Captain!" Thurvin called.

Quiam rushed over.

"Open the gate and clear out this area. We are about to receive guests. I wish to show them a proper reception."

Quiam issued orders, the portcullis rising, the area inside it opening as guards backed away to form an arc, Thurvin at the apex. There he stood, his shield still blocking the rain, arms crossed over his chest, feet shoulder width apart, glare intense. Everyone else was wet, but his silver-trimmed, midnight blue robes remained dry.

The three riders passed through the gate. The first was a tall man in glistening wet plate, his crested helmet marking him as an officer. Judging by his height, age, and appearance, Thurvin guessed him to be Theodin Rahal,

Captain of the Gleam Guard. The next was a thickly built man in chainmail and cloak. His long hair and grimace had Thurvin assuming it was Bosinger Aeduant, personal guard to Queen Priella. The third rider wore a gray cloak, hood up, only her exposed lower legs informing him it was a woman.

The three riders stopped and dismounted. The woman strode forward, pulled her hood down, and threw her cloak back to reveal herself.

Queen Ariella stood tall for a woman, a silver crown with a sparkling aquamarine jewel at the front nestled in her fiery red hair. Emerald green eyes stared back at him, brow arched in a silent challenge. Her skin was pale and perfect, red lips full and pursed. A pale blue dress clung to her curves, of which there were plenty, the neckline plunging to expose generous cleavage. She was simply the most beautiful woman he had ever seen.

"Lord Thurvin." Priella dipped her head. "Thank you for receiving us. I am flattered you ventured out to meet with me personally."

Thurvin gathered himself, dismissing his lust and focusing on his anger. "Why have you brought an army to my doorstep, Priella?" He purposely avoided using a term befitting her station.

Her eyes narrowed for a beat before a relaxed smirk spread across her face. "Are you not flattered by my gift?"

He blinked. "Gift?"

"You seek to conquer the world, with Ghealdor already beneath your thumb. I intend to spare my people the suffering of war." She knelt. "I would pledge myself to you here and now, my troops serving you as Farrowen turns her attention upon Orenth."

Thurvin was taken aback. "You seek an alliance?"

"I do. Leave Pallanar alone, and I will help you conquer the world."

She looked up at him and took a deep breath, his eyes drawn to the gap down the front of her dress, revealing far too much for propriety. His heart raced, both at her beauty and the thought of gaining additional forces without cost.

Thurvin dismissed his magic and smiled. "I accept your offer. Please, rise. Let us discuss this further someplace private."

Priella smiled, and it were as if the sun had broken through the mist. She took his hand, stood, and allowed him to lead her toward his carriage.

"Tell me," Thurvin said. "How could you do it?"

"Do what, Lord Thurvin?"

"How could you leave Illustan and remain bereft of prayers for so many days. Do you not long for Devotion?"

"Leaving Illustan was not as difficult as you might suspect."

A soldier opened the carriage door, and she climbed inside. Thurvin followed and sat across from her.

"As for Devotion, it continues. I have not missed a single evening."

He frowned in confusion. "How is that possible?"

Priella smiled. "There is much others deem impossible simply because it has never been done. When Pherelyn took the throne of Farrowen, for example."

Thurvin's expression darkened. "Her rule proved to be a tragic mistake. I only pray yours proves to be different."

She laughed. "Oh, Thurvin. How little you understand."

Ire stirred, he growled, "What does that mean?"

"I was destined to claim the throne of Pallan, just as I am destined to rule the world."

He shook his head. "While our alliance spares Pallanar, it does not include you gaining power."

She smiled, head tilted, finger running down her chest, his eyes following. "You don't know it yet, but soon will. Anything that is yours will be mine."

"Are you suggesting marriage?"

She laughed again and sat forward, placing a hand on his knee. "No, you silly man. I am suggesting far more than that."

Her hand on his knee, her beauty stirred his blood, lust fogging his mind. A blinding glow of magic suddenly surrounded her. He tried to react with his own, but it was too late.

A dominating force struck, his mind reeling. Thurvin's head slammed backward, mouth open in a silent scream as he fought to regain control. Horrified, he struggled as she divided his mind into pieces, segregating his free will and sealing it away.

"Ahh..." She smiled. "How wonderful. Even a wizard lord is not immune to compulsion."

What have you done to me? He could not voice the words, his body reacting against his will. "Yes, My Queen."

Priella chuckled. "Marriage." She shook her head. "Funny thought, me marrying a little weasel like yourself. My intentions for you lie in a quite different direction. You might be the most powerful wizard of all time, but your strength now belongs to me. With such power at my disposal, I will rule the world." She leaned close to him and whispered, "You get to watch, helplessly trapped in your own mind, while I use your abilities as I see fit. You see, we have a war to fight, but not the one you expected."

The adventure continues in Wizardoms: Rise of a Wizard Queen.

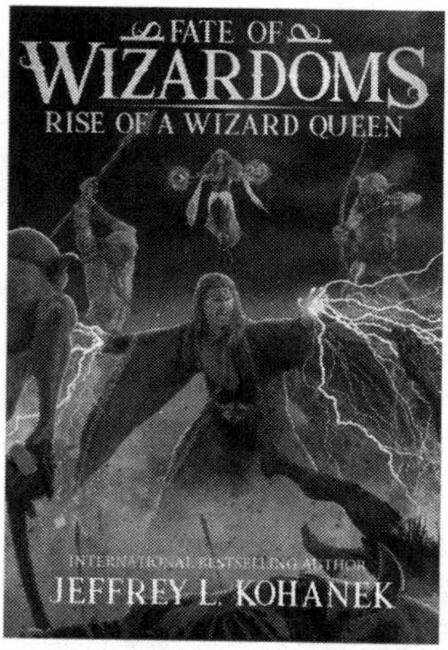

NOTE FROM THE AUTHOR

I hope you have enjoyed the story thus far. Two more books remain in the **Fate of Wizardoms** epic, and I would love for you to join me for the entire saga.

Not only does this adventure continue in **Wizardoms: Rise of a Wizard Queen** in July 2020, there are other tales to tell, including three companion novellas featuring Jace, Narine, and Brogan, each set long before Lord Taladain's death.

I give those stories out for free to anyone who joins my author newsletter. In those emails, I share exclusive insights on my characters, my stories, and myself in addition to weekly giveaways and fantasy book promotions. If you are interested, proceed to www.JeffreyLKohanek.com.

Best Wishes,
Jeff
www.jeffreylkohanek.com

ALSO BY JEFFREY L. KOHANEK

Fate of Wizardoms

Book One: Eye of Obscurance

Book Two: Balance of Magic

Book Three: Temple of the Oracle

Book Four: Objects of Power

Book Five: Rise of a Wizard Queen

Book Six: A Contest of Gods

* * *

Warriors, Wizards, & Rogues (Fate of Wizardoms 0)

Fate of Wizardoms Boxed Set: Books 1-3

Runes of Issalia

The Buried Symbol: Runes of Issalia 1

The Emblem Throne: Runes of Issalia 2

An Empire in Runes: Runes of Issalia 3

Rogue Legacy: Runes of Issalia Prequel

* * *

Runes of Issalia Bonus Box

Wardens of Issalia

A Warden's Purpose: Wardens of Issalia 1

The Arcane Ward: Wardens of Issalia 2

An Imperial Gambit: Wardens of Issalia 3

A Kingdom Under Siege: Wardens of Issalia 4

ICON: A Wardens of Issalia Companion Tale

* * *

Wardens of Issalia Boxed Set

Made in the USA
Columbia, SC
24 July 2021

42366417R00178